THE MIDAS EFFECT

Copyright©2019 T M Nantier
ISBN 9781090153685

With appreciation to Marina, Beka, Stephen, and Alexandra.
A special thanks to Victor Vartanian for his insight.

CHAPTER 1

The bullet was traveling at a subsonic speed of only 650 feet per second, silent in the cool nighttime air, its rotation stabilizing it with arrow-like precision. The silencer attached to the muzzle of the futuristic assault rifle, equipped with infrared technology, absorbed its sound wave. For the split second it took to reach its target, the only sound was a high-pitched hiss. Steve Ross and Jim Ragan were Immigration Agents, Special Investigations Unit, on assignment in Key West. They had been crouching beside a low brick wall at the estate of Jason Boulez, owner of the world's largest cargo shipping company. Trained in clandestine information gathering techniques from their days as Army Rangers, they made their way to a communications interface cabinet mounted in a secure outbuilding near the rear of the exclusive property. Cryptic messages sent to South Florida over a satellite communication system intercepted from Boulez's overseas operations triggered a department terrorism alert. Authorization to attempt infiltration of the system came from the highest levels in the department. The electronic security system on the outbuilding presented no problem for the sophisticated equipment Steve and Jim carried. Within seconds, the lock and alarms were de-activated, and they slipped inside. They found an interface cabinet the size of a two-drawer file mounted to the wall, with several rows of green LCDs showing the operational status of the system. With adept precision, Steve inserted a data recorder connector into the external diagnostic port of the interface. It only took seconds for the computer chip embedded in his equipment to disabled the interface's alarm and downloaded the information stored within. Jim kept watch at the door, his service weapon drawn, and ready.

"It's as easy as taking candy from a baby," Steve whispered. "Hurry, and don't wake that baby up, or there'll be hell to pay," Jim responded.

A few seconds later, Steve finished. "I've got it, let's get out of here." He said as he wrapped the cord to the recording disc up and stuffed it in its pouch, "you ready?"

Jim waited for Steve's to finish and cracked the door open a little further, stepping out into the humid night air.

1

As Steve and Jim exited the outbuilding, they paused for a second to get their bearings. Steve reached up, realizing he had not pulled his heat containing Kevlar mask down over his face. As he reached up to pull it down, the first bullet passing over his right shoulder, shattering into the wall beside him. Small pieces of brick and lead shrapnel from the impact pierced the skin on his forehead and left cheek. He hit the dirt, pulling Jim down with him, knowing if the shooter had wanted to kill him, he would be dead already.

Rodney Best, second in command of the compound's security, was zeroing in the computerized infrared scope on his new toy, known as a SABR. The Selectable Assault Battle Rifle has not only a 5.56 mm carbine, but a 20 mm auxiliary munitions launcher, and laser sighting with high-resolution infrared targeting. Swinging it around towards the perimeter he spied a feral cat at 100 yards, scrambling up a tree, its fuzzy outline confirmed as a hot target by a blinking light in the scope display, and a low-pitched blip-blip-blip sound in the scopes attached ear set. Steadying his aim, he zeroed in on the cat through the viewfinder, but he decided not to pull the trigger. Even though the compound was almost 35 acres, he did not want to risk a ricochet finding its way to a neighboring window over a scroungy fur-ball. As he held the rifle on point, a second, quicker blip-blip-blip started, showing another target. It surprised Rodney to see the image of a man's head pass through the scope's viewfinder.

"What the hell?" He thought to himself.

Eager to try out his new weapon, Rodney planted two rounds as close as possible to the intruder, hoping to pin him down until help arrived.

"Get down! Get down!" Steve cautioned Jim under his breath. Looking around for the shooter, his mind raced, "How'd they see us?"

His stealth suit, with its cooled black Kevlar outer layer, should have protected him any infrared or night vision equipment. Then, as he lay in the dirt, he realized it was his fault. He chastised himself for not pulling the mask down on leaving the outbuilding, a stupid mistake. The little things always got you, one small detail, or one moment of inattention Those few seconds of exposure, and a little luck were all Rodney needed, allowing the automatic infrared targeting in his SABR to lock on to the heat signature. A second bullet thudded into the dirt behind Jim.

2

"Damn!" Steve muttered as he sucked in a quick breath. Jim did not bother to answer. Pointing his second and third fingers at his eyes, he then pointed them over to a shallow ravine which led to a storm drain about thirty inches in diameter. Steve nodded in silent agreement, knowing they had to move, time was their enemy now. He pulled his semi-auto out of its holster and gave Jim a gentle shove towards the ravine.

CHAPTER 2

Jason Boulez was of Algerian descent. He got his start in the shipping industry in the late sixties, by purchasing a derelict freighter from a bankrupt Jordanian merchant. Fifty thousand dollars and the promise to look the other way when the merchant needed to transport small amounts of contraband was all it took. After slapping a coat of paint on the rusty hull, and naming his company 'Global Shipping', he made millions shipping cargo to ports all around the Middle East. Boulez's fleet grew, helped along by the embryonic terrorist organizations developing in the region who realized with containerized shipping, it was easy to move weapons, currency, even personnel undetected. His empire comprised44 super freighters carrying containerized freight to and from ports from all areas of the world. The Chinese and South Koreans were his primary customers, however with the lowest rates in the shipping industry, his fleet kept busy with no problem.

Any of his freighters entering U. S. waters came under scrutiny from Immigration and Customs, who did not understand his uncanny ability to keep his ships running at discounted rates. Although he owned the largest and most modern freighters in the worldwide maritime system, they always embarked at only three-quarters of known capacity. Authorities knew he had a previous affiliation with factions of the Red Brigades terrorist group during his youth, and that brought additional scrutiny from Home Land Security, which felt there was no such thing as a 'reformed' terrorist. He had no direct proven link to any terrorist organization, yet his Middle Eastern connections had earned him a position on all the watch lists.

He had homes around the world, Switzerland, France, Brazil, and on both coasts of the United States. His private jet and helicopters afforded him almost unlimited freedom to travel between those homes and many other countries where he had business ventures. The cargoes of his ships drew the interest of the Customs Service. When searched for contraband, they were clean except for small amounts of marijuana crew members smuggled aboard from time to time. So well run and efficient were his fleet and the Coast Guard rarely cited him for a safety violation. Since his compound was the largest in Ocean Haven, Florida, the most exclusive of exclusive residential areas in Key West, Boulez feared little interference from his neighbors. They comprised retired dotcommers and the rich spawn of any number of entrepreneurial geriatrics. Their hedonistic pursuits kept them busy, and busy

4

neighbors are good neighbors. What he feared was government surveillance. He swept his communication system for bugs, and sophisticated encryption programs protected his telephones, computers, and fax communication. He knew the government has sensitive listening devices using windows and flat surfaces to amplify conversations inside a building, and even able to monitor keystrokes on a computer. Seeing a dark-colored van parked on the side of the road near the compound was a common occurrence.

"Moronic infidels!" He would laugh as he passed by in his limousine. It took a lot of time and expense to stay ahead of them, all part of doing business in the US. Knowing they were under surveillance kept his security personnel on their toes.

Benny Chavez was Boulez's head of security in Key West. It had been a long day. Security was not a nine-to-five job, and he was up twenty hours at a time. He was preparing for bed when his ever-present Blackberry chirped with the tone programmed for an urgent message. Snatching the device from his dresser, he saw a diagram of the compound on the screen, with a dot blinking at station seven, in the southwest corner, a low area often flooded in heavy rains. He picked up the security phone, one of the 34 in the main house. The phone rang to the blinking station, and he was talking to Rodney.

"What's going on?" he asked, expecting yet another incident of local teenagers trying to get a peep of the other rich and famous walking naked out by the pool.

"Someone got inside," Rodney said, under his breath. "I put a round beside his head, and one almost up his ass, he's pinned down now at the drainage ditch. I can't see him; he might try to get to the road."

"Notify stations 4 & 12 to block him on both ends," ordered Benny, "Don't shoot him, yet, I want to find out who it is, and what he wants!"

"It's done," Rodney replied, anticipating the hunt already focused his thoughts on a plan of action.

By now, Steve and Jim were at the bottom of the shallow ravine. They knew security would soon close the perimeter, and there would bring several ill-tempered canines along with them for exercise. This should have been a simple twenty-minute in and out operation. Steve's adrenalin always began flowing with the start of an operation; he

5

needed the challenge to stay sharp. You never feel as alive as when an adversary is trying to take your life from you. You focus, react, and implement procedures developed over years of trial and error. Men paid for those errors with their lives. He did not plan to be one, at least not tonight. His Ranger training gave him the mental and physical tools to overcome almost any situation, even his own mistakes. Now, his exit plan: get in, get out, and get down the beach unseen, was history. It was time to improvise.

They lay on the wet grass, both thinking the same thing: The security forces had the ravine covered up by the road, and the dogs would be here as soon as they traced blood scent on the brick wall. This would get nasty real soon. Just then several perimeter lights came on, bathing the wall and about twenty feet from it in unflattering High-Pressure Sodium daylight.

"Piss!" Steve scowled, and looking around, he saw he was only six feet from a storm drainpipe, Jim right beside him. He figured it must come out in a better place than this. The dogs were barking and whining now, and low, almost unintelligible voices were urging the dogs on:

"Find 'em boy, get 'em now, go on!"

Steve hated small places, being a little claustrophobic, but the sound of the dogs getting nearer left little time to waste. Thirty inches of pipe was not much room, and to make it worse, the bottom was slick with silt and slimy vegetation. He cursed under his breath as he slithered in headfirst, making sure the information he downloaded was secure inside its waterproof carry bag. Jim was right behind him, and after crawling in about ten feet, he reached into one of his thigh pockets and brought out a small canister of pepper spray. Bending behind, he sprayed the canister around the opening and on the leaves and debris in the pipe. It surprised him at how much the canister held, enough to coat everything, almost eight feet into the pipe. Scooting into the dark pipe, he caught up to Steve, all the while trying not to let himself think what might lurk up ahead in the darkness. After about forty feet, the pipe veered right, and Steve felt a piece of thin metal wedged into the pipe, blocking his progress. Reaching for his mini Mag-Lite, he saw it was a trashcan lid pushed into the drain by the last rainstorm. By pushing it over flat and bending it in the middle, he could scramble over it. Jim followed and rolling over on his back, he used his feet to push the lid up and hold it in place, a makeshift hatch door. With a good swift kick of his boot, the lid wedged tight. The dogs were at the pipe entrance barking at the echoing sound of boot to metal. The pepper spray was causing them to sneeze and hesitate to enter the pipe. Steve figured it would only be a few seconds before their natural aggression took over and they rushed past the pepper spray. Holding the flashlight in his mouth, he crawled on his knees and elbows as fast as possible, mud and slime wetting his nice black stealth suit.

"Come on, this must come out at the road!" He whispered to Jim. The dogs were past the spray now, and Steve heard them pawing at the trash can lid, urging each other into a canine frenzy. If they broke through, the only option would be to shoot them with the silenced .40 Smith & Wesson semi-auto he had strapped to his chest. Two hundred feet further in, they came to an intersection of a larger pipe, almost 5 feet in diameter. Popping into the larger pipe, Steve discovered he could crouch to make better time, but he was not sure which way to go.

"They'll expect us to get down to the bay. Let's go uphill, there has to be a manhole up ahead." Jim agreed with a nod, digging his own Mag-Lite from his sleeve pocket. The growling and barking of the dogs had subsided now, and Steve stopped and held up his hand to Jim, needing quiet. Listening, he did not hear the dogs at all.

"They must go around trying to come up from the bay. Let's hope it's high tide; they won't be able to get in. One way or the other, it will get us about ten minutes. We have to get back to the bikes before those dogs find them."

They had come up the beach on dirt bikes earlier, hiding them in the tall grass about a mile down the beach. If they found the way out of the pipe, and make an eight-minute jog to the bikes, they would make it.

Turning, he shined the Mag-Lite up the pipe to see only about 10 feet ahead. There had to be a way out ahead, these pipes all started somewhere. Steve led the way up the pipe, his sweat dripping in the humid dank air. Bending over was putting a strain on his back, which still ached from time to time because of a teenage traffic accident. A drunk driver had forced Steve's pickup truck into the ditch and ejected his girlfriend, Grace Spencer. Steve often remembered that horrible night, how he felt kneeling beside Grace, holding her lifeless hand in his as she died in the ditch in front of him. The plans they had to marry would be forever unfulfilled. Although he had had several girlfriends in the ensuing twelve years, he never allowed himself a deep level of emotional commitment again. Denial was his only solace, a misguided attempt to honor her memory.

Back at the ravine entrance, Chavez knew this was no sightseer. Telling one of his security details to stay at the pipe opening, he called the dogs back and headed toward the bay outlet with one, and told Rodney to take the other dog and go up the street to intercept whoever was screwing with his beauty sleep.

Steve, breathing hard now, came upon an intersection; four pipes all going different directions. His sense of direction told him to take the pipe on his left, which he did, pulling Jim's sleeve around the corner, and following it for 100 yards until it ended at a manhole.

"Sit tight." He directed Jim. Climbing up the ladder embedded in the wall, he waited under the lid for twenty or thirty seconds, which seemed to be an eternity, listening for any sounds telling him someone was there. He heard nothing, nothing but the distant vibration of traffic. He figured he must be near the main road.

"*Don't hesitate,*" he cautioned himself, "*don't give them time to find you.*" His training told him first inclinations are usually correct. Instinct is always stronger than reasoning; don't psyche yourself out with 'what ifs'. Decide a course of action and then execute it. Determined, he pushed against the manhole lid, which was heavy. He had hoped to lift it up enough to peek out, but he realized now it was too awkward to hold it and balance on the ladder rungs. He would heave it off and jump out. Looking down, he said, "Stay put, I'll scope it out, but be ready." The thought passing through his mind he trusted Jim, in a situation such as this, he would pick Jim over anybody to back him up. Then, gathering all the strength his sore back would allow, he shoved the lid up with all his might.

CHAPTER 3

Beth Williams was driving her Ford Explorer down the Coastal Highway in Key West, at 4:30 AM, going back to her sister's beach house after a disappointing blind date. Her sister Jill and brother-in-law Howard own a summerhouse here. They had set her up on a date with a friend of Howard's, one they considered a promising romantic opportunity.

Brian Hoag was an up-and-coming lawyer with a large firm in Atlanta. He was a college friend of Howard's, and by coincidence, he was in Key West on a short vacation. Beth, refusing his request to pick her up at the beach house, met him at Lamar's, the local fish house/bar, where, over a drink, he monopolized the conversation by recounting his plans to shake up the legal fraternity with his Darrow-Esque prowess. A cell phone call halfway through dinner altered the standard first date dinner and a movie routine.

"Sorry, it was a client of mine from Atlanta. He sold a computer integration company for a zillion dollars. Anyway, he is having a party at his house tonight... about a half an hour from here. You want to go check it out?"

Although not impressed with him, Beth's curiosity with the local rich and famous compelled her to accept his invitation. Taking Brian's car, they arrived at the estate near midnight, finding a raucous party in full swing. Groups of young professionals trying to one-up each other with stories of office intrigue and business acumen dominated the bar. Brian, no stranger to self-aggrandizement, sidled into the largest group, launching into a treatise on how to get rich suing doctors and priests. Beth wandered away, making small talk here and there with the wait staff, nibbling the fresh exotic fruits offered at various service stations. The evening ended when Brian, head spinning from too much vodka, passed out on an overstuffed chaise lounge. She accepted a ride back to her car in the caterer's van; it disappointed Beth that she wasted her evening. Driving along the featureless highway, her mind drifted back to the previous spring. The long relationship with Tom Ayers, her fiancée, had ended when he accepted a position at a college in Chicago. Almost as soon as he moved, the communication between them stopped. In an act of confidence, Beth flew to St. Louis, expecting to discover the man she loved immersed in his work, perhaps too busy,

9

too distracted to realize their relationship was in trouble. Hoping to surprise him with an impromptu lunch date, she took a taxi from the airport, a pleasant half-hour to his office. Tom's receptionist informed Beth he was in a staff meeting but would be back in a few minutes, welcoming her to wait in the lounge area. Soon, Tom rounded the corner with several colleagues. He looked surprised, and a little confused. He excused himself to his coworkers and led Beth into his office. After an enthusiastic embrace and kiss started by Beth, she realized Tom seemed very uncomfortable at her unexpected appearance. Glancing down at his desk, she spotted a framed snapshot of Tom and an attractive young woman at a cookout, sitting on his lap and kissing his cheek. It explained all Beth needed to know.

"Well, well, well... I feel so foolish." She murmured as she picked up the small frame.

"She's pretty, a student?" It was a subtle dig for a thirty-two-year-old man.

Tom saw the futility of lying. "No, she works in the medical lab. Listen, It's not any big deal. I was lonely. I made a mistake, I can end it."

"No, you already ended it!" She replied, trying not to show her broken heart. As the tears welled in her eyes, she slipped the engagement ring off he had given her only four months earlier, laying it, and the snapshot on the desk. Cursing herself for displaying such emotional weakness, she turned to leave. The look of betrayal on her face told Tom he would never hear from her again. His inaction when she left told her she had made the right decision.

There was an explosive jolt, and the Explorer launched into the air, coming down hard with the horrifying sound of metal grinding into asphalt, sending sparks flying from the undercarriage. It was all Beth did to hang on to the wheel, but as the Explorer skidded sideways on the shoulder, she slammed on the brakes, which resulted in the car sliding sideways onto the shoulder, perpendicular to the road.

As Steve heaved the manhole lid up, it shocked him to see the white blur of a vehicle right in front of his face. He ducked his head, as the vehicle caught the suspension protruding from under the car, and with a loud bang, the heavy disc flew off, causing a tremendous clatter of metal and squealing rubber. With the lid gone, Steve looked over the rim. It was dark, only the twin daggers of headlights shone across the road.

With a quick heave, he propelled himself up and out, calling to Jim, "Let's go!"

10

Reaching down in the open manhole, he yanked Jim up by the shoulder as soon his head popped up. Then he turned to the white Explorer sat idling on the shoulder, the acrid smell of burnt rubber hanging in the humid night air.

Beth sat stunned for a few seconds, not understanding what had happened. She thought she must have dozed off and hit the curb; she got out to see if there was any damage. As she cracked the door open, a black shadow startled her appearing at her side.

Pulling the door open, Steve said, "We need this car, now!"

"Okay," Beth recoiled, still dazed from the impact, but knowing better than to argue with a carjacker. "Can I take my cell phone?"

"Keep it, slide over! We need to," Steve told her they wanted to get down the beach about three miles, and then she could go. However, before he had time to explain, there was a loud THWACK, and the backside window disintegrated in a shower of glass.

"Get in and get down!" he yelled, pushing her across the front seat as he slid behind the wheel. Jim whipped open the rear door and with a quick swipe of his hand slid the broken glass to the floor and got in., the vehicle was still running, so Steve cranked it into drive and floored it. While only a V-6, the motor whined as it spun gravel and fishtailed down the road.

Rodney stopped running, and took quick aim with at the rear license plate with his rifle's scope, knowing he had little chance to stop the SUV from his distance.

"Virginia ADF-3016. Alpha Delta Foxtrot 30-16", he repeated it to himself three times. By now, Chavez and two other security personnel arrived.

"Whoever it was, they had help," Rodney offered. "I got a tag number, a Virginia tag."

"Get Rahim; find out who it belongs to. This is too close to the operation. I want to know if this is the Feds, and if so, why. Mr. Boulez will not be happy."

Steve kept glancing in the rear-view mirror, expecting headlights, but seeing nothing after a few minutes, his adrenaline subsided. Looking over at Beth, he noticed a knot on her forehead the size of a walnut.

"Are you okay?"

11

"Please let me go," her voice sounded slurred, "I have a little cash, but there are three credit cards in my purse, take them and let me go, please!"

"Wait a minute, calm down," Jim responded from the back seat. "We're not here to take anything. All we need is to do is get to Crab Cove, it's two miles down the beach."

Earlier they hid the dirt bikes in the marsh grass down the beach from Boulez's compound. They would have to backtrack to pick them up. Although they were untraceable to the Department, Steve did not want to tell his boss he had put them in a position not to recover the bikes.

"We need to get there before it gets too light." Steve explained, "When we get there, you can drop us off on the side of the road and go on your way."

Rubbing her forehead, Beth said, "I feel so a-dizzy... nauseated. I, I'm," Beth's head rolled back against the headrest, her eyes half shut and glazed over.

"Damn it!" Steve pulled off the road into a small boutique mall's parking area. Looking over at Beth, he realized Beth was pretty and exotic. She was not a classic American beauty. Her dark almond-shaped eyes were not Asian, but from a place over the pond.

"Greek? No, Italian?" Maybe, he thought.

"I'll get you help," He whispered. Noticing her cell phone on the console, he picked it up and dialed 911. An operator picked up after two rings. "I want to report an accident on Coastal Highway at the Sea Scape Shopping center, a white Explorer ran off the road, and can you send an ambulance?" he asked. Looking back in the mirror, he saw Jim watching the highway through the broken window.

"See anything?" He asked holding his hand over the phone's mouthpiece.

"Headlights up the road, half a mile, it could be anybody," Jim replied.

"Okay sir, can you stay on the line until we get there?" the operator queried.

Jim watched as the car passed by, slowed a little, and then sped up the road, buildings blocking it from view.

"Can you let me know the injuries; is this an emergency, sir?" The operator sounded impatient.

As Steve described Beth's injury, Jim grabbed his shoulder, and a light flashed in the rearview mirror. Looking back through the broken window, he saw the same car they saw a few minutes earlier pull in across the street and cut off its lights.

"Too early to show up for work at a used car lot isn't it?" Jim asked.

Steve had already set the phone on the dashboard, still connected to the operator. He heard the faint 'Sir? Sir?' emanating from the small speaker. Keeping his eyes on the mirror, Steve considered his options. They would engage whoever was in the car, but he did not want to put this woman in any more danger. Besides, they have backup coming. The second option was to lose them. The beach was their way out.

"Sorry, we gotta go!" he apologized to Beth.

CHAPTER 4

Benny Chavez got lucky. Driving up the coastal highway in his dark blue Mercedes, he spotted the back of a white Explorer to the side of the old boutique mall. He passed by, noticing the rear window of the SUV was missing. Chavez radioed Rodney and told him where he was.

"Get here now," he instructed. The next turn around was several hundred yards up the road, and he gunned the Mercedes around it, returning to the used car lot across the street from where he saw the Explorer. Pulling in, he cut his lights, and eased into an empty parking space, his motor idling. Watching the car for a few seconds, he wondered if they had abandoned it already. His answer came in a flash of brake lights, and a puff of smoke from the tailpipe, as the Explorer started across the parking lot.

"I got you!" Chavez muttered to himself, as he connected his two-way to Rodney again.

"They're taking off, I need you here now!"

Rodney Responded. "Give me a minute."

Reaching into his center console, Chavez removed the Browning 45 ACP he always carried there, knowing there was no better handgun for stopping power. Pushing the slide mechanism back, he chambered a round and laid the gun on the seat next to him. Although a close-range gun, a 45 round to the chest would put almost anyone or anything down for good. Yanking the shifter to reverse, the powerful car swung back and out of the parking space in one fluid motion. He knew the Mercedes would have no problem keeping up with the SUV, but he did not expect what happened next. As the Explorer reached the end of the parking lot, it jumped the curb and headed across the sand and marsh grass towards the beach.

"Damn!" Chavez yelled spinning across the highway and sliding up to the curb. He lost sight of the four-wheeler as it turned up the beach, back toward the Boulez compound. Rodney careened into the lot in less than a minute. Seeing what had happened, he jumped into the passenger side of the Mercedes, as Chavez screamed out of the parking lot, back on to the coastal highway. They glimpsed the beach between the buildings, as sunup was only about fifteen minutes away. As they raced up the coastal highway, Rodney spotted the Explorer up ahead, churning up the beach, sand, and mist trailing behind it. It helped the commercial buildings were getting farther and farther apart, development had not encroached on this section of the beach yet.

14

It worried Steve. As he looked back over his shoulder and spotted headlights through the breaks in the dunes, keeping pace with the SUV. Jim confirmed what he already knew. "It's them, we might have to ditch the car, ride out on the bikes. You think she can hang on?" Steve's mind was racing, soon he would be at the dirt bikes, what then? Beth was still woozy, her head rolling back and forth with each pitch of the SUV.

"Lady, are you all right?" He asked with urgency.

"I'm okay, better. I... please stop, please let me out."

"Love to," Steve said, "but if we stop now, whoever is chasing us will think you are with us. It would be very unhealthy for you. Stay down, do what I tell you."

"What's this all about?" Beth exclaimed, contemplating opening the door and jumping.

Steve saw thick marsh grass up ahead and knew the dirt bikes would lay it over the next rise. Jim was bouncing in the back seat, checking the magazine of his gun. He made sure both of his extra magazines were secure in their pouches.

Ignoring Beth's question Steve instructed, "When I stop the car, we have to get out and run towards the dunes. You stay close I'll get you away from here, trust me, I'll explain later."

Beth sensed these men were not trying to do her harm; she sensed an aura of confidence she knew had to come from military or police training.

"All right," She agreed. "Just get me out of here."

Steve crested a large dune, and over the top, he slid the SUV to a halt. From the road, Chavez and Roger saw the Explorer stop, the white roof visible over the ridge of a dune.

"They will hide in the marsh grass... idiots!" Chavez sneered to Rodney as he slid the Mercedes to the shoulder. "Let's go, stick close to the dune, they won't be able to see us until we get close. Remember, we want them alive. I will enjoy making these guys pay for keeping me up."

While Jim covered them, Steve and Beth broke from the Explorer and ran towards the thick marsh grass. The sand filled Beth's shoes with every step until one fell off behind her. Breaking Steve's grip, she stopped, taking several steps back to retrieve it.

"Come on, come on, leave it!" Steve reacted, reaching back and grabbing her elbow with a firm grip.

"These are my favorite Farragamos." Beth gasped.

"They'll be your last Fagaramos if you don't hurry!" Steve countered.

As they reached the marsh grass, Steve saw the dirt bikes, right where they left them. Jumping on one, he kick-started it, and in a flash spun it into the open.

"Get on!" he ordered. Beth looked hesitant, but Steve's no-nonsense look of urgency put her in motion. Her skirt was a little tight, but she slid it up and hopped on the back as Steve revved the two-stroke. Following close behind, Jim stood his bike up, and with a quick slam of his heel on the starter pedal bringing it to life, and he pulled up even with the other bike.

While Chavez and Rodney approached the Explorer, the two dirt bikes plowed through the marsh grass headed straight for the coastal highway. Rodney fired off several rounds to persuade them to stop, with Jim returning fire. Steve knew they were almost out of handgun range, so he concentrated on keeping the bike upright in the soft sand, not an easy task with a passenger. With a loud 'whump', the dirt bikes jumped the shoulder of the road, tires squealing on the asphalt.

Wasting no time, Steve made a sharp right turn and cranked hard on the throttle, he yelled back to Beth, "Hold on!"

Jim, an expert bike handler, did a 180 and stopped facing the dunes, leveling his gun at the area he last saw Boulez's men. He squeezed off eight quick rounds, hoping to immobilize them for a few minutes. Clutching Steve around the waist as they took off in a blur, Beth noticed three large crosses made of wooden poles sitting on the opposite side of the road, a hanging board announced "Jesus Saves" attached to the top of one. She hoped it was not an omen. Jim kicked his bike around to follow them, and passing the Mercedes parked on the shoulder, he slowed enough to put two well-aimed rounds into two very expensive tires.

16

A wave of relief seemed to blow through Beth's head along with the rushing wind from the speeding dirt bike. When she looked back, she was unable to see the Mercedes and Jim had caught up to them. Two miles down the road, they slowed down to a safer speed, riding two abreast, with Jim keeping an eye on the road behind them.

"It's Ferragamos," Beth yelled over the roar of the dirt bike's motor. "Not Fagaramos!"

"What?" Ross replied in manly ignorance.

"My shoes, they're Ferra, never mind." Feeling silly, she would never have brought it up. Still a little stunned from the jolt against the steering wheel, she was grasping at any fact she knew. As the cool morning air rushing by cleared her head, Beth wanted answers.

"Who are those guys, who are you?"

"They're the bad guys, we're the good guys. I'm Steve Ross, U. S. Customs, and he's my partner, Jim Ragan. Jim and I were on an assignment when we ran into you. I'm sorry for all the trouble if you can give me a few minutes I will take care of everything."

"What about my car? I can't leave it on the beach."

"I'll deal with it. We have to get away from Boulez's men."

"Boulez?" The name fired a synapse of memory in her brain. "I know that name, why do I know that name?" A vague memory, of an article she read in a professional paper last week about harvesting gold from the ocean, crossed her mind. She swore it mentioned a person named Boulez.

They screamed down the road at eighty miles an hour, soon reaching the downtown area of Key West, such as it was, within fifteen minutes. The hotels and restaurants were but crowded with tourists to afford Steve and Jim an opportunity to get to the safe house which was the second-story apartment over a cyber cafe.

"Listen," Steve said as he turned the bike into the alley of the café, "I need you to wait in the cafe for a few minutes, have a cup of coffee. I've got to change, make a call, and I'll be right back and try to explain what's going on."

He could not bring her up to the apartment; it was against policy to allow civilian access to the safe house.

17

He circled the block to make sure no one was following, as Jim pulled up behind. The wind had restyled his hair into a messy punk hairdo. Steve had to grin.

"Jim, buy her a cup of coffee, I'll be right back."

"Make it quick," Jim returned, "I need a shower. I smell like that sewer!"

"It's an improvement!" Steve joked, but realizing Jim saw no humor in the situation, he retreated with an apologetic, "Okay, okay!"

Steve looked around and found nothing out of place. He trotted to the rear of the building, and up the back steps to the safe house. After pushing the buttons on the combination lock, he entered and pulled out the watertight pouch, removing the data recorder he had stored the information he downloaded at Boulez's on. Going over to his computer, he slipped in the mini-CD, copied it to his hard drive, and forwarded a copy to Dave Spellman at the Customs computer lab. He also sent a copy by email to his boss's office, noting the lab should work on it. Within minutes, he had showered and dressed in jeans and a tee-shirt.

Down in front of the cafe, Jim peeled off his dirty stealth jersey, revealing a black undershirt, damp but not muddy. Holding out his hand, he introduced himself as he threw the jersey over the dirt bike seat, and led Beth through the door. The cafe was empty, still a little early for a resort town. Picking out a booth near the back, Jim pointed to the seat.

"Let's sit here. You want coffee?"

"No, just water, thanks. I think I have an aspirin." She was rummaging through her purse, looking for the little foil packet she kept there.

Jim got a bottle of water out of the display, setting it on the table.

"If you don't mind, I need to use the facilities. I'll be right back. Sit tight, when Steve gets down, we'll get your car back."

"All right," she said as she uncapped the water, "but I need to get home." She knew her sister would worry about her; she never stayed out all night.

Upstairs, Steve dialed his office, the switchboard putting him through to his boss, Gene Tyson, who was at his desk by 6:00 AM. Gene spoke five languages and had a Ph.D. in economics. Boredom with the corporate world had led him to a new challenge, and ICE had always intrigued him. It had taken him ten years, but now he was head of the southern Florida district, in charge of one hundred and seventy-two agents.

"We got a big problem, Gene." Steve and Gene were close enough associates to dispense with formalities.

"What's going on?" Gene responded, sensing Steve's concern.

"I ran into interference at Boulez's compound. Got a civilian involved, she's down here in the cafe."

"Uh-oh," Gene cringed, "a civilian... how bad is it?"

"His security picked us up on the way out. They tossed a couple of rounds at us, tried to corner us, but we got out. I'll brief you about this later, but we had to appropriate a set of wheels, and she was driving by. We must have hurt their feelings because they gave chase and they weren't fooling around. They wanted us bad; they followed us all the way to the shopping district. Shot up the lady's car and we had to leave it on the beach."

"What do you mean they picked you up, Steve?" It was a question would have to explain later.

"We were leaving, and they got lucky, Gene. Shit happens in this line of work, you know that."

It was not a flippant remark, rather an acknowledgment many operations affected by the slightest unforeseen circumstance. Still, he was not eager to bring up the facemask slip up.

"Anyway we had to grab the lady's wheels, and they ended up on the beach a few miles down from Boulez's. The girl is downstairs with Jim waiting for answers."

"Did you get anything from the interface?" Gene wondered.

"Whatever they had, I got it, I emailed it to you, and the lab. I'm worried about the girl now, they have her tag number. It's a Virginia tag, it might slow them down, but you can bet they'll be able to find her. I'll put her in a safe place until we can get things sorted out," He paused for a second. "I don't know what to say, Gene, I had to react when they shot. They don't know she had no involvement in this."

"Yeah," Gene sighed, hating complications. "I'll get her up to the Miami house. Don't beat yourself up over it."

The Miami house was an oceanfront apartment a drug importer forfeited last year.

"You guys stay with her I will send agents Barnes and Graves down to pick her up. They'll call you as soon as I contact them to set up a rendezvous."

"Thanks, Gene."

19

As Steve hung up, he thought he sensed the disappointment in Gene's voice. Gene was a perfectionist, expecting the same from his agents. Losing an agent working this case earlier in the year had put a special burden on him to make sure the department covered all its bases. This operation had gone south, Boulez knew they compromised his data, and now a civilian was in the middle.

As soon as Jim disappeared around the corner towards the restroom, Beth noticed a bright orange cab outside, having dropped a fare off at the motel next door. Without giving it a second thought, she tossed her business card on the table, ran out and hailed the cab.

Beth opened the rear door and plopped down on the seat, "Can you take me to Bay Vista Terrace?"

The cabby, looked up into her rearview mirror, nodding, "No problem honey, I know where it is." With a glance in the rearview mirror, she turned around, concern showing in the older woman's face.

"You okay, honey, been in a fight? You got a big bump there."

As she pulled across the road, Beth sat back, not even minding the stale air reeking of pine freshener.

"I'm okay, thanks. You should see the other guy." She gave the standard cliché response, as the cabby chuckled. Lost in thought and exhausted, she settled into the back seat and dozed off.

CHAPTER 6

Jim came out of the restroom, shaking his wet hands, "This place has no paper towels." He complained to the teenage boy behind the counter. Scanning the cafe, he saw the booth Beth had been sitting at was empty, except for the business card. He ran over and picked up the card, cursing under his breath. The only other customers were an older couple in another booth, and two biker chicks, sitting on stools at the front window.

"Excuse me; did any of you guys happen to see what happened to the lady I was with?"

The couple shook their heads no, while one of the biker chicks sneered at Jim, with his hair uncombed, and mud on his pants. She had watched him come in on the dirt bike earlier, laughing with her friend, making a joke about the dirt bike he was riding.

"A Harley starter set," she sneered, making both girls snigger.

Not hiding her disdain, she offered, "The chick booked, pal, you know what they say, little bike, little…"

"Yeah, yeah, thanks." Not waiting for the end of the innuendo, Jim ran out to the parking lot looking for any sign of Beth. He saw nothing, no cars on the road, no way to know where she was. A sinking feeling started to brew in his stomach.

"I'll be a son-of-a-bitch! What a friggin night." Shaking his head, he ran around to the back of the building. Taking the steps two at a time, he punched the code on the lock and shoved the door open.

"Can tonight get any worse?" Jim asked a startled Steve as he burst into the room. "She took off!"

"How did she do that?" Steve looked annoyed, "What happened?"

"Hell, I don't know, I had to take a piss, so I told her to wait in the booth and when I came out, she left. I was only gone for a couple of minutes. At least she had enough sense to leave her card."

Holding the card up for Steve to see, he read aloud:

Professor Elizabeth D. Williams, Ph.D.
Assistant Dean - Microbiology Department
University of Virginia Charlottesville, Virginia

21

"Ph.D., no kidding? The woman has a brain. And microbiology, heavy stuff." He took the card from Jim, noticing the formal, almost old-fashioned layout compared to the business cards in vogue. "Let's call UVA, maybe they can help us locate her."

Grabbing the phone, he dialed the number, which rang several times before it connected.

A woman answered, "Dean Williams's office."

"Hi," Steve replied, "my name is Steve Ross, with US Customs in Key West. I was speaking to a Beth, I guess Elizabeth, Williams this morning and she left me this number, but no local number. I was wondering if you had a cell phone number on file."

"Can you hold on a second?" The voice did not wait for an answer, clicking the line to hold.

After a few seconds, the phone clicked again, "This is Beth Williams, hello?"

"Beth Williams?" Steve hesitated, "You're Beth Williams?"

"Um... yes, and I'm very busy so how can I help you?" She thought to herself it may have been a little curt, but she felt having to work early on a Saturday morning to make the department's funding report deadline, instead of tending her beloved garden, gave her license.

"Sorry," Steve backpedaled, "let me start over. My name is Stephen Ross. I'm with Customs and Immigration in Key West. Earlier today, I spoke with a woman who told me her name is Beth Williams. I got this number from her business card. Do you have any idea why she would use your identity? She may have put you in danger."

"Oh give me a break, sir. If she didn't want to give you her cell number, take it as a hint. She is my daughter, she has been through a lot, and she does not need or want any complications."

The elder Beth Williams was always a little overprotective of her daughter, suspecting this might be a ploy from a rejected suitor. "I will give you credit for an original line, though."

"Your daughter? Okay, I see now. Sorry, but this is an official call. I can give you my supervisor's number. If you call it, he will patch it through on an official line. I'm afraid your daughter may be in danger, through no fault of her own." Steve's voice had a businesslike air, and it gave the elder Beth Williams pause.

"What sort of danger is she in? She's in Key West, not Mexico City!"

"I had a little run-in with the local undesirables last night," Steve explained. "Your daughter was in the wrong place at the wrong time. I needed her help, and she gave it." Steve exaggerated a little. "It may be

22

possible to trace her tag number, and I want to make sure she is okay. I need her contact number."

The elder Beth Williams took a few seconds to consider his request, then compromised. "Okay, Mr. Ross is it? I will call her and relay your information. It's her decision to call you back. Is that fair enough?"

Steve agreed. With no other immediate choice, he gave Mrs. Williams his cell phone and office numbers. Looking up at Jim, he said, "Come on, we have to go get that Explorer!"

CHAPTER 7

It aggravated Chavez and Rodney as they waited for help to change the front tire of the Mercedes. Over the cell phone, Rodney gave Rahim the tag number of the white Explorer, telling him to do a quick Internet search. Within minutes, Rahim called back with the information they wanted.

"The car is registered to an Elizabeth Williams; she lives in Virginia, Charlottesville. Single, twenty-eight."

Rodney took the information and relayed it to Chavez, "Microbiologist, on staff at UVA. It might be a coincidence."

Chavez looked weary. In his business, coincidences did not exist. "Let's find her. Tell Rahim to get a rundown on any family or relatives in the area. Check the conference schedules, hell, check the hotels. If she's stupid enough to drive their own car, she might have registered under their own name."

"What about the other two, any ideas?" Rodney asked.

"Professional. FBI, CIA, ATF, who knows? Get back in the pipe and see if they dropped anything. Find out what they did in the communication building, do a thorough sweep for bugs. See if you can get a sample of blood off the wall. We have a man on the inside that can cross-reference DNA with the FBI archives, but it takes time. We need to get the girl, she's the key. Find her and I will make her talk. Maybe we can do a little fishin' with her as bait."

Beth exited the taxi at Bay Vista Bay Terrace and entered the side door of her sister's beach house. The ocean seemed to send an invitation to her, so calm and serene in the early morning light; she considered going down to the private beach and climbing into the hammock. A note propped up on a fruit bowl sitting on the kitchen counter changed her mind. Her sister- and brother-in-law had left an hour ago to visit a friend whose baby had been born two weeks early yesterday in Ft. Lauderdale. They were planning to return late Sunday evening or Monday morning. Grateful to have the house to herself, she sat on a stool at the kitchen counter, probing the bump on her forehead. A dull ache was throbbing behind her eye sockets. Beth headed upstairs to her bathroom and rummaged in the medicine cabinet until she found a bottle of Tylenol. After popping three pills, she turned on the shower and slipped out of her clothes, examining the bump on her forehead in the mirror with disappointment.

"I bet I get a black eye." She groaned, wiping the accumulating fog off the mirror for a closer look. Stepping into the shower, she stood motionless as the hot water soothed her back and shoulders. Indulging herself after the harrowing night she had endured, Beth lingered under the relaxing spray for a while longer than she might have had her hosts been home. As the hot water softened her skin, she allowed her mind to wander back to the evening's events. Her impression of Steve Ross was he was a take-charge guy, a man who felt comfortable in stressful situations. She felt he was not prone to excess verbosity, a trait she admired in men. As an academic, she knew it is a lot harder to think when your mouth is in gear. The adage if you remain quiet, people may think you are a fool, but if you open your mouth, they will be sure, came to mind.

"It's just my luck to meet a man like Steve Ross under such bizarre circumstances." She thought. Beth allowed herself a little curiosity as she lathered the shampoo into her thick hair. *"I wonder what he's like when he's not out shooting at bad guys."*

The sudden temperature drop of the shower, the cold water poking needles into her skin, interrupted her daydream. Feeling sheepish for using an entire tank of hot water, she toweled off and threw on a pair of cut-offs and a tee shirt. In the bedroom, she sat on a small dressing stool in front of the full-length mirror, the blow dryer emitting a steady blast of hot air as she pulled a brush through her hair. Drying her hair was always a relaxing time for Beth, with the sound of the telephone or TV drowned out, she used the time for planning her day. Today, however, the conversation she had with Steve was nagging her thoughts.

"I know I've heard that name, Boulez... Boulez... Boulez. Wasn't he the person involved in funding a microbial research project at Indiana State? Or was his name Peña?" Using a tactic she often used to help jog her memory, she closed her eyes and repeated several keywords from what she remembered.

"Microbes, some type of microbes, no Peña was a researcher, now I remember, he was doing research, and he disappeared suddenly."

CHAPTER 9

Back at Boulez's compound, Rahim was doing a simple Internet search on Beth Williams. Williams is a common name, so he expected a lot of hits, and was not surprised to get two million hits on his first search. Narrowing it down to Elizabeth Williams, Ph.D., Virginia, returned a paltry sixty-five hits, of which only the first forty or fifty had any relevance. One article drew his attention, a technical paper on microbial applications for cleaning oil spills. The Author was a Dr. Elizabeth Williams, Assistant Dean, Microbiology, University of Virginia.

"This is almost too easy!" Rahim congratulated himself. Next, a white pages search located six Elizabeth Williams's in Charlottesville, Virginia. Rahim dialed, getting an answer on the first call. Beth Williams was at work, her husband stated, and would be home around four.

"One down," Rahim counted. The second call didn't pick up, and the third line was not in service. On the fourth call, Rahim hit pay dirt.

"This is Doctor Beth Williams," the voice announced, "please leave a message."

Just to make sure, Rahim dialed the last two numbers, on his list, both turned out to be not in service. Calling the emergency number, Rahim was almost unprepared when a sleepy-sounding woman's voice said, "Hello?"

"Um... uh, I'm trying to reach Elizabeth Williams," he stammered.

"This is her," Beth answered, wakened from a short nap.

"Uh, hi, Ms. Williams. My name is, uh, Rahim al-Moussad," Rahim recovered, giving a common Arabic surname, not his own. "Would you be the same Elizabeth Williams who wrote an article on microbes and oil spills, by any chance?"

"Yes, I wrote an article earlier this year for Scientific Review. What can I do for you?" Her curiosity piqued by the Arabic sounding name.

"I have some information I think you should see. I need to get it to you. Your answering machine message says you will not be back until the fifteenth, and I was hoping you would look at it before then."

27

"Well, I'm on vacation, Mr. al-Moussad, what is it? Can you send it to our office in Virginia? My assistant can review it and call me if she feels it's necessary."

"No, no, no," Rahim refused, lowering his voice. "This must be for your eyes only. I should not discuss it over the phone. I should overnight it to you." An accomplished liar, he made it sound urgent.

"All right, all right, you can send it to my sister's house in Key West, Florida; do you have a pen?"

"Yes, go ahead, please." Rahim was grinning at his ruse, as Beth gave him the street address on Bay Vista Terrace.

As soon as she hung up with Rahim, her cell phone rang again.

"Jeeze, come on," she exhaled. She picked it up and flipped open the cover. The caller ID displayed the familiar number of her mother's office, so she pushed the connection button.

"Hi, Mom."

After a quick how are you, Beth's mother related to her the story Steve Ross had given her, and Beth gave her mother a brief rundown of the previous evenings' misadventure, leaving out the part about getting shot at, not wanting to cause her Mother any additional angst.

"It's over, Mom. I hit a manhole cover in the road and bumped my head. I only got back here two hours ago. How did he find you?"

"He claimed he has your business card, so he called here. I think you should call the police now. Go with them to get your car maybe you want to come back early." She suggested.

"No, no, I'll be all right, Mother. I will call a tow truck, and they can bring the car here. I do not want to drive back to Virginia yet, I still have three weeks. I need the quiet if I will ever finish my paper." Then she added, "I'll call this Ross guy. He wants to see if I'm okay. He seemed like a nice guy, so don't worry."

Beth hung up, her mind spinning. Who was Steve Ross? Why was he involved with this Boulez guy? The name Boulez struck a vague memory in her subconscious, she was sure she knew it. What was so important his men would chase them down and shoot at them? Why should she be in danger, what is it they want with her? This was supposed to be a working sabbatical, forty-five days to finish a research paper on pollution-eating ocean microbes. Concentration would take a lot of effort now. Returning downstairs, she brewed a fresh pot of coffee and looked through the refrigerator for her yogurt. She made plans to call Steve Ross after she had breakfast, and grabbing the phone book, turned to the yellow pages to look up a towing company.

28

CHAPTER 10

After arriving back at the compound, Chavez met with Rodney and
Rahim in the security office. Rahim filled them in on the information
he had conned from Beth, giving Chavez a computer map with the
location of the beach house highlighted in yellow, and a grainy black
and white satellite photo.

"It's not a built-up area, as near as I can tell the closest house is
about two hundred yards away, there are empty lots on both sides. The
satellite photo is two years old; it's the latest I found on the Terra
Server."

"What's a Terra Server?" It always amazed Rodney the stuff
Rahim came up with on short notice.

"It's a website, U.S. Geological Survey," Rahim explained. "Type
in an address and it downloads a satellite photo of the site. The problem
is it only gets around renewing them about every four years."

Chavez glanced at the photo, handing the map to Rodney. "I'll go
over to the equipment room. Let's see what they got access to, and how
they did it. I want you to take Jose and go pick up the woman. Be
careful, the other two guys might be there with her. If so, all the better,
get them too."

The phlegmatic Jose was the ablest of the staff thugs doubling as
security for Boulez in Key West. He followed orders without question,
even showing a little initiative. Most importantly, his loyalty was
unquestioned. Chavez and Jose, both being of Latin descent, had a
contradictory relationship. On one hand, their common ancestry
instilled the responsibilities of brotherhood, and on the other, they had
a respectful caution of each other, almost but not quite, distrust. Jose
knew the bonds of ancestry only took him so far. Loyalty and
discretion would pay off big later.

Map in hand, Rodney clicked his walkie-talkie to Jose's frequency.
"Jose, I need you to meet me out front. Hurry and make sure you have
heat. Bring a box of forty-fives with you; I have target practice this
morning."

"I'm on the way, amigo."

Checking the magazine in his handgun as he walked across the
parking lot, Rodney got behind the wheel of a beige-colored van,
starting it and turning the air conditioning up to full blast. Within a

29

minute, Jose appeared with the box of ammunition, taking a seat on the passenger side. Rodney whipped the van out of the driveway, back toward the coastal highway, not wasting any time. As soon as they reached the highway, Rodney tossed his gun in Jose's lap with an ominous glance, "Make yourself useful hombre and load this up. I have the feeling we might need it soon."

It took almost 45 minutes to find the beach house, and then another few to find a secluded spot across the road where they huddled to a vantage point. The house looked deserted as Rodney scanned it with high power binoculars from the front seat of the van.

"There are no cars around, so we better wait a while, see if anybody shows up."

"Why don't we wait for her in the house?" Jose asked.

"Don't be stupid, amigo." Rodney answered, "We don't even know who they are, or how many of them might be in there. What are we going to do, blow in there and shoot it out with twenty people? Not me. I'll wait and see who shows up, or who comes out. We got time. Besides, they don't know that we know where they are, so I'm betting they will try to keep this quiet too. They screwed up and got caught last night."

"Yeah, you're right man, you watch, I'll bet we're gonna have to sit here and sweat our balls off all day." Jose leaned back in the seat and stretched his legs as much as the van would allow, trying to get comfortable. When he cranked the window down, a gentle breeze was blowing through the dunes, and with the windows down it was making him sleepy. Pulling a toothpick from his shirt pocket and slipping it into his mouth, he made the best of it. It would be a short rest.

CHAPTER 11

Jim showered and changed while Steve waited, going over in his mind the events of the evening. Once Jim dressed, they hurried down to the parking lot. Checking to make sure there was a towrope in the bed of the Department's four-wheel-drive pickup, Steve got behind the wheel and slid out into the morning beach traffic. Vacationers were heading to their favorite beaches now, stopping at the local convenience stores to stock up on ice and beer. The sun would be brutal in south Florida today, and it always amazed Steve how people sat for hours in the hot sun, summer after summer, baking their skin into leather, and then wonder why they developed skin cancer when they turned forty years old. Traffic was slowing, and soon they came upon signs warning of roadwork ahead. "Right Lane Closed Ahead" and "Merge Left" signs directed them into the left lane, as the usual idiots whose time was always more valuable than anyone else's, ran up the right side to the last moment before cutting in, causing the backup. They were close to the entrance to the gated enclave of Ocean Haven, and as they passed, Steve noticed the DOT work crew examining a manhole cover sitting about thirty feet off the shoulder.

Steve and Jim were best friends, close friends as only those who often had to trust each other with their lives become. They had come up through the ranks together, meeting in Ranger school. Both men were always in the top five percent of their peers in physical evaluations, but Steve's strength was his analytical mind, math and computer skills, and Jim was an expert survivalist, a demolition expert, and a damn good barbequer. When his military service was over, the Treasury department recruited Steve for their mandated antiterrorist investigation division. While building his team, his first request was to get Jim Regan. They were close enough friends he told Jim he would take the responsibility for screwing up last nights' operation. Admitting he slipped up by not pulling his facemask down, a rookie mistake. Jim tried to ease his buddy's self-flagellation.

"With a face like yours, you should keep it covered all the time!"

"Screw you too," Steve grinned.

Traffic was picking up as Steve pushed the pickup past slower traffic, weaving past the local retirees who were never in a hurry. It was farther than Steve remembered to the Explorer, almost ten miles. Steve

31

directed Jim to pull off the road when he saw it sitting in the dunes, right where they had left it. Sliding out of the truck, Steve looked over at Jim.

"Cover me; I'll go check it out." Jogging through the marsh grass, he paused at the dunes, looking both ways on the beach. There was nobody around the deserted beach. As he made making his way to the passenger side door, he saw the key still in the ignition. The door was wide open, so he slid in, and turned the key. It dismayed him to find the ignition silent, not even as much as a click.

"Damn." Getting back out, he gave a loud whistle, catching Jim's attention, while spinning his hand in the air. Jim had been watching Steve through the marsh grass, and waved, knowing what Steve wanted. He put the pickup into four-wheel drive, coming up to the rear of the SUV. After connecting a towrope, Steve steered the dead vehicle while Jim dragged it back to the shoulder. On solid ground again, Jim rummaged behind the pickup's seat for a pair of jumper cables as Steve looked through Beth's glove box and console, hoping to find a clue where she might be staying.

It didn't surprise Steve when Jim approached the Explorer with a terse, "No cables."

The Department would spend hundreds of thousands on a consultant, often ignoring the advice they paid for, while money for maintaining the basic surveillance infrastructure took an act of Congress. As he looked up at Jim, a bright yellow tow truck made a screeching U-Turn and pulled in behind them. Ever on alert, Jim put his hand on his service weapon, tucked beneath his arm under his light jacket.

"How y'all doin'?" A heavy-set driver shuffled out of the truck, eyeing the towrope attached to the rear tow hooks of the SUV. "A lady called and asked me to pick up a white Explorer said it was in the sand near the crosses. Is this it?"

"Depends... where did she tell you to take it?" Steve pulled out his Government ID and held it up for the driver. While Jim threw the tow rope in the bed.

"Hold on, hold on," the driver reached back into his cab and pulled out a well-worn ticket dispenser. "855 Bay Vista Terrace. It's up towards Key West. She said she'd leave the garage door open, to put it inside."

"Did she give you a phone number?" Jim asked.

32

"A phone number? Yeah, it's local, 555-7712," the driver wheezed, the increasing humidity making it a little harder for the overweight man to breathe.

"Let's go, Jim." Steve tried to sound casual, but Jim was already hurrying towards the passenger door of the pickup.

Looking back from the driver's seat, Jim announced, "we'll let her know you're on the way, thanks."

"I know Bay Vista Terrace, Steve. It's up by Mako Bay." Jim offered.

"Maybe we can get lucky," Steve suggested, as he unclipped his cell phone, and dialed the number the tow truck driver gave them. It rang four times and as Steve was about to give up, a familiar voice answered.

"Hello?" Steve guessed she had been asleep.

"Hello? Hi, this is Steve Ross. Is this Elizabeth Williams?"

"Oh yes, hi Mr. Ross, this is she. I'm sorry, I meant to call you a little while ago, I must have fallen asleep. I have such a headache. My mother called and told me you contacted her. Sorry about leaving this morning, but I wasn't thinking straight. I wanted to get home."

Apprehension was evident in Steve's voice, "You don't have to apologize, I got you into this, but I wish you had let me know. You might be in danger. I don't know if those guys traced your tag yet, but I'm sure they are trying. Are you okay?"

"Yes, I guess, this bump must have affected me more than I thought. What kind of danger am I in? What do they want with me? I didn't even see anything! I don't understand what's going on," Beth sounded annoyed.

"If you don't mind, my partner and I want to stop by to explain. When we went back to get your car, the tow truck you called showed up. The driver gave me your number and address. We're about five miles down the road." Steve did not want to sound too concerned, "We need to discuss a way to get you out of this mess."

"I don't want to get involved any deeper in this Mr. Ross. I am here on a working vacation and I do not have time for all this crap. This is your problem, not mine. Whoever was chasing you, they must have seen I was just a passerby!"

"I can't take a chance, Ms. Williams, I..."

"Beth, call me Beth," she interrupted with a hint of exasperation in her voice.

"Okay, Beth, I'm sorry I got you involved, but these are bad people. They act first and ask questions later. You are a loose end to them, and they don't want loose ends. We have a safe place for you; work with me, please!"

Not waiting for the answer, he told her, "We'll be there in a couple of minutes; we'll be in a black pickup truck. I'll blow the horn twice in the driveway, come out and talk to us, okay?"

"Oh all right, but *you* better listen, I'm warning you, I-DON'T-WANT-TO-GET-INVOLVED!"

Steve held the phone away from his ear in mock pain, as Jim smiled, able to hear Beth's words over the speaker. Pressing the speed dial button for Gene Tyson's office, he got a recorded message from the secretary requesting the caller to leave a message.

"Gene, it's Steve Ross. We found out where the woman is staying. It's a house out on the South side of Key West. We are heading over that way now. I will give Angie Graves a call as soon as I get the details. Talk to you later."

CHAPTER 12

The muted sound of a horn's quick 'beep-beep' roused Jose from his overheated stupor. Sweating from the humidity, he opened his eyes to see Rodney peering with the binoculars at the beach house.

Rodney put a finger to his lips warning Jose to stay silent and exited the sedan. Crouching low, he crept to the edge of a small dune. Stretched out in the sand, he trained his binoculars on the black pickup truck. Two men exited and scanned the surrounding dunes. He recognized their faces, as the men he chased last night. Now he remembered one of them from a recent inspection at the Fort Lauderdale pier. He was an ICE Agent that did a contraband search of Boulez's ship, the Voyager.

Rodney watched them leave the house by the side door. A woman came out of the house, walked up to the men and shook their hands. Each man offered what must have been IDs as she stood at arms-length. Whatever they were talking about, it was obvious the woman disagreed, shaking her head, and spreading her arms, palms up.

Rodney watched as all three turned to look down the driveway. Following their gazes, he spied a bright yellow tow truck bringing the Explorer to the garage. He knew he found whoever had been poking around. He hit the two-way button on his cell phone.

"Go ahead," Chavez answered.

"I've got her!" Rodney said under his breath. "She's with two Feds. As far as I can tell, they are alone. What do you want to do?"

"Do what I pay you to do! Find out what they were doing. Get them down to the pier, to the Global Trader docked at number fifty-four. Find out what they know and chop them into bait. No trace!"

The Global Trader was one of Boulez's largest freighters. A container ship, it held 90,000 tons of cargo when loaded, which was seldom. Loaded for ports in South America, the ship had a departure date two days hence, and an estimated voyage of eighty days. It contained a sophisticated onboard laboratory, similar to those installed on every one of Boulez's ships.

The cover story was they used the laboratories for research to improve the company's compliance with new rigorous offshore ballast waste and bilge dumping regulations.

CHAPTER 13

Steve and Jim pulled into the driveway at Bay Vista Terrace, their experienced eyes looking around for any sign of danger. The beach house was not big, although it had a homey, lived-in look. A pleasant sight of faded cypress clapboards, several close palm trees, and an undulating porch hammock gave it an aura of a tropical bungalow from the front. Dropping over the dunes at the rear, two-story expanses of tinted glass showed its more modern pedigree. A long wooden walk wound down to the beach, small lights protruded from the sand next to it, no doubt lighting the way to many a bonfire on the beach.

Approaching the house, Steve tapped the horn, thinking it was a wimpy sound for such a powerful truck. As they slowed to a stop, Beth slipped out of the side door and approached the pickup.

Opening the doors, Steve and Jim got out and walked toward Beth.

"Well, we meet again." Beth was the first to speak. Shielding her eyes from the midmorning sun with her hand, she seemed smaller to Steve than he remembered. She wore cut-off jeans and a crisp white tee-shirt, rolled up at the sleeves, which set off her golden complexion, perfect except for a reddish lump above her left eye.

"Hello, Beth. As I told you last night, I'm Steve Ross, and you met Jim Ragan. We work for Immigration and Customs Enforcement; we have been investigating now for several weeks near where I ran into you. Or I should say where you ran into me." Steve smiled at his feeble attempt at humor.

"Let's get to the point, Mr. Ross." It did not amuse Beth. "This is not funny. You say I'm in danger?"

"Yes," Steve said, "I will tell you things I shouldn't, but I need you to understand the situation, and why you are in danger."

"Well, then I guess I should invite you inside… out of the heat at least." She gestured to the house, leading the way as Steve continued with the basics of the story.

"The men we ran into last night work are security for a local shipping magnate, who has ties to extremist groups in Europe. ICE has been investigating activities involving him in Florida. We could never prove his involvement, but an agent disappeared last year after he stumbled onto information about this guy. Our agent, Tom Miller, undercover on one of Boulez's freighters, sent to investigate the onboard lab; suspecting it was a front for designer drug manufacturing. Our guy didn't make a connection to drugs, but what he found he

36

thought was very interesting. Before he filed a full report, he turned up missing. His last communication was a weird voice mail message to his office. Sounded as if he was calling from his cell phone, he sounded excited, but all he said was 'Boulez is growing old, notify Treasury'."

"Growing old, so what? It makes no sense. Everybody is growing old," Beth said. "Why would you have to notify the Treasury Department? Why would it be a reason to harm anybody?"

Steve looked down at the ground, "We don't know. He did not show up at the office the next day. We never saw him alive again. He had a wife and two kids. His mother lived with them. He floated up in Tampa Bay three months later."

"He was a good agent, a good biologist," Jim added. "When we found him, he had a bullet hole in his eye, and they crushed every finger and toe. I cannot imagine what the bastards did to him, they have no regard for human life. Whatever he knew, I'm sure they found out. We don't want them to believe you are working with us."

"That's why you need to stay at the safe house. The Department has one in Miami, a nice place. I think we can make them realize that this does not involve you." Steve reasoned.

"This is crazy!" Beth backed up, her voice animated. "Why would you involve me in this? No way! I will leave for Virginia tomorrow. I can't get my work done here. If they come here, they will see I'm an everyday professor. No threat to them!" As she was turning enter the house, she noticed the yellow tow truck pulling into the driveway.

"There's my car now." She ran back down the steps, pointing towards the garage. The sun was bearing down now, and she noticed glistening sweat bubbling up on both men's foreheads. "Come in while I get my checkbook." she offered, "I'll get you a cold drink before you go."

Steve and Jim glanced at each other, uncertain of how to proceed. Beth's involvement was Steve's fault, but they could force her to go to the safe house. She seemed confident, but Steve and Jim both knew all about the ruthless people they met. It would not matter to them if Beth was working for Customs or not, it was easier to eliminate her, and let God sort out any mistakes. Beth poured them each a large tumbler of iced tea and ran back outside with her checkbook. Jim watched from the doorway until she returned.

Entering the kitchen she said, "I was thinking about what you said. I mean about the agent killed, the biologist. Last night you mentioned a man by the name of Boulez, didn't you Steve?"

"Yeah, I might have." He realized Jim would have not approved of that information going out. "It's his estate we were at, I can't tell you anything more than I already have, and it's an ongoing investigation."

"Maybe I can tell you something." She frowned as if trying by force of will to float information to the surface of her memory.

"I'm a microbiologist studying microorganisms and their impact on our environment. I read many technical papers, things you would find boring. It is research on genetic coding of microbes, mutations, and developing new beneficial microbes. I recall a few weeks ago that I was reading about a scientist at Indiana State University. I believe his name was Peña. He was doing a preliminary study of microbes reproducing in the water surrounding hydrothermal vents at the bottom of the ocean. The water is hot, over 350 degrees, where these microbes thrive and reproduce. As I recall, the reproduction process of these microbes involved a byproduct of pure gold, which would be precious, assuming you amassed enough. Funding for the research came from someone named Boulez. Of that, I am positive. Anyway, after publishing his initial findings, two years ago, Peña disappeared, no one has heard from since, and Boulez discontinued funding the project."

"It might mean something." Steve was not optimistic, "You mean there are bugs making gold?"

"No, you can't make gold. It's already there, billions and billions of ounces, suspended in the ocean water. The problem is it's dispersed over the whole ocean in such small amounts, a few parts per billion, it isn't economically feasible to extract it." Beth explained, "The salt in an amount of seawater is more valuable than the gold." You would need a tremendous volume of water to get enough gold to make it worthwhile. Germans attempted it during World War Two, but they had trouble pumping enough water through their system. They diluted the water around their intakes with the discharge, creating a vicious cycle of diminishing returns. The energy required to pump the water was costing more than they realized from the process.

Steve was about to answer when a quick motion registered in his peripheral vision. He jerked around to hear a loud bang accompanied the sudden implosion of the side door. Two men, semi-automatics drawn, burst into the room.

38

Startled, Steve pushed Beth down behind the kitchen counter, the only cover between them and the intruders. In an instant, Jim reached for his weapon, trying to crouch beside an armchair.

Jose was ready, firing twice, the first bullet lodging in the back of the chair, but the second finding Jim's chest, shattering two ribs. The exit wound was the size of a tangerine, and blood and lung tissue splattered on the wall behind him. The sudden drop in blood pressure caused him to fall, semiconscious to the floor, his damaged lung sucking blood and air into a foamy mixture. Steve reached for his Smith & Wesson, as Beth and he fell to the floor, but Rodney was taking dead aim at his chest.

"Don't move asshole!" He yelled with a menacing gaze.

"Okay! Okay! Hold on!" Steve exclaimed, calculating his next move. He had no way to draw his weapon. His adversary was smart enough to stay back from his legs. He heard Jim gasping for breath, a distressed moan coming with each exhale, and Beth curled up beside him whimpering, as she covered her head with her hands.

After shoving Jim's gun across the floor with his boot, Jose approached Steve, "Turn over! Both of you!" and kicked Steve on the hip. Reaching down, he unclipped Steve's gun and put it in his back pocket. From another pocket, he pulled out two plastic ties. Grabbing Steve's wrist, he tied his hands behind his back, making sure he threaded the tie through his belt loop. He gave it a quick tug, as Steve winced at the pressure on his wrists. The flick of his gun towards Beth was all the encouragement she needed to roll over. Jose did not show her any mercy as he tightened the tie on her thin wrists. He hoped Rodney would let him have her for a while before they killed her.

"Come on, get up, asshole!" Rodney ordered.

Struggling to his feet, Steve looked over at Jim, the moans coming farther and farther apart now.

Beth stood, risking a glance at Jim. "Oh my God, oh my God!"

"Shut up!" Rodney was pushing them towards the door. "Don't move or I swear I'll plug both of you!" he hissed. Jose was already heading back across the road to get the van. On the way, he stopped at the Department four-wheeler sitting in the driveway. Climbing into the driver's seat, he started the truck up and shifted the automatic transmission to drive. Pointing it towards the wooded area beside the house, he gassed it and jumped out. The pickup rolled up and over a dune and mired itself, rear wheels spinning, in a marshy area, out of sight from the road.

Rodney stood at the window, keeping careful watch, waiting for Jose to return with the van.

"That man is a Federal Agent, he needs help," Steve said through clenched teeth.

Whipping around, Rodney pushed his gun deep into the soft tissue under Steve's chin. He grasped Steve's shirt, pulling his face close, his eyes closed and last night's garlic still pungent on his hot breath.

"Screw him, asshole! You think I give a shit about him?" Rodney snarled. "Don't make another sound, either of you, or you'll end up as dead."

Steve glanced at Beth. She was trembling, with terror showing in her eyes. He tried to reassure her by mouthing, "it's okay" after Rodney looked away. His own mind was racing, looking for any angle, or possibility of extricating them from this situation. He feared for Jim, looking over and seeing a growing pool of blood and a trickle dripping from the corner of his mouth.

Rodney turned at the sight of the van coming up the driveway. "Get in the van. Any heroics and I will leave your brains in the sand. You understand?" With a slight "Yeah" from under Steve's breath, they started for the driveway; his desperation for Jim was filling his stomach with a putrid taste. Jose rolled the van to a stop, and ran to the back, opening the double doors. Inside was empty except for two empty milk crates, and four cargo rings mounted on the carpeted floor. The cab area separated from the back by a metal barrier behind the seats. A small, meshed opening gave the occupants a view of the rear. Rodney shoved Steve into the back, and then climbed in behind him, securing his wrists to the cargo rings with another large plastic tie. Once he secured Steve, Jose reached over and grabbed Beth's butt with one hand, lifting her into the van in a vulgar shove, pushing her alongside Steve. Jose waited as Rodney secured Beth to the cargo hooks. He needed no explanation when Rodney looked up and nodded his head towards the house.

Steve pulled against his restraints, as Beth cried beside him. They both reacted in horror as they heard two sharp cracks of gunfire. Realizing what Jose had done, Ross struggled with all his might, craning his head with a look of hatred and disbelief.

"You bastard, you lousy bastard!" Steve sneered at Rodney. "I swear I'll make you pay you…" Before he finished the sentence,

Rodney slammed him in the temple with the butt of his gun, and Steve fell to the side, a large gash flowing blood onto the van's carpet.

Beth stifled a scream. The horror at what was happening unfathomable to her. As Rodney got out and slammed the doors shut, she closed her eyes, praying for the nightmare to end. She did not realize it was only the beginning.

CHAPTER 14

Jason Boulez was sitting in his office, staring out at the ocean through large sliding glass doors. A bright midday view was a painting framed in contrast with the decor of his offices, all soothing earth tones, and muted lighting. The report from the World Gold Council lying on his desk caused a slight smile to crease his face. The latest IMF gold auction resulted in a $7.23 per ounce drop in the price of gold. The value of the worldwide gold supply had dropped by about fifteen billion dollars, with the United States losing two billion alone.

Through his contacts in Dubai, he had been borrowing tens of thousands of ounces of gold each month. Selling the gold short, he benefited when the price fell, repaying his loans with ounces worth less than what he paid. Each month's profits allowed him to borrow even more gold to sell short, a cycle bringing huge profits. As long as the price of gold fell, his profits grew. He knew the price would continue to fall and he would make sure it did. However, profits were secondary to his goal. Whatever short-term pleasures they brought, his cause was Islam, and his mission was to put Islam and its followers in their rightful place. Western influence and Jews had blinded man to the truths of the Koran, corrupting whole nations with filth and greed. He envisioned a world of prayer and reflection, with all of Allah's enemies lying dead. Peace came only with eliminating the infidels. Peace would only come when Islam controlled the Holy Land.

Thinking back to when he was a young man, remembering the well-deserved hatred for the crimes against Islam by infidels drove him to violent acts, condoned by the Imam as necessary and honorable in a holy war. Allah's army had no real access to modern weaponry, determination, and martyrdom made for an effective alternative. Becoming an expert in concealing ever-smaller explosive devices, he took part in many successful sabotages and bombings, garnering a reputation as a man able to plan and organize difficult operations.

During the spring of 1978, certain Palestinians were trying to put together a cooperative link between the PLO, the Brigate Rosse, or Red Brigade as it is better known, and the German Red Army Faction. Its purpose would be to institute attacks against Zionist and Western interests in their respective countries. The leader of a Marxist faction of the PLO was a man known as Abu Iyyad who was familiar with Boulez's activities. After the brutal kidnapping and murder of the former Italian Prime Minister, Aldo Moro gave the Brigate Rosse status in the terrorist underworld. Iyyad contacted Boulez and requested he be his liaison with the Brigate Rosse. Boulez, a Palestinian sympathizer, agreed, and soon made his way from Algeria, across the Mediterranean, to southern Italy. One doctrine the PLO and the Brigate Rosse had in common was the necessity to de-structuralize the capitalist economy. It knew it had little hope of defeating the established imperialist government's militarily; therefore, its best hope for achieving its Marxist-Leninist utopia was for repeated attacks on factories, industrial infrastructure, and trade unions, and the police and the judicial system. The goal was the disintegration of the State's political process, leaving a vacuum which they were preparing to fill.

During his time in Italy, Boulez learned his lessons well. While bombs and kidnapping had their intended effect, the sheer size of the western imperialist empires and their ability to overcome the financial repercussions of terrorist attacks made him realize it would not be bombs to destroy them. Allah would smother them with their own success. He would heap coals on their heads as they wallowed in the decadence of western culture. From the outside, it would be impossible to kill them. It seems as if now, Allah has provided a way.

The soft chirp of his secure telephone interrupted his thoughts.

"Yes?" He always answered with a question rather than a greeting.

Chavez was on the line, worrying Boulez would consider the break-in by the Treasury agent and the girl his shortcoming. "We have them, as you said; we took them to the Trader. It got a little messy; my guys had to kill one."

"And the others?"

"They needed instruction on how to behave, but they're alive. Rahim is doing a rundown on the agent, I doubt if we find out much. We traced the girl earlier. She is a civilian, a biologist. I figure she's a consultant."

Boulez took a few seconds to consider the situation.

"This will be a problem after they nosed around when we got rid of the undercover agent last year. Get them off the Trader as soon as possible. I don't want to take any chance of them being found on my ship in US waters. Fly them out on the chopper to the Global Express. She's scheduled to disembark from Havana tomorrow, on her way to Aden. Find out what they know and get rid of them. No trace, do you understand?"

"Consider it done, Sir."

43

Steve struggled to wake up as he sensed a burning on the side of his head. His hands and feet were leaden, the ties binding them cutting the blood flow to a trickle. Rising from the stupor of unconsciousness, he looked at the ceiling of the van, the only light a small opaque Plexiglas vent cover. His mouth was dry, and the faint smell of exhaust filled the back of the van. Beside him, facing away was Beth, hands and feet bound behind her also, and then fastened to the cargo hooks. He saw the black dried blood on the thin carpet beside him, and the memory of the last few minutes of consciousness flooding back into his brain. The bastards! He thought to himself. The two shots he heard was Jose finishing Jim. His eyes moistened as he thought of the waste. Any man would want Jim a buddy. He would out brag you, out drink you, and outfight you, but he would never leave you behind when things got tough. Fury replacing sorrow, he vowed to himself he would make them pay! A slight groan from Beth brought Steve out of his thoughts.

Glancing up at the piece of metal separating them from the cab, Steve whispered, "Beth, are you all right, have they hurt you?"

Struggling to turn towards him, her restraints holding her arms in an awkward position, her staccato answers seemed labored, "My hands hurt from these straps. They haven't touched me, yet. I'm scared. What are they going to do?" Tears were dripping from the corners of her eyes now, "What did they do to your partner?"

"We have to stay calm, don't panic." Steve tried to sound confident. "If they wanted us dead, they would have left us there with Jim."

"You mean he's...?" A look of horror came over her face.

A dejected nod, "They didn't want to leave a witness, but holy hell will rain down on them when Customs finds out about this."

Then trying to get closer to her face, he whispered, "They will get information from us my guess is with chemicals. Try to be strong; they will let you go when they realize you are not with us. They don't want to make this even worse for themselves by killing a civilian." Steve hoped the lie sounded reassuring, but Beth's face showed she was unconvinced, as tears once again flowed from her almond eyes.

A gruff, "Shut up back there!" from the mesh window, and Steve rolled his head back, pulling against the restraints. Looking down, he saw Beth's watch, the large dial face catching the rays of light from the vent. It read twelve forty-five. He was unconscious for over two hours.

Although his head was aching, he assessed their situation, making a mental checklist of what he knew. They had to be heading north; the only logical direction from the Keys. Boulez's operation needed to be kept quiet at all costs, even the cost of bringing the full force of ICE down on him to investigate the murder of an agent. They were not dead, which meant Boulez must think we have information, or they might need us to negotiate. The van slowed and made a series of quick stops and turns. Steve heard the unmistakable sound of a ship's horn, giving two extended blasts. He knew right away, where they were. The Fort Lauderdale pier was the only shipyard close enough to reach in three hours. A few more turns and the van came to a lurching halt, Rodney and Jose exiting, slamming the doors as they left. Steve heard voices talking in a barely audible voice, the stilted cadence recognizable to Steve from his time in Iraq as Pashtu.

As they lay waiting for the rear doors to open, he felt the fear in Beth's rapid breaths. With a clunk, the back doors unlatched, swinging open. Two men of middle-eastern descent peered into the back of the van, now backed up to an open shipping container, a large grin crossing the face of the younger one. Malek the older of the two held an ominous-looking Russian AK-47 aimed at Steve's chest. Steve stared into his eyes as Malek hissed "Akmed, the woman first."

Beth recoiled as Akmed jumped into the back of the van and pulled a folding hunting knife from his back pocket. With a flick of his wrist, the six-inch blade snapped open, the blade glistening in the dim light. Steve eyed the knife as, while Akmed sliced through the ties holding Beth's feet, leaving her wrists tied.

"Get out!" Malek ordered Beth. "Get to the back." He thrust his thumb over his shoulder towards the back of the shipping container. Beth clambered out, her ankles weak from the ties; she stumbled to the back of the container, sitting as directed by Malek.

Akmed turned to Steve with a bloodthirsty look in his eyes. He would as soon cut Steve's throat as look at him.

Steve did not give him an excuse, lying still as Akmed cut his bindings. Akmed grabbed him by the collar and dragged him out of the van. The short drop to the ground knocked the wind out of Steve. Malek kicked him in the kidney with a heavy boot and then pushed him to the rear of the container beside Beth. As the van pulled away from the front of the container, Rodney and Jose appeared at the doors.

45

"Enjoy your cruise suckers," Jose swung the doors shut with a muffled taunt. The grinding of the locking levers on the door and the sound of a padlock snapping shut left Beth and Steve in almost total darkness. Steve looked around the dark container, his eyes adjusting to the darkness with the help of small shafts of sunlight streaming through several holes drilled in the container's side, near the top of the wall. Struggling to his feet, he turned his back to the wall, feeling along its surface with his fingertips.

"Where are they taking us?" Beth's voice was quiet as she pushed herself up the wall and the blood returned to her feet.

"I don't know, but the heat will come down on them when our team finds Jim. Did you live there alone? Were you expecting any visitors?"

"My sister and her husband own the house. I was visiting, and they're not coming back until Sunday night. Don't you have to report where you are going? What about your supervisor? Won't he be expecting you to report in?"

"We had no time; we had to be certain they didn't find you. I gave him a quick briefing when you were in the cafe, but he has no way to know what's happened until they find Jim."

Steve explored the container, on the front door he found what he was looking for. Several bolts passed through the door, securing the four outside lock levers to the doors. Feeling at each one he reached, he found one with about a half-inch of coarse threads exposed. By squatting down, he worked the heavy plastic slip tie against the sharp threads, grinding away a section of plastic. It took a while, the strap broke, and Jim's hands snapped free. He could barely bend his blood-starved fingers, but rubbing them and shaking his hands brought relief.

"Can you get mine off?" While Steve had been exploring, Beth had slipped her hands under her feet, bringing her bound hands to her front. Her shoulders felt a wave of relief as she rotated them to help the circulation. Jim searched the floor, spying a paper bag he had thought was trash. Kicking it, two small plastic bottles of water rolled out and hit the wall with a thud.

"The room service here leaves a lot to be desired." He stated. Picking up one bottle, he opened it up, smelled it, and offered Beth a drink. "It's okay, just water."

Beth took several swallows, while Steve examined the bottle cap. He found a small detachable ring along its bottom edge, so he removed it and pressed the strip into the keyed slot on the band holding Beth's wrists. The binder came loose and fell away from her swollen wrists.

46

He took her wrists between his hands rubbing them; he traced the deep indentations left from the ties.

"Give it a few minutes; you'll be good as new." Placing his hand on her shoulder, he tried to encourage her. "We will be all right. If they separate us, cooperate all you can, do not challenge them. They expect women to defer to them, to show respect. Don't be afraid to tell them what you know. They already know as much as you. They found you at your sister's house so they know who you are, and a lot more. A twenty-dollar internet search will give them all the information they need."

"I know nothing, what can I say?" her voice tense.

Steve was in the corner by the shafts of light. Wedging his foot into a ridge on the door, he pushed himself up to look through the small holes. Outside were row upon row of corrugated shipping containers, each one almost identical to the one surrounding them. They heard distant voices and a loud clanking against the bottom of the container. With a jolt, the container shifted, throwing Steve to the floor, Beth catching herself with outstretched arms. A moment of stillness and the container rose high into the air, gripped by the claws of a giant crane. Beth felt the same sensation as when she rode an elevator, an uneasy feeling in the pit of her stomach. Swinging as if a carnival ride, the metal box dropped three stories, and then landed with a gentle thud, metal to metal, on the deck of a huge cargo ship. Unseen deckhands attached clamps to keep it from sliding, and within moments, they heard other containers attaching to the side of theirs, the echoes of clanging metal, and the whine of cranes diminishing, as they got further and further away.

Steve scrambled back up to look out of the holes again, "They loaded us onto a container ship." Steve announced. "We might be here for a while."

He slid down the wall and sat on the dirty floor.

As Beth's eyes adjusted to the light, she came to sit beside him and noticed a trail of dried blood tracing a line down his cheek.

The gash where Rodney had pistol-whipped him was open and seeping.

Determined to help, she tore off a strip from the bottom of her Tee shirt and dabbed at the dried blood.

47

"I'll be okay." he tried to wave her off, not wanting to give in to her concern.

"Sit still or this will hurt. At least let me get the blood off your face." He didn't want to admit he needed attention, but the touch of a strange woman's hand on his face was pleasant, almost calming, and his protest was half-hearted. He winced as she got too close to the broken skin, not saying a word.

"I never imagined I would die in a shipping crate, I always hoped it would in the bed of a mountain cabin, surrounded by family and grandchildren." She said.

Steve interrupted, "Don't say that. As long as we are alive, we have hope. I have been in situations as hopeless and made it. They already made a big mistake putting us together. I would have separated us. They may let their guard down on the ship, knowing we can't get off. When they come to get us, most likely for interrogation, they will take us. It will be our best opportunity. This is a big ship. If you get away, go down to the lower decks. There will be dozens of corridors and all kinds of storage rooms and such, you name it. People have stowed away on these ships for months, raiding containers for food, necessities. Ports are never more than a couple weeks away, often less. These ships don't have a need for a big crew, so I would bet there are only ten to fifteen people on board, including the jerks who got us."

"You are asking a lot of a college professor. The most excitement I've had since I visited Sea World." Exhausted, she sat down on the floor leaned into the corner. "At least they gave us water-it must mean something."

Steve looked at her and nodded. Putting his head in his hands, he replayed the events of the last few hours in his mind. He knew Jim must be dead, he knew Gene Tyson would have to call his family and tell them. Although not married, Jim had a longtime girlfriend who lived in Orlando. It would devastate her. Just thinking of the way they shot Jim, he could not hide his anger. He promised himself he would avenge Jim's death ten times over.

CHAPTER 16

It was hot in Dubai, and the sun reflecting off the blue water seemed to amplify the temperature. Rippling heat mirages were visible across the vast expanse of a concrete pier.

As white-clad workers scurried among the many rows of containers, maneuvering huge dock lines, a powerful tugboat was nudging the rear of the great ship close to the pier. The Global Star was home in the Jebel Ali Free Zone port, after a voyage of almost ten thousand miles.

The Government of the United Arab Emirates in Dubai established the Jebel Ali Free Port. The port allowed foreign-owned companies to operate without State regulation. With hundreds of acres of warehouses, chemical storage facilities and offices, the ports were bustling 24 hours a day. There were no currency restrictions, making it an attractive port for Global Shipping.

Once secure at its berth, the massive twin 42,000 horsepower diesel engines of the Global Star shut down.

From his glass-walled office 200 meters away, Abdul Rahman watched two large tanker trucks parked near the rear of the ship.

The cargo supervisor communicated with the operators of several huge overhead cranes, ordering them back and forth, as if he was directing an army of huge spiders. Bar codes read from a hand-held device directed each crane to a specific container and after locking on, delivered the steel box to a predetermined location on the pier, or placed it on a waiting flatbed trailer.

The Global Star had a capacity of about six thousand containers, however, on this cruise only forty-two hundred were on board. Still, it would take at least two days, working around the clock, to unload her.

Rahman stopped at the door to his office, looking in the full-length mirror. He adjusted the fit of his tailored Saville Row sharkskin suit, one of at least fifty hanging in his wardrobe room of the elegant apartment he shared with his wife, Fatya.

He hurried past the receptionist, "Send for my car," were his curt instructions, feeling no need for courtesy. Rahman's driver was polishing the dashboard of the immaculate Maybach when a loud buzzer notified him his boss was descending the elevator. Two bodyguards exited the small office where they were watching television

49

and got in a black Suburban. As Rahman's driver pulled up to the elevator vestibule, the guards pulled up behind him, got out and flanked each side of the doorway. The entire operation performed with the timing and coordination of a Broadway stage show.

Rahman glanced at his watch as the elevator doors opened. He stopped near the open rear door of his limousine, nodding a demure greeting to his security detail as he slid onto the plush leather seat. .

"The Star, Hasan," confirming what his driver expected. The small convoy exited the underground garage and made the short trip to the ship. Hasan often wondered why the Operations Manager of Global Shipping in Dubai would need bodyguards, but he knew better than to inquire. Allah was kind to him, supplying him with a well-paying job, allowing him to support his family at a level of privilege unknown to most drivers.

Easing the limo into a shady area near the great ship, Hasan got out and opened the door for Rahman, the bodyguards at his side to escort him aboard. Near dock level, a short gangplank led up to a hatch door in the ship's side. The ship's Captain and a crewmember, both Indonesians, were waiting as Rahman and entourage ascended the gangplank, greeting the captain.

"Salaam Aleichem Budi, another profitable voyage I hope!"

"Yes, Sir!" Budi gave an enthusiastic response, knowing Rahman would soon reward him for bringing the great ship to port as scheduled. Overhead, a graceful ballet of cranes was unloading, and then reloading new containers as spaces came available.

Rahman whispered in his ear. "The usual protocol, no one enters or leaves this ship without my approval. Shore service will deliver a treat for you and the crew when we finish."

Budi smiled, the feast Abdul Rahman supplied his crew was always a welcome treat after eating the cooking dished from the ship's galley for a month.

"Insha'Allah, Insha'Allah," Budi offered, motioning the group of men to follow him. They walked in silence, single file down the narrow corridors, descending several deck levels into the hold of the gargantuan ship. The air temperature rose and brushing his hand against the thick bulkheads Rahman started to sweat from the heat radiating from inside.

They arrived at a hatch labeled in large letters: LABORATORY. Budi reached into his shirt and withdrew a lanyard from around his neck. Attached was an electronic key which he inserted into a small keypad. After punching in several digits, and twisting the key, a distinct click emanated from the hatch, a green LED came on to show the hatch was unlocked.

One bodyguard and the crewmember remained outside the hatch while Rahman, Budi, and the other guard entered the hatch, closing it behind them with a solid 'clunk'. Budi led them through a pair of wooden doors, into a laboratory. While not large, it had sophisticated equipment lining the walls, several computer workstations, a large lab desk, and a floor-mounted digital scale large enough to drive over with a forklift.

Along one wall were eight centrifuges, each about twice the size of a household washing machine.

Looking up from a computer screen, where he was examining an image relayed by a digital microscope, Alejandro Peña, a sturdy-looking man in his mid-thirties, looked up at the men as he slid off his stool.

"Hello, Mr. Rahman." Alejandro extended his hand, trying not to show his true feelings.

Brought to the ship with the harbor pilot as it waited for its turn to dock earlier in the day, he worked out of the large lab next to Rahman's office building. Today he needed to check the progress of his new adjustments to the 'process', as he called it.

He was a virtual captive here, his family living under the threat of death if he did not cooperate. He had no choice other than to play along. Although Rahman always treated him well, he realized his cooperation was not negotiable. Boulez's minions had met with his wife, warning her any action she might take to notify the authorities would bring dire consequences.

Peña demanded to at the least to receive candid photos of his wife and children every six weeks; it assured him of their safety. They afforded no such courtesy to Mrs. Peña. She had to take the shadowy figures Boulez sent at their word her husband was alive. A generous sum wired to her bank account every month was the only sign it was true. When they finished with him, they promised to reunite him with his family and to endow a research facility at a university of his choice. Hoping to see them again was the only thing keeping him from killing himself.

Enriching these bastards was not the reason he had invested seven years of his life experimenting and engineering his special microbes.

51

His goal had been to discover a way to help supply the gold requirements of the modern world without using the destructive and pollution causing chemical processes used for mining. He knew his research was of Nobel Prize quality, and he despised Boulez for stealing it for a misguided scheme.

With an over firm grip, intended to remind the scientist of Rahman's authority over him, he took the scientist's hand in his, placing the other on Alejandro's shoulder. "Thank you, Alejandro, you look well. Budi told me you are making good progress. Show me what you have."

As always, Rahman's coal-black eyes betrayed no emotion; neither hate nor acceptance was clear in their icy gaze. Peña felt as if he was a microbe, observed under a microscope by Rahman, the value of his life dictated only by the selfish usefulness assigned to it by this inhuman vermin.

"Oh, yes," Alejandro forced a weak smile, having already gone over in his mind the lies he would tell Rahman, "the new generation of microbes are reproducing in less than forty-eight hours. I have changed the temperature curve, along with a slight modification and configuration of the mats. So far, it has been quite successful, and to duplicate it will not cause any great modifications to the other labs. Come over here, I will show you." Walking to a large window, Alejandro pushed the light switch, and a large chamber became illuminated behind the thick glass window. "Sorry, I can only leave the lights on for a few minutes or it will kill the microbes." Inside the flooded chamber were dozens of racks containing what looked to Rahman to be large, thick window screens.

"Each rack holds 24 of those microbial mats, the oily-looking panels. We can fit fifty-six racks in this chamber, and we have four chambers on the Global Star. It gives us about 48,000 square feet of mat. On this voyage, each square foot of mat was producing at a rate of over a half-gram per 24 hours, or 25,000 grams per day."

"Our latest voyage lasted 32 days, which means we have 800,000 grams, which is 25,720 troy ounces." Rahman did a rough calculation in his head, as his eyes were gazing into the depths of the chamber. *"38 million dollars' worth of gold,"* he said to himself. *"And only one ship!"*

"Let our little friends sleep, Budi." He said to the captain, reaching out to shut the lights off. The faintest hint of a smile creased his face as he turned to leave.

CHAPTER 17

It was getting stuffy in the container as the late afternoon sun baked the dark green paint on the doors. Steve drifted off to a fitful sleep for two hours, and Beth sat in silence, every shipboard noise filling her with dread. She allowed herself to look over at Steve in the dim light while he slept; noticing the dark blue polo shirt he wore stressed the muscular build of his chest. It gave a preppy look. She looked away as he stirred, using the back of his hand to rub the gash on the side of his temple.

"Don't touch it. You'll make it bleed again."

Steve looked over at her, the foggy feeling in his brain dissipating, "Sorry, I must have dozed off. Have you heard anything?"

"There's someone talking outside, too far away to make out anything."

Within a few minutes, they felt several small vibrations through the floor, causing them to lock eyes. "The ship is underway, it's moving!" Steve announced. Jumping to his feet, he wedged his foot into the door again, straining to see out. "We're about half a mile into the bay and moving. That was the propeller kicking in."

"I hope they let us out of here soon, I've got to pee." Beth sounded anxious, and Steve tried not to look too embarrassed at her unexpected revelation. Another hour passed before muffled voices and grinding of the locking levers startled them to attention. With a loud snap, the doors swung open, and light from the early evening sun flooded the container. Standing as far back as possible, they had to squint, holding up hands to shield their eyes.

Malek yelled, "Turn around, put your hands on the wall."

As Steve hesitated, Malek pointed an AK-47 toward him, yelling louder, "Do it now, kalb." The word in Arabic was an insult, meaning 'dog'.

Steve turned to the wall, as Akmed came up behind him with a roll of duct tape, grabbing his wrists and binding them behind his back. Beth received the same treatment and once secured led out by the collar onto the deck. Looking at the horizon, Steve saw they were about 15 miles offshore, the buildings on the skyline almost lost in the haze. Malek directed them toward the stern with the muzzle of his rifle.

Walking towards the huge superstructure at the rear, Beth stopped as she noticed a hatchway in the bulkhead labeled HEAD, standing ajar.

"I have to go." She turned, gesturing her head towards the door, looking into Akmed's eyes. "I can't wait." Surprised at her boldness, he hesitated.

Not giving him time to consider, she turned back around, holding up her arms "You will have to untie me."

Looking back at Malek for approval, it surprised him when Malek gave an exasperated flick of his hand. Taking a razor-sharp knife from his pocket, he flipped it open and sliced the tape on her wrists.

"Don't lock it, you have two minutes. Two minutes and I'm coming in, done or not." The door slammed shut before he finished his threat.

While they waited, Steve heard the unmistakable sound of helicopter rotors winding up. Glancing to the top of the superstructure, he caught sight of a spinning tail rotor.

Soon, Steve broke the uncomfortable silence. "She has nothing to do with this. You have a chopper. If you drop her off on the beach, I will cooperate."

"You'll cooperate anyway, I'll see to it!" It was Rodney, coming down a steep stairway, Jose following close behind.

"Don't make this worse. You have already killed a federal officer. My office knows what I was doing; they will put two and two together and come up Boulez. US Customs will board every one of his ships in US water tonight."

Rodney looked over at Jose and gave a smirk, "I guess we must make sure we're not in US waters, now won't we!"

Akmed banged on the hatchway, "Let's go, now!"

Beth pulled the door open, surprised and disappointed to see Rodney and Jose standing with the others. "Oh how nice to see you, again." The sarcasm was thick.

"Upstairs, hurry" Malek directed, pushing the barrel of the AK-47 into Steve's backbone and shoving hard. Akmed grabbed Beth by the arm, not taking the time to re-tape her wrists, pulling her up the steep stairway. Reaching the upper deck, the helicopter was ready to take off. Rodney climbed in beside the pilot, Akmed pushed Steve into the rearmost seat and Beth to the front with Malek beside her. Jose sat beside Akmed, who had laid the AK-47 on the floor at his feet, and pulled out a small semi-auto, holding it up as a warning to Steve. Lying across both seats in the back, Steve was glad as he stretched out.

Putting on a pair of headphones, Rodney spoke to the pilot. "How long will it take, Carlos?"

"About two-and-a-half hours, if we're lucky, sir. He replied. With seven people, this baby will only get 100, 110 miles an hour. The Global Express is about 230 nautical miles from us, by the time we get there, she'll put another 40 or 50."

Nodding, Rodney leaned back, stretched out his legs as far as possible, "Okay, vamoose."

CHAPTER 18

Steve looked around the cabin of the Bell 206 Lone Ranger, amazed at how outfitted it was. He was familiar with the 206; the army used it for MEDEVAC during the first gulf war. He flew ones that were stripped down to the bare essentials to improve range and speed.

Shifting to gain a more comfortable position, he earned an angry stare from Akmed. He saw the side of Beth's face reflected in the small window, her shoulder leaning against the bulkhead of the helicopter two rows ahead.

It was still light as the chopper started a slow bank, shaking a little in the turbulence from in the sub-tropical air. Far below Steve spied a huge container ship, its deck stacked high with colored metal boxes, looking like a display of Pez candy from their altitude. His ears popped as the helicopter circled the ship, and he read 'Global Express' in letters twenty feet high across the broad stern.

Guiding the Bell to a soft landing, Carlos shook Rodney awake, "We made good time, two hours forty-five."

"That's why we pay you the big bucks, Carlos!" Rodney smiled, "Get it gassed up, I want to go back tonight." Then he turned to face the cabin, shouting, "Everybody out, step on it!" His smile disappeared into a nasty sneer.

Rodney had radio telephoned Captain Rene, the Master of the Global Express during the flight, telling him to prepare a secure area for two of Mr. Boulez's 'guests'. There would be no questions from the ship's Master.

Boulez handpicked all the captains on his ships and recruited Rene as a young man. His progress through the ranks of responsibility watched and his loyalty tested. He had full authority for the ship while underway, except for the laboratory which was autonomous.

Two biologists and their helpers, stayed in the lab, their quarters comfortable, even plush, by ship's standards, and self-contained.

Captain Rene's duty was to fulfill a simple mission: Keep the great ship moving at sea for the greatest number of days possible, maintain a steady 23 knots. It was necessary to complete port calls as required and it would process only freight available for immediate loading. Other container ships might wait in port for several days to get loaded, but not a Global ship. Competitors of Global Shipping could not imagine how the company sent the great ships to sea, loaded to less than full capacity. How did they discount shipping costs on the freight they carried and never hear a hint of financial difficulty? Rumors circulated Boulez paid for fuel with gold bullion.

Standing on the superstructure, the first mate joined them, as the Bell's rotors came to a stop. He recognized Rodney; he met him earlier in the year when he accompanied Mr. Boulez on visits to the ship's laboratory.

"We have an area secured for your guests, sir." Rodney waved the barrel of his semiautomatic pistol, pointing out Steve and Beth to the first mate.

"Good, take them below. Have the steward fix us dinner, and then we'll deal these two."

"Should I bring dinner for your guests?"

Bending closer to the first mate's ear, Rodney sounded ominous under his breath, "They won't need it."

The helicopter fell silent, only the sound of a muted warning buzzer from the control panel breaking the stillness of the landing pad.

"Akmed, help Carlos fuel her back up, then meet us in the mess hall." Pushing Steve and Beth by the shoulders, the group headed for the stairs, Malek and Jose keeping their weapons trained on Steve. Several decks down, the First Mate opened the thick wooden door to a small berth, the inside devoid of furnishings, except for a lumpy cot, the thin mattress pad covered by a clean sheet. Shoving Beth inside, Jose warned, "I'll be back to see you later." A large brass slide bolt on the outside ensured she would be there when they got back. Down the corridor, a steel hatch door was ajar; a brass plaque overhead read 'VALVE CABINET 15.'

Leading everyone to the cabinet, the first mate gave an apologetic look to Rodney. "It's the best we can do, Sir. We've never needed a lock-up. We removed the screw handle from the inside."

Rodney entered the cabinet, measuring six feet by twelve, the two bright lamps mounted to the ceiling giving ample light. Along the outside wall were two dozen large pipes running from floor to ceiling, labeled for contents and flow direction. Large gate valves on each pipe controlled those flows, and saucer-sized gauges, displayed various temperature and pressure readings. Swinging on a hook was a clipboard with several sheets of paper, the top page noting the readings from each gauge at four-hour intervals. A small air vent near the ceiling was the only opening. Four solid steel walls, welded to the deck and ceiling, a steel door, and no way to open the locking dogs from the inside.

"This will do. There's no way out of here." Again, Carlos was the one who pushed Steve into the room, raising his eyebrow to challenge him when Steve turned and glared at him. Closing the hatch door, Rodney turned the screw handle and pushed down on the locking lever. Grabbing a nearby fire ax from a recessed cabinet in the bulkhead, he wedged its fiberglass handle into the latch as an added measure of security.

"He's not going anywhere. Let's go eat, I'm starving."

CHAPTER 19

Steve listened at the door with his ear pressed flat, the sounds of footsteps fading in the distance, and a bulkhead door being secured. He knew there was not much time. Sitting on the floor, he worked his bound hands under his butt, then with a struggle over his boots, and up past his knees to freedom. Using his teeth, he unwound the several layers of duct tape on his wrists, until his hands were also free. Thankful they had not thought to shut off the lights, he explored his small prison. It did not take long, the small crew kept a spotless ship. This cabinet was no exception. Aside from the clipboard, the only loose item was a roll of electrical tape.

With a swift smack of the clipboard against a valve handle, the metal clipping mechanism separated from the board. The main metal clip was about seven inches long, rounded on both ends. Bending one end back towards the middle, Steve took the roll of tape and wound it around, using the entire roll. The makeshift knife wasn't sharp, but with enough force, the point would put out an eye, or puncture a lung. He took the duct tape that had bound his hands, tearing off short lengths to wrap around each wrist. Gathering the broken clipboard, and excess tape, he stashed them out of sight on the ledge where he found the electrical tape. It had been a long day, and easing himself down against the wall, he sat, willing himself to gather his focus, and conserve energy. He felt extra responsibility for Beth; she is an innocent bystander in these events, vowing to himself to get her away or die trying.

An hour passed before the clatter of footsteps echoed in the corridor again, unintelligible voices resonating fear ahead of them. Beth was sitting on the cot, the warmth of the thin fitted sheet she had draped around her shoulders comforting her against a blowing air conditioner vent. The door bolt sliding away caused her to cower in fear at the back of the cot, dread filling her throat with a bitter taste.

The door opened to the chilling faces of Rodney and Jose, the latter's eyes giving Beth a creepy feeling, as they took no shame in the obvious appraisal of their expected reward. Malek was right behind them, also trying to get a glimpse of the girl from the hallway.

"Wait outside," Rodney instructed the two men, stepping inside and shutting the door behind him. The pause had its desired effect.

Beth asked, "What do you want?"

Rodney pulled her to a standing position, brushing the hair from her cheek with the back of his hand. "It would be a shame to let Jose defile such a nice lady. Rumor has it he is maybe HIV positive, he doesn't have much of a conscience, you know."

She remembered Steve's advice to cooperate.

"As I tried to tell you before, I was driving by when Steve, Mr. Ross, uh, hijacked me. How could I know what he was doing at Boulez's estate?"

"Oh, but you know it was Boulez's estate? What else do you know about Mr. Boulez? Ross had to give you an explanation for what happened!"

"No, nothing, nothing at all." Tears were rolling from the corner of her eyes.

"Nothing at all? Tell me, you are a biologist, are you not?"

"Yes, I'm a microbiologist, so what?"

"I'll tell you *so what*," he emphasized her words, "the thieves in the United States Government are trying to interfere in a biological research project we have, research Mr. Boulez has paid quite a lot of money to undertake. The Government seems to think they can monitor our research, which takes place in international waters, and therefore is none of their business. Their pitiful attempts at infiltrating our operations have ended in disaster for them. We hoped they might get the message after one of their operatives, who got in a lab, met with an unfortunate accident. Now *you* show up, another biologist, along with your friends, all snooping around Mr. Boulez's personal residence. Mr. Boulez is a private man; the word coincidence is not in his dictionary. As you can see, we have good reason to believe you are part of their operation. If you tell me everything, and I mean everything you know, I promise you I will let you live. I will instruct the Captain to put you ashore in San Juan tomorrow. If not..." He glanced at the door separating them from Jose, implying her fate.

"I can't tell you what I don't know!" She wailed.

His patience was running out as he gripped her throat with a strong hand, squeezing, and lifting her weight at the same time. "Can't or won't? You will talk; it's up to you how unpleasant it gets. Is this worth your life?"

Fighting against his steel grip, she used up what little oxygen she had in her lungs, causing her body to go limp. Rodney let her fall to the cot.

60

"Lying little bitch, I'll be back." Kicking the door open, he fumed to Jose, "I'm not playing around. Either he tells me what I want to know, or I'll hang him off the stern for shark bait until he does!"

Steve heard the voices in the corridor, and he knew they were near the berth where they had put Beth.

"If they laid a hand on her..." He felt the anger percolating in his gut. Breathing deep, he willed himself to relax, concentrate, and focus. He repeated the mantra while the loud talk filtered in from unseen crevices in the walls. It did not last long. It was a hopeful sign; they would not give up and kill her so soon. Soon he heard the footsteps approaching, outside the valve cabinet door. It was Rodney, his voice loud and menacing.

"Open it and keep the guns on him. If he gets funny, plug him, I'm not playing around."

Steve was standing against the wall, facing the door. He tucked the homemade knife into his waistband in the center of his back, only an inch protruding above his belt line. He held his hands together behind him to hide the hilt of the shiv. It would take a close examination to tell the duct tape was not binding his wrists.

Jose turned the latch mechanism while Rodney kept his .45 ACP aimed at the door. When he pulled it open a few inches, Rodney saw Steve standing against the wall, hands behind him.

"Don't move, prick. Not a hair or I'll drop you!" He and Malek edged through the door, as the other two men watched from the hallway. Surprised to see the tape still binding his wrists, Rodney grabbed Steve by the sleeve, yanking him back to the door, a gun pressed into the flesh beside his spine. "Let's take him down to the girl's room. We will need space"

Jose was across the narrow hallway, pointing his weapon at Steve's chest. The opportunity was minuscule, but when it presented itself, Steve reacted with the speed of a cobra. As Rodney pushed Steve ahead of him through the doorway, he stepped sideways to allow Malek space to exit the room. Steve spun around, deflecting Rodney's gun with his elbow, and with one swift movement, pulled the knife from his waistband. An ungraceful pirouette put him behind Rodney, holding him between Jose and himself. Kicking back against the door, he slammed it shut, knocking a surprised Malek off his feet inside the valve room.

61

Pushing his foot against the closed door for leverage, Steve jammed Rodney up against Jose, pinning both men against the wall. Then, with a powerful thrust, Steve brought the knife up and through Rodney's suit coat and shirt, burying the blunt shank it into his kidney, severing the renal artery. The excruciating pain buckled Rodney's knees, causing his finger to contract on the trigger of his gun, which discharged a round into the wall near Jose's head. So startled was Jose, he ducked sideways holding his hand out in front of him in an instinctive move to block the next bullet. Another hard push to the back sent Rodney to the floor in a crumpled heap, knocking Jose off balance. Rodney's limp body fell in front of the valve room door, blocking Malek from opening the door, while his gun skittering down the metal deck, out of Steve's reach. With no time to think, Steve picked up the only weapon available, the fire ax, and took a vicious swing at Jose, aiming for the gun he was raising for a shot. The ax clipped the barrel of Jose's gun, knocking it from his grip and sending it up the hallway in the opposite direction. A moment of fear showed in Jose's eyes, watching paralyzed as Steve waved the fire ax ready to bash in the smaller man's head. It was necessary for Steve to step over Rodney's body to get closer to Jose, and as he did, a shaky hand reached up from the floor and grabbed his boot. In his last act alive on this earth, Rodney Best tripped Steve, causing him to fall towards Jose. Falling onto his hands and knees, the impact knocking the ax from his grip, as Jose backed up, he retreated up the hallway, bending to scoop up his gun as he ran by.

Scrambling back to his feet, Steve took three large strides back towards Rodney's gun, and dove to the floor, pivoting on his hip. He spun around grabbing the .45 as he slid by. In one motion, he rolled over to the opposite side of the hallway. Malek shoved at the door, trying to slide Rodney's body over to let him out. Jose was almost to the end of the hallway, firing behind him as he ran, bullets ricocheting off the walls and floor. Forced to stay behind, Malek ducked down to avoid catching a stray bullet. Steve, using Rodney's body for cover, fired several shots after Jose. A cloud of smoke from the gunfire obscured his vision, and the sound of a distant door slamming shut and the hurried echo of footsteps on the stairway told him he had missed.

Jumping up, for a second he considered dealing with Malek, but thought better, remembering Falstaff's axiom "Discretion is the better part of valor". Spinning the lock mechanism, he secured the Arab in his former prison.

"Sit tight, I'll be back for you!"

Blood was soaking through Rodney's clothes and streaming across the hallway. Steve slipped in the viscid fluid, and hovered over the ashen face for a second, gun ready, confirming the hollow stare of death.

"No time to waste!" was his only thought as he wiped the blood from the sole of his shoe onto Rodney's pant leg and ran up the hallway to the locked berth. Working the stubborn slide bolt down, he opened the door to see Beth standing in the corner, holding the sheet in front of her as if it would afford a little protection. Purplish and yellow bruises on each side of her neck contrasted with her even tan.

"Steve! You're okay! I was sure they'd shot you!" She ran to him, burying her head on his shoulder as she hugged his neck.

Taken aback, he brought his free hand up and patted her back. She felt so tiny to him, so much smaller than she looked, he considered holding her for a moment, as reality snapped him back to attention.

"They tried. I killed one, but the Latino got away. He'll be bringing help soon. We have to get away from here." Holding his hand up for silence, he heard several men running in a distant stairwell. "They're coming, let's go." He grabbed her small hand and led her into the hallway. Beth gasped she saw Rodney motionless on the floor, copious amounts of black blood draining into the gutter running along the base of the hallway. Steve paused over Rodney, reaching down to extract the knife, sliding it into the rear pocket of his jeans. His other hand was squeezing the pockets of the dead man's jacket, hoping to find a spare magazine for the .45. A pat or two on an inside pocket yielded the magazine, and as Steve wrestled it out, a gray plastic card fell out onto the floor. Computer circuits embossed on one side converged at a clear square area in the center. Picking up both items, Steve looked over at Beth, pointing down the hall.

"Run over there, hurry! I'll catch up in a second..."

"But..." she hesitated.

"Run damn it, NOW!" He gave her a gentle shove.

As Beth ran down the hallway, the long hallway, Steve reached into Rodney's breast pocket, removing a cloth handkerchief. Stepping on the dead man's hand to flatten it, he picked up the fire ax, and with a one-handed chop, severed the lifeless thumb from Rodney's right hand. He picked it up and wrapping it in the handkerchief; he stuffed it down his front pocket and ran after Beth.

63

Catching up to her as they neared the end of the hallway, they rushed through the steel door and slammed it behind them, as two rounds thudded into it, one shattering, but not penetrating, the reinforced glass panel. An aluminum stepladder leaning against the wall caught Steve's eye. Just a few inches taller than the width of the hallway which turned at a 90-degree angle from the door; he could wedge it between the wall and the bottom of the door, jumping on it to lock it in place. Now, no one could open the door from the other side. Pulling her hand again towards a nearby stairway his voice was businesslike. "Remember what we talked about in the container? Go below to find a hiding place."

CHAPTER 20

Donald Ferlazzo had been the Treasury Secretary for six years under President Peter Branson's administration. A Harvard Business School graduate, he made his mark in the pharmaceutical industry, amassing a fortune worth an estimated half a billion dollars by the time he was 48 years old. While professing his acceptance of the appointment to Treasury Secretary as altruism, a way to give back to the people, his ego played a bigger role. He wanted recognition and respect. Over the last several months, whatever his stock with the public had been, it was diminishing in lockstep with the decline in the price of gold.

Sitting in a cabinet meeting, he was going over the report he would have to give today. Herbert Bergamore, the head of the Security and Exchange Commission (SEC), and Robert Rayson of the Commodity Futures Trading Commission (CFTC), would be at his side to help clarify recent events in the world gold markets. A large LCD video screen at the far end of the room would display the charts and projections they had prepared.

Ferlazzo and his associates talked for almost two hours. Gold bullion and gold futures had been in a steady free fall since early in the year. While far from a catastrophe, the trends showed no optimism for improvement in the near term. An influx of gold was flooding the world markets, driving the price down to lows not seen in decades. Gold bullion was over thirty-eight dollars lower than last year, reducing the value of the country's bullion by thirty and a half-billion dollars. This was meaningless to a trillion-dollar economy not based on gold; however, it was still ten percent of the value of US reserves.

Ferlazzo rose to make his conclusions, hoping not to sound too alarmist, "Our problem is not the value of our gold reserves. We already own enough gold bullion to back every physical dollar. As you know back in 1971 when Richard Nixon abandoned the gold standard, the United States entered the floating currency system. We no longer set the gold value of a dollar, nor does any other country. It rises or falls according to the demand for the metal."

Walking to the screen, he pointed to a map of the African Continent. "The problems we face are the difficulties arising with the social turmoil produced when nations such as Lesotho, Eswatini and

Ethiopia, to name a few, have their gold industries devastated by prices too low to sustain the labor force. Most of these nations are fertile breeding grounds for the radical Islamic movement. We would face tremendous pressure to provide aid, financial, humanitarian and military, to prevent these governments and populations from turning to our enemies for help. It's the proverbial 'Catch 22'. This would cause our economy to tank trying to provide the massive aid required to keep our economy from tanking." He continued, "If you look at the model of Afghanistan, the coming to power of the Taliban, and the costs associated with cleaning that mess up, you will see the danger this situation presents. We need to find out who is flooding the markets with gold. Then we need to stop it. I see this as a matter of the utmost National Security."

The President thanked Ferlazzo and his associates and turned to Ned Watley the interim CIA director.

"Ned, what do you know about this situation, have you had any discussions with our friends at the KGB or the MI-6 boys?"

"Yes, we have got feelers from several gold producers," Mr. President, "In fact we received a call this week from Alexi Goudrov, Russia's Deputy Finance Minister."

"Isn't he the Minister we helped with the Chechen oil well sabotage problem last year?" Peter Branson had a talent for remembering names.

"He's the one. Seems the price drop has hit them hard. They have 82 billion in reserves but worry about their mining industry. If the decline in prices continues much further, the viability of producing one of their major cash producing exports comes into question. Russian gold has been receiving stiff competition from Middle Eastern gold sources. He didn't come out and say it, I got the distinct impression he thinks Britain and the United States are dumping reserves to help pay for our military operations in the middle east."

Mulling the information for a few seconds, the President's tone was serious. "The gold is coming from somewhere. If there's smoke indicating Middle Eastern involvement, we should look for fire there, first. We know there are certain factions who have no compunction against operating outside the purview of the IMF or World Bank. As I understand Mr. Rayson, the world's gold production is static, around twelve hundred tons a year. A large influx means two things. One, a bad actor is releasing bullion outside of the regular established international channels, or two, there is a new source we are not privy to. Either way, I will not allow this disruption to have a ripple effect on the United States' economy."

66

Branson stood up, gathering the reports laying on the conference table in front of him, and handing them to his aide. Preparing to leave the cabinet chambers, he turned, speaking with the clear baritone, no-nonsense voice that had helped him to be a two-term president. The formal addresses conveyed the seriousness he felt." Mr. Watley, Mr. Ferlazzo, I want to know who is doing this, and what they hope to achieve. Let's get to work."

CHAPTER 21

The kicking and yelling at the blocked doorway grew fainter as Steve and Beth made their way into the bowels of the great ship. With only fourteen crewmembers on board, the chance of running across anybody was remote, but Steve wanted to be cautious. Bypassing the mechanical deck which included the engine room, machine shop, and anchor rooms, he led Beth to the container deck. One of four large caverns on this ship, each one having a mechanized roller system allowing it to push selected containers onto an elevator platform, and then transports them to the top deck.

It took close to fifteen minutes to traverse the length of the great ship, almost a quarter of a mile. Steve thought it seemed hot in the belly of the Global Explorer, and reaching out to touch the bulkhead beside him, noticed it was hot. Reaching the end of the cavern, they were at the front of the ship. Steve looked up at a ladder, welded to the bulkhead, rising over sixty feet from where they were, to a small landing. They supported the first ten feet above the deck by a chain mechanism. Pulling on the chain would lower the bottom section to a slot in the deck. As Steve cranked the ladder down, the faint sound of men's voices far behind them meant Jose and friends were doing a sweep on this deck level. They might have ten minutes until they arrived.

"We have to go up, can you climb this ladder?" Steve pointed up as Beth bent over, her hands on her knees, trying to catch her breath.

Craning her neck upwards, Beth shook her head, "I'll never make it, and it's too high."

"You'll be fine, take it one rung at a time, and don't look down."

The dim overhead light shone on the bruises surrounding Beth's neck, which had grown larger and darker over the last few minutes, the distinct pattern of thumb and fingers evidence to the violent method of questioning Rodney used.

"That jerk did a number on you." Genuine concern showing in Steve's dark eyes, he reached over and cupped Beth's neck, brushing against a bruise with his thumb, as if trying to wipe it away. Beth felt a strange but comforting sensation from Steve's touch, the gentle invasion of her personal space was pleasant.

"I feel better now. He promised to put me off in San Juan tomorrow if I told him everything I know. When I told him the truth, I don't have a clue what's going on, he got so mad I thought he would kill me on the spot."

Reacting to a noise behind them, Steve nudged her, as he looked back over his shoulder. "I don't think we want to wait for those guys." Showing the palm of his and offering a quick, "After you."

It was not as difficult as Beth had imagined, and she ascended the first twenty feet. Steve waited until she cleared the bottom section, and then pulled on the chain to raise the ladder back up, locking it into place on the chain dog.

Looking down, He surprised Beth. "What are you doing?"

"Just keep going, I'm coming right now!"

Steve jumped up and grabbed the chain, climbing hand over hand until he reached the lowest rung of the ladder. He pulled his weight onto the first rung, catching his breath for a second while reaching into his back pocket for the clipboard knife he had stashed there after dispatching Rodney. The chain wrapped around a circular chain wheel welded to a bracket on the bulkhead. Steve worked the knife into the small space between the wheel and the chain. If anybody pulled the chain from below, it would rotate the wheel, pulling the blade up into the mechanism, jamming it.

Beth was nearing the top, and Steve caught up, encouraging her on up the last few rungs. It took all her strength, as she pulled herself up onto the landing, the blisters formed on the fingers of both hands stinging and burning.

Steve was right behind her. "Good job, I'm proud of you." He helped her to her feet, as he looked below for any sign someone had spotted them. He heard their pursuers getting closer, although he still did not see them in the poorly lit cargo cavern. The landing was large enough for both of them so as Steve sidled by he warned her under his breath, "Careful, hold on tight." He didn't need to tell Beth, who had her arm locked around the railing in a death grip. Cracking the door open, Steve saw it opened to the main deck, very near the bow of the ship. He opened the door further, glancing both ways, gun ready in his right hand. He saw containers stacked above him four high, air scoops to ventilate the hold, and two lifeboat stations, one on each side of the bow. Two containers were missing. They made room for the swing arc of the small derrick in the bow. The base of the derrick contained an open bin where Steve saw a coiled rope with a hook attached to one end. Stepping out into the travel way he crept towards the gunwale of the ship looking back over the top of the stacks of containers. He could

69

not see the windows of the bridge from his angle, which meant if anyone were watching from the bridge, they wouldn't be able to see them either. Steve motioned for Beth to join him on deck, as he slipped over and retrieved the rope.

"I have an idea, to make it work I'll need your help. You told me they offered to let you off the boat tomorrow in San Juan, right?"

"Yes." She said.

"We have to make them think we escaped. That we made a run for it." Steve was whispering. "If we can convince them of it, they'll stop looking for us. They wanted to fly home tonight, so maybe if they think we escaped, they'll go."

Curiosity in her eyes, Beth responded, "How can we do it? The helicopter is the only way off this boat. Can you fly it?"

"I can, I may have a better way. Wait here for a minute."

Looping the rope over his shoulder, he could climb up to the top of the second container above his head, using the external hinges and lever locks of two containers as handholds. Hauling himself up, surrounded on three sides by containers sixteen feet tall, the open side facing the ocean. Walking back as far as he thought safe, he determined no one could see them from either the bridge or the deck if they stayed low. Next, he slipped the hook end of the rope into the cable slot each container had at the four corners of its roof and threw it down to the deck where Beth was waiting. With the rope in hand, Steve backed off the container and rappelled down to the main deck.

Once down, Steve led her over to the nearest lifeboat pod. Because they limited the crew size, the lifeboats didn't need to have a large seating capacity, leaving room to outfit them with an enclosed cabin, complete with a small galley, and a private head. The seating was convertible to tables and bunks. A small outboard motor mounted on the stern would help it get clear of the ship, although it's limited to a range to a few miles. The lifeboats were hooked to large steel arms released by pulling a pin in a center stanchion mounted to the deck. Counterweights on the steel arms would allow them to lower the lifeboat over the gunwale of the ship. An electric winch with dual controls, one in the stanchion, and the others aboard the lifeboat would then lower the craft on steel cables into the ocean alongside the ship, for release.

"We will do this fast," Steve explained. "I'm sure the alarm will tell them up in the bridge we have launched a lifeboat."

"Just tell me what to do, Steve, I'll try my best."

70

"I'll ride down in the lifeboat and release it. You keep a watch on me over the side. When I signal you, press the red button to release the cables, and then push the green one to raise them back up. I'll grab a ride back up on the cable. Once they figure out what's happening, they will come running. I think we have plenty of time. By the time I get can get back, they'll be close. You climb up and hide on the top of those containers." He pointed.

Beth looked puzzled, "Why don't we get in the lifeboat and leave? Why pass up the opportunity to escape?"

"They have radar on this ship, they can locate it. Once the alarm sounds because we have released a lifeboat, they will either turn this tub around or try to snag it, or they will use the helicopter to run it down and shoot the hell out it. It's made of flotation material so they will come up with a way to sink it. They don't want a lifeboat full of bullet holes turning up off the coast of Cuba. Our safest bet is to get them to stop looking for us. If they think they killed us, they have no reason to keep looking. We can hide below until tomorrow, and it will be easy to get off in San Juan, assuming our dead friend wasn't lying."

"You're right Steve, I'm glad one of us is thinking. Make sure you get back, I don't know what I'd do without you."

He ran the implications of that statement over in his mind for a second. For now, he needed to act. He reached into his waistband and pulled out the gun he picked up from Rodney, handing it to Beth.

"I want you to take this. It's on safety, push this little lever down and it will fire."

She tried to refuse, not taking the gun. "I can't. I'd never be able to shoot."

"Take it as a last resort." Not waiting for an answer, he placed the gun in her hand and then climbed up a short ladder into the rear of the lifeboat. Pulling the release pin from the stanchion, the small lifeboat glided to its launch position.

71

CHAPTER 22

Jose ran as if a wild dog was chasing him, up the five deck levels to the small mess hall. Akmed and Carlos were just finishing their meal after the difficult job of pumping fuel into the helicopter from 55-gallon drums stored on deck. Bursting through the mess hall door gun in hand, the look of urgency on his face caused the diners to jump up from their seats.

Instantly alert, Akmed ran over to Jose, "What happened, what's going on?"

Jose gasped for breath, as he looked back towards the stairs. "The son of a bitch killed Rodney! We were taking him out of the room, and the next thing I know Rodney's down and he's got his gun blasting away at me."

"Where's Malek?" Akmed asked.

"I don't know, he could be dead. I had to leave him down there. We have to find the customs guy before he finds us. You know he will come looking. Either way, when Chavez finds out about this we're dead, anyway. We can our asses if we come up with the customs guy and the chick."

Regaining his composure, he directed Akmed. "Go get some firepower from the chopper. I will get someone to show us around the boat. Meet back here in five minutes. GO!"

Meeting back at the mess hall as agreed, they made their way down into the ship, one deck at a time until they reached the deck where the shootout occurred. Still lying on the deck where he dropped, Rodney was a sick yellowish-white, his eyes rolled back in his head. The amount of blood coagulating in the hallway gutter showed he had died, his heart pumping all his blood out of his body through the severed artery in his kidney. Malek was on edge as he heard footsteps approach, and the familiar voices of Akmed and Jose caused him to beat against the door.

"Akmed! Akmed! Let me out!" Jose pulled the limp body away from the hatch door, feeling no remorse at the death of his associate, only a misplaced sense of superiority for not falling victim himself. Akmed freed Malek from the valve cabinet, and Jose didn't wait to see who would take charge now.

"Leave him. We'll come back later. Fan out and stay in sight. They must try to get down to the container deck, that's where I'd go. We'll check the crew decks as we go down, maybe we can push them ahead of us and corner them."

72

The crew decks weren't big since cargo took up as much space as possible, and the lab took up one entire deck level. They worked their way down each deck level, searching any equipment lockers, mechanical rooms, and storage closets as they descended. When they got to the deck labeled "LABORATORY" Jose pushed the intercom button several times, as he beat on the steel door with his fist. Shortly, a tired-sounding voice responded over the small speaker.

"What do you want? We have no deliveries scheduled today. Go away."

"I'm with security; we're looking for two people. Have you let anybody inside tonight? Have you seen anybody on this level?"

"No nobody has been in here, it's impossible. We haven't been out in four days. Only Captain Rene has access to the lab, if you're Security you should know that."

"You don't have to get smart, asshole. If you have any problems I want you to call the bridge, do you understand?" Jose didn't wait for the answer. He smacked the speaker and turned to the group, "Let's go!"

The lab was on the bottom deck, running the full width of the ship. It was on the same level as the container deck, the only area that remained to search. Jose wasn't high enough on the security ladder to know the lab was self-contained for the duration of the voyage. They could not leave the sealed rooms until the Captain or one of Boulez's security personnel opened it up. A watertight hatch door at each end of the hallway gave access to the area. They were the only way out at the aft end of the ship, and someone watched the long hallway that opened from either end.

"Carlos, stay here and make sure they don't double back. Nobody comes out unless it's with me, got it?" Jose gave him a small walkie-talkie supplied by the crewmember. "Call me if you have any problems."

Jose realized it would be difficult to find anybody in the huge cargo hold and even more difficult to find those who did not want to be found. The stacked containers, row after row, the only breaks were several freight elevators spaced at equal intervals around the perimeter. A passageway between containers left enough room for a large forklift to move containers. Stopping to listen, he heard faint metallic knocks emanating from the front of the ship, however, the slight movement of the ship caused the containers to groan and click with eerie dissonance, so no clear direction was obvious. Pushing on towards the bow, it was a dangerous dance, jumping and covering each other at each gap or intersection in the containers. Searching the first large compartment, sweat was dripping off the three pursuers. Twenty minutes had passed by when a chirp on the walkie-talkie stopped the procession. It was the first mate, on the bridge, sounding excited.

"Mr. Jose, Sir, they have launched a lifeboat, do you copy? They have launched a lifeboat near the bow!"

Jose held up his hand to silence the group. "What the hell, it's them! Can you stop the ship? Tell the Captain to stop the ship. We're coming up."

"But Sir, it will take at least a half-hour to stop."

"I don't care, throw the anchor out! Stop this damn ship!" Jose looked to the deckhand, "How can we get up top?"

Pointing towards the bow, he said in his broken English, "Ladder, ladder go top deck, go this way."

Running in line behind the deckhand, Jose had a sick feeling in the pit of his stomach. His life might depend on getting the boat back, or at the least destroying it. How did they mess everything up so fast?

Even though it wasn't far, everybody was sucking wind upon arrival at the base of the ladder. The deckhand unhooked the chain dog and cranked the chain with all his might. Spinning only a half revolution, the chain locked up on the chain wheel, the knife jamming the gear as Steve had expected. Aggravated, Jose pushed the deckhand aside, and cranked the chain himself, to no avail.

Jose grabbed the deckhand by the front of his shirt, "It figures, he jimmied it. Is this the only way up?"

"No, we can take an elevator. Follow me!"

CHAPTER 23

Steve wasted no time as the lifeboat smacked the water beside the behemoth hull of the Global Express. Two quick pulls of the starter rope and the small outboard fired right up. *"Remind me to thank your maintenance people, Boulez,"* he thought as he stripped the safety belt off of a bulky lifejacket. In the small cabin, he found the emergency transmitter and clicked it on. Next, he strapped the steering wheel tight with the safety belt, so the little boat would travel in a straight line. He pulled the throttle open, and the motor whined against its restraints, a cloud of oily white smoke billowing from the small muffler. Back outside Steve looked up, Beth's face only an outline, visible over the side of the ship, her dark hair blowing in the stiff wind. Locking his arm around the cable, he waved his other arm around in a circle to signal her, to no avail.

"Beth, push the release! PUSH THE RELEASE!" The thunder of the bow wave was stealing his shouts and dashing them against the side of the ship, unheard from above. *"Why won't she release the damn boat? She's looking right at me..."* His frustration was growing with each wasted second. He was sure Jose and friends would descend on them and he couldn't release the cables from the control panel of the lifeboat. He could never make it back to grab onto the cable before the boat moved away.

As Beth looked over the edge, she made out the shape of the lifeboat in the dusk; the cloud of smoke from the small two-stroke motor hid its white top. *"Where was Steve? There, was that him?"* Was it the vague shape of Steve waving, or was it her imagination? Indecision and panic were setting in. They had not expected it would be 35 feet to the waterline. If she released the lifeboat too soon, Steve would float away, and she would be alone with Boulez's men. The thought made her blood run cold.

Steve realized Beth couldn't see him, and he knew what to do. Picking up the discarded lifejacket he had removed the strap from, he yanked the chemical light off the thin cord securing it. With a quick snap, he broke it and shook it to combine the chemicals. A bright yellow-green light shined against the hull. Steve ran back and caught the cable, as he waved the light back and forth in a large arc. Within seconds a signal from above released the on-load cable clamp, with

Steve clinging to the cable, his feet gripping the clamp for support. Fighting to maintain his grip on the oily cable, he watched as the empty lifeboat made quick headway to the port side of the ship.

Beth was trying to watch in three directions at once, holding the firearm with both hands, hoping against hope she would never have to use it. Taking quick glances over the gunwale, she saw Steve clinging to the cable as it flopped him around the side of the ship. It seemed an eternity, the cable winch rewinding as if in slow motion, its methodical pace seemed to be taunting her, exploiting her patience.

"Come on, come on, come on, while I'm still young," she beseeched the inanimate mechanism.

Nearing the top, Steve yelled out to Beth. "When I get to the top, pull the retraction lever to swing me over. Wait, a few more seconds!" Looking behind him to the black ocean below, he saw the top of the lifeboat about 100 yards away.

"It should have at least an hour's worth of fuel." He said to himself. *"If they get this tub turned around, it should be at least five miles away."*

The cable slowed near the end, and Beth pulled the retraction lever, causing the davit arms to glide back over the deck. As Steve cleared the gunwale, the views down the side of the ship not give him much reassurance. Toward the center of the ship, a large elevator hatch was rising on its hydraulic rams, and Steve would not wait around to see who got off.

Jumping to the deck, he took his gun back from Beth and led her over to the rope he had left dangling from the top of the container. There was no time to spare. Jose would be there soon. With the excess rope, he tied a loop around Beth, across her chest, and under her arms, curious what had almost gone wrong.

"What happened? Why didn't you release the cable?"

"I had a hard time seeing you down there, Steve. There was smoke covering the lifeboat. I didn't know what to do until I saw the light!"

"No pun intended I'm sure. You had me worried for a second, we'll be okay now. Let's get out of here. I'll go up first, and then I'll pull you up, hang on."

They heard shouts from amidships as Steve climbed the side of the containers. Thankful for the hours he spent at the gym on the rock-climbing wall, he was standing on top of the second container within a few seconds. Pulling the slack out of the rope, he glanced down at Beth, "Are you ready?"

Flashing a quick thumbs-up, Beth wrapped her blistered fingers around the rope, grimacing in pain as Steve hauled her 110 pounds up to his level. The sounds of footsteps were right below them as Steve slipped the remaining rope over the top of the container, and they crouched in the black shadows of the containers.

Jose, Malek, and Akmed arrived at the lifeboat davit in a rush, searching the water below the ship for any sign of the boat. Akmed spotted it bobbing over the top of the waves, spotting the small flashing white light activated by the release of the cable.

"There! Look! It's out there!" Akmed yelled as he brought the AK-47 up, firing off several rounds.

The gunshots startled Jose, who gave Akmed an angry glance, "What the hell are you doing? Christ, they're a hundred miles out there, give it a rest." At least he knew where his former captives were. It was time to end this. Turning to block the wind noise from his walkie-talkie, he paged the bridge.

"Yes, this is Captain Rene."

"Captain, they are three hundred meters off the port side. Can we keep them in sight? How long to turn around?"

The captain answered. "Well, I have them on the radar, we can track them no problem. I ordered a full stop, but it takes an hour to get back. The lifeboat only has a powered range of about twenty miles; we are looking at two hours minimum. I have a port schedule to make in San Juan. I cannot afford to lose four or five hours, Mr. Jose."

"Screw your schedule. I've got a better idea." Changing the frequency on his walkie-talkie, he paged Carlos.

"Carlos, get up here, time to go!"

There was a short pause as Carlos responded, "I'm on the way."

The captain came back on. "Mr. Jose, it seems we might have another problem."

"What is it?" Jose was losing patience.

"I'm picking up an SOS beacon. They must have tripped the emergency transmitter on the lifeboat. Radar shows none other boats within range, but any airplane or a satellite flying over will pick it up and relay it to whatever is closest. We might get a visit from the Coast Guard, a patrol from Cuba, anything."

"Well we had better get there before anybody else, or you can kiss your ass goodbye, Captain."

77

The underground needed no air conditioning. Its temperature at the depth of forty feet remained a constant fifty-two degrees. A heavy-duty freight elevator designed to hold the weight of a forklift and an equal amount of product was the only way into the vault. The temperature difference from the surface seemed magnified to Rahman, although the chill was not unpleasant, as he rode the elevator down three stories into the ground. He had overseen the design and construction of the vault himself, specifying six-foot thick super strength concrete walls, floor, and ceiling, and a vault door of thick stainless steel. A perfect cube, it was small, only five meters on each side. The steel reinforcing bars in the concrete adding enough strength to repel anything short of a bunker-busting bomb. They located it in the bottom of the three-level parking garage under his office building. Aside from the airtight vault door, the only openings in the vault were two vent pipes installed to allow fresh air to circulate through the vault and to exhaust the air displaced from the elevator's movement. The pipes ran up the elevator shaft to the wall to the parking area where they nestled among other similar looking sewer and drainpipes. They connected one other pipe to a floor drain, designed to take any water seeping through the concrete from the parking structure above, and divert it to a daylight outlet beneath the nearby pier.

On the elevator besides Rahman, were one of his two bodyguards, and the forklift operator, and two trusted employees. Rahman's other bodyguard remained at the top entrance to the elevator to ensure no surprises when the group exited the shaft. Gliding to a gentle stop, the large double elevator doors parted, revealing a gleaming solid stainless steel vault door, its massive frame and hinges machined to a mirror finish.

A niche near the door held an iris scanner and a small keypad. There was a small square of metal embedded into the concrete floor, in front of the scanner. Rahman had a similar metal plate covered by a flap of carpet in a corner of his office. Before leaving to come to the vault, he had uncovered the metal plate, which was a sensitive scale. Weighing himself, including his clothes, watch, even the cash in his pocket, the information sent to the vault computer, where it was valid for twenty-two minutes, the time allotted to leave his office and make his way to the vault. To open the vault door, he needed to weigh the exact amount he weighed when he left his office, his iris had to match the data stored in the eye scanner, and he had to have a numerical code.

A coin dropping from his pocket would be enough weight difference to start a system reset.

Rahman stepped onto the scale, triggering a green light to flash with the message "Data Accepted" on the LED screen in front of him. Nesting his face into the scanner rest allowed a scanner to match the pattern of his iris with the file copy, triggering the second green light. A pleasant female voice sounded from the small speaker.

"Please enter the daily code at the tone; system reset will occur in twenty seconds."

They limited the system to three resets in a twenty-four-hour period, so it was imperative to follow the procedure. A system reset meant a two-hour delay, so Rahman entered the seven-digit number he had memorized from the codebook in his office, triggering the third green light.

The system was foolproof. The three levels of security are impossible for a thief to overcome.

A motor whining followed by a loud click was the only sign the door had unlocked. The bodyguard stepped forward and pulled the sturdy handle, opening the chamber, causing a whoosh of air to blow out as the pressure equalized.

Directing the forklift driver where to set the box, Rahman made small talk with his bodyguard as the lift operator and his helper unloaded and stacked three dozen ingots.

A satisfied grin crossed his face as Rahman looked at the gold stacked in neat piles, the last load bringing the vaults contents value to 965 million US dollars. Buyers at the upcoming World Bank auction would soon be very unhappy to see the price drop by at least another twenty dollars an ounce.

CHAPTER 25

Steve and Beth huddled in the darkness, listening to the angry voices below growing fainter. His ploy was working; Jose and associates believed Steve and Beth were on the lifeboat. Even if they got the ship back to the lifeboat, it would be difficult to maneuver the ship close enough to snag the small vessel.

Crouching side by side atop the container, there was only dim starlight to help distinguish shapes in the dark. The feverish tension eased a little, as they sat in silence, listening for any sign of Jose below. The breeze at the front of the ship was constant, and Steve felt briskness to the late-night air. Beth shivered in her tee-shirt and shorts. They afforded no protection against the wind.

"Are you cold?" He whispered.

Beth nodded her head, "Yeah, the wind has a bit of spray in it, but I'll live."

Moving around to block the wind with his body, he said, "You did a great job, Beth, a lot of women wouldn't have been able to handle all you've been through the last twenty-four hours.."

"I don't want to be alone. I'm glad you waved the light, I was about to come down and get you."

Steve smiled, knowing she wasn't serious.

"What are we going to do? Can we get off this ship?"

"Let's hope we are heading to San Juan, it's the best scenario for us. Customs has a field office there, so they can get us back to Florida. These guys will have a big problem if they don't head back in the helicopter soon. It doesn't have enough range to fly them back from San Juan, so they're stuck on board until the ship gets back within range of the mainland. They can't take the chance of leaving us alive since we know who is to blame for all this. They don't want us coming after them on U. S. territory. If the next port is San Juan, I'd almost bet the next scheduled port after is in the Mediterranean or the East coast of Africa. It would be stupid to divert from San Juan an extra two days each way, to get them back into range, so I figure they will leave as soon as they deal with the lifeboat."

Beth was shaking, "I hope your right…"

"We'll go below after things cool off a little, I'm sure we…" his thought interrupted by the unmistakable whine of the helicopter motor starting. "Hang on, things will get interesting now!"

"I wouldn't say what's happened so far has been boring!"

80

CHAPTER 26

Carlos was spinning up the powerful helicopter, glad to be in his element. Even though he was an expert pilot, he didn't appreciate flying over the ocean when it was this dark. It was very hard to have faith in your instruments when they showed a thousand feet of altitude, and you can look out and swear the ocean was only ten feet below your landing struts. That's what darkness did, it fooled you, caused you to lose your orientation. Many an experienced pilot has flown full speed into the water, thinking the whole time he was gaining altitude. Ever since he trained to fly helicopters in Viet Nam as a young man, he kept the good luck charm one of his buddies gave him dangling from a control knob overhead of whatever aircraft he was flying. A small vial filled with colored water, hanging by a piece of fishing line. The vial had helped save his life once when a shoulder-fired rocket hit his Huey. It was night then too, and the rocket severed the wires connected to his instrument panel, putting the cockpit in the pitch black. With no lights on the ground for guidance, the only way he made sure he was maintaining altitude was to watch his little vial. It worked similar to a plumb bob and told him all he needed to know. Clipped in the center of an overhead control, if it moved toward the front of the chopper, he knew to pull up, or when it moved towards the rear, he knew to level off. The vial and a glow in the dark compass got him back to base and saved his life. It was a little primitive, when the ride was rough it was useless, but he wouldn't dream of flying without it.

Jose slamming the door behind him woke him from his thoughts. "Let's get this pony in the air, Carlos, we don't have all night."

Akmed loaded a crate containing several plastic milk jugs between the seats. Carlos's first thought was it was apple juice, and after smelling the gasoline Akmed had spilled on his shoes filling the jugs, he realized what they were, and why they were there.

"I hope you have the lids tight on those, or you will blow us all to hell."

"Don't worry," Malek replied from outside, "you fly, and we do the hard work. We all go home soon." He opened a compartment, removed a long plastic case, and tossed it into the rear seat. Climbing in beside Akmed, he opened the case and withdrew one of the new SABRs

81

Boulez was issuing to his security forces. He also removed two fifty round magazines and a strap of 20 MM incendiary rounds, similar to large metal-tipped shotgun shells.

He and Akmed sat in the back seats, not bothering to strap in. They would need mobility.

The roar of the blades intensified as the Bell lifted off from the heliport. Carlos banked low over the water following the high-intensity spotlight beam the Captain had directed to the little vessel. Looking below, they saw several crewmen lined up at the gunwale of the ship, ready for the unusual entertainment.

"There it is, Jose. Two o'clock." Carlos pointed towards the light.

"Be careful, he has Rodney's gun. I don't know how much ammo he has. Try to come in from the front. We have the SABR; we can stay back a little."

Carlos agreed, hovering ahead of the lifeboat which was still motoring away from the ship. Upon Jose's signal, Akmed slid the door of the helicopter back about halfway, opening a slot where he felt comfortable firing. An annoying buzzer activated in the cockpit to announce the door was ajar.

Carlos knew how to position the aircraft. He never dreamed his experience in Viet Nam would come in handy again after all these years. Coming as close as they dared, Jose nodded a go-ahead to Akmed, who fired with the SABR. The water around the boat jumped to life with the splashing bullets, and several direct hits to the enclosed cabin shattered the windows and left a pattern of black dots on the roof. Akmed replaced his spent magazine with a fresh one and handed the assault rifle over to Jose who took a boyish joy in emptying another full magazine into the craft. Black smoke was coming from the outboard motor area, filling the cabin, and drifting from the many bullet holes.

"No way had anyone lived through that. Too bad, I wanted the girl. I would have shown her my Latino moves..." Jose poked his index finger through the circled fingers of his other hand in a crude sexual simulation.

"Carlos, bring her down over the boat, get as low as you can, I want to finish this job!"

Carlos had trouble maintaining the chopper over the lifeboat. A stiff wind was buffeting the chopper, its aerodynamics compromised by the open door. When he felt they were in as good a position as possible, they bombed the lifeboat with the plastic jugs. The first two missed, falling into the ocean, and floating beside the boat, the third bounced off the fiberglass roof and fell into the water. Waiting for the perfect moment, Akmed lobbed the two remaining jugs into the small open area behind the cockpit. Having unscrewed the caps to the last thread, the impact blew the caps off, and two gallons of gasoline-soaked the cockpit and ran down into the cabin area.

"Take her up Carlos!" Jose was playing with fire, he was eager to see how his plan would work. He loaded the SABR with three incendiary rounds and tried to hold it steady out the window, aiming for the cockpit. It would be a difficult shot. Closing one eye, Jose zeroed in and pulled the trigger. The first round was high and wide, the flash from the incendiary round glowed orange under the water for a few seconds, before sinking from sight.

"Hold it steady, damn it!" He snapped at Carlos, "Get lower, get lower!"

The helicopter descended to a few feet above the waves, as low as Carlos dared. Jose flipped on the SABR's automatic targeting and braced his foot against the doorframe. The rifle beeped almost, gaining the heat signature from the outboard motor. Jose squeezed the trigger as soon as he saw green 'Target Confirmed' light in the scope and sent another 20-millimeter incendiary round into the rear of the lifeboat. With a loud "WHOOF" and a blinding flash, the lifeboat blew to pieces, its violent shock wave catching the helicopter in its sudden updraft. Before Carlos had time to react, the updraft blew the helicopter's nose up, causing the tail rotor to dip into the crest of a wave. The blades bent by the contact with the water, forcing the metal pin holding them to the rotor shaft to shear off. Wobbling on the shaft, the rotors loosened and lost speed. Losing full rotor power brought on an unstable counter-rotation of the helicopter surprising Akmed, who was leaning out of the open door, only his shoulder and one hand steadying him. His boot slipped on the aluminum doorsill, throwing him off balance. Terror showed in his eyes as he realized he was falling, and he attempted to grab onto the doorframe. The smooth vinyl trim afforded no grip, and the oily residue on his hands from handling the gun was enough to seal his fate.

Malek made a lunge from his seat, but it was too little, too late. Akmed fell forward out of the helicopter, striking the landing strut below his rib cage. The impact broke both of his bottom-most ribs and knocked the wind from his lungs. He let out a high-pitched screech as he fell shoulders first into the blackness of the ocean. His nostrils filled with the horrible stench of gasoline mixed with saltwater, its fumes choking what little air he had from his lungs. Panic welled up from deep inside his gut, the pain in his chest as sharp as a twisting knife blade. He was not a strong swimmer to begin with, and the added handicaps diminished what little ability he had.

The water covered him as he floated on his back and burst the capillaries in his lungs as it replaced his air. He convulsed, grasping for the surface, the struggle against the weight of the ocean not winnable. He vomited his last meal as his body sunk to join the multitudes, deserved or not, who live at Neptune's depths.

Malek was incredulous, searching the dark water for any sign of Akmed. "Go lower, go lower!" He yelled at Carlos.

Carlos ignored the screams, realizing what had happened; he knew he had only a few seconds to get control of the chopper would fall into the ocean. He was fighting for control, as Malek and Jose hung on in terror, the chopper trying to spin them out into the blackness beyond the open door. Carlos pulled back on the stick to gain altitude, thankful what little of tail rotor he had was enough to keep the chopper from spinning out of control. As soon as the rear deck of the ship came into view, he edged the chopper over the helipad, his head moving back and forth as if it were a metronome, trying to judge the distance to the landing area as it rotated back into view every couple of seconds. Calling on his combat experience, where he would have to land so close to trees he would cut off a few limbs, he could line up over the helipad and cut the engine before the aircraft drifted into the superstructure at the front of the helipad. It only fell a few feet, and as it did, it slammed into the deck, collapsing one landing strut with the combined weight and force of the fall. When the big machine tilted over on the collapsed strut, the main rotor struck the deck, sending pieces of shrapnel from the blade screaming in all directions.

The three men lay moaning inside, alive but stunned from the collision with the deck. As smoke drifted from the engine cowling, several deckhands arrived with fire extinguishers, spraying their contents over the engine vents. Carlos switched off the electronics as he unbuckled his safety harness. His flight helmet had kept him unharmed, and the smell of raw fuel gave him a sense of urgency. He climbed out of the passenger side door and saw the crewmen dragging Jose and Malek by the arms to a safe distance. It only took a few moments for the shock to wear off, as Jose and Malek stumbled to their feet.

What the hell are you trying to do, kill us all?" It incensed Jose as he pulled Carlos by the shirt collar.

84

Carlos wasn't having any of it. He pushed Carlos away, "You're the one who can't hit the side of a barn. If I didn't need to get your dumb ass so close, we'd be on the way home by now." He yelled to the deckhands watching the argument, "Get the hoses up here and spray the fuel down!"

Jose gave him a disgusted look and headed over to the gunwale to see the remains of the lifeboat. The burning fiberglass was almost out. He snatched a radio from a nearby hand and scrolled the menu to bridge frequency. "This is Jose. Put the spotlights back on the lifeboat." He waited as the bridge repositioned the powerful lights to light up the wreckage, sweeping across the deck on their way to reveal a few pieces of fiberglass floating on the low waves. As he followed the course of the light traveling across the containers stacked on the deck, he swore he saw the figure of a man, for a split second, crouching on top of a container near the front of the ship.

Clicking to the bridge again, he yelled into the small transceiver, "Go back, and shine the light up front! Shine it on the containers at the front of the damn boat!" Jose guided the light to the spot he wanted. There was no sign of anybody. He stared for a few moments, deep in thought.

"That son of a bitch." He cursed under his breath. "I must be crazy!"

Malek came alongside him, looking over the gunwale, "What about Akmed?" He's my cousin, we have to get him!"

Jose said, "Forget him, we've they played us!"

85

Steve and Beth watched their supposed executions from the safety of the shadows, the distant shooting and explosions seemed to be a surreal video game. With each burst of gunfire, they heard shouts and whistles from behind them, as if the crewmembers were attending a holiday fireworks display. Their front row seats enabled them to watch the chain reaction of the helicopter blowing the lifeboat up, and the ensuing drama. Although they were too far away to see Akmed fall in the ocean, Steve thought he saw the chopper strike water.

"They're in trouble, look, they're going down!" Steve jumped to his feet, pointing.

Beth watched in awe, breathing "Oh my God!" against the helicopter's motor odd-sounding whine, as it tried to gain altitude. While the disabled aircraft spun towards the stern of the boat, and out of their sight, Steve scrambled up to the top of the containers concealing them. He crouched low; sure the darkness hid him, gaining a view as the machine slammed into the deck. From the awkward way the chopper had hit, he was expecting an explosion at any moment.

Below him Beth was calling up, "What happened, did they crash?"

"They crashed on the helipad... the crew is trying to get them out. The chopper could blow any second!" He continued watching the unfolding events, until, a huge spotlight came on, passing over him for a split second in its arc to the lifeboat. He took one last quick glance before climbing back down, seeing one man walking away and two dragged from the wreckage, both still alive. Beth waited for him to come down, aghast at the level of violence she experienced in the last day, her gentle academic lifestyle turned upside down by an indifference to human life she had never imagined possible. The smoldering wreckage visible in the distance off the port bow was a testimony of how far they will go to protect their fanatical interests. They both retreated to the dark corner again as the light returned and played over the place Steve had been standing moments before, snapping Steve to attention.

"Uh oh, damn, we will get out of here. They must have seen me. I saw at least three make it out alive from the helicopter, so once they get themselves together it won't take long for them to look for us again. We should go below to hide. It's way too open here."

"Thank God for that. What about the rest of the crew? Won't they come looking?"

"We don't have to worry too much about them, this is not their fight. They don't train for this, so as long as we are careful to keep out of sight, we'll be okay."

"Okay, I'm ready to get out of this wind." Beth shivered.

Steve tied the rope around Beth again and lowered her to the deck. Following her, he threw the rope up onto the container in case anybody came by.

Steve noticed Beth examining her blistered hands when he got to the deck, the pained look on her face obvious. Taking them in his hands, he examined her palms. Several small blisters were on her fingers, the skin ready to burst with any touch.

"I have a callus on my writing finger, but I'm not used to climbing ladders and ropes."

Steve looked sympathetic, "Ouch, I'm sorry. Maybe we can find a first aid kit below. Wait here a second."

He stepped over to the crane derrick from where he had taken the rope earlier and poked around in the attached toolbox, finding a large screwdriver and a pair of greasy gloves. Taking the screwdriver and the cleaner of the two gloves, he walked back over to Beth.

"No first aid kit here. These gloves will help a little." He said opening the hatch door to the ladder well.

Beth cringed as she put on the dirty gloves, and followed Steve to the landing, not eager to climb back down the ladder. Glad at least be out of the chilly breeze, Steve cranked the door shut and bolted the lock.

"Wait here, I'll come back up for you when I get the ladder down." He descended the ladder to the chain wheel he had jammed earlier with the makeshift knife. Taking the screwdriver, he tried to work the wedged piece of metal loose, again noticing the elevated temperature in the hold. *What generates all the heat down here?* The cool surface area of the hull alone makes the hold of a freighter a cool damp place, but this boat felt like a sauna. He resigned himself to find out why. At last, he could work the metal knife free, releasing the ladder with a sudden rush of spinning chain, slamming it into the deck below.

Heading back to the top, Beth waited on the landing, ready to descend.

"Come on down now, Beth, I'll be right here underneath you. Remember don't look down. Just come down nice and steady. You can do it!"

"I'll do my best, but we may be here all night." She said as she started down the ladder. The blisters soon broke open in her gloves, and she bit her lip against the burning pain, feeling the water from them seeping into the oily leather of the gloves. As they neared the bottom, she did not have the strength to resist anymore. The blisters were acid on her fingers, her tears clouding her vision. She stopped to steady herself, wrapping the ladder in a frantic bear hug.

"I won't make it, I can't do it."

Looking down, Steve saw they were above the chain wheel. It wasn't much farther. "You hold on tight, stay right where you are!"

Steve half-climbed, half-slid the remaining distance to the floor. Grabbing the chain again, he raised the ladder up, stopping it below Beth's feet.   "Just a few rungs Beth, come down a few and I'll lower you down."

Beth summoned everything she had left, descending five rungs to the sliding section. The pain was making her faint headed, and she let out a weak scream as she felt herself falling. Steve cranked the ladder down, bracing himself as Beth let go above his head, and he caught Beth's limp body in his arms.

CHAPTER 28

ICE Agent Robert Graves had his feet up on his desk as he and Agent Angela Barnes were discussing the schedule for the next day.

Their assignment was to transport a drug runner who they had arrested in a stolen boat sting operation, upstate for his arraignment.

The drug runners would pay top dollar for stolen boats, knowing their owners often lived out of state and were unaware, and therefore unable to report it stolen. They would relay drugs from boat to boat, with much less chance of the documented vessel drawing attention from the DEA or Customs. After a couple of weeks, they would either scuttle the boat or sell it to a chop shop for quick cash.

Florida had no end to the fresh supply of boats, and the wealthy population was putting pressure on the legislature to act.

Gene Tyson was returning from an afternoon meeting when he passed by the door to the office agents Barnes and Graves shared with four other agents. A little surprised to see them still there, he stopped to inquire about the status of the woman about whom Steve Ross called him.

"We've been trying to locate both Steve and Jim all day, Mr. Tyson," Barnes said. "They're not answering their cell phones, and there was no sign of them at the safe house. It seems they must have left in a hurry."

Graves explained further, "The department four-wheeler wasn't there, so we ordered a GPS vehicle locate, but the damn system is down for maintenance until four this afternoon. Your secretary wasn't in, and there is a do not disturb sign on the conference room door. We've been waiting here for you to finish up."

"Yeah, I was in a teleconference with Director Ferlazzo. There are very interesting things going on. I will schedule a briefing tomorrow morning." Gene looked at his watch, "The systems going to be up in fifteen minutes, see if you can push them a little while I check for messages... maybe he called. Let's meet at my office in twenty minutes."

Back at his office, Gene saw there were fourteen messages queued on his desk phone. He would have to trudge through every message, most of them mundane bureau matters, for which he had little patience.

Fast-forwarding through ten messages, he got to the one from Steve. He noted the incoming time on a yellow legal pad, as he listened to Steve's short message. It had been six hours since the message had posted, with no further communication. Gene feared that if Boulez's people had compromised his agents, they would be in a serious situation.

Opening his email, the file Steve had sent him was as he had expected. He found several columns of gibberish over three pages. Dialing the computer lab, he hoped they had been working on it.

"Dave Spellman," a distracted sounding voice answered on the first ring.

"Dave, its Gene Tyson."

"Gene Tyson? Well, how are you, old man? I don't get to talk to the main man often, it must be important!"

"I'm fine Dave, thanks for asking. The reason I'm calling is I've been wondering if you have looked at the information one of my agents downloaded to you earlier today. Steve Ross sent you a file he got on a surveillance OP. I think it may contain important information."

"Well, speak of the devil. I was going over the preliminary info. Two of my best guys started on it as soon as it came in today."

"Great Dave, what have you got?"

"Can you hold on a second? Let me get my computer to that screen."

Dave came back on the line, "Gene, I have good news. The equipment this information came from has what we call a Clipper Chip. I'm sure you know the NSA mandated any encryption devices sold by or imported to the States have the chip."

"I'm familiar with it, Dave. We had authorization from the Attorney General to use a LEAF (Law Enforcement Access Field) key to get the information."

The Clipper Chip contains an algorithm code called 'SKIPJACK'. It has a specific configuration, unobtainable as software and tampering with the chip renders the encryption device unusable.. Unauthorized users cannot bypass the chip. More important, it is illegal to provide the technology to any foreign nationals.

Dave continued, "So far we have found nothing earthshaking, although we pulled an interesting page from a secure transmission log. If you're at your computer, I can email it to you."

Moving to his desk chair, he told Dave to go ahead. Soon a short spreadsheet entitled **'MUSA'** appeared on Tyson's monitor.

GSL	JEBEL	AU	GSL	JEBEL	AU
STAR	4/10	1,221	TROPHY	6/23	2,017
EXPLORER	4/14	1,794	HALO	6/25	1,933
ADVENTURER	4/16	1,894	DISTANCE	6/30	1,114
EXPRESS	4/16	3,014	SUN	7/1	2,054
TRAVELER	4/20	2,983	VANGARD	7/3	2,112
WANDERER	4/24	1,446	MESSENGER	7/2	2,194
NOMAD	5/1	1,542	SHADOW	7/4	2,167
SIDAM	5/7	5,456	HERALD	7/15	2,093
PILGRIM	5/7	1,454	RUNNER	4/16	1,922
ROVER	5/9	601	DIRECT	4/18	2,459
MARATHON	5/10	556	CLOUD	7/18	2,574
VOYAGER	5/15	2,421	PRIZE	7/19	1,993
INTREPID	5/22	1,440	JOURNEY	7/22	1,597
WAYFARER	5/26	2,717	HERALD	7/28	2,777
DANCER	5/30	276	ENVOY	8/2	2,201
SPIRIT	6/1	1,422	COURIER	8/5	2,641
CREST	6/2	270	VANGARD	8/14	2,084
EMMISARY	6/14	1,814	SUNRISE	8/15	2,955
DRIFTER	6/14	1,826	MAJESTIC	8/15	1,429
EXCURSION	6/17	1,062	THUNDER	8/20	1,894
	K	35,209		K	42,210
	Oz	1,241,962		Oz	1,488,916
	Val	1,383,620,482.06		Val	1,658,741,246

"MUSA? Any idea what it means?" Tyson asked.

"Not yet. Our people are working on it as we speak. They have an interesting theory on the data. I'm assuming MUSA is an acronym for M-something. The 'M' could be anything, use your own imagination. Murder, Muslim, Monday, Mickey Mouse, you name it."

"I recognize most of the other names, they are all ships owned by Global Shipping, and we've done inspections on most," Gene said. "I can't say what the numbers mean. It looks to be a total at the bottom of each column. Doesn't 'K' stand for kilometer? Can it be distances?"

"Kilometer is a good guess Gene, although the bottom figure caught my analysts' eye. It adds up to almost three billion. That's a lot, and I think I know what it is. They label the line VAL, and VAL is an abbreviation for value or money."

Doing a quick calculation in his head, Gene offered "It must be the value of the cargo, Dave, it figures to about, what seventy-five million a pop? It sounds about right for a big container ship."

"You're right. It's not cargo, at least not TVs and washing machines," Gene agreed.

"Yep. The clue is in the column heading labeled 'AU'" Dave replied.

"Could it be an abbreviation for Austria, maybe Australia, or another destination?" Gene asked.

It's an abbreviation, Gene, but not for a place. All the numbers are circling around one commodity. K stands for Kilos, oz. is the number of troy ounces in those kilos, and VAL is what it's worth in dollars if it's gold at eleven hundred an ounce. AU is the periodic table designation for gold. AU stands for gold, and we think these ships have something to do with three billion dollars' worth of gold!"

"Damn! I got off the phone with Director Ferlazzo, not twenty minutes ago. We are seeing an influx of gold to the markets. Prices are dropping like a rock. We have orders from the highest levels to find out how and why, before it sets off a chain reaction affecting the gold-producing countries."

"This makes no sense. If this is gold, it's over eighty tons. That much gold doesn't appear out of thin air. Someone controls the world gold markets. The civilized world sells through the World Bank and the IMF and has to follow strict procedures to sell gold. If it came through those channels, you will trace it. From what I understand, they buy and sell most gold only on paper. Nobody's dragging tons of gold around the globe." Dave explained.

"You're right," Gene agreed, "but we may not be dealing with the civilized world."

Gene instructed Spellman to continue working on the information, as he sat on the edge of his desk, trying to make sense of the information he had discussed.

A few minutes later Angie Barnes poked her head around the open door, tapping on the frame. He waved her and agent Graves in and motioned for them to sit down.

"Thanks for coming back. What have you found out?"

"No communication yet, the GPS got a location on the pickup truck. It looks as if it's on the beach about twelve miles out of Key West," Barnes explained. "We got a GPS vehicle history for today. We had a two hour blackout period while they did the system maintenance, as far as we can tell, it hasn't moved since this morning."

"Let's get a START unit (Special Tactics Agent Rescue Team) down there. Angie, I want you and agent Graves to coordinate enough people to back them up. Cover the entire area, beach, roads, and water. Seal it off and close the perimeter until you find them. I'll want a status report every half hour."

Both agents were already on their feet as Gene finished with his instructions, knowing their boss had a good reason for concern.

"Don't worry Mr. Tyson. You know Ross and Ragan can take care of themselves," Barnes tried to reassure him.

"I hope you're right, Angie. I have a bad feeling about this, after what happened to Tommy Miller. Boulez and his people are serious people, with serious reasons to protect the privacy of their operations. We may have found out why."

CHAPTER 29

Steve looked around the cargo area as he carried Beth in his arms, finding an open area between two rows of containers where he eased her to the deck.

She was regaining her composure as he propped her feet up on the edge of the walkway to elevate her legs. Her tanned face had turned pale for a few moments, but her color returned with a rush.

"I don't know what came over me," she whispered to Steve, "It's so warm down here. I've never fainted before in my life. My blood sugar might be too low, I should eat something."

"You've been through a lot. Most people would have passed out long ago. Truth told I didn't peg you to be a tough lady, but you fooled me, so far."

A slight smile and a roll of her eyes told him she was coming around. "I wouldn't refuse a little something to eat either. Let me see what I can find. You keep watch down the aisle." He pointed to the long travel way between the several rows of containers.

Steve picked a nearby container and cranked the levers on the large door. Pulling it open, he saw it stuffed full of stacked boxes labeled 'Misushiro VCR'.

"Nothing here," he announced, "let me try another one." He opened several containers, trying to be as quiet as possible, finding each full of household electronics, laundry detergent, or barbeque grills. One was full of cases of cheap wine, and another was full of tee shirts and sweat suits. Then a container with the words "DO NOT TIP - THIS SIDE UP" caught his eye. When he opened the door, he saw it contained three automobiles. A beautiful midnight blue Porsche was at the rear, a Jaguar sedan in the middle, and in the front, a Mercedes ML55 SUV. Each had a clear plastic pouch containing the ignition keys hanging from the inside rearview mirrors.

"Well, we have a place to sleep." He told Beth as he squeezed past the first two cars. He opened the front door wide enough to slip into the Mercedes. Once in, he found the owner's manual in the glove box. The glossary directed him to the first aid kit mounted behind a small plastic panel in the cargo area of the car. He clambered over the seats and found a brand new first aid kit in a small compartment.

"I'll be right out!" He yelled to Beth as he saw her peering into the dark container. He released the lock on the rear hatch door and it rose on its pistons. The cars were bumper to bumper, so Steve got out and walked over the tops of the two cars, leaving small dents where his heels dug in.

"Someone steals these cars," he said, noticing Beth's surprised look. "The buyers will be disappointed with the quality." He gave a mischievous glance as he opened the first aid kit and motioned Beth to sit on the back of the Porsche. She felt a sense of security around Steve. He was unassuming, yet confident. Several times, she noticed a hint satire in his voice.

94

"How do you keep a sense of humor after all we've been through?"

"Well, believe it or not, I don't spend every day being chased, or killing people. My work is what you might describe as 'run of the mill'. It's a lot of paperwork, a lot of planning in the office. I've seen things nobody should have to see. These assholes killed Jim for no good reason. Children killed by bombs, people maimed, lives ruined by terrorists. If you don't keep a sense of humor, you can let things you have no control over eat away at you. It's a defense mechanism."

The mention of Jim brought a more serious tone. "Now let me see those hands."

Beth raised her hands, palm up, and Steve held each one muttering, "Uh, uh, uh," and shaking his head when he saw how the skin was raw and exposed.

"I'm sure you know this will sting," Steve said as he prepared to swab them with alcohol wipes. Beth nodded and bit her lip as Steve dabbed at them with the wipe, her eyes watered from the pain and smell of alcohol. When they were clean, he squirted antiseptic lotion on them and wrapped a gauze bandage around each hand. He finished with a few wraps of medical tape.

"That feels so much better, I can't believe it. Thanks." She was smiling as she touched his forearm. She gave him a look of genuine appreciation which caught Steve a little off guard, bringing a flush of red to his face. His eyes lingered on her face a half-second too long as he noticed her pretty smile, always a turn on for him. He averted his gaze, hoping she hadn't noticed.

"Now it's your turn, get over here." She guided him and gave him a gentle shove onto the back of the Porsche. "You don't look so good." She cleaned the dried blood from the gash on his temple and the spots where the shattered brick had made small punctures in his cheek. "You will need stitches on your head. That's going to leave a mark."

"I know, I know. It seems as if I've been collecting them," he said as he tried to stand.

She examined the large spots of blood on his shirt, and front pants pocket, she asked, "What happened here, are you hurt?"

Looking down at his pants, Steve remembered where the blood came from, "No, it's not my blood. It's from the guy I took out in the hallway."

He walked over to the container of clothes and searched around, tossing packages aside until he found a package of extra-large tee shirts. When he broke it open, it dismayed him to see all of them covered in graphics of the latest American hip-hop groups. He had never heard of the groups, and the graphics of men wearing large jewelry, standing with their arms crossed in front of several exotic sports cars, was not his style. Peeling off his bloody polo shirt, he picked out the least adorned tee shirt he found and pulled it over his head. Beth let out a little snicker when he displayed his new fashion statement. The front emblazoned with large letters reading: "You Da Bomb, B-B-Baby!"

95

"Don't say a word," he warned, feigning anger.

"Well, so much for that vaunted sense of humor," she responded with a grin.

Steve took the good-natured dig in stride as he looked towards the aft end of the ship. "I have some business to take care of. You can wait here. I'll fold the rear seat down in the Mercedes and you can try to get some sleep. Don't worry you're safe here. It would take them forever to search all these containers."

"No way, you got me into this mess, now you're stuck with me. It's spooky enough down here. I don't want you to leave me here by myself."

Steve contemplated refusing for a second before deciding where he was going, she might be useful. Besides, he was getting used to her company. "Okay, but stay close behind me, and be quiet."

CHAPTER 30

It was almost 7:00 PM as a convoy of four sedans and a van made its way down the coastal highway. Angie Barnes and Bob Graves were in the lead car with the other vehicles following close behind.

Angie had a bad feeling in the pit of her stomach. Steve Ross and Jim Ragan were not the kinds of agents to take off on a lark. There is a good reason they hadn't checked in. Graves was in radio contact with an agency speedboat, following the GPS signal from shore to direct it to the beach house.

The convoy slowed as they neared the address, and Angie briefed everybody on a group radio channel on the way, to save time. As planned, two sedans and the van pulled to the shoulder near the driveway, as the two remaining sedans pulled past and parked on the shoulder.

The rear doors on the van popped open, releasing five men in black stealth suits, high tech armor protection showing beneath their suits at critical spots. As the START unit fanned out and headed for the beach house, the remaining twelve agents covered the perimeter, keeping at least 50 yards between the START unit and themselves. Once the vehicles were stationary, a GPS signal relayed coordinates to the speedboat to guide it into the vicinity, making sure there would be no escape from the beach.

The rescue team made its way toward the house, with the two men on the right flank encountering the department's pickup truck lodged in a hole at the bottom of a steep, grassy sand dune. Lights on the dashboard indicated the ignition was on, and the truck had run out of gas.

A quick communication from them to agent Barnes notified her they found the vehicle with no obvious evidence of the fate of the two agents.

Within seconds, the rescue team was at the clearing containing the beach house and the detached garage. The only vehicle present was a white Explorer parked in the open garage. They did a quick check on it, noting nothing remarkable other than a rear window broken out. The screen door banging against the doorjamb was the only noise coming from the house.

Ben Driver was the team leader on this mission. He approached the house and sensed an aura of evil in the atmosphere, in contrast with the peaceful, idyllic setting.

A former New York City homicide detective, he had had the same feeling several times before, when assigned to investigate a violent murder.

He was a sentimental man, he never put it into words, he never explained the feeling he got at a murder scene. He always felt there was a disturbance in the fabric of human dignity lingering around violent crime. The physical silence of a dead body seemed to him to be a photographic negative. An opposite realm fighting to make itself heard. Maybe it was the spirits of those victims, trying to call attention to their violation, he didn't know. He had the same feeling now, and it was making the hair stand up on the back of his neck.

His team members had surrounded the house and popped up like prairie dogs to take quick glances into the lower windows.

Each agent cleared his assigned area converging on the side porch. Creeping low to the swinging door, one team member slipping his fingers under the bottom and opened it wide, pinning it between his foot and the house. A short safety chain with a spring on one end dangled from the top, the other end was ripped from its bracket on the doorframe. Ben Driver saw the entrance door was ajar, so he reached over and gave it a shove as he and the rest of the team readied their weapons.

The door swung open with a bang, breaking a small pane of glass as the rescue team flooded in, swinging and ducking to cover any ambush points.

Ben was the first to see Jim Ragan, lying on his side, a large pool of blood surrounding his lifeless body. He realized the body had been there for quite a while. He kneeled to check for a pulse anyway, knowing it was a waste of time. "Damn!" he muttered. "Search the house, guys." He instructed the team through clenched jaws, knowing if they found anyone else, they would most likely be dead.

Unclipping his radio, he clicked to Angie Barnes, "Angie, you and Graves need to get in here, but keep your agents at a safe perimeter from the house, for the time being," he paused, not even bothering to hide his sorrow. "We have a murder scene here. We will need a CSI unit."

The rescue team members returned from searching the house within a minute to tell Ben there were no other people, dead or alive in the house. They filed out through the front door in reverential silence, taking care not to contaminate the crime scene on the way out.

Ben waited for Barnes and Graves on the porch, taking deep breaths of the salty breeze. As he stared at the ocean, the thought passed his mind how fragile life is. Many times, it might have been him lying on the floor, guts sprayed on the wall. He looked up at a small cloud hanging in the air, thousands of feet above him, and for a moment he swore he saw Jim Ragan's face superimposed on it. *"You're getting too old for this."* He thought to himself as he watched the cloud disappear into a larger cloud.

Ben watched as the two Customs agents jogged up to the porch, the sweat beading up on their brows from the run down the driveway. He tried his best to force himself to mask his sadness over the dead agent, considering the emotion a hindrance to what needed to happen next. There were people missing. His assignment was to find them and get them back. Although he was working under the auspices Agents Barnes and Graves, the START unit was his baby, so he held them up on the porch to fill them in.

"We have a dead agent in here. It's Jim Ragan. It looks as if he's been there for several hours. There's nobody else in the house. You should take a look before the CSI team gets here for their investigation."

Barnes gave Graves an angry look as she shook her head. "This is unbelievable. Boulez isn't stupid enough to think he can get away with blowing away a Federal Agent."

"Yeah, dumb." Graves seemed unaffected.

"This makes two, don't forget Tommy Miller," Angie continued. "Whatever he's doing, he's not taking any chances. You don't kill a Federal Agent over bullshit unless you're a fool, and Boulez is no fool. This is a declaration of war against ICE, and I hope Gene Tyson will rain down hell on him for this."

They followed Ben Driver into the side door the kitchen where Jim lay. The sour smell of dried blood was permeating the room, and a few flies had made their way onto the body as Angie walked up and squatted beside Jims' head.

She saw his service weapon was missing from its small holster. There was a small neat hole in Jim's forehead above his right eye, but little blood had flowed from it. His shirt soaked both front and back, and small gray pieces of tissue splattered the wall surrounding an obvious bullet hole.

"Did you find his gun?" Angie asked Driver.

"No gun and no evidence. There is nothing else disturbed in the house. They must not have been here long."

Angie was scrolling the contacts on her cell phone as she talked. "From the size of the exit wound, they must have shot him with a hollow point. He was already dead when they shot him in the head. It looks as if he had already bled out, and they came back to finish him. They made sure there were no witnesses. I guess I better call Gene Tyson."

It surprised her when Gene answered on the second ring, only remembering his secretary was off that day when his voice came on the line.

"Tyson here."

"Mr. Tyson, it's Angie Barnes. You asked me to report back to you."

"Thanks, Angie. What do you have for me?"

"No good news. We found Jim Ragan dead at the site where we tracked the pickup. It's a beach house near Key West. Someone shot him at least twice. It was an execution. There was no evidence of a struggle. We found no sign of Steve Ross and the civilian. We have a CSI unit and the State Police on the way to secure the crime scene."

"Ah, jeez, I'm sorry to hear it, Angie. I should notify the FBI. How can this not be Boulez? Who else could it be? Sorry, I have too many questions, and not enough answers. We've been working on the data Ross downloaded last night, and there is amazing stuff there. If Boulez thinks Ross might have compromised the data, there would be plenty of motive for him to go after Ross and the civilian.

He needs to find out what Ross knows. Probably why there aren't three bodies on the floor, at least not yet."

"I agree, sir. What's our next move?"

"As you know, we've been monitoring Boulez and his whereabouts for several months. We keep track of the movements of his private plane and both of his helicopters. We also monitor his ships' communications when possible. It's the normal mundane, day-to-day operations any business would have. Boulez always files a flight plan and keeps the proper transponder frequency deployed while his aircraft is in the air. He follows the rules because he knows if he flies, and doesn't, it will draw our attention."

"Right, the drug interdiction program keeps a close watch on aircraft in our area," Angie replied. "Boulez has been clean in that regard. Why does that matter now?"

"A report I received about ten minutes ago was red-flagged. It seems one of his choppers left Ft. Lauderdale a few hours ago, without filing a flight plan. We tracked the transponder for a half-hour until it died. The only ship on its flight path large enough for it to land on was the Global Explorer, one of Boulez's ships had left Havana earlier today." Tyson explained.

"Went dead? Maybe they had to ditch at sea. It takes more than a half-hour to get a helicopter from Lauderdale to Cuba."

"No, we think they turned it off to hide their destination."

"Where the ship is now?"

"The Coast Guard has it in international waters off Cuba. It's scheduled to make port in San Juan tomorrow, early afternoon. Oh, and one other thing, Angie, the Coast Guard said they tracked an emergency beacon from the same ship that activated for a few minutes. The ship's captain maintains it was an accidental deployment in a lifeboat drill."

"Okay, not sure what that might mean, but a lot of crazy stuff going on," she replied.

Tyson ignored the comment, "We might be pissing in the wind, but in case, I will send teams to all of Boulez's ships in U.S. waters within 500 miles of here. I want you to get the START unit and get to San Juan. As soon as the Global Explorer gets back into U. S. waters, I will have the Coast Guard stop her so your team can board her. She's our best shot."

CHAPTER 31

They made their way in silence through the bowels of the ship, stopping to listen for any sounds of human activity. Steve made sure they stayed out of the field of view of several cameras mounted high on the bulkheads, even though he suspected they were inoperable from the awkward positions they hung. They hugged the outside bulkhead as much as possible, the unusual heat radiating from it causing perspiration to form on both their brows.

Running her hand on the warm metal, Beth's curiosity caused her to break the silence with a whispered question: "Steve, why is the wall so warm? It feels as hot as a furnace pipe."

"I don't know," he replied, "It's weird. The ocean water temperature around here is in the low eighties. This is not the hull. There must be a room behind it. It feels the same on both sides. I noticed the other side when we were running from Boulez's guys, it was hot too."

Nearing the rear bulkhead of the freight hold, Steve saw the door that opened to the hallway containing the lab. Holding his finger to his lips for quiet, he pointed to the door.

"This is where we have to be careful," he cautioned her. "You stay here and wait for my signal."

Steve crept up to the hatch door, inching his eye to the edge of the reinforced window panel in the center. He spotted part of the hallway and the door labeled 'LABORATORY', all looked quiet. Twisting the hatch mechanism, he cringed as its threads squealed with the announcement the door was about to open.

Steve looked back at Beth, holding his hand up for her to wait, as he cracked the hatch open, and peered down the hallway. Keeping low, he pulled the hatch open and glanced down the dim hallway. The only lights were several small round fixtures mounted high on the bulkhead.

Without looking back, he motioned for Beth to join him. Within seconds, she was at the hatch, tension causing her breaths to come in a quick, shallow rhythm.

"It looks clear," Steve spoke in a low tone. "There are no cameras. I imagine everybody's sleeping except whoever is in control of the bridge. It only takes a few people to run this ship, if you can believe it."

"Where are we going?"

"Right over here. Stay close." Steve walked over the laboratory door. A solid steel door, it had a mirror in the center. Near the side, a small panel reminded Steve of an ATM.

Beth came around beside him as he stared at the panel, pointing to the mirror. "That's one-way glass, isn't it? Are you going to get in? I've seen similar security doors in a nuclear lab at the University of New Mexico. You need a passcode to turn on the scanner, and then your fingerprint has to match one in the computer file. It's simple but effective, and almost impossible to hack."

That's right, and unless I'm mistaken, I have the passkey." Reaching in his back pocket, he withdrew the card he had removed from Rodney's pocket, as he lay dead in the hallway.

"How did you get it? I don't imagine they are passing those out to the U.S.Customs Service, are they?"

"Let's say one of Boulez's employees didn't need it anymore."

"Oh, I think I get it. Ugh!" She shuddered, remembering Steve bending over the body back in the hallway.

Steve continued with an explanation, "Boulez takes no chances. He makes frequent spot checks on his boats. We had inside information the security people he sends can override the lab security with a special card." He inserted the card into the slot, but nothing happened. "Damn, it doesn't work."

"You're doing it wrong."

Steve looked at her, "What do you mean?"

She held her hand out for the card, "I saw them do it once at UNM, let me have it." Holding it flat, she noticed three corners were round, and one was square. "This card has a registration key in the corner, see?" It fits over this scanner window." She placed it flat over the scanner window, into a recessed area, which fit the card. The clear area in the middle of the card was the same size as the scanner window.

Reddish light glowed from the tiny scanner window, about an inch and a half square.

"You need to scan an authorized fingerprint to operate the lock."

Reaching into the front pocket of his jeans, Steve withdrew the bloody handkerchief and unwrapped the unsavory package.

"You know what they say; a good Boy Scout always comes prepared. Don't look if you have a weak stomach."

Beth tried to avert her eyes although she could not overcome her curiosity. She watched in morbid amazement as Steve uncovered the handkerchief from around the thumb he had severed from Rodney and placed it on the scanner.

A soft beep acknowledged the authorized fingerprint, and with a click, it unlocked the lab door.

"Oh my God! Where did you, how did?" Beth sputtered, as she gave Steve a stunned look of disbelief.

"I knew the guy I had to kill in the hallway had to be high in Boulez's security force, it's why they gave us to him. Lets' say he donated to the cause. We have to go." He nodded towards the door.

Steve pulled the gun from his waistband and pushed the door open. They found a small, dim vestibule waiting. He grabbed Beth's hand, and they entered and shut the door behind them.

The vestibule opened onto a dim hallway where they paused, waiting for any sign their intrusion had triggered an alarm. It surprised them to find no sign of life.

"Everybody must be asleep," Steve whispered. He scanned the hallway, and he saw each door labeled with a small back-lit sign. At one end, was a door labeled 'Personnel Quarters', and at the far end one labeled 'Galley'. In between were three doors marked 'Laboratory', one marked 'Control', and one labeled 'Stock'. A stairway at each end gave access to a second-level mezzanine.

Steve pointed to the galley door, "Let's see if we can find the restaurant."

They crept down the hallway keeping low, under the windows in the lab doors, just in case. The only sounds they heard came from machinery running in the distance. It sounded to Steve like a washing machine on its spin cycle. They entered the small galley, finding it was not much bigger than a standard residential kitchen.

Once inside Beth turned to Steve. "You watch the door, and. I'll check the menu." Opening the commercial refrigerator, the bright light seemed to light the entire room. She didn't find much. A dozen cans of assorted soda, a few packages of American made cheese, several unappetizing containers of leftovers and a few slices of raisin bread. The fruit drawer at least contained several large apples and oranges, along with a tropical fruit not familiar to Beth.

"Not much here, Steve, I hope you didn't want steak and potatoes."

"Just grab anything, we have to go. I saw shadows from the lab window. There are people moving around in there!"

Beth looked around and spotted a canvas shopping bag lying on top of an empty milk crate. She filled it with sodas, fruit, and two packages of cheese.

On a counter were several loaves of bread. She took the softest loaf and headed for the door, not before taking a serrated steak knife she found on the drying rack. Steve held the door open for her and pointed to the mezzanine stairs.

"Look, there's a storage area at the top. Let's go up."

Plastic containers filled with old crowded the mezzanine, along with obsolete electronic equipment and several racks of large gas bottles. The floor was solid over the first half of the lab area, which must have contained offices. However, the metal grid floor was open to the other half below, affording a view of a large open bathed in red light. The area contained several large machines, and a row of lab desks with all types of lab glass, monitors and computers spread out on them.

They waited a few moments, with no evidence of who was causing the motion Steve saw from the galley door. Steve led the way to the center of the mezzanine area, finding a place large enough to sit down. The glow of reddish light allowed Steve to move a few boxes around to make seating. Beth found a solid feeling box, and spread the food out on it, taking care to place the soda cans on the floor, lest they roll off and make a noise.

103

Too hungry to talk at first, they devoured the bread and cheese, washing it down with the cold soda, the only sounds a few appreciative animalistic grunts as they devoured their first meal in over twenty-four hours.

Soon Beth broke the silence, "I can't believe how good crappy cheese and two-day-old bread can taste."

Steve agreed with her, "You're right. This reminds of one of our Ranger training missions. We had to go 72 hours without food, and travel 30 miles over rough terrain, out West. The only thing we had was water, and whatever bugs and plants we found along the way. When we made it to our rendezvous, they had dried up cereal bars and lukewarm coffee waiting for us. I'll never forget how good it tasted."

"What is a Ranger? It's a military thing right?"

"You could say that. We were a special operations team trained for an anti-terrorism squad. I made it four years until an old back injury from a car accident caught up with me. It was time to get out. Anyway, the younger guys were kicking my butt."

"I doubt it," Beth responded with a raised eyebrow.

"Well, anyway and an old friend talked me into coming over to ICE, and I've been there ever since."

"At least it *sounds* as if you have had an interesting career. People assume my work must be boring."

"You're a microbiologist, right? Your business card said you work at UVA. I'd be willing to bet you are in research."

"Yes, I am. I'm the assistant dean. We have a research grant to improve a strain of pollution-eating bacteria. It's why I remember the man's name you said yesterday, Boulez. I was telling you he is or has been, involved in microbiological research at the University of Indiana, it had to do with using microbes to precipitate gold. As I remember, he discontinued the grant when his main researcher disappeared."

A sudden loud noise brought them back to attention. Voices below told them someone had entered the lab.

They surprised Steve. He didn't think anybody could come down the hall without hearing them. "Where did they come from?" he said under his breath as he and Beth froze in place.

They waited in silence for a few minutes as the voices continued talking in low tones, and the sounds of metal banging against metal echoed off the ceiling above. It was too noisy to make out any specific conversation, the sounds of whirring machinery providing enough of a cover mask the words.

"I need to see what's happening. You stay here." Crouching low, he made his way around the boxes they had stacked, and soon he came to a long tank rack. There were several tanks were missing from the lowest section, allowing him to

104

crawl in beside a tank labeled 'Hydrogen', far enough in to see through the metal grid floor of the mezzanine.

He looked down and realized what made the sudden noise. There were two shirtless men working below. They did not come from the hallway. They entered through a hidden side door. A large window was giving off the same reddish glow that lit the lab area, and Steve observed the men wheeling racks full of metal frames, across the area lit only by the red lights. A sign above the door read "Caution High Pressure - High Temperature"

He watched for a few minutes when a brush against his boot startled him. Beth had found her way around the maze of boxes, finding him lying prone in the cylinder rack.

"Sorry," she whispered as she sidled in beside him, "I was worried something had happened."

Holding his index finger to his lips, he motioned for her to come and join his observations.

They lay side by side, watching as the men took the metal frames from the rolling racks they had transported them on, over to the large white machines.

Although it was dark, their eyes were adjusting to the red light, and they saw the individual frames coated with what looked to be heavy oil. The two workers opened the lids of the machines, enabling Steve and Beth to see the same metal racks arranged in a circular pattern inside.

"Centrifuge," Beth whispered in Steve's ear.

The workers removed the frames from the centrifuges. Spun clean to remove the oily substance, they revealed a fuzzy mesh substrate. One by one, the clean frames were unloaded and replaced with the oily frames.

After removing the clean frames from the centrifuges, one man took them over to a large vat full of the dark slime and stacked them in a loose pile inside. When necessary, he would reach into a small toolbox sitting on the floor to pull out a tool for adjusting and tightening a loose connection on the frame. The other man retrieved an open bucket from beneath each centrifuge, containing the spun-off slime from the previous racks. He took the buckets two at a time and dumped them over the clean racks lying in the vat, immersing them in the slime. Working swiftly, he used a large paint roller to make sure the entire substrate received a layer of the slime, before removing them and reinserting them into the rolling racks.

Turning the centrifuges on, they pushed the racks to the door they had come out of earlier, stopping to drink from large plastic bottles of water.

When they opened the thick door to the chamber, a cloud of steam wafted into the lab, enveloping them in the mist.

The men repeated the process three more times, before coming out and sealing the watertight hatch they had been using with a series of levers and handles. Then, they turned the overhead lighting on, causing Steve and Beth to freeze while they waited for their eyes to adjust.

Steve and Beth stayed still, curious about what would happen next. After resting for a few minutes, the men walked over to a bank of valves on the wall, turning several large round handles, which resulted in muffled alarm bells coming from inside the chamber. Steve and Beth watched in quiet amazement as seawater filled the chamber, rising past the observation windows. The digital readout displayed above the door showed the rising temperature of the water.

"What in the hell are they doing?" Steve asked under his breath.

"I think I know the process, but I don't know what they're after," Beth answered.

When the lights came on a third man joined the first two, this one older, and dressed in a white lab coat. The men returned to the centrifuges, which had become quiet.

Taking a key attached to a lanyard from around his neck, the older man reached to a floor level compartment in the first machine and unlocked it. Inside sat a large glass beaker filled about halfway with a dull yellow substance. A hose connected the beaker to a vacuum pressure pump, and then to a mechanism on the bottom of the machine.

One man opened a lever releasing the pressure in the beaker with a short hiss. Next, he removed it and stoppered it with a rubber plug. In succession, they repeated the process on the seven remaining machines.

Steve and Beth remained quiet; their vantage point enabled them to watch the process developing below. Once the men collected all eight bottles, the older man wheeled them over to a lab desk, and the two workers placed them on the table. They watched as he logged on to a computer, and then weighed each beaker on a digital scale, recording the information. From the effort it took to move the beakers, Steve realized they must be heavy. Inserting a long thin metal instrument into a beaker, the man took a sample from one and inserted it into a small spectrometer. Noting the readings in his computer, he wiped the instrument clean with a paper towel, and proceeded to the next beaker, repeating the process, sampling each one. Next, with a nod, he directed the two helpers to pour the contents of the beakers into a funnel on the top of a short heavy piece of equipment mounted on sturdy legs. He adjusted a simple dial on the front, and, a bluish color light coming from beneath the equipment reflected against the floor. Next, they repeated the process in the chamber at the opposite side of the lab.

Steve turned to Beth. "I don't think it was a liquid, it looks granular. What do you think it is?"

"I think I don't believe my eyes." Beth looked incredulous." I thought it was impossible to do what he's doing in such large quantities, but it all fits together.

"What fits together?"

"The Midas Effect," she said under her breath.

106

"What the hell is that?" He looked confused by the excited look on her face.

"Steve, didn't you tell me someone killed one of your agents after he discovered the lab on a ship owned by Boulez?"

"Yes, Tommy Miller. What about it?"

"It's what you said he left a voice mail message about. I'm sure you told me he said Boulez was growing old."

"Yes, that's what he said. We never figured out what Boulez growing old meant. What's your angle?"

"Well, I don't think growing old has anything to do with it, I'll bet I know what the message meant. If you say it quick, you'll get it too."

"If I say what quick?" Steve did not grasp what she was saying.

Beth's eyes were wide with disbelief, "Growing old, growing old, growing GOLD! What he must have said was Boulez was *growing gold.* When you say it fast it sounds the same, you didn't understand it"

"Growing old... growing gold. You're right; if you say it a few times, it sounds the same. I know it's impossible to make gold, so how can they be growing it?"

"They're not growing it, but it looks as if they are harvesting it. The oily substance on the racks must be a culture, a concentrated microbial breeding environment. They *must* be deep ocean microbes," Beth said. "It has to be why the chamber and the lab use red light when they are handling the microbes, white light would kill them. If these are the microbes I think they are, they originate from the deepest parts of the ocean, around the super-hot thermal vents. Scientists theorized no life could survive at the pressure and temperature found at those depths. In addition, to make it worse, no light can reach that far down either. We do not understand how microbes have adapted to those conditions. Since their environment is so harsh, the microbes can't rely on organic methods, or even on photosynthesis for reproduction."

"I still don't get where the gold comes from." Steve looked confused.

"It's a lot more complicated than this," Beth said, "In a nutshell, their reproduction process involves an electrochemical reaction enabling the microbes to amass gold on special membranes. Precipitating the gold gives them an energy source to reproduce, leaving a byproduct of pure gold. Scientists studied the process and called it the *Midas Effect.* On a tiny scale, everything the microbes touch turns to gold. If you have four things, enough microbes, enough 'fresh' seawater, and high enough pressure and temperature, you can produce all the gold you want. They must use the paste to facilitate the growth of the microbes, a culture medium on a large scale. They grow and reproduce in it by the trillions upon trillions. After harvesting the gold with the centrifuges, they return the microbes to a hospitable environment to begin the process all over again. The centrifuge is separating gold residue from the culture, and then they load the culture back on those frames and reuse it. I can tell from the sound of the centrifuge they are only spinning at low speed. We use the procedure for spinning out living organisms we want to keep alive. If you spin too fast, the microbes separate into their components and die. They spin the culture out in the centrifuge, and then they collect whatever byproducts they are after. Again, unless I am mistaken, it is gold. When the slime containing the live microbes drops into the bucket at the bottom and they collect it and put it back on the racks to start the cycle over again."

"I see now," Steve nodded his head, "it accumulates on those frames, and they spin them in a centrifuge, like a beekeeper. The frames are the honeycombs."

The lights in the lab switching over to red again interrupted his thought. They watched again as the two workers toiled in silence. They opened a hatch door on the side of the lab to a puff of steam and rolled racks to the centrifuges.

It excited Beth with scientific curiosity as she whispered, "Right, and it looks as if they can reproduce all the microbes they want, each generation producing enough to replace any killed, plus a large percentage of new ones. With the system in use, the mortality rate would be minor. The microbes would reproduce exponentially. They can reproduce an unending supply. They must control the flow of seawater from outside the ship, to inside the chambers. It takes the right amount of flow across the microbes. Too fast and they wash away, too slow and there is not enough gold available in the water to collect in their cells. A ship moving through the ocean would give them an unending supply of 'undiluted' seawater. It makes sense except for the temperature. Look at the gauge." She pointed out the digital readout, over the first hatchway. "It's reading 312 degrees now, it was at 86 when they filled the chamber. How do they keep the water in those huge compartments heated? It seems unless this is a nuclear-powered ship, it would be unfeasible to maintain the temperatures needed to go through the microbial reproductive cycle. It can be two weeks or longer for some species."

An explanation flashed into Steve's head. "Oh, it's feasible all right. They have this down to real science. There is only one way to generate that much heat, and it doesn't cost them so much as an extra dime."

"Okay…" Beth was waiting for the explanation.

"There are three huge diesel engines powering this ship. I'll bet you a nickel to a doughnut they have an exhaust heat exchangers connected to those chambers. As long as the engines are running, hot water at over 500 degrees is coming out. Those chambers are full of hot water. See how thick the doors are?" He pointed to the entrance door to the chamber.

"I hadn't noticed, but yes, you are right. They insulate the walls, and still, there is a lot of heat loss through the walls. It must be why everything is so hot in the hold," Beth offered. "If I remember what I read, the microbes live in temperatures of about 350-400 degrees Fahrenheit, so if the engine can generate heat and sustain it at that level, they have a viable environment for reproducing these microbes."

They continued to observe the men work until they processed the racks in the last chamber.

It seemed the man in the white lab coat was in charge of keeping the records for the gold. After turning the laboratory lights on again, he repeated the procedure with the remaining bottles, dumping them into the top of the heavy piece of equipment, as he had done earlier.

Their work finished, for the time being, the workers pulled up lab stools to the table and sat down as if expecting a meal. One of them pulled a deck of cards from his pocket, and after a brief discussion, dealt cards to the other two.

It was quieter now that the centrifuges were not running, and their conversation was audible. However, they were speaking a language neither Steve nor Beth understood.

"*That* was a lot of gold," Beth whispered the obvious, "each one of those beakers had to weigh at least ten pounds, I'd guess over 160 pounds of gold!"

Steve nodded in agreement. He was deep in thought, thinking it all didn't add up. Why is Boulez hiding all this? Why kill at least two federal agents?

As far as he knew, it wasn't illegal to produce gold, even in large quantities. He had the legal means to protect his process and any proprietary information if he felt it necessary. There can only be one explanation... Boulez wants no governing body to know what he is doing.

They lay watching, waiting for almost twenty minutes until a loud buzzer sounded.

The men put the cards away, and one worker retrieved a dolly from the corner with two rows of heavy metal containers the size of shallow bread pans, lined up in two rows. He wheeled it over to the piece of equipment they had poured the beakers into, parking it beside a small spout protruding from the side, near the bottom. Once in place, the other worker twisted a lever, and a bright golden river of thick molten metal ran out of the spout, filling each of the metal molds.

"No doubt about it now, they are making gold ingots!" Beth whispered.

They watched in fascination at the methodical and routine operation unfolding before their eyes.

Leaving the ingots to cool, the men left the lab, switching the lights back to the eerie red glow.

Steve and Beth lay still for several more minutes until they were sure the men had left the lab area.

"Gold is almost undetectable," Steve whispered. "We can't know much gold's on the ship. It's the perfect contraband, no smell, not magnetic. No known sensors available to a customs agent would find gold, except a metal detector. When gold enters U.S. territory, unless it's declared, it becomes contraband. There is plenty to bring federal charges to put Boulez behind bars for a hundred years. We've been trying to pin a big charge on him for years."

"You've won, Steve, all we have to do is get off this ship and tell everyone."

Steve believed there was more here than met the eye. "What's his reason to make all this gold? If what you say is true, then he has an unending supply of money. Why would he need it? He's a billionaire now, how much more can he spend?"

Beth nodded in agreement, "There is something else… think about it, if he makes too much gold, he will reduce its value. For Boulez, who has a lot, it seems counterproductive."

Steve stared at the dolly full of gold ingots, thinking to himself, "*this is counterproductive… if Boulez is smart enough to accumulate this, and who knows how much other gold, he will not do anything to make the value drop, or would he? No… that is stupid, the gold ends up somewhere. Now we have to find out where.*"

"Let's go, I need to sleep." Steve took Beth's arm and led her back to the stairway. All was quiet in the hallway. There was no sign of the workers.

"Nobody home," Steve said, glancing at his watch, "it's after one A.M." They worked their way back to the exit without encountering a soul. Steve glanced through the one-way glass in the door and found the hallway empty. They were safe for now.

110

A few minutes later and they were back at the containers they had examined earlier. The door to the one containing the three cars was still ajar.

"It's not exactly first-class accommodations, but I'll fold down the rear seats in the SUV and you can bunk out in there, I'll use the Jag." He said as he clambered over the hood.

"Okay, I forgot how tired I am. I haven't stayed up for over twenty-four hours since college." She said through a yawn. "Excuse me!"

Jim grunted as he struggled to release the seats in the tight confines of the storage container. Almost resorting to reading the owner's manual, he finally figured out how to flatten them, noticing it was a large enough area for two. *"Don't even think that, fool,"* he admonished himself.

While Steve was wrestling with the seats, Beth had made her way to the container filled with the tee shirts. Picking out two large ones, she stuffed them with more shirts and tied off the bottoms, making two halfway decent pillows. Looking around as she waited, she spied the container filled with cases of wine. "Why not?" she said under her breath and ripped the top off one. It was full of bottles labeled Punta Del Este, Rioja Uruguay. "How bad can it be?" She removed a bottle, noticing it was too warm and carried it back over to Steve, who was climbing down from the back of the blue Porsche with the tool kit from the Mercedes in one hand.

He smiled at her boldness, not knowing which to appreciate more, the pillow or the wine.

"I don't know about you, but my nerves are about shot. I'm exhausted, but not sleepy yet. Would you have a drink with me? We should at least make a toast for getting this far alive." Beth held up the wine with a shy smile.

Steve smiled his wide grin and pointed to the Jaguar. "Go have a seat in my living room. I'll be there in a minute."

Steve made a quick check of the containers, and then secured the doors. He returned to the container where they would spend the rest of the night and took an adjustable wrench from the tool kit, removing the bolts holding the locking lever on the container doors. He didn't want any surprises, and now it would be impossible for anybody to lock them in if they wandered by and noticed the door ajar. After he entered he pulled the door almost shut, leaving a crack for ventilation. It would take more than a casual look to see the container was unlatched. As Beth sat in the passenger seat of the Jag and watched Steve work, the exhaustion seemed to flow over her in waves. She was strangely numb, not able to place her emotions. She knew she should be a basket case after all she had seen today. Murder, killing, violence... it was all such a nightmare. She wanted a moment of peace, a little time to push the fear to the back of her mind, and enjoy a small distraction, even if it was in the most bizarre manner.

Steve finished his chore and then entered the opposite side of the Jag. He had to squeeze past the partially opened the door into the front seat. The seat felt uncommonly plush as he fumbled with the tool kit, selecting a screwdriver and using it to push the cork down into the wine bottle. While Steve occupied himself with the wine, Beth fished around in the center console, finding several CDs in their diamond cases.

"I feel as if I'm stealing."

"Don't worry. The insurance company will make the owner whole... except for his CDs. There's a huge market in South America for these stolen cars. With a little help from an insider at the vehicle administration office, you get a new title, clean car history, and Voila! You own a fifty thousand dollar car for about half price."

It looked to Beth as if the CDs were all show tunes, so she reached in and took one from the middle of the stack. Since the thieves had gone to the trouble of installing new ignitions and leaving the keys, she could switch to an accessory and insert the CD. To her embarrassment, the speakers filled with the sound of Barry Manilow singing one of his well-known hits, albeit from twenty-five years ago.

Steve laughed, as he smelled the wine, and then took a sip from the bottle. "It's not too bad." He offered her a taste. "The wine, I mean..."

Beth smiled and took a sip. "To tell you the truth, I'm a closet Manilow fan. I can't help singing along when I listen to the oldies station."

They took turns sipping the wine and discussing the amazing process they had witnessed earlier, as the music flowed almost imperceptibly from hidden speakers beneath the dashboard.

"There's an aspect about all this I can't figure out," Steve said as he rubbed his tired eyes and tried to stifle a yawn.

"Oh, please don't yawn, it's contagious," she responded, offering Steve the wine. "What don't you understand?"

"I don't understand this. Boulez has similar labs on every ship we have boarded. I believe the last report I saw said he has about forty ships operating worldwide. We have inspected seventeen of them and have found labs similar to the one here. He also has a very hush-hush, highly advanced security system. Ships we don't know about since they don't come into U.S. waters, so my guess is every one of his ships has a lab, or at the very least, is being outfitted with one. We never figured out what he was doing. He claimed it was ecological research, a way to clean the bilge water before pumping it overboard. Because he has had ties to terrorist organizations, we thought he might develop a biological or chemical weapon."

"So now you know, he's after money and a lot of it." Beth surmised.

"It still doesn't add up. He already has money and lots of it. A comment you made back at the lab has been eating at me. You said making that much gold

112

would be counterproductive because he would drive the price of gold down. We know the more gold he puts into the market place, the less rare it becomes. The less rare it becomes, the more the price drops. If he's making similar amounts of gold on another forty ships, it will have a big impact on the world's gold markets. Why would he want to devalue his own holdings? It is definitely counterproductive, not to mention stupid." Steve said between sips of wine.

"He's not stupid. Believe me, I know it's almost impossible to put together the research, facilities, and funding necessary to develop the state-of-the-art technology required, and then profitably commercialize an extremely delicate biological process. That's smart. To replicate it forty times over, in the bottom of ships as they travel around the world, is pure genius. I can't believe he doesn't know what he is doing. His purpose must be other than to maximize profits."

Steve considered the bit of information for a few seconds. "Precious metal can be used as a financial weapon. The Hunt brothers manipulated the silver markets for several years back in the seventies. I remember they made billions and eventually lost it all. One of their schemes involved convincing Saudis to invest big money in silver futures. The theory, never proven conclusively, was the U.S.Government influenced the Commodities Exchange Commission to manipulate their regulations, reducing the amount of silver any one person can own to a few million ounces. It drove the price way down because it required large investors to liquidate their holdings. A few Saudis high in the government lost hundreds of millions of dollars, and it came close to causing a revolt within the royal family. The Royal Family claimed it was the intent of the U.S. Government, saying it was retribution for the 1973 oil embargo. Maybe Boulez realizes a flood of gold will create the destabilization of certain governments in third world countries, making it easier for terrorist elements to operate."

Beth arched her eye at Steve as they sat in the near darkness. "What if he works directly with the terrorists, have you thought about this from that angle?" She leaned her head back against the headrest, surprised the few sips of wine had made her head spin a little. Her mind wandered as Steve answered, his soothing low voice bringing an aura of calm. She lost her concentration as he talked, wild thoughts drifting through her mind, and flashes of fantasy trying to push their way into the dreamlike trance into which she had descended. Her mental inhibitions faded with the realization she longed for human contact for the safety of an embrace, the security of a soothing voice. She lapsed into a semi-unconscious state, her muscles seemed paralyzed, yet her thoughts demanded she considered the man beside her. She let herself admit an attraction to him. It was a losing battle she fought with herself to block those thoughts and concentrate on the voice speaking near her ear. Even though she heard his voice, even though she smelled the sweet wine on his breath, her brain would not allow her to process the sounds into intelligible words. Sleep seduced her with peaceful surrender.

"How do you mean, financial terrorists?" Steve quizzed. "You have a point. If they have that much money, they can finance a hundred attacks similar to the World Trade Center, anywhere in the world. I suppose it's possible for Boulez to move terrorists around the world on his ships and deliver them to the doorstep of an unsuspecting country. He can even move nuclear material, say in a lead-lined container. They inspect less than one percent of the containers entering the States, and many ports worldwide have no inspection at all. We have been aware for... some..."

He stopped talking, realizing he had been running on, and sensing Beth had become still. With the dim light coming in from the crack in the door opening, he watched her eyes closing. Her head nested between the corner of the door and the headrest. She had fallen asleep during Steve's hypothesis.

"I guess my theory didn't interest her," Steve mumbled to himself, as he stretched out his tired body. He was hoping to get a little sleep, although he knew the stillness would bring waves of grief through his mind. The memory of Jim's brutal murder caused an uneasy tension in his bones.

CHAPTER 33

It took half an hour for the stunned men to regain their faculties after crawling out of the twisted wreckage of the helicopter. Jose awoke to an ache in his ankle making it hard to walk. He forced Malek and Carlos to follow him into the container hold to search for the man he had seen in the spotlight. He was sure it had to be the ICE agent. The crew was all accounted for, and they prohibited the lab techs from leaving their secure area during the voyage unless it was an emergency. Jose was getting pissed. Malek and Carlos were complaining there was no way to check all the containers. They didn't believe Jose had seen anybody. They tried to tell him he hit his head, he would have none of that. He was sure he saw a man on the container, and he would damn well find him. Malek tried to convince Jose to wait until the ship made port in San Juan, where they would get help to search. His distress over Akmed's terrible demise brought tears welling in his eyes every few minutes.

"*A hundred of these blue-eyed devils are not worth my brother Akmed! He is a hero and died for our cause! Allah is good, Allah is great!*" He repeated it again to himself following Jose down a passageway between rows of containers.

"Just shut up and keep a watch behind. Don't forget he has a gun and knows how to use it." Jose ordered.

Carlos didn't have a lot of respect for Jose, and, he was the only one who had any real training that would help them find the Customs agent. He blamed Jose for what had happened to the helicopter. If he had been a better shot, they wouldn't have had to get so close to the lifeboat, the tail rotor wouldn't have hit the water, and they wouldn't be in the mess they were in now. Now, what was he going to tell Mr. Boulez? He wrecked his three million dollar helicopter because he had listened to Rodney's gofer. If the ICE agent had escaped, their only hope to save their own ass was to find him. He had his doubts about what he saw on the containers earlier, but at least it was a chance. They would do everything in their power to avoid a bullet in the head.

Jose's ankle was swelling as they had walked the length of the container hold twice now, down the outside passageway, and back up the inside. They found every container they tested locked. There were two more passageways on the other side of the ship to inspect, all stacked to the upper side of the top deck. It would be impossible to open any container not sitting on the deck, so they concentrated on everything down low. Jose figured it would take at least an hour per passageway, so they would hurry to finish before daybreak. The creaking of the containers rubbing together from the slight rocking of the ship caused them to pause and take up defensive positions several times.

It took an hour and a half to get to the last passageway. Jose let his guard down a trying to walk a little faster. He needed to get this finished so he could get

115

off his ankle. He pulled down his sock to inspect a dark purple bruise surrounding the anklebone.

"It's broken," Carlos said when he saw the grimace of pain on Jose's face. "I saw it a million times in Nam. Those morons would get anxious and jump out of the chopper when it was ten feet off the deck. It never failed."

Jose shot him a glaring sneer, "You calling me a moron?"

Tempers were running short now. Carlos wanted to challenge him, but Jose was holding his gun, and looking as if Carlos had meant to insult him. He bit his tongue and replied through clenched teeth. "I didn't call you anything. I said your ankle is most likely broken. The pain will get a lot worse."

"You let me worry about that. Let's go. I want to check to the end of this row, and then we'll go back on deck."

Carlos glanced at Malek and shrugged. "You heard him, let's go."

They walked in silence as they got to the midpoint of the passageway. He almost disregarded it, but as Jose walked by one container, a small reflection sparkled from the center of the door. He stopped the men as he kneeled to examine a piece of plastic protruding from the center of the double door sealing the container. Jose held his hand up for silence, and pointing to the locking lever, he motioned for Malek to unlatch the box. Malek tried to be as quiet as possible, but the metal handle made a loud clank when the pressure released from the locking clamps. Jose and Carlos flanked the doors from across the passageway; guns aimed at the container, as Malek yanked one door open. He jumped back in surprise as two open cases of tee shirts slid out of the door and spilled onto the deck in front.

Steve had been dozing, a fitful almost-sleep, the persistent images of Jim being gunned down kept surfacing in his semi-conscious state, as if they were globules in a lava lamp. Hushed voices and the sounds of a container opening near their lair snapped Steve to full alertness. He reached over and shook Beth with one hand, holding the other over her mouth. If Jose noticed the door to the container cracked open, he would realize they might be inside, and have them trapped. There would be only one chance to escape, and Steve was ready to act.

With a quiet whisper in Beth's ear, he said, "Get in the passenger seat of the Porsche, and buckle up."

"What? What are you going to do?"

"We don't have time to discuss it right now Beth, we have to move!" Steve slid out of the Jag, making sure the door didn't bang the side of the container. He shuffled back to the rear of the Porsche, where he snuck a glimpse of Malek and Carlos examining the container of tee shirts. They had thrown several boxes of shirts out, just to make sure nobody was hiding inside. There was no way they would miss the unlatched door if they came further up the passageway. Jose came into view holding his handgun at his side, limping as he crossed from side to side, and examining containers for any sign anything else was amiss. It would only be

116

seconds until the group would be at the door. Steve worked his way around to the driver's side of the Porsche and slid in the seat. In one swift motion, he removed the ignition key from its plastic sleeve and inserted it into the ignition. Reaching into his waistband, he withdrew the full spare magazine he had taken from Rodney and replaced the used one in the gun. Then he flipped off the safety and loaded a round into the chamber.

"Take this." He said to Beth, "Hold it with both hands." He showed her how, and then handed it to her, wrapped her fingers around the thick butt.

"I can't shoot this! I've never even touched a gun." Her protestation was too loud.

"Shh… it doesn't matter. All you need to do is to stay down as low as you can and shoot right through the back window, or the roof, anywhere behind the car, as fast as you can… just close your eyes and pull the trigger when I say shoot!" Her eyes were wide with apprehension. "You can do it, can't you? I need your help here, just wait for me to say shoot and then let it rip!"

"What if…?" She didn't finish as Steve shushed her.

"Get ready!"

He heard the men talking nearby. They must not have noticed the unlatched door yet, and Steve didn't want them to. The element of surprise belonged to him for the next few seconds only, and he intended to take advantage. Waiting with his fingers on the key in the ignition, realizing if the car didn't start, they would be dead before they could get out of the car.

"Remember, wait until I say shoot!" It was now or never, Jose would be at the door any second. He twisted the key, and the powerful Porsche kicked to life with a throaty VROOM. He stomped the clutch, and slammed the transmission into reverse, hoping for as much smoke and noise to confuse his pursuers as possible. With a motion a professional car driver might admire, he popped the clutch and spun the wheel, sending the dark blue speedster slamming back through the container doors, splaying them wide open.

Carlos was the closest to the door… too close. As the door flew open with the car's powerful thrust, it caught him in its arc and slammed him into the adjacent container. Sprawled spread eagle as his head bounced off the corner of the metal box, the disturbing sound of skull-shattering heard above the screeching of the spinning tires.

Jose and Malek spun around in shock, the sight of the small sports car slamming backward through the doors, and the shrill complaint of the tires spinning on metal froze them in slack-jawed amazement. Steve shoved the gear lever to first and rammed the gas pedal with all his might. A split second of spinning was all it took for the high-performance tires to heat and grab the metal deck, propelling the little blue rocket past Jose and Malek in a flash, as they jumped out of its path. Steve felt a pair of thumps accompanied by two quick bumps, running over Carlos's outstretched legs.

117

"SHOOT, SHOOT, SHOOT!" Steve yelled at the top of his lungs, as he fought to control the tremendous torque that wanted to slide the rear end of the car from side to side. Beth hung on to the butt of the gun for dear life as Beth squeezed off four wild rounds, the bullets bouncing off the containers with the intended effect. Jose and Malek ducked as ricocheting bullets whizzed around, and the pungent smoke from the tires filled their nostrils. They fired a disorganized volley into the smoke-filled passageway; however, the dark color of the car rendered it invisible as it sped away.

Steve hunched down in the seat watching the containers lining the passageway fly by as if they were cars on a speeding freight train.

"Get down, get down!" He was yelling again, over the screech of the brakes, and the whine of the decelerating motor. The Porsche reached the end of the eight hundred foot passageway after a few seconds. The faint echoes of footsteps running toward them from afar met Steve's ears as he switched the ignition off. He snatched the gun from Beth and fired off several more blind shots towards the sounds as they got out of the car.

The echoes stopped, as a fusillade of bullets sprayed the end of the passageway as they ducked around the corner.

Back at the doors leading to the hallway containing the laboratories, there would be no way to gain access now as Steve had discarded Rodney's thumb in a lab trashcan. Steve looked back at the little Porsche sitting there, a beautiful machine Steve thought to himself, too bad he had to sacrifice her.

He stuck his head through the door into the hallway, glad to find it. He accounted for three of his captors, but he had not seen the one they had called Akmed, so he wanted to be careful. Satisfied there was nobody waiting for them in the hallway, he pulled Beth in beside the door.

"Wait right here, don't move, okay? And yell if you see anyone!"

Beth was shaking in fear from the wild escape, and all she could do was nod her head in assent as she leaned against the wall, breathless.

Steve slipped back out of the door towards the Porsche. In a squat at the corner, he heard footsteps getting nearer. They were still far enough away to be invisible through the cordite and rubber haze hanging in the air. Watching down the passageway, he knew Jose and Malek wouldn't be able to make out the car or him for a few minutes. He crept to the driver's side, reached in the open window, and unlatched the trunk, in the car's front. He also grabbed a pack of cigarettes he had noticed tucked beside the seat. Steve pushed the cigarette lighter in as he fished a cigarette out of the pack and put it to his lips. It only took a few seconds for the lighter to heat, and Steve lit the cigarette and took two deep puffs to make sure it was burning well. He knelt at the front of the car, placing the lit cigarette on the bumper. Finding the hood release latch protruding from the small grille, he opened the hood enough for the little lamp that lit the inside to display the storage area contents. He spied the object of his search almost, a short steel lug wrench clipped to the sidewall. He unsnapped the wrench and felt the beveled end he was hoping to find. The car turned at an angle to the passageway so as he crawled to the side of the car and lay on his back near the front wheel, the car shielded him from any potential of approach from behind.

The light was very dim in the passageway, he would have to find what he wanted by touch. He reached up behind the front tire, probing, running his hand over the smooth surfaces of the underside of the car, so new it had only accumulated a small amount of road grime. Soon his hand felt what he had been trying to find, the cold steel of the fuel tank. The other metal on the car was almost warm to the touch, but the fuel tank felt cool to the touch, and there was enough room to maneuver his lug wrench. He had to hurry, cautious footsteps were closing in, and he might only have seconds. Steve rolled over to his side as he stuck the beveled end of the lug wrench into the gap between the frame and the gas tank. A glance under the car towards the approaching footsteps shocked him into dropping the wrench. There, not more than a few feet from him was the battered face of the helicopter pilot! His face distorted, as he lay on his back, motionless, behind the Porsche. Steve craned his neck around to find the man's foot and trouser leg tangled in the rear suspension. A chill ran up his spine as he returned to his task with a sarcastic comment: "Sorry to get you dragged into this, pal." Again, he reached into the spot he hoped to gain the most leverage and placed the beveled end of the wrench against the fuel tank. With all his might he pulled it back, it surprised him as the wrench pierced the tank, allowing a steady stream of gasoline to drain from the tank. He removed the wrench and returned to the front of the car to retrieve the cigarette that had burned half of its length away.

He heard Jose shout to Malek. "It's him, it's him, get down!" Quickly, they fired two rounds into the wall behind him. He dove for the door where Beth was waiting, sticking his head in to find Beth in the same spot as when he left. "Run, I'll catch up!" He pointed down the hallway. She didn't bother to ask why she turned and ran. Steve jogged back out and slammed the door hard, getting the desired effect.

The footsteps were coming more now, and he caught Jose's pained voice. "That's the door. They must have gone into the hallway, hurry!"

Steve stayed low and stole a quick glance around the corner. He saw them approaching in a low squat, less than a hundred feet away. Jose was limping, and Malek was giving him a shoulder for support.

Steve returned to the doorway, counting to himself as he waited, six... seven... eight... nine... ten. He took a long puff on the glowing stub and reaching around the door, flicked it under the Porsche, and then ran after Beth. He had made it halfway up the hallway when the cigarette lit off the gasoline on the floor with a resounding WHUMP knocking Steve to his knees. The gasoline was still draining through the hole in the tank, and when the fire raced up the stream into the empty tank, it set off a loud explosion rocking the huge ship. Steve gazed

119

back down the hallway as he caught up to Beth, just in time to watch the door he had come through blown from its hinges and slam across the hallway in a great cloud of black smoke. Jose and Malek were unaware of the gasoline pooling under the vehicle as they made their way up the passageway.

"Hold on, something's not right, I don't trust him!" Jose said through a grimace, as he dropped to one knee.

"I think this is the only way out unless we go all the way back around the containers." Malek pointed back the way they had come.

"That's just what he wants, two dumb asses to walk right into his line of fire. If we go through the door, he might wait for us anywhere. We have to go back around."

"Or, what if he's waiting for us at the other end?" Malek asked frowning. He was always the hunter, not used to being the hunted.

"Well, we can't just sit here and wa..." Something interrupted Jose's words as the cigarette ignited the gasoline on the deck. A huge fireball and a wall of heat pushed both men back against the wall as it filled the end of the passageway, not thirty feet from them.

"Run! It will blow... get out!" Malek took off back down the passageway, as Jose struggled to his feet; his ankle slowed him down as he ran away from the car. When the gas tank exploded, the Porsche blew into several large chunks, which crashed into the surrounding containers with a deafening cacophony of loose metal, plastic, and glass. It blew Jose face-first down the passageway, rolling until he came to a stop against a container. Malek was a little luckier, having put a little distance between himself and the explosion. He ended up thrown against a container also but maintained his balance. Disoriented from the blast, the pressure wave stopping up their ears with such force Malek at first thought he was deaf. Jose groaned as he sat up, greeted with a blast of filthy water spraying from the ship's automatic sprinkler system. The water had been lying in the sprinkler's pipes for over three years, and its stagnant oily smell was almost enough to make him retch. Malek worked his way back to Jose and helped him to his feet. Thick black smoke was hanging over their heads as the water continued to spray the entire area. For a second Jose considered going after Steve, but only for a second. The Customs agent had now killed both Rodney and Carlos, and if it weren't for Jose's slight hesitation back there, Malek and he would suffer the same fate.

"To hell with him, Malek," Jose spat. "Let's see if we can get up to the bridge. Call Chavez and find out what to do. We're screwed now; they scheduled this ship to get to San Juan soon. We need help."

Malek hesitated as he pulled Jose up and searched for the gun he had dropped in the blast. It would be just as easy for him to shoot Jose and blame it on the ICE agent. His ass was on the line now, if this was the only story that got back to Mr. Boulez, he might have a better chance of surviving this nightmare. He spied the gun in the corner and gave Jose a furtive glance as he bent down to pick it up.

Jose noticed the hesitation and also the glance. His years of street smarts gave him an intuition that would have passed by most people. As Malek reached to pick up the gun, Jose stepped on his hand and put his own gun to Malek's temple. "You wouldn't be thinking of a way to save your ass, now would you?" Malek squinted, the coal-black of his eyes visible in the dim light. "You know Mr. Jose, if I wanted to, I had time to shoot you in the back a hundred times in the last two hours. What would I have to gain from killing you?" He stared into Jose's eyes, with the eyes of a man who was even a more practiced liar than he was himself.

Jose thought for a second and released his foot. "You can never be too careful... go ahead, *you* lead the way," distrust obvious in his tone

121

Angie Barnes was trying to sleep, but the Coast Guard troop transport plane was cold and noisy. They strapped her into a jump seat in civilian clothes, alongside Robert Graves, trying to find a comfortable position to allow for a short nap. Through her open eyes, she watched as Ben Driver and his START unit members were discussing the upcoming operation, writing on notepads the procedure they would be using. Each man would switch his notes with another to review prior to the deployment, a tactic Driver always used to emphasize the strategic importance of everybody being on the same page. He believed when you had to read the plan in someone else's handwriting, it demanded more concentration and made a more lasting impression. His plan was to board the Global Explorer as soon as it crossed into U.S. waters, which should be in a few hours. He wanted to make a fast approach on a Coast Guard cutter, arriving with a show of power to avoid any 'discussion' the captain may want to institute. It would take a mile for the ship to stop, depending on its speed, and in the meantime, the crew of the cutter would deploy in several inflatable speedboats to patrol the perimeter of the ship. Once the START team boarded and secured the bridge, they would perform a methodical search of the ship for any evidence of Agent Ross and his civilian associate. The Coast Guard Station in San Juan is at a place named Sickbay. They had offered access to a cadaver-smelling dog and agreed to have the dog and its trainer available. Almost as soon as Agent Barnes drifted off into unconsciousness, a period of rough turbulence shook her out of her stupor, the cool air circulating in the cabin blowing the fog from her brain. She stared out the small window, watching the faint first rays of dawn trying to creep above the eastern horizon. Graves was beside her, his head rolled back against his headrest, and his eyes closed.

His deep voice startled her, "It'll be about another hour to San Juan."

"Good, I'm ready to get off this tin can. It's cold as hell in here."

Graves stretched his legs out, and unbuckled his harness, "I'll grab us a coffee."

"That would be nice, thanks, Bob."

Graves returned after a few moments with two Styrofoam cups, and they sipped the strong coffee, trying to time the calm spells between the turbulence to avoid spilling it.

It wasn't long before Agent Barnes noticed a difference in the pitch the motors were making, telling her they were preparing to land. The pilot came on the intercom to instruct everyone to secure all equipment and to strap in. Angie was always a white-knuckle flier, even on commercial airlines. She had flown into Sickbay two years ago, so she knew the runway was short, and it was always a nail biter to get this size plane on the ground there. She scanned her fellow travelers, and seeing nobody appeared concerned, she gained a little confidence.

They were descending now, everybody's ears popping as they braced for landing. Angie leaned back and closed her eyes as the plane hit the pavement with a solid bump, the four engines whining as soon as the pilot stood on the brakes. She was more relieved than she wanted to show as she stepped off onto the tarmac from the mobile stairs, the early morning sunlight lifting her spirits. The Coast Guard attaché was waiting for them on the tarmac with a dark gray bus, and the team unloaded their gear and stowed it in the side compartments. It was only a ten-minute drive to the docks, the men and one woman riding in virtual silence as they approached a modern cutter. Several Guardsmen were visible attending to their duties on the deck and on the pier, nearby. Several Guardsmen rolled to a stop near the gangplank and surrounded the bus offering to help the team load their equipment onto the boat. With their help, it only took a few minutes for everybody to get aboard. The Captain briefed earlier, had his command ready to depart within the hour. This would be a routine drill for his crew. They often boarded ships entering U.S. waters, and container ships such as the Global Explorer were drawing extra scrutiny as tighter restrictions on port entry were coming down from Homeland Security. There were millions of mysterious containers entering U.S. ports each year, and it was up to the Coast Guard to protect the motherland from assault facilitated by the insidious importation of dangerous elements.

The START unit met in the situation room to ready their equipment. Each man field stripped his weapon and checked to make sure they loaded all its magazines to full capacity. They also gave a final check to radio and flashlight batteries, rappelling gear, and even shoelaces.

A loud blast on the klaxon announced the ship was underway. Once clear of the port and making headway out of Sickbay Coast Guard Station, the Captain came down to brief them on their target. He looked as if central casting chose him for the part of the captain. Six feet four inches tall, wide shoulders and an athletic build. At forty-six years old, he had just enough gray on his temples to suggest his experience, and his square chin and broad smile relayed his confidence.

"Good morning, ladies and gentlemen," he gave Angie a respectful nod. "I am Captain Brown, Dennis Brown. As you know, we have orders to assist ICE on this mission, which we take great pleasure in doing. Your target vessel is now about 225 nautical miles North Northwest of Puerto Rico and heading for the Port of San Juan. Her speed is twenty-four knots, and with this tailwind, we will make just under thirty knots. It means the target will enter U.S. territorial waters at nine hundred hours, and we should have a visual no later than eleven hundred fifty hours. We will notify you as soon as we make visual contact so you can prepare for boarding. I recognize you are all professionals, so let me remind you of one thing. This ship and everybody on it is under my command until we land back at Sickbay. Our first concern is the safety of the crew, and the ship, in that order. If

123

anything goes south, I will determine whether we end, I will expect your full cooperation. Are there questions?"

Pausing, as he looked around the room, satisfied they understood the pecking order. "Good. Now can I invite you all to join us in the mess hall? We will show you the breakfast that keeps our re-enlistment ratio one of the highest of any service."

"This is the hardest part," Angie thought to herself as she ate scrambled eggs and biscuits covered with rich creamy gravy, *"the waiting and anticipation."* While she and Bob Graves wouldn't be a part of the initial boarding party, their apprehension in the face of what had happened to Jim Ragan was palpable. To her surprise, the hours flew by, and it surprised her when a loud klaxon sounded the alarm. Again, Captain Brown came on the intercom.

"Target vessel sighted off the Starboard bow, range fifteen miles, ETA thirty minutes. Boarding party please report to the main deck with your gear."

"This is it, Ben. Go get our boys." Angie said to the START unit commander.

Dan Driver saw the concern on her face, and he put his big hand on her shoulder. "Don't worry, if they're on the boat they're mine."

124

Steve caught up with Beth at the stairway to the next level, sliding to where she was waiting on a waxed, tile floor. The ship's fire alarm system sounded a bell, and the emergency lights in the hallway had come on, flashing their warning with bright strobe lights.

"What happened, are you all right?" Beth asked as Steve led her up the stairway, his gun pointed ahead.

"I had to remind our friends about how unhealthy it can be to smoke!"

"That was horrible. I hope... do you think you killed them?" Beth felt a pang of guilt for a second for wishing harm on another human being, it passed when she thought of how brutal those 'human beings' had been to her earlier.

"I didn't wait around to find out, if they were anywhere near the car when it blew, they are wallpaper now. Since I didn't see them get it, we have to assume they are still after us. And don't forget the other one who wasn't with them, he must be on deck to cover their backs." Steve had no way to know Akmed had been lying on the bottom of the ocean since last night.

"What are we going to do now?"

"I will take over the bridge. If I can get a radio or satellite phone call out, I'm sure the Coast Guard can send a chopper. There's a Coast Guard base in San Juan, so let's hope we are heading there. Stay close." Steve led the way up the several flights of steps connecting the decks, stopping at every level to peer through the small glass window in each door. The hallways appeared deserted, except at one deck where a crewmember was polishing the floor with a buffer machine, oblivious to his surroundings.

While Steve and Beth made their way towards the bridge deck, Jose and Malek ran up the stairways on the other side of the ship. Jose was having difficulty putting any weight on his ankle, so he had to resort to leaning on a broom handle he had fashioned as a crutch. He had to admonish Malek to slow down several times, still wary about letting him out of his sight for now. Several crewmembers assigned to the fire brigade met them running in the opposite direction, smoke masks and heavy rubber coats in tow. Jose stopped the first man, telling him the fire was on the lowest deck and told them to call him on the bridge if they saw anybody who didn't belong on the ship. After arriving on the bridge deck, there was a flurry of activity. The Captain was communicating with the fire brigade, and his Chief Engineer, who was trying to determine if it was safe to turn the sprinkler system off. Malek helped Jose limp into the bridge on one foot, as the pain was now shooting up his leg and into his hip. Accessed from the bridge, the ship's infirmary was down a short passageway to the port side. There was no doctor on board, so the Navigation Engineer doubled as the paramedic. His basic medical training enabled him to treat the injuries and maladies common to a seafaring crew.

Upon seeing Malek helping Jose to the bridge, he hurried over to assist him, directing him down the passageway to a small treatment room. Jose eased back on a cot, while the paramedic took off the injured man's shoe and sock, revealing an ankle joint purple and swollen twice its normal size. He tried to make small talk with his patient. "You had a rough landing last night. I am surprised nobody was more hurt. You have gotten the worst."

"Yeah, well check with Akmed. He's not feeling too good right now either."

Jose ignored the paramedic's unsuspecting advice to tell Akmed to stop by, and groaned to Malek, "Go check the stairwells at both ends of the hallway. Make sure you lock the doors. I don't need surprises in here."

Malek was all too happy to put a little distance between him and the Mexican for a while. He headed out of the bridge, expecting the customs agent to be behind every door. When they go to the door he and Jose had just come up, he looked through the glass to the small landing. It was empty, so he spun the locking mechanism and threw the bolt securing the door. He turned and headed for the other end of the hallway, his sweaty hand wrapped around his gun in anticipation.

There was a small x-ray machine attached to the wall, similar to one in any dentist's office, which the paramedic used to take several pictures of the ankle. The small negatives slid out of the machine, and Jose reclined as the paramedic held them up to a lighted panel.

"It's broken, Sir. There is a hairline fracture, see here?" He pointed out the evidence to Jose, who rose up on one elbow.

"Okay, so what do I do? It hurts like hell, what pills do you have?" He lay back down, thinking this would put him at a big disadvantage for finding the man who caused his pain.

"Not much I can do here, I'll wrap it up tight with ice packs. It should help the swelling go down if you stay off it. I can give you Percocet for the pain, and as soon as we get to San Juan you will need to visit a doctor."

The paramedic saw the barrel of Jose's gun sticking from a small holster under his jacket. He had been in his quarters last evening when the helicopter arrived, so he wasn't aware of the two prisoners Rodney and Jose had brought aboard. Having witnessed Boulez's security men on the ship before, he knew there was something secret happening in the lab, although he did not understand what. He knew it was strange they often ordered him to take a longer than necessary route between ports. The Captain had given him a cryptic explanation of needing time for the lab to complete its experiments. It made little sense to him, and he didn't care. For what they paid him, he would sail this damn ship around in circles for a month, if they wanted. When he heard the shooting last night while watching a video in his cabin, he made his way to the top deck just in time to observe the helicopter crash land on the helipad. He helped drag Malek out of the wrecked chopper, and in the confusion, never found out what had

126

happened. The Captain had given him a fairy tale about trying out a new weapon, and a look conveying an unmistakable suggestion: Don't-ask-questions. Seeing Jose's gun reminded piqued his curiosity again.

"What the hell was going on last night? It sounded like World War Three out there."

Jose let his impatience show as he popped two Percocet, "Are you done?"

The paramedic held up his palms in a sign of surrender.

"Sorry, I'll mind my business. I have to get back out to the bridge. You need to stay off the ankle as much as you can, so hang in here as long as you want. Those Percocet should kick in a few minutes."

CHAPTER 36

A faint haze of oily smelling smoke was visible in the shafts of the morning light shining through the windows along the hallway leading to the bridge. Although there were three or four men visible in the pilothouse Steve saw from the far end of the hallway, none of them armed. Confident if he got control of the bridge, Beth and he could defend it against attack until help arrived. He was sure they must have found Jim by now, and he knew the murder of a Federal agent would trigger an all-out search of Boulez's assets anywhere near Florida. If they were lucky, this ship would be on the list. If not, he would put it there. While watching the hallway from the safety of the stair landing, he merged the remaining bullets in the two magazines he had. Nine bullets in total. He would make each one count.

"Are you ready?" He asked Beth.

She shrugged her shoulders, "Do I have a choice? I am not staying here by myself. I'll be right on your tail."

Steve managed a smile as he opened the door. Malek coming out of the bridge door, gun in hand, froze him in mid-stride. He ducked back into the stair landing, inching his eyes around the edge of the window to see what Malek was doing. He watched him walk in the opposite direction, slowing to point his gun at each door as he passed by. When he got to the end, Steve saw him lock the door, one of only two ways up to the bridge deck. Steve realized they were standing at the only unsecured door to the bridge, and, Malek would come to seal this door off as well. Steve jerked his head back just as Malek turned to head his way. The landing Beth and he were on was small, big enough for two people. If Malek came and checked through the window, there would be no way for him to miss them.

"Beth, one of them is coming this way. I will take him out. Go back down to the next landing and stay where you can see me. When I wave, come up the stairs. I *want* him to see you. Now go, hurry, hurry, hurry!"

Beth realized she didn't have time to ask questions, so she gave Steve a confused expression, as she slipped down the seven steps to the next landing. Up through the railing, she saw Steve with his hand held high, signaling her to be still. Steve heard Malek's footsteps in the hallway, heading for the door. He squatted as low on one knee, forcing himself to the farthest edge of the landing. He was out of the swing of the door, and because Malek was short, it would be difficult for him to see below the window without great effort. He attempted to time Malek's look through the glass, he held his breath as he waited. It only took a few seconds for him to sense Malek was a step away. Catching Beth's eyes, he motioned for Beth to come up. His timing was perfect. Malek had been extra cautious, noticing the door was ajar. He squinted through the glass, surprised to see Beth coming up from below, and alone. Amazed at his good fortune, he jerked his head back and scanned around the hallway. There was no place for him to hide and wait, the best thing for him to do was to shove the door open and grab her. Had he more time to think, it might have occurred to him this was all too convenient. After all the right moves the customs agent had made, the woman was now wandering around alone. The immediacy of the situation clouded his judgment, and he smiled with the satisfaction he would soon be the one to absolve them of the consequences of their bumbling the night before. He saw the shadow of the woman's head on the wall behind the window and knew it was time to surprise her. Malek sprang from his crouch; he pushed the door open, extending his open all the way. There wasn't even enough time for him to shout. The door slammed into his elbow, causing excruciating pain. Looking over his shoulder through the window, he was face-to-face, with the customs agent!

A mixture of fear and pain caused him to expel a loud "Ahhggg!", as Steve twisted the gun from forearm and gun through the opening. He knew there was a problem as soon as he realized the door wouldn't his hand, dropped it to the floor, and jerked him halfway through the door. The force of the door pinning him to the jamb didn't allow him to duck when Steve swung a mighty roundhouse punch into his temple. It dazed him, struggling as Steve pulled him the rest of the way onto the landing, the door shutting behind them. Soon, Malek regained his senses, swinging at the larger man; the fear of death brought an adrenalin rush to the smaller man's muscles that surprised Steve. They rotated on the landing now, as Beth watched, cowering from below.

Malek attempted to knee Steve in the groin, a tactic that infuriated Steve. "You little prick!" Steve hissed, as he punched, catching Malek on the chin, following it with an elbow to the eye. It hurt Malek, his knees buckling as Steve bent him backward over the railing. The smaller man clutched at Steve's shirt as Steve reached down and hooked an arm behind Malek's knee, raising him up as he clawed for a handhold on anything within his grasp. Hatred was in Malek's black eyes as he realized what Steve would do. As Malek sucked in a breath of air to spit in Steve's face, Steve shoved his head back with a flat palm and sent the screaming terrorist plunging downward, his body bouncing off the steel staircases as it fell seven levels to a painful death.

The sickening sound of flesh colliding with steel turned Beth's stomach, and she fell to her knees, dry heaving with painful convulsions. Steve gathered the guns up, and after a quick glance back down the hallway to make sure no one had heard the commotion, ran down the steps to Beth's side. She was trying to cover her face, tears welling in her eyes, no shame in her revulsion at what she had just observed.

Steve wrapped his arm around her shoulders, helping her to her feet. With the back of his hand, he wiped the tears from her cheek; a pronounced empathy for the nightmare she endured welled up inside him. Still hugging her, he sensed her vulnerability.

She felt weak hanging to his arm, appreciating his strength and comfort.

"It's okay, it's okay, Beth." He said, rubbing her shoulder. "We have the advantage now. I believe we can get to the bridge, it's down the hallway here, and we'll be able to hold them off until we can get help."

"Sorry... I'm trying to hold it together. I realize I'm a pain in the..."

"Hey, don't even go there. I got you into this, and it's my responsibility to get you out. I know it's a lot to ask, but I will need your help one more time. We have to storm the bridge and get control of the ship. There are only two more bad guys, the little guy we haven't seen for a while, and the Mexican." He handed her Malek's gun.

"When we go up, just point it at anybody who you think is threatening, it'll be enough to keep them away. I'll take care of everything else. Can you do it?"

"What is it with this guy?" She asked herself. His confidence was so reassuring she was almost eager to go. "You will owe me big time for all this, you know don't you?"

"I surrender, you name your price!" He was giving her a big smile. The lighthearted banter helped reduce their tension, as they made their way to the top landing. A quick glimpse through the window showed a deserted hallway. No one had noticed the scuffle on the landing, and with one more look, Steve was sure Beth had regained her composure.

"Let's show these people who they're messing with."

Beth gave a halfhearted nod as they opened the door and stepped into the hallway. They hugged the wall as they made the short distance down the passageway to the bridge. As he stole a look in the door, Steve saw the pilot at his control station, sitting in a large comfortable swivel chair. The Captain was on the telephone beside him staring at a bank of video monitors, adjusting the images to compensate for the shifting morning light. Everyone was facing away from the door. Steve managed another quick glance, just to make sure. He could not observe the passageway to the treatment room from his vantage point.

"This will be a piece of cake, come on," Steve whispered.

They hustled through the door, both holding their guns extended in front. If Steve had not ordered everybody to freeze, the people on the bridge wouldn't have even known they were there. All three men looked around in disbelief at the dirty couple. Steve's "Da Bomb" shirt would have been comical had there not been two guns pointed at them.

"Don't move, any of you. I'm with ICE. I am taking command of this ship. If you do as I say, you will not get hurt. Nobody has to get hurt here, do you understand?"

Trying to keep the wall to his back, Steve had not noticed the passageway to the infirmary, and Beth was standing in the doorway where they had entered.

"I want you to get on the radio and issue a Mayday." He jutted his chin at the pilot. "Do it now!"

It startled Jose as he lay back on the cot to make out a strange voice coming from the bridge. As soon as he heard the words 'ICE Agent', he knew to whom it belonged. He jumped up and hobbled to the door, his view unimpeded to the end of the short passageway. His gun at the ready, he saw the custom agent's back in front of him, not eight feet away. He thought he could drop him from where he was, but something worried him about the girl. He didn't know where she was, and he might not find her by the time they reached San Juan. If she found a way off, he would be in deep shit. Where was Malek?

"Worthless jackass," he hissed under his breath as he kept his eye on Steve. *"I'll bet he parked his fat ass in the head. Anyway, I can take care of this you myself. Just stay right where you are."* He coached himself as he crept the few steps to Steve's back, his shoeless feet helping to ensure silence. As the pilot turned to the radio, Steve noticed the Captain's and the other man's gazes diverted, and their eyes open wider with surprise. Before he could react, the shocking cold steel of a gun muzzle pressed into the muscle at the back of his neck.

Beth inhaled a surprised gasp, "Steve!"

"You're gonna drop the gun, or I will spray your brains all over this room. Now you don't want that do you, *Steve?*" Jose's voice was above a whisper, as he mocked the sound of Beth's voice.

"No, you drop it!" Beth shouted in high-pitched anger, as she pointed her gun at Jose. "No, you drop it, or I swear I'll shoot!"

Jose laughed, as he put his arm around Steve's neck, pulling him closer to use him as a shield. "Got that Stevie? She's gonna shoot! How much you wanna bet I can put one in your head and drop her before you hit the floor?"

It was a dangerous game now. Steve saw Beth's gun was on safety. Even if she had the ability how to flick it to ready, there was no way she could hit Jose. He tried a little schoolyard psychology.

"Shoot him, Beth! He yelled. He will kill me anyway!"

It mortified her at the thought of pulling the trigger. What is he trying to do? She thought to herself. Her hands trembled, the gun weighed a ton, and she realized lives were hanging in the balance. With a sudden rush of courage, an animalistic urge rose in her, and she made her move.

She gathered every ounce of strength she had and pointed the gun at Jose's face. With three quick steps at him, she yelled, "Drop the gun, DROP IT!"

Jose, surprised by her audacity, had only a split second to decide. If she took another couple of steps, she would have the gun so close to his head he would never have time to shoot them both.

He pulled the gun away from the base of Steve's skull and started his arm in a defensive arc towards Beth. The other men on the bridge ducked when they saw the gun in motion, diving for any available cover. When the gun came into his line of sight, Steve reached over and grabbed Jose's wrist, while kicking straight

131

back with his right leg. Jose pulled the trigger, sending a spray of bullets into the large glass windows at the front of the bridge area. The one-inch thick Plexiglass withstood hurricane-force wind and waves, and it seemed to absorb the bullets. A muted 'thunk' was the only sound made as each bullet hit, leaving a trail of smoke rising from melted plastic craters.

Beth clapped her hands over her ears and screamed as she half fell, half dove, for the door, the bang-bang-bang of the semiautomatic amplified to painful decibels in the confines of the small room. Jose fell down in a heap, with Steve wrestling his arm behind his back as if he was hog tying a prize steer. Shouts of agony bellowed from the Mexican's throat as Steve yelled.

"Drop it, or I'll break your arm too, DROP IT!" The fight went out of the man as Steve yanked the gun from his grip and pointed it at the officers on deck. "Stay back, stay right where you are!" He backed up to keep them all in front of him.

Beth picked herself up from the floor, fearing the worst. When she saw Steve standing, uninjured, a wave of relief cascaded over her, propelling her to his side, knocking him off balance, as she hugged him, sobbing.

"Steve, I'm sorry, I had none idea what to do, I thought he would kill you! I've never been so scared in my life!"

"It's over, we did it, Beth. You were great. That was the bravest thing I've ever seen, you did what you had to do. Now let's get the hell off this ship."

He frisked Jose, and finding no other weapons, kicked him to the corner, the odd bend in his knee joint ensuring he wasn't going anywhere. Still wary, he remembered there was still a loose end. "Where's the other guy you had with you? There were five of you, where's the other one?" Jose didn't respond, he appeared to go into shock, his color was a pale yellow, and the sweat was pouring from his brow.

"He's dead." The Captain offered. "He fell out of the helicopter last night, just before it crashed. They never told us how it happened."

Steve considered the information for a second, reasoning it made sense. They hadn't seen him for a while, something must have happened to him. Pointing his gun to the captain he said, "If he shows up, I'll make sure you get it first, understand?"

The Captain shrugged as Steve pointed to the satellite radio, "Now, as I was saying before we were so interrupted, get on the radio and get a Mayday out."

"It won't be necessary, Sir." The Captain responded, pointing to the starboard side of the ship where a dark-colored ship flying the Stars and Stripes plowed through the water, headed right for them. "Your Coast Guard has notified us they will board us at oh one hundred. I have already stopped the engines. We have standing orders from our employer to comply with all U.S. regulations while in your waters. Since we have not passed the two hundred mile limit, I submit this ship is under the authority of the Coast Guard."

Steve took the radio transceiver from the captain, still holding the three men at gunpoint. He would not take any chances now. He told Beth to monitor the hallway, as he pressed the button to talk: "Coast Guard cutter 1079, Coast Guard cutter 1079, do you read me? This is Global Explorer, come in, please."

"We read you, Sir. Can you identify yourself?" The tinny response was audible on the bridge.

"This is Special Agent Steve Ross with Immigration and Customs Enforcement. I can't tell you how glad I am to see the big gray fish you're riding on."

"What's your status, Agent Ross? We have a team of your buddies on standby, preparing to board the vessel. Is there danger close?" Came the no-nonsense reply.

"I'm requesting your immediate help, Sir." Steve answered, "I have control of the bridge, and I'm not sure how many hostiles may be onboard. Consider anyone you see armed and dangerous. I have one in custody with me, and at least three more KIA."

"Roger, Agent Ross. Standby, I'm preparing to come alongside her now. I'll keep this channel open."

"Roger that, Sir, thank you, I'm standing by."

Steve did a quick frisk of the three crew members on the bridge and told them to resume their duties, and not to leave the room. Keeping the immobile Jose in his sights, he also did a quick check of the small rooms in the infirmary, verifying there were no other people hiding there. He snatched a roll of medical tape from a counter and returned to tape the wrists of Jose's limp arms, noticing his breathing was shallow and labored.

Calling Beth back into the room, he escorted her to the treatment room, pointing to the cot. "Why don't you take a rest for a few minutes? My friends are on the way now, we'll be off this tub in a half an hour, and get you to safety."

"Thanks… I'm so tired." Beth didn't quite know what else to say. Although they had only known each other two days, she was feeling an attraction for him beyond the closeness the struggle for mutual survival had brought to them. She would miss his company. He left the room with a smile and a half wink, as she lay back, unable to stop herself from fantasizing about what it would be like to be in a relationship with him. Talk about opposites. She was a quiet researcher, spending her days in classrooms and labs, while he was an undercover agent for the Customs Service. *"Get real!"* She said to herself, *"Never in a million years!"* She lay back in utter exhaustion, closing her eyes for the first time in over forty-eight hours without a sense of foreboding evil hanging over her.

Beth was resting for only ten minutes when the voices of several men at the door startled her back to reality.

She sat up to the sight of an armed man, dressed in black, much the way she had seen Steve and Jim when this began. Steve stepped in the room and took Beth's hand, allaying the slight fear he saw in her eyes at the sight of more armed men.

"Dan, I want you to meet one of the bravest women I've ever known, this is Beth Williams."

Dan held out a big paw and shook Beth's fingers as he introduced himself, while Steve recounted a small part of the story.

"She faced down the Mexican dude out there like she had been training for it all her life. If it weren't for her, I'd be dead, no question about it. She's a tough lady, I'm thinking about signing her up!"

"Now that's a real compliment, coming from this guy!" Dan joked. "He still thinks a woman's place is barefoot and pregnant!"

Steve gave Dan a good-natured shove on the shoulder. "Get out of here; don't you have bad guys to catch?"

"Well hell, you guys did all my work for me. So far all we found is three stiffs, and the other guy won't be doing any running soon." He glanced back at Jose, slumped on the floor. "I have a team rounding up the crew, so you can look at them. The guy you say was helping the others may not be dead; he might try to pass himself off as a crew member. We will check all their immigration papers, he will not slide by me, and I guarantee it. If not, then let's hope he's fish food. In the meantime, I will station a man on the bridge until the harbor pilot arrives from San Juan. There's no point in transferring you to the Coast Guard ship, the only way over is a rope line, and I think you two have been through enough. You're safe now, and when we get to San Juan, Angie Barnes and Bob Graves will wait for you. I'm sure you have a lot of catching up to do."

Steve and Beth agreed with him, and as he turned to go, Steve grabbed his sleeve.

"I want you to take special care of the idiot on the floor, Dan. I will have him charged him with first-degree murder. He's the scumbag who shot Jim Ragan."

Dan gave a fierce look in Jose's direction, his tone serious and said, "don't worry. He ain't ever going to see the light of day again, Steve. You have my word, now you two kids chill out and let me do my job."

He nodded over at Beth as he left the room, giving Steve a friendly pat on the shoulder.

Later, Steve and Beth walked topside and were leaning on the railing of the observation deck, the early afternoon sun shining on the Port of San Juan's waters, cooking the humidity out of the undulating waves. A stiff breeze blew as they enjoyed a clear view of the old fort, and the domed minaret styled observation posts dotting the wall of the fort. It was a peaceful sight, in stark contrast to the miserable conditions Boulez and his security forces subjected them to. The armed escort Dan Driver had assigned to them was pacing on the far side

134

of the deck, keeping a careful watch on any movement of the crew on the decks below, as they prepared for docking. Steve had been in contact with Angie Barnes over on the Coast Guard cutter, and they had made plans for a briefing once everybody returned safely to shore. For now, it satisfied them soaking up the sunlight, as the pilot maneuvered the huge ship, with the help of several tugboats, into the assigned pier. There was a haze of smoke emanating from several open hatchways on the main deck. The smoke came from textiles still smoldering in containers touched off by the fire that blew up the Porsche. A thirty-foot patrol boat met the Coast Guard cutter as it escorted the Global Explorer into the harbor. Agents Barnes and Graves climbed down a rope ladder from the cutter into the patrol boat, which took them the rest of the way to the pier. Once the START team had determined there was no further danger to its agents, they secured the vessel and turned the search over to the Coast Guard personnel waiting for it at the pier. It would be up to the Coast Guard to do a thorough search for illegal aliens, and contraband, once the ship had docked.

CHAPTER 38

Agent Graves traveled to the local field office to set up a briefing for Steve later in the afternoon. His assignment was to work out the protocol with the other investigative agencies present. An agreement would call for briefing Steve later in the afternoon, giving him time to clean up, eat, and maybe even catch a nap. Angie Barnes was waiting on the pier, along with several colleagues from Customs, representatives from the FBI field office, a Coast Guard response team, the local police, an ambulance, and the coroner. She watched as Steve and Beth walked down the gangplank, both looking neat and trim in the crisp blue crew overalls they had appropriated from the ship's laundry. Although it may have seemed unprofessional, she gave Steve a generous hug when he walked up to greet her.

"Sorry Steve, sorry about Jim, you two were close. I always had great respect for him... both of you, you made a great team." She was trying to choke back the emotion filling her throat, keeping her hand on his arm in a small gesture of consolation.

"Thanks, Angie, I appreciate it. The only thing that makes it any better is I got the bastard who killed him. It was hard to resist putting a bullet in his head." They watched as the ambulance crew carried Jose from the ship on a litter, federal Marshals meeting them at the dock, and escorting him along the way.

Seeing the look of concern on his face as they loaded Jose into the ambulance, she offered: "Don't worry, he's not going anywhere. Marshals will babysit him until we get him in a secure lock-up. He won't be going to a local jail. They will take him to the military hospital at Vieques, patch him up, and then throw him in the brig until we can arrange transport back to Miami."

Steve scowled at the ambulance until the doors shut, and it left the area under heavy escort.

"I hope to hell we can make a death penalty charge stick."

"It shouldn't be a problem. He has so many charges, kidnapping, murder, assaulting a federal officer, not to mention whatever terrorism charges they come up with. Hell, he's dead meat." Angie ticked off the information on her fingers. "Let's let everyone else worry about that for now. You people deserve a break. Let's get out of here. The Department has a few rooms at the Sheraton for us to use. We have a secure perimeter with spotters around the outside, so you are not in any danger there. It's not fancy, but it is on the beach. I'll drop you off."

"Wait a minute, Angie," Steve hesitated, "I have... or I should say we have important information about what is going on in the ship's lab. Can you have it sealed it off until we can get back? I believe it should be at the highest level of national security. Nobody will believe it, or even find out about it if we don't show them what's going on."

136

"It's not nuclear, or biological, or a WMD is it Steve? If it is, you know I will have to notify the CIA and shut this area down."

"Well it might be a weapon of mass destruction, but not unless we let them get out of this port with it. It's harmless as long as it stays here on the ship."

"You want to explain?" Angie asked.

"It will be a long story, and part of it is just a theory. Just make sure we hold the people working in the lab in custody and keep everybody else out for now. Oh, and one other thing, you must keep the light off on in the lab." Steve looked back at Beth, who showed her agreement with a nod. Steve opened the door to the Ford Crown Vic Angie had led them to, seating Beth in the back, while he took the front passenger seat. Angie was already on her cell phone to the head of the field investigation unit, relaying Steve's instructions. They left the pier area, watching the bustle of law enforcement agencies entering and leaving the ship. Steve looked back as they rounded the corner, stifling a pang of guilt as the coroner wheeled a body bag down the gangplank. Although he had killed in the line of duty several times before, it was always troubling for him to take a human life. "They brought the fight to me, they asked for it." He acquitted himself as they sped out of sight of the pier, his thoughts interrupted by the sound of Beth's voice from the back seat.

"Can I borrow a cell phone for a minute? I should call my mother and my sister, I'm sure they are frantic by now."

"Sure." Angie said, handing it back to Beth, with cautioning her: "Whatever you do, tell no one where you are. Until we get this situation under control, you are still in danger."

Beth agreed, and as she dialed Steve leaned his head back against the headrest, he felt hungry, dirty, and drained. He was looking forward to a long hot shower on Uncle Sam's tab.

Local traffic crowded the island roads with local traffic, many vehicles weaving in and out, double-parking, and ignoring every traffic regulation. It was a picturesque ride along the coast, and after leaving the main road, a short ride down a sandy lane brought them to a smallish, pastel green building. A few faded wooden rocking chairs were visible on a side porch, and beyond, a narrow beach, with endless miles of ocean stretching in front. The entrance area between the street and the hotel covered with vines and colorful plants provided a barrier to the sounds of the nearby road. A local Customs Agent was waiting on a bench near the lobby, a cold soda in one hand as he enjoyed the breeze blowing in from the surrounding hillsides. He jumped up to open the door as Angie pulled the car to a halt in the circular driveway. After offering condolences regarding Jim Ragan, he directed Steve and Beth into the hotel.

"You're already checked in under aliases." He said as opened the door and led them inside, handing each of them a plastic room key. "You're Joe Smith, and Ms. Williams is Linda Green. Sorry, it was short notice." He smiled as Steve groaned. "I also have this for you." He handed them both long white envelopes. "Just a little cash and an American Express card with your aliases on it. I would imagine you want to get clean clothes and a few necessities. Anyway, you know the drill, Steve. You will answer for everything you charge, so don't go crazy."

"You don't have to worry about me. A pair of shorts and some Nikes and I'll be okay. I can't imagine we will be here for a long time, anyway. Once the Government closes down the operation, we saw on the ship last night, I'm sure they will not complain about two extra beers missing from the mini-bar." Steve joked.

"Is there a department store around here?" Beth asked. "I will need a little more than shorts. I don't think I've never been this filthy."

"They have shops on the beach level... one down. They should have anything you need. If not, we have agents occupying the rooms next to yours. Just use the house phone and let them know what you want."

Angie broke in, "If we can get you both briefed later today, you can be on a plane to Miami tomorrow... or the next day. Oh, Steve, Gene Tyson is arriving on a military jet at three-thirty. He wants to meet with both of you on the ship. Do you think you can be ready around four?"

Steve looked at Beth, "I know it's a lot to ask..."

"It's okay. I guess so... who is Gene Tyson?" Beth asked.

"I'll explain it to her after we get cleaned up" Steve started towards the rear of the lobby, a wall of glass drawing his eye to a spectacular ocean view, as he pushed the elevator button.

Beth followed close behind, "Not bad... not bad at all!"

Angie held the door open as Steve and Beth entered the elevator. "One more thing you two, please don't leave this hotel until the meeting without telling us. We're not set up for traveling security. So, is there anything else I can do for you right now?"

"No, just send a car for us at four-thirty," Steve said, hitting the button for the lower level as Angie backed away from the door.

"Okay, we'll see you then."

"Oh, I almost forgot, there is one other thing I need, Angie. They took my gun... I need a backup weapon."

"Leave it to me; I'm sure I can come up with one."

The elevator descended to the lower level, opening to an open-air pavilion containing several beach shops, a drugstore, and a liquor store. They agreed to meet back at the elevator in twenty minutes. Steve wasted no time in finding several plain tee shirts, shorts, a shaving kit, the toiletries, and a well-made pair of island sandals. Beth took a little longer, having a few more items to buy, finding everything she needed. Steve killed a few minutes perusing the myriad offerings in the liquor store as he waited for Beth to finish paying for her purchases. When she met up with Steve, she had several small bags on her arm.

138

"You find everything you needed?"

"Yes, I did. There's a bit of everything here." She said. Steve took her bags as they headed back to the elevator. The hotel only had five floors, and their rooms were on the uppermost level. They found their side-by-side rooms near the end of the hallway, and Steve opened the door for her, depositing her bags on the colorful bedspread, as she walked over to the balcony door and pulled the curtains back. At the foot of the bed, there was a rolling table with a tray holding a covered plate sandwich, chips and a fruit salad was waiting beside a thick white bathrobe folded to the side

"Such a different world from what we have been dealing with." She said looking down at the beach umbrellas dotting the shoreline. "It's so peaceful here. I never knew such terrible people live and operate with such hatred, right in our own backyard. I suppose I have led a very sheltered existence."

"You're right. The world has become a much more dangerous place in the last few years. Our department's attention used to focus on drug interdiction, and believe me; the drug consortiums are full of very violent people. I suspect they recruited the guy who killed Jim from a cartel. Ever since 9-11 we've had to concentrate our efforts on people who make most of those drug runners look like Girl Scouts. At least the drug dealers were just trying to make money and protect their turf. These terrorists have a misguided desire to please Allah, and they don't care how they do it, or how many of us 'blue-eyed devils' they take with them. It's…"

"Steve?" She interrupted, pulling his attention back into the room. "You're tired, you need to get your rest, we both do." His smile softened the gentle chastisement.

He felt a little sheepish now, realizing his rambling discourse was keeping her from her well-earned rest.

"I'm sorry." He paused on the way out of the door, "You know, I will need your expertise when we try to convince them about this 'Midas Effect" fairy tale. I hope we weren't hallucinating."

"It was real, don't worry, the gold is still there."

"I'm sure you're right. Anyhow, I'll leave you alone now, why don't you clean up and try to catch a nap. I'll call you at four." He said as pulled the door almost shut. "If you need anything, just call room service, have it delivered to my room, I'll bring it over. Oh, and a couple of things, whatever you do, do not open this door for anybody but me, and please don't make calls to the States. We can't take the chance of him tracing the call back to here. I wouldn't put it past them to bug your relative's phones."

"I'm too tired to dial a phone, all I want is a shower and to go to sleep."

Steve agreed as he shut her door, "See you at four."

He returned to his room, entering with a vague sense of uneasiness. It was the last room on the fifth-floor hallway, so it was secure… at least for a hotel. The day's events were eating at him though, lingering in the back of his mind. He glanced over at the tray of sandwiches room service had left on the coffee table; they brought to mind the small café on the bottom floor of the safe house in Key West. He and Jim Ragan had stopped there for many a time to grab a quick sandwich during one investigation or another. An image of Jim's face presented itself in his mind's eye as he sat on the side of the bed, weary. Not sentimental, disbelief and grief over what happened to Jim caused him to let down his emotional guard. Without thinking, he reached for the telephone and dialed Jim's cell phone. It seemed to ring forever until Jim's simple prerecorded greeting played.

"Hi, this is the number you called. Leave a message, thanks." It was typical Jim... to the point with a touch of sarcasm. Steve squeezed his eyes shut, hearing Jim's voice as if he were in the next room.

"Jim, buddy, I... I wanted to hear your voice one last time. You're up there laughing at what a pussy I am, but hey, what can I say? I wanted to tell you I got the guy who shot you, but I'm sure you already know. Anyway... take care." Unable to finish, he fought to control his emotions, waiting in despair until the 'beep' signaled the recording was over. He hung the phone up, cradling his head between his hands.

CHAPTER 39

Steve was in a fitful sleep after showering and attempting to choke down one sandwich on the tray. He lay on top of the bed in his new boxers when the sound of an unfamiliar phone rang, disturbing his subconscious world. A disjointed dream about Jim Ragan ran through his mind. He was outside, on a sandy beach, watching as a man was firing a gun at Jim. Jim just stood there with a blank look on his face, paying no attention as the bullets bounced off, and drop into the sand at his feet. Steve was sitting on a dirt bike, and when the shooting stopped, Jim walked over to him, smiling.

"You see, Steve? I'm okay! I'm stronger than any bullet!" Steve looked up in horror as Jim's face neared, his eyes solid black orbs, his bright smile now a mass of cragged yellow looking stumps. As he recoiled, he heard the soft ringing again, off in the distance.

The persistent ringing chased the dream from Steve's mind. He opened his eyes to a stippled ceiling, a fan spinning overhead. His heart was throbbing, his mouth dry, and an arm he had slept on was tingling with the new rush of blood. He sat up rubbing his eyes, with a creepy feeling lingering around him as he reached for the phone.

"Yeah?"

"It's Angie, Steve. You sound rough, are you okay? Did I wake you up?"

"No, no, I was just about to get up." For no good reason, it embarrassed him to admit he was asleep as if it were somehow a weakness.

"It's a little after four, are you ready to go?" Angie surmised he had been asleep.

Steve fought to clear his head, blinking at the clock to bring it into focus.

"Give me a few minutes. I'll get Beth and meet you in the lobby in twenty minutes."

"Okay, no big deal. I'll get a cold drink in the lounge. Just come get me when you're ready."

When Steve called Beth's room, she answered on the first ring.

"Hi, it's Steve. You ready to go?"

"Anytime, I only slept for a half an hour, I guess I'm too keyed up for sleep." She explained.

After Steve met up with Beth, they found Angie sipping a Coke in the lounge, and writing on the keyboard of a laptop which lay open on the table.

"I've already got so much information on this case for my report, I might have to write a book before it's all over," she joked as she placed the laptop in her satchel.

"You better hold a few chapters for what you will see today. If what we think we saw is true, we are all going to be spending a lot of time writing reports." Steve replied.

141

"And I will need to write the most unbelievable papers as well," Beth added. "My colleagues just may think I fell off the deep end!"

"You two have got my curiosity up. Let's head out, I am looking forward to finding out what all this crazy talk is all about."

The trio settled into Angie's rental car for the short trip to the piers. Angie had become the unofficial liaison between ICE, who had jurisdiction, and the multitude of law enforcement and investigative agencies assembled to work on this case. With her cell phone glued to her ear, she was putting out fires and soothing egos as each autonomous section wrangled for positioning and inside information. She was becoming frustrated with the attitude of non-cooperation. The protocol Agent Barnes worked so hard on was being manipulated for agency one-upmanship, and she didn't like it. As they neared the pier, she turned the phone off aggravated.

"To hell with them," she complained. "We have a dead agent and all they care about is when they can file their reports and get back to the beach. I've got news for them, we're first and they can sweep up the crumbs when we're done."

Steve looked at Beth, sitting in the back seat, and laughed.

"I'm surrounded by tough ladies. I need to watch my step!"

Arriving at the pier, the size the fleet of government vehicles amassed alongside the ship amazed Steve. Agent Graves was waiting for them there, pulling Steve to the side as they got out of the car. He handed Steve a small black handgun encased in a nylon concealment holster, along with a screw-on silencer.

"Angie asked me to get this for you. Sorry, it's only a thirty-eight; it's the best I can do on such short notice."

Steve pulled the small black gun from its holster, checking the magazine and loading a round into the chamber.

"It'll do for now, Bob, keep the silencer. If I have to use this while I'm here, I want plenty of attention. Thanks, I appreciate it." He clipped the holster to the waistband of his jeans and covered it with his shirttail. You would have to look very hard to notice the slight bulge it made. Graves led the group up the gangplank, back up several deck levels to the mess hall. While not large, it was the largest room on the ship, and it had about twenty chairs strewn around at various tables.

Steve followed Agent Graves into the room, seeing Gene Tyson wearing a borrowed Navy flight suit. They hugged as Gene offered his condolences, taking Steve into a small antechamber used as the captain's private dining room, to speak with him.

"I know it's not much, but I will see Jim gets the highest commendation possible for the sacrifice he made for our homeland security." Tyson continued, "He died a hero, doing what he loved. From what we know there was nothing you could have done differently, so I don't want you to beat yourself up over this.

You got the guy who killed him, and I know if he was here he would agree that makes you are a hero as well."

"The Mexican is just a pimple on the ass of this whole operation, Gene," Steve explained. "It goes to Boulez, and who knows who else. I should have killed the jerk just to save the taxpayers the cost of a trial. I guess it's what separates us from these terrorists. We at least have a sense of honor. The best way to avenge Jim's death is for the authorities to come down hard on Boulez and his whole operation, and I think we may have found out how to do it. If everyone is ready, I say we get this dog and pony show rolling."

They hugged again, and Steve turned to face the assemblage of a dozen law enforcement personnel gathered in the room, sitting as he introduced himself, and then asked each of the attendees to introduce themselves and give their position within their respective government departments. Steve was a little surprised to find out the CIA had bypassed the local headquarters and brought a representative there direct from Langley. He was an intense man, about forty years old, named Robert Beebe.

"I have asked you all to come here for a briefing on a situation my supervisor, Gene Tyson, and I, believe involves grave national consequences," Steve explained. "As you know, our department has been investigating Jason Boulez for several years now. He has ties to a defunct branch of the Red Brigade we have been receiving information about through intermediaries. Our information suggests a well-funded attempt is being made to resurrect a faction of the Red Brigade, with the purpose of carrying out terrorist attacks against western, and in particular, US interests. Through various surveillance methods, which you are all aware of, our department learned of an opportunity to gain sensitive information from an interface at Mr. Boulez's estate. Jim Ragan and I were on an assignment early Saturday morning when Boulez's security compromised the operation. Because of circumstances, I will not go into how Beth Williams, the nice person sitting beside me here, became involved. To make a long story short, Jim and I had to appropriate her vehicle, which they traced to her sister's house in Key West. They discovered Miss Williams is a microbiologist who would have sent up tons of red flags in their organization. She is an uninterested party, and an unwilling participant in the events that transpired, which lead to the murder of my partner, Jim Ragan at her sister's house. The perp who murdered Jim is in our custody and charged with the capital murder of a federal agent. They kidnapped Miss Williams and me from the murder scene and flew us by helicopter to a container ship owned by Jason Boulez, the Global Explorer. The ship was off the coast of Cuba headed for San Juan. We escaped from our captors, neutralized them, and took control of the vessel earlier this morning."

"Way to kick ass, Steve!" A voice shouted from across the room, accompanied by an appreciative murmur from the group.

143

"Thanks, it wasn't all me, by a long shot. Jim Ragan was instrumental in the assignment's success. When they ambushed us, he never had a chance. Boulez's men murdered him in cold blood." He paused with emotion as the room became silent. "And Miss Williams, well, let's say I wouldn't be talking to you now if it weren't for her. For a civilian, I was damn impressed with her, and believe me, they put her through the wringer."

One of the FBI agents interrupted, "Can you explain a little about what you said about Miss Williams, her being a microbiologist raising red flags. Why would they even care?"

"At first I didn't know why. After Ms. Williams and I infiltrated the lab aboard this ship, it became clear what concerned them. If what we think we saw is going on, then they would have good reason to worry we know about it." Steve answered.

The same FBI agent responded, "Our information says Boulez claims to be studying a method for filtering ballast water to make it acceptable to the EPA for discharge in territorial waters. We all know that's a load of bullshit."

"Boulez had one of our undercover agents killed earlier this year when he discovered what was going on in another ship's lab. You don't kill people over bilge water." Gene Tyson added.

"They didn't kill him over bilge water, Gene," Steve responded. "Beth and I believe they killed him because he discovered Boulez had perfected a process for removing gold from seawater. Ms. Williams is familiar with the process, and if I understand her explanation, there are certain microbes, which use a chemical reaction to precipitate minute particles of gold out of seawater. She said scientists have studied these microbes, and they call their reaction to seawater heated under certain conditions, the 'Midas Effect'. I think the best thing to do would be to go down to the lab and let her explain to you what we saw, and how it works."

As the group rose to its feet, Robert Graves seemed to be playing the devil's advocate.

"Steve, why would Boulez resort to murder to hide what is a legal operation? If he was worried about industrial espionage, there are legal means to protect his process. It makes little sense to bring the heat down he's getting on himself for what little gold he might get out of a few gallons of seawater."

"It's the same question I had, Bob." Steve replied, "All I can say is when you *see* the operation, I think you will understand why."

The group headed down the several flights of stairs towards the lower level housing the laboratories. ICE processed the three men Steve and Beth had watched in the lab upon arrival in San Juan. All three were traveling on legal passports, with all visas and immigration certificates in perfect order. They claimed to be doing research to improve the cleanliness of the ship's ballast. A quick sweep of the lab turned up no evidence of contraband, no evidence of any illegal activity, and no gold. The captain, first mate, and two crewmembers

144

assisting Jose were in ICE custody, and the rest of the crew, including the lab workers, returned to the ship after the investigation.

When the group arrived at the lab, it surprised Steve to see lights on through the door. They entered with the Captain's key card, and to his dismay, Steve saw lights on in the hallway, and in the lab area. The doors were open to the two large compartments holding the metal racks, and the entire area bathed in bright light, the racks looking clean enough to eat off.

"What the hell happened here, Angie?" Steve looked disappointed, "All the lights are on!"

"Sorry, this is the way we found the lab, Steve. Lights on, and they were in those chambers with those fire hoses, washing everything down. We got everybody out and sealed it up."

"I should have known. They must have orders to sterilize everything if there is any hint of trouble." Steve looked dejected.

"What happened to the gold?" Beth inquired. "It has to be here," she speculated.

"What gold? You saw gold in here?" Tyson asked.

"We saw them pour out eight ingots, right out of this oven!" Steve pointed out the small smelter they observed the previous night. "I know it's here…"

"Right, they had no way to get it off the ship, unless they threw it overboard," Beth added.

"I'm guessing the lab workers weren't eager to explain anything?" Steve looked at Tyson, already knowing the answer.

"No luck there, at least not yet. These people fear what Boulez will do to them if they talk, not what the U.S. government will do if they do not. All they will say is what they poured out of the beakers was an organic residue from bilge cleaning microbes."

CHAPTER 40

Robert Beebe was skilled at blending in with the crowd. He has been with the CIA since even before graduating from the university, working as an intern at CIA headquarters in Langley during his summers, while he lived with his parents in nearby Falls Church, Virginia. He had been waiting in traffic behind several cars in January 1993, as a Pakistani national opened fire on vehicles waiting at a stoplight in front of the CIA entrance. The Pakistani killed two people, fled the scene and escaped back to Pakistan. The license plate number Beebe wrote as the murderer sped past him helped to identify the suspect and in his eventual capture and execution. It was also instrumental in Beebe's offer of a full-time job upon his graduation, a job he took to heart.

While the other representatives from various agencies crowded and jostled for positions, he hung to the back, ever observant, analyzing every question, every statement. The rumors tying Boulez to terrorist activities were surfacing with greater and greater frequency. Now the murder of one U.S.Customs agent and abducting another involved in information which seemed to point to Boulez being involved with large quantities of gold, set alarm bells off at the highest levels. It was his job to judge, to assess, and test people. He determined Steve Ross and Beth Williams were no nut cases, whatever they said they saw, they had seen. The story they had given seemed plausible, the timeline matched, and most importantly, they both believed it. If they witnessed the production of large quantities of gold from seawater, it would be prudent to find out how and why. Robert Beebe defined prudence, and he was an excellent judge of character. Hearing how Ross had overcome and escaped from his captors, he realized Ross was the man who got things done. He had made a few mistakes, gotten himself in real trouble, and found a way out. No agency asked for more of its people. People will always make mistakes. How you overcome those mistakes sets you apart from the ordinary man. Unlucky men end up dead, and smart men end up smarter. Steve Ross ended up smarter. He knew he needed a man like Steve Ross.

Gene Tyson wrapped up with solicitations for cooperation among the various agencies involved in the investigation. In theory, Homeland Security required each agency responsible for their 'niche'. Requiring them to share whatever pertinent information they uncovered with any other agency, as requested unless there was a damn good reason for not sharing. The new era of interagency cooperation was off to a rocky start, after many versions of 'who knew what, and when they knew it' in response to 9-11 investigations suggested an entrenched attitude. A few agencies were famous for their policies of no cooperation of any kind.

Beebe waited for everyone else to leave before he walked up to the trio of Steve, Beth, and Gene Tyson, who were discussing plans to have the entire lab searched for hidden compartments, and trace amounts of gold. After introducing himself, he got to the point.

"Your theory was very interesting, Ms. Williams. It's hard to believe anybody can get gold from microbes. You called it the Midas Effect?"

Beth nodded in agreement, "Yes."

Gene continued, "I'm wondering if I might ask both of you a few questions? Just a nagging feeling I have there is a way to explain what happened to the gold."

"Oh, so you believe us? I got the impression many people think we wasted their time today."

"I have no reason not to believe you, you are an educated scientist, and Mr. Ross is an experienced investigator, not people prone to hyperbole, I would say."

"It is possible we are wrong," Steve replied. "We have no real way to prove we saw gold, although a lot of circumstantial evidence points to it."

"I agree, it seems fantastic, however as Mr. Tyson knows, our government has a great concern about reports of a large influx of gold coming on the market through unconventional channels," Beebe said. "We know how much gold is available in the world markets, and we know the world's mining capacity. Those two things control the market. Since mining has been supplying less gold than in recent years, and demand is higher, the price of gold should go up. The World Bank and the IMF control the amount of bullion offered for sale through traditional channels, and they have not increased the amount to any substantial degree, yet in the last year, the price of gold has dropped twenty-five percent. At that rate, gold will be worthless as a monetary instrument in less than four years. Only one thing can cause that price drop. It has to be an oversupply, a glut, so to speak. I think what you have described here today merits serious investigation."

"We appreciate your confidence, Mr. Beebe."

"Forget the 'Mr.', everybody calls me Bob."

Steve smiled. At least he wasn't one of the usual self-important stuffed shirts the CIA sent around to quote regulations and procedure.

"Okay, Bob, how can we help?"

"I was standing near the back of the room while you were briefing our colleagues, and I noticed that." Beebe walked to the corner of the lab, pointing to an unobtrusive black plastic dome, not much bigger than a soccer ball, attached to the ceiling. They located it above the lab table where the man had weighed and logged in the suspected golden sand.

"Unless I miss my guess, there is a video camera inside the dome. It's just if there is a recorder on the other end, and if they haven't erased the tape, we can all watch what you saw."

"There's only one way to find out," Steve said, pushing a lab stool under the dome. He took the now dry broom handle he had used to check the acid-filled tank and broke it over his knee. The result was a wedge-shaped piece of wood, which he wiggled under the lip of the plastic dome. Four screws secured the corners, which pulled through the plastic as Steve yanked down on the broom handle. The dome clattered to the floor, revealing a small video camera, pointed at the lab table.

"Nice!" Gene Tyson exclaimed, "Let's get the captain down here to tell us where the other end of this thing is."

"It might not be necessary. I believe I saw where it ends up. There is a bank of video monitors up on the bridge, twenty or more." Steve said, leading the way back out.

They all hurried to the bridge, still under the control of the Coast Guard. Steve sat down in front of the bank of small monitors. The only images showing were fore and aft, starboard and port views from cameras mounted on the ship's exterior. The group gathered around as he switched on every monitor, from a computer touch screen, waiting for the vertical hold to stabilize on several monitors. Once they were all on, they realized the lab camera was not transmitting.

"I don't see the lab here. This thing will switch to different cameras, but I don't see how it works. It will take a while to figure this out," he said.

"Sir, may I be of help? We have a similar system on the cutter." The Coast Guard Petty Officer stationed on the bridge asked, noticing their confusion.

"Can you work this system?" Tyson asked.

"I believe so, Sir," the Petty Officer sat down in the chair Steve offered, accessing a menu from the file system.

"Here it is," he announced after a minute, "Location Selection Mode". As he directed the computer's cursor to highlight the selection, an outline of the ship appeared on the screen, red circles denoting camera locations.

"Which deck are you looking for?" he asked Steve.

"I need the lower deck, aft, the laboratory area."

The Petty Officer scrolled through the decks, reaching the area in question. There highlighted in yellow was the floor plan of the lab, showing cameras at the entrance, and the one over the lab table.

"Here it is." Steve pointed to the circle in the lab. "Is there any way to determine if there is a tape from that camera?"

"There's no tape, Sir. These systems record to a hard drive. It's recorded over when it reaches capacity. This one's motion-activated, so it lasts a long time, and if we're lucky, we have several days of activity on it. It will burn a DVD of the time parameters you put in."

The Petty Officer brought the camera's history up on the monitor. A few seconds of the CPU churning and the image of the lab table popped up on the screen.

There it is!" Steve exclaimed as they huddled around the monitor.

After showing the controls for fast forward, reverse and freeze frame, the Petty Officer resumed his post, to the heartfelt thanks from everyone else.

Everybody pulled up a chair, watching as the lab workers appeared in the periphery of the recorded image, most of their labors not recorded by the stationary camera. Steve and Beth narrated, as Tyson and Beebe watched with rapt attention. Although the picture was in black and white, it was clear. After a while, the work progressed to the weighing procedure. The operation recorded with clear detail, the camera pointed at an angle making even the scale readings legible.

"The camera always recorded this part." Beebe theorized, "Someone wants to monitor whatever it is they're doing."

They watched as the lab technician inserted the metal rod into the beaker for a sample, analyzed it in the spectrometer, and recorded the information into the computer. When finished, he poured the contents of the beaker down the funnel.

"That's it. Do you see the sandy looking stuff?" Steve touched the screen. That's gold!"

"Interesting," Tyson added. "If it is gold, where is it now?"

"I don't know, the camera is at the wrong angle to pick up the little smelter spout and the ingots. Let's keep watching." They watched for several minutes, with only images of the tops of the lab worker's heads popping in and out of the picture.

"Hold on a second, stop it right there, Steve." Beth blurted, the pause in action giving her time to think. "Can you go back a few minutes, back to when the technician took the sample?"

"Give me a second." He replied, running the image back to the place she requested, and restarted the video at normal speed.

"Stop right there! Watch what he does." Beth said as the picture on the screen showed the technician extracting the sample on the metal rod, cleaning the rod with a paper lab towel, and sampling the next beaker. Each beaker was the same. Every time the worker wiped off the metal rod, the paper towel he disposed of into a bin beside the lab table.

"I see nothing unusual. It's a simple procedure. Take a sample, put it in the spectrometer, remove it, and put it back in the beaker." Tyson seemed perplexed.

Beth had Steve run it back again, this time in slow motion.

"Stop playing with them, Miss Williams." Beebe insisted, as he also noticed what had caught Beth's eye. "Have you ever considered a career change? You would make an excellent video analyst."

Steve looked puzzled. "Do you guys want to let us dummies in on the secret?"

"It's simple housecleaning Steve, simple housecleaning!" Beth answered.

"Can you give us a live shot on the lab?" Beebe asked.

With a shrug of his shoulders, Steve switched to a live feed, and the lab area and desk came into view, just as it was last night. "Okay, so what gives?"

"The paper towels, it looks as if they have not emptied the bin, see?" Beth pointed to the top of a trash basket just in the picture, beside the table. "He wiped the metal rod each time he took a sample and threw the paper in the trash."

"And whatever is in those beakers is on those paper towels," Tyson noted.

"It's always the simplest thing that trips you up, how many times have you drummed it into our heads, Gene?" Steve smiled as they began another trip to the lab.

They ran down the stairways to the lab, arriving breathless with anticipation. Steve hurried to the metal trash bin, sliding it from under the table, and dumping its contents out onto the top of the lab table. After flattening out several wads of paper towels, all streaked with a dark brownish substance, Steve rubbed one stain on his finger and held it up to the light.

"It looks like gold dust…"

"Let's find out." Beth found a small clean beaker on the shelf, along with a long glass tube, and brought them to the lab table. Pulling on a pair of thick rubber gloves she found draped over the end of the table, she approached a shelf containing several bottles of chemicals. Looking through several samples, she found what he was looking for, bottles labeled sulphuric, and nitric acid. She inserted the tube into the liquids several times, each time holding her thumb over the end of the tube to draw the acid out, and then depositing it into the beaker. After repeating this several times, she had half a beaker of mixed acid.

"Try to shake as much of the powder off those towels onto the table as you can, we won't need a lot." She directed the others, pointing to the pile of crumpled up towels removed from the waste bin.

While the other three wiggled the minute amounts of dust from each towel, Beth finished taking the acid from the bottle and returned to them. She took out the credit card Barnes had given her earlier and scraped the small dusting of granules laying on the lab table onto a pile. "This isn't very scientific, but I know from high school chemistry acid has no effect on gold, let's see what happens." She scraped the gold into the card, and then into the beaker, watching the shiny grains fall to the bottom. Holding it up to the light, she swirled the beaker twice and set it on the table. Everyone watched, as the grains settled on the bottom unharmed.

"Gold," Beebe announced after watching for half a minute, "Pure gold. Ms. Williams is right, if it was anything else, it would have dissolved by now."

He turned back to look at them, scooping the paper towels up and putting them back in the trash can. As he did, one towel fell to the floor, catching Steve's eye.

"And you were right about what they did. They made a lot of gold here last night. We have good evidence, now all we have to do is figure out is where it is. We'll get a team to check every nook and cranny in this lab. Hell, we might have to open every one of those shipping containers out there. I don't care if we're here a month, we will find the gold."

Steve stared at the towel, his mind trained to notice even the smallest oddity. He bent to look at the towel lying on the clean floor. The towel lay beside a dull arched pattern on the floor, an arc ending at the rear leg of the lab table, tracing a semicircle of almost ninety degrees. He knelt, feeling the bottom of the leg, and seeing instead of a metal foot, there was a small rubber wheel encased at the bottom of not only that leg and the two others.

"This table rolls!" He stood up. "Look, they rotated it so many times it left a track on the floor."

He realized now. The table could pivot on a rear leg, swinging out from the wall in a wide arc. After further examination, Steve noticed a latch tucked up onto the underside of the table's top. With an easy pull, he unlatched the table that swung out two inches from the wall. It took almost no effort to swing the table away, perpendicular to its furthest position. Once the table swung out of the way, it revealed a large panel on the wall secured by at least two dozen well- worn screws.

"We need a few tools," Tyson observed, pulling close by drawers open, and rummaging for a screwdriver.

"Look over by the big vat." Beth pointed, "They had a little toolbox last night!"

Beebe was there first and soon found the box stored on a low shelf. Opening it on the way back, he found a large handled screwdriver laying on top and handed it to Steve who was kneeling in front of the panel. The screws backed out without difficulty, and upon removing the last screw, Steve lifted the panel off as everyone gathered around. The entire group looked into the compartment in stunned silence. In front of them was a solid looking stainless steel safe door.

"I don't suppose you have anybody hanging around, who can crack this?" Beebe asked Tyson.

"Not here. We have people back in Miami; I might put together a team and get them here tomorrow afternoon."

Steve was still on his knees, examining the safe door. He realized the safe door had an airtight gasket, and otherwise, the thick stainless steel shell had no openings or connections. He stopped, looking back over his shoulder at the mezzanine area where Beth and he lay spying on the lab workers last night.

"I have an idea. With a little luck, I think I can get this safe open." He announced. "Make it a little luck and a few odds and ends."

"How're you going to open it, don't tell me you're a safecracker too?" Beebe smiled.

"I might surprise you at what I can do."

"I've learned not to doubt it."

151

"Tell us what you need, Steve. I'll send someone from the local office to round it up." Tyson offered, taking out a pen and the small notebook he carried everywhere.

"I'll need a drill, a good heavy drill, with a quarter-inch bit. One of those good cobalt drill bits. About thirty feet of quarter-inch plastic tubing, and a spool of small electrical wire, you know the kind you used to hook up speakers."

"That's it?" Tyson raised a brow.

"That's it. Oh, except for a battery. I need a nine-volt battery."

Tyson shook his head in disbelief as he took out his cell phone, calling the agent responsible for processing the immigration papers for the crew.

"This is Tyson. I need you to get the ship's machinist down here on the double. Tell him we're about to make his life a lot easier."

"Are you telling me you will crack the safe with a battery and a roll of tubing?" Beebe looked doubtful.

"And luck, don't forget. I will try a thing we learned back in Ranger school. Keep your fingers crossed and come with me."

Steve led Beebe into the hall and up the stairs to the mezzanine overlooking the lab. He led him to the tank rack they had laid in the night before, spinning the tanks and reading the contents until he found the one he was looking for.

"Oxygen, no, Acetylene, no, CO2, no, here it is!" Stenciled on the side of a small green tank in white letters was the word 'HYDROGEN'.

"Hydrogen?" Beebe sounded cautious. "What are you going to do? This is nasty stuff. Just ask anybody on the Hindenburg."

"You guessed it; I'm going to Hindenburg the hell out of the safe!"

They wrestled the tank of gas down the steps and carried it back into the lab where Beth and Tyson were waiting. After a few minutes, the agent Tyson had talked with entered with the machinist in tow.

"Do you speak English?" Tyson asked him. "If I can get a little cooperation from you, I might forget you were helping the people who tried to kill my agent and his friend. Do you understand?"

The man nodded, fear showing in his eyes. Even though he had been in the engine room all night and did not know what had gone on, Tyson's ploy worked.

"We need a drill, a big drill, a roll of tubing and wire. Do you have that on board?"

"Yes sir, we have drills and such in the maintenance room. I will take you there?"

The trip to the maintenance locker had been fruitful. Steve found a good drill, an array of drill bits, and two rolls of small wire, one red and one white. He also cut a long length of clear vinyl tubing from an air conditioner drain. It was enough for Steve to begin work. He found a low stool, and after inserting a drill bit into the drill, he drilled on the door of the safe. The steel was much harder than Steve had imagined. After wearing out several bits, he only had a hole bored about a half-inch deep. It was slow going, and a profuse sweat rolled off him. After an hour of drilling, a small hole penetrated the door.

"Wow, the steel was over an inch thick!" He exclaimed, wiping the sweat from his brow with a roll of towels Beth provided. "Now for the fun part," He grinned.

"Beth, can you look around, maybe in the office and find me a battery?"

"Yes, Sir! On the double, Sir." She joked, grateful to help.

Steve continued, connecting the tubing to the valve on the hydrogen tank, and inserted the other end into the hole he had drilled in the safes' door. Turning the valve, they all listened to the faint hiss, as the hydrogen flowed out of the tank and filled the safe. Once it was full, Steve plugged the hole with a small rubber stopper he found lying on a lab table. Next, Steve took the rolls of electrical wire, unwinding two lengths as long as his tubing, and threaded them through the plastic tubing. When they were through, he took the ends and stripped a short length of insulation from each wire. Bending the white wire back, and taped it to the outside of the tubing, so half of the stripped part was inside the tube. Now, he had his detonator. He pulled the red wire about six inches farther through the tubing than the white wire, leaving it loose, spreading its uninsulated strands in a fan shape. Next, he asked Tyson to roll the tubing through the door into the hallway. Removing the stopper from the safe door, he fed the wires and a short length of tubing into the safe.

Beth had perfect timing. As soon as Steve was ready, she returned with a shiny black and copper-colored battery. "Is this OK? It was in the clock radio."

"Perfect," Steve said, taking the battery and leading Beth into the hallway with Tyson and Beebe. He taped the ends of the wire to the terminals on the battery and shut the laboratory door.

"Everybody needs to go out in the main hallway and stay down. I don't know how this will go. No sense in everybody being this close."

It was true; Steve did not understand how powerful an explosion would occur. It depended on how much space was in the safe. The emptier it was, the more gas would be present to explode, and there was only one way to find out, Steve waited until they were away, then crouching behind a structural support, he gave the red wire a sudden jerk, pulling it a short way back through the tubing. When the bare metal of one wire contacted the bare metal of the other, it produced a spark setting off a violent explosion of the hydrogen gas. The door of the safe blew off, slamming into the bulkhead above Steve's head, leaving a large dent protruding into the hallway. A cacophony of flying metal and glass echoed from inside, sounding as if a box full of silverware had spilled on the floor. An acrid smell filled the room as Steve opened the lab door, a haze of smoke hiding the opening containing the safe, he saw see several gold ingots strewn about on the floor. Beth, Tyson, and Beebe ran in as Steve knelt on the floor in front of the

153

safe, and waved the smoke away with his hand. They stared in amazement as they saw more ingots inside the safe, still neatly stacked.

"How many are there?" Beebe asked, amazed at the amount of destruction to the safe and surrounding equipment.

Steve counted the ingots in the safe. "Twenty-one in here, and I can see another eight or nine on the floor."

"Ouch!" Beth exclaimed, picking up an ingot leaning against the wall, and placing it on one of the few tables still upright. "This must weigh at least twenty pounds!"

"Good guess," Steve agreed, picking up one brick, "I'd say twenty pounds, easy."

"That would make each ingot worth about 350 grand!" Tyson calculated. "We're looking at about ten million dollars' worth of gold."

"And that's just on this ship, what about the other forty-plus he has floating around? What if there is this much gold on those as well?" Beebe said.

Tyson was thinking back to the conversation he had with Dave Spellman the day before. They were sure the MUSA spreadsheet had listed amounts of gold on Boulez's ships, and this was confirmation.

"I can see why Boulez was so determined to find out what information Steve got from his communications interface. You don't know it yet, Steve, but the information you got tells us how much gold it involves. We thought we had it figured out, and now we have confirmation. He's sitting on almost eighty billion dollars' worth of gold!"

CHAPTER 41

Jason Boulez was not happy. He was aboard his private jet, cruising over the azure blue Mediterranean, and from the window, he gazed out at the coastline of Northern Africa. On the other side of the aisle, Benny Chavez was asleep, his head lolling in response to the slight turbulence. Although he wasn't sure of their current position, he imagined the dark line on the horizon he was seeing was Algeria. Unfortunately, his schedule would not allow a stopover in his native land; there were pressing matters to tend to elsewhere. He envisioned his boyhood home, in the port city of Oran, a humble place he returned to years later, buying it from its current owner for three times its real worth. The small house reminded him of the time spent there with his mother and father, and his childhood. The sandy yard contained a tiny garden area where his where mother used to grow herbs and spices. His father had been a gentleman, a religious man. He had worked himself to death in the southern oil fields, pumping oil from the ground allowing the Infidels to wallow in their culture of decadence. Before he died, the elder Boulez planted the seed in young Jason's mind driving him to seek to destroy a culture so pervasive, it was destroying the purity of Islam. He often prayed with his father in the local Mosque, seeking guidance. Because the rich American oil company his father worked for provided no medical benefits. Stricken with a blood disorder, his father died within the year. Boulez remembered the sorrow etched in his mother's face and still felt the hatred for the people he was sure caused his father's death. The Mosque they attended converted into a theater years ago had burned down and now lay in quiet rubble. He did not allow the same with his home, not wishing for anyone to change it, or alter it in any way breaking. The house remained the only connection he had to his dead family.

A great sense of satisfaction came over him as he reminded himself he had infiltrated the enemy, became one with them, and would destroy them with the wealth they had built on the bones of countless humble fathers, including his.

A steward broke his concentration with an offer of strong Arabic coffee. Boulez waved him off; already feeling an extra tension in the base of his skull a dose of caffeine would amplify.

It had been fortunate Captain Rene could slip in a short encrypted satellite telephone call to Chavez and alert him of the fact the Coast Guard was approaching the Global Explorer and would take control of the ship soon. He had established procedures to deal with it, as it was happening with a greater frequency of late. More disturbing was the news the ICE agent and the woman with him were still alive. This would present a huge problem. Boulez knew the FBI would want to question him and want to charge him as an accessory to the murder of the agent in Key West. He would not leave it to chance. He had an associate in San Juan, a man who was 'retired'. Abraham Azziz had been living in

155

San Juan under the name Yousef Fahd for almost three years. He found himself on several terrorist watch lists for his previous activities in Germany and Spain. He had blended in well with the local community, operating a gasoline station under a false identity. Fahd was beholden to Boulez for establishing his identity, and for fronting the money necessary to establish the gas station. Boulez knew eventually he would call in the marker, and this was the perfect time. As soon as he had learned the ICE agent and the woman were alive, he had Chavez order Fahd to watch for them on the pier and make every attempt to eliminate them. They were the only two witnesses to the murder of the other agent, except for Jose Benitez, and he knew Jose would not talk. Chavez had let him down; his people had botched the simple task he had given them. In an earlier time, he would have had Chavez killed for allowing such a screw-up, for now, he did not want to cause himself any further problems. Chavez was loyal, if nothing else, and that counted for a lot. It was still possible to redeem him, although it would require assassinating the two witnesses. How could one man and an untrained woman make such fools of his security? How they were stupid enough to get themselves killed or captured, and destroy his favorite helicopters, also?

A small part of him respected this ICE Agent, just as all men who consider themselves warriors pay homage to a worthy adversary who overcomes great odds. No matter about the helicopter, Boulez could buy twenty tomorrow if he wanted to. The Customs Service was another matter. Soon he would give special people an assignment to avenge the loss of his employees, however bumbling they might have been. Unless Chavez takes care of this problem, he will fear for his life also, and with good reason. An undercover agent had infiltrated his security last year, and stole data, although useless, from right under his nose. They had captured the people responsible, only to lose them again, this was inexcusable.

"Many people will soon find the answer to the great mystery!" He promised himself, the hatred for his Western adversaries causing his fists to clench. At least on this side of the ocean, things were proceeding well. Gold was being distributed to trusted intermediaries in ever-increasing amounts and filtering down through the system of underground banking known as hawala. The markets headed in the right direction: down. While he felt responsible for the hardship, this was causing his brethren in the poorer countries, once he brought the Western powers to their knees, the Islamic world would assert its rightful place, and all of Islam would benefit. It was the will of Allah.

The jet landed with a soft bump, rolling to a stop on a private tarmac at the Dubai International Airport. Rahman was waiting for him, along with his contingent of security people, ready to whisk Boulez to his plush offices at the top of the office complex near the pier.

After the customary greetings, Boulez showed no desire for any small talk on the drive from the airport. He wanted a full accounting of the operation, and he wanted to implement a plan to speed up the distribution of the gold as quickly as possible. He was sure the gold aboard the Global Explorer was safe, but it did not matter much, if they found it, they would classify it as contraband, and he would get a proportionate slap on the wrist. There were plenty of other ships, all equipped to produce similar amounts. What worried him most was the Americans might discover he was producing the gold. If so, it would only take few well-placed torpedoes to send every ship in his fleet to a watery grave.

"Rahman, we have problems back in the States. We will have to accelerate MUSA, and we have to get as much product out as possible. What is the status, what do we have?"

"It's very close to two billion dollars in the vault, Mr. Boulez. And we have another five hundred fifty million coming in from the sea."

"And it doesn't include what is already in transit to our friends, am I right?"

'Yes, we have done as you have instructed. We have been working very hard."

"Not to worry, my friend. We will not be working for much longer." Boulez smiled, "I have an ambitious plan. I want to get rid of three billion dollars' worth of gold by Ramadan… in less than three weeks. Is it possible?"

Rahman hesitated, "If Allah wills it, we will do it. Inshallah."

Boulez sensed hesitation. "Allah will help those who help themselves. Is there a problem?"

"It may be nothing. I have indications the gold is leveling off, even declining on four ships. I have spoken with Peña, and he claims it is a matter of a few adjustments. Fine-tuning, I believe he called it. He has assured me it is no problem, so I want you to be aware."

"I see." Boulez sighed. "Then we will discuss this matter with Mr. Peña. If it is as he says, then we should have no problem accumulating the same amount of gold again within a few months. It will be a deathblow to the west. When we release another few billion, it will bring them to their pitiful knees!" He had a deranged, far-away look in his eyes. "The world will be in an upheaval never before imagined. When we crush their economic system, we will step in to lead all the people of the world they have stepped on to attain their position. Their wealth will disappear into the smoke it is made up of, and Islam will rise to power from their ruin!"

"And if not?" Rahman asked quietly.

Boulez did not answer. He had a chilling look in his eyes even Rahman had never seen in him before. Moral indignation combined with pure hatred.

CHAPTER 42

Beebe stared at the gold ingots, realizing what the implications of such an amount of bullion were. An ominous feeling was penetrating his gut. Director Watley had sent him a memo with the Agencies' concerns concerning the severe downtrend in the price of gold over the last year. The downtrend was causing huge problems for Western countries and the United States in particular. If they produced that much gold on one ship, there might be a few billion or more in gold floating around. What if there were more stockpiled at various ports, or even worse, flowing into unregulated markets?

"Mr. Tyson, we have a serious problem here," Beebe said.

"We? I don't want to seem skeptical, but the CIA has a bad reputation for its interagency cooperation. I didn't think 'we' is in your vocabulary, so it will not surprise me when I hear the CIA is taking over this investigation." Beebe was a little surprised at Tyson's sudden display of pique, having attempted to stay low key, even though he had the authorization to shut ICE out if he had wanted to. He knew Tyson was a good man, understanding it was necessary for him to protect his turf in front of his people. Just a little interagency rivalry over what he knew might be a career-making investigation.

"Why all the sudden hostility?" Beebe asked. "I'm not interested in any jurisdictional fight. I know this is your baby, you've lost a man, and your people have got us this far. As far as it concerns the Agency, we're willing to work together on this. Understand, as much as we need you, need us."

Tyson considered Beebe's answer for a few seconds, realizing he may have been premature in judging Beebe.

"I'll agree with you, it's hard to be the one giving up authority, so I'll take you at your word. I just want to make sure my people, and my Department, get the credit they deserve."

"Understood and agreed. You have my word." Beebe held out his hand, which Tyson took, giving it a firm handshake.

"Okay, where do we go from here?" Tyson asked.

"We have one or two ideas, scenarios we want to discuss with you. Mr. Ross seems to have a good understanding of the situation. What are the possibilities of sharing him with us, as a liaison?"

Beebe replied, "In my briefing, I mandated full cooperation between all Homeland Security agencies. We intend to honor the mandate on our side. Mr. Ross is at your disposal for as long as you need him, providing he doesn't have a problem with it." Tyson raised a brow questioningly at Steve, waiting for his answer.

"What are we talking about here, a liaison? I'm not looking for a new job, undercover and clandestine investigations are my thing. I can't sit in an office, staring out a window, Sir." Steve seemed flustered.

158

"No, no, no, you misunderstand me." Beebe backpedaled, "This has become a matter of the highest national priority. We need boots on the ground, people who know what's going on, a person who can take whatever plan we come up with to neutralize this threat and implement it. 'We' meaning all involved here, not just the wonks sitting at the analysts' desks back at Langley. I don't have the luxury of time to bring an outsider up to speed, so we need to take action in days, not weeks. You can't put the genie back in the bottle once he's out, and if this pile of bricks is any sign, they are ready to disperse a large quantity of gold into world markets. Once it's out, it's out, there's no getting it back. This gold is part of the plan. Mr. Ross, you are the man we need now, I can't say it any plainer."

"What about it, are you in?" Tyson asked, seeing Steve was unsure.

"Just wait a minute. What do you mean 'whatever plan we come up with'? That's wide open. Why do I suspect you already have a plan?" Steve sounded skeptical.

"No, we don't have a plan, per se; however, we have ideas. That's why we need you and Ms. Williams. You're both on top of this, that's why we need you both to help develop those ideas into a workable plan." Beebe explained.

"You know, Jim would have wanted it this way, had things been the other way around," Tyson added. Steve thought of Jim, lying in a pool of his own blood, gasping for air through a lung destroyed by a bullet fired by one of Boulez's hired help. His jaw clenched, and he knew what he had to do.

"All right, I'm in, if it means getting Boulez, I'm in."

Tyson stepped in. "Hold on, please. Steve is a government employee, and he can decide for himself. However, Ms. Williams is a civilian. Our intention was to put her in WITSEC as soon as possible. She must decide if she wants otherwise."

Beth looked at Tyson, "WITSEC? Isn't that witness protection? I'm sorry, I'm not going into any witness protection program, I have a life, or at least I had one until this week. I'm going home, and the sooner I get there, the better."

Steve pulled Beth to the side, "Don't worry about it now, we can figure this out later. I can use a friendly face to help us figure out what's going on here. I know it's a lot to ask, I need your help."

Steve's doleful look was having its intended effect. "Well, I want to know how they are developing the microbes," her tone softened, "maybe I can help."

"Good, it's settled then!" Beebe jumped in to dissuade any further discussion of the matter. "I still have the arrangements to take care of with Mr. Tyson and others, so if it's all right with him, why don't you two take a few hours off and we will all meet back up tomorrow afternoon. Uncle Sam is generous enough to put a very nice jet at my disposal. It can put us back in Washington in about four hours."

Steve looked at Tyson, who nodded his approval. "He's right, you look as if you can use the time off, Steve. In fact, I'm ordering you to stand down for the time being. I need time to get a team in here to do a thorough search... for all we

159

know there is more gold stashed here. It will take most of the morning, so I'll get in touch with you as soon as Beebe and I work out a schedule. Oh, one other thing, Steve, was Agent Graves able to find you a weapon?"

"Yes, if you call a thirty-eight a weapon. Good for shooting squirrels."

Tyson grunted as he picked an ingot up from the floor. "Well, I was hoping you I'd say after we log this in, we should have a real good chance of getting a budget increase next year. We'll get you the shiny new toy of your choice!" They all laughed as he put the ingot down on the table with a dull 'clunk'!

"All kidding aside, I know I don't have to tell you Ms. Williams is still in danger, so I'm putting her in your protective custody until we can determine her status. I want you to take responsibility for her until we get back to the mainland."

Beth looked taken aback. "No offense to Steve, but I don't think I need a babysitter. As a matter of fact..."

Tyson interrupted before she finished her sentence. "I'm sorry, but I will insist. You are a material witness to at least one murder, abduction, and illegal contraband smuggling. The list goes on and on. Boulez and his people have good reason to believe we compromised their entire operation. They have already shown a penchant for overreaction, so we know they'll kill not only to silence, they'll kill to intimidate. It's how you define terrorism. You need protection, and we need to have you protected."

Steve took Beth's arm and pulled her towards the door. "Come on, don't fight it. Let's get out of here before they change their minds and lock you in the dungeon."

She relented as the thought crossed her mind it might be pleasant to be around Steve for a while without having to run for their lives every couple of hours.

"Oh, all right, but I'm telling you, no witness protection!"

They left Tyson and Beebe behind to arrange for confiscating the cache of gold. The stairway to the gangplank deck was becoming all too familiar now, and when they made their way outside, the early evening sunlight was casting golden hues on everything it touched.

Steve spotted Robert Graves standing beside a burgundy sedan, talking with two of the FBI agents who had attended the briefing. "Is this your ride, Bob?"

"Well, it's signed out to Barnes..."

The glint of sunlight reflecting off the face of Grave's watch caught Steve's eye. He recognized it as a Rolex Submariner, a watch that would cost a big chunk of Grave's annual salary - before taxes. Steve noticed the keys dangling from the ignition switch. He opened the passenger door for Beth and trotted around to the other side.

"Nice watch, Graves. You hit the lottery?"

Graves stared back at Steve, no humor in his tone. "No, an investment paid off. What am I going to tell Barnes?"

"Tell her something important came up, and I needed the car for a couple of hours, will you? We're just going to the old town, I'm sure she won't mind!" He didn't wait for an answer as he backed the car out of its space to Grave's halfhearted protestations, and threaded his way out among the many official cars parked along the edge of the pier.

Graves waited a few seconds, turning his back to the two FBI agents, as he pulled out his cell phone. He typed three letters into his keypad, and watching the sedan leave, he hesitated just a split second before pushing the send button.

"Can I buy you dinner? Or better yet, can Uncle Sam buy you dinner?" He asked Beth with a wide grin, as he pulled the white envelope from his back pocket.

"I thought you'd never ask...I'm starving. I think I could eat a horse!"

"From what I've heard, we must be careful where we go or it's what you might eat!"

On the far side of the pier, two men slouched sweating in a dusty brown Toyota Corolla, watching everyone come and go from the gangplank of the ship. So far, all they had seen were people in military uniforms, and people in sports jackets, their department identification badges displayed on their front pocket or clipped to their belt. The passengers kept the tinted windows rolled all the way up, and the motor was not running. They drew no attention to the beat-up vehicle parked in a line of a dozen similar cars, most of them belonging to locals who helped with the various loading and maintenance operations of the pier. Fahd was smoking his fifth cigarette in the last ninety minutes as he became alert, nudging the man beside him, a disheveled looking man named Ali. Ali worked for Fahd as a cashier in his gas station and did not know of what was going on, because Fahd had told him he was tracking a customer who had taken his car from the gas station and had not paid a large repair bill. Fahd had used Ali as a driver a few times, whenever he felt he would need to 'lose himself', always making up a story to explain his actions. The Toyota was legal and not linked to him, so all he had to do was find a deserted corner, step out and he was anonymous. Fahd planned to take a taxi home after his night's work.

A chirp on his cell phone notified Fahd he had received a text message. He looked at the display to see three letters: NOW. Fahd squinted with pleasure when the burgundy car approached the parking lot exit. Through the lightly tinted windows, he saw two people, the man driving, and a dark-haired young woman. Smiling, he started the Toyota and waited for the government sedan to exit the pier before falling in behind it, taking care to maintain a safe distance. Soon he would pay his debt to Boulez in full.

Steve and Beth cruised toward the light of downtown San Juan. When they neared the narrow streets of Old San Juan, they pulled to the curb to ask a man selling straw hats and various nick-nacks from a folding table in the corner, for advice on where to find a good island restaurant. They had no reason to suspect

161

the unwashed Toyota turning into a fast food place across the street, although it bypassed the drive-thru and rounded the building, parking in a spot near the curb.

The street vendor cracked a crooked smile, his too white false teeth beaming with genuine pleasure at the opportunity to make small talk with anyone on a slow day, not to mention a sale. He held a finger into the air, and craned his head towards the lights of San Juan, just coming on in the early dusk.

"Listen, Mon, listen!" The old man spoke with a singsong Jamaican accent.

Beth and Steve looked at each other, neither on understanding what he meant.

"Listen to da music, mon! It's gonna be a beautiful night! You need to leave yo' car parked right dere, and follow the music... you will see, Mon! Many, many good places to be eaten'!" He pointed to a small grassy lot beside the road with several cars lined up along a weathered fence. "Dere's no parkin' downtown tonight, mon... it's festival time, you be spendin' two hours lookin' when I can help ya... only five dolla'!"

He seemed to be such a harmless good-natured soul, infusing the area with his happy-sounding banter, that Steve was having a hard time refusing his sales pitch. Traffic appeared backed up on the road ahead, and it was a beautiful evening.

After refusing his offer to try on several hats, Steve relented, paid him the five dollars to park, and backed the sedan into the lot. Steve told him there would be another ten when they returned if the car was in the same condition as when they left it. The old man assured them it would be with a wide grin and a wave, as they walked toward the sounds of a steel band in the distance.

They were on the narrow streets of Old San Juan, the oldest city on any U.S. territory. Tour buses and cars inched by on the main roads, and the side roads mostly closed to traffic, allowed the restaurants to set up tables in the street. A multitude of street performers plied their trade in an effort to relieve tourists of their vacation dollars. Their stroll took them to the top of a large hill within the city which was the site of the El Morro, a beautiful sixteenth-century fort on the Northern point of the old city. Steve loved the solid feeling of the old stone architecture, marveling at how difficult the work must have been to construct such a large fort without the use of forklifts, cranes, and modern digging equipment. There were few tourists about at the dinner hour, which is why Steve noticed a man standing across the street, leaning on the building and glancing in their direction. Steve avoided a direct look at the man, pretending to pan the scenery from the top of the hill. He had no reason to suspect the man for any reason, he only noticed him because he would notice any man with dark glasses and Middle Eastern features after the last couple of day's events. When he stole a quick glance back, the man had moved on down the block, stopping to look in a jewelry store window. Steve filed it away in his mind as over-caution and he resumed their walk. From the top of the hill, they encountered a street lined with restaurants, and the band whose music they had followed started up again, with a raucous Caribbean beat. It took only a few minutes for them to make their way to a sidewalk table, sitting right in the middle of a closed street. The old residences along the street long ago converted to shops and restaurants, with each dining establishment staking a claim to a section of the street closed to vehicles every night at five. Pulling up two flimsy chairs, they didn't realize how far they had walked until they sat down in exhausted relief. Sliding a seat out for Beth, Steve again noticed the same Arabic looking man he had seen earlier, entering a nearby liquor store. The man looked around directly at the couple as they took their seats. Was it his imagination or did he look in their direction again? Nothing about the scene seemed right to him, although he didn't dwell on it, people checked out each other, commenting on their choice of clothing, or hairstyle, or many unusual peculiarities. He was with a beautiful woman. *"Come on, you're spooking yourself, calm down."* He said to himself. After a few minutes, the waiter brought the menus. They ordered two martinis, and Steve slid his chair around closer to Beth, so they could talk over the sounds of the band. Although Beth had avoided the topic while they had wandered the streets, content to remark about the scenery and architecture, the conversation back on the ship was foremost in her mind.

"What happens now, Steve? Am I being held hostage by my government?"

"Are we holding you hostage?"

"You know what I mean."

"Yeah, it's not us, it's Boulez. Until we can neutralize him, we're both targets."

"Neutralize him? It sounds so… antiseptic. What does 'neutralize' mean? Are you saying they will kill him? Is that what's it going to take to get him off our backs?"

"It's that, or dismantle his entire operation. He needs money to operate, and we know he makes no money hauling cargo around on half-empty ships. The cargo industry is competitive, and there is an oversupply of ships right now. It's one reason we were so interested in him, we knew he had to be hauling special cargo to make money. At first, we thought it was drugs… heroin, cocaine, whatever. We found nothing on any of his ships to amount to anything except a few kilos of hash or coke in a container now and then. He wasn't putting gas in those ships with that kind of money. Until you came along, we did not understand he was pumping out gold by the bucketful."

"You had one clue, remember? Growing old?" She teased him a little.

"Right… I have to give you credit. Beebe was right. You would make a good information analyst."

"I was just lucky. What I don't understand is why Boulez is so determined to kill us. What good is it going to do Boulez to kill us now?"

"He wants revenge for killing his hired help. Remember he is a terrorist and intimidation is the only thing he has. He needed to know what we knew, so he kidnapped us. I'm sure he planned to get whatever he thought we had and then put a bullet in our heads before he threw us overboard. He might even have just thrown us over and let the sharks take care of us. He had no way to know that grabbing us for interrogation would go so wrong for him." Steve allowed himself to gloat just a little.

Beth nodded in agreement. "Also, if you think of it, he has no way to know we have figured out what he's doing in the labs, the Midas Effect. The lab people never knew we were there, they didn't see us, so how did they tell the captain?"

"See? I need you around… you always seem to make sense!"

Beth waved off the unexpected compliment as if it was no big deal. Steve continued, "For what it's worth, we don't even know if he knows whether we're alive, it's only logical his people have a procedure to deal with a Coast Guard boarding. We have done dozens on his ships, and there has been no gold lying around in the open. If they got the word out they were being boarded, I'm sure they would tell whoever they report to we were still wandering around alive."

"It's crazy, I feel as if I woke up in a different world. I hit my head, and when I woke up, everything went nuts. I can't wake up from this nightmare. Any minute I will see a witch pedaling by on a bicycle… Auntie Em, Auntie Em!"

"Try clicking your heels together."

The drinks came as they laughed together at the image, surprised by the bar's efficiency. Steve sipped his drink; eager for the satisfying feeling of numbness, he knew would soon flow through his veins. Not a heavy drinker, the alcohol had an almost immediate effect on Steve, easing any inhibitions he may have felt making personal small talk. "Let's forget about all this for now and enjoy a nice dinner." He held up his glass, offering a silent toast.

"Agreed." Beth held up her glass to the toast. "What should we talk about?"

"Hmm, well, I don't think I ever asked you about yourself. Would I be getting too nosy if I asked you if you have a boyfriend?" He leaned in a little closer to the adjoining tables wouldn't hear the conversation.

She shrugged, "No boyfriend. I had a fiancée, and it didn't work out well. That is why I was in Key West; I needed a change of venue. Now it's your turn. Do you have a girlfriend, wife, significant other?"

"No Ma'am, so far none of the above. At least not anything you would consider serious. My friends are always trying to play matchmaker, with this job, you know, it's difficult."

Beth sensed he wasn't being honest, and she felt just a little ashamed for her voyeuristic desire to probe further for information on Steve's love life, this man she had only known for two days. The waiter interrupted her thoughts, bearing their order of two generous plates of steaming hot fish and rice. Little did she know Steve was weighing the same thoughts about her. He ordered them another drink, stealing glances at her as they ate. The skin on her face was smooth and clear, its soft tone highlighted by the glow of lanterns strung from poles along the street. He had to resist the urge to reach out and touch her cheek.

164

Neither of them had realized they were so hungry, as the warm night combined with the music and drink, brought out a ravenous hunger, which they sated to the sights and sounds of an idyllic Caribbean evening. After a while, their eyes locked together for a split second, lingering just long enough for each of them to conclude there was a connection developing between them, more than a professional friendship, not long enough to signal an overtly sexual attraction. Steve was the first to look away, uncomfortable displaying any attraction for Beth. He knew she was with him through no real choice of her own. Beth continued to watch him, as he looked away, bemused at his shyness. She was not the type to use the power of her femininity to manipulate a man, although she realized it often was. He fumbled with the saltshaker for a few seconds, before looking back to her, his smile almost an unspoken apology.

"These drinks must have been a lot stronger than I thought."

"Why do you say that?" Her innocent tone belied the fact she knew what he was talking about.

"I'm not the guy who can 'talk women up' as they say. I have no gift of gab, but for whatever reason, you seem easy to talk to."

"And you're blaming it on the alcohol?" She was teasing him a little now, her face showing a look of mock indignation.

"No, no, no it's not the alcohol. I will make an ass of myself now, but I was just thinking…"

"Go on…" She encouraged, not knowing quite what to expect.

He hesitated, weighing the benefit of exposing his thoughts. The alcohol was affecting him. His natural self-protection instinct was under assault from within, the two martinis opening a crack in his macho defense mechanism deep down he wanted to break wide open.

"What were you thinking about, Agent Ross?"

Her voice brought him back from the recesses of his mind. He studied her in the lantern light, as a breeze blew her hair across her eyes.

"It's just, well, I was thinking how impressed I am with you, how you have handled this whole situation. I don't want to get all, ah…"

"Maudlin?" She offered when she saw he was struggling. "So, what 'situation' are we talking about? Getting abducted, or having dinner with you?"

"Yes, maudlin is a good word." He acknowledged her wordplay with a smile. "Anyway, I am around strong women all the time. There are women in the Department who can kick just about any man's ass, and they are not afraid to let you know it. It's a necessary trait in this line of business."

"And you're telling me this because…" She waited for an answer with a raised eyebrow.

"Because what I'm trying to say is, there's an attitude about you I find very attractive, I can't quite put my finger on it. Few women can figure out a strange lab process one minute, and face down a bad character with a gun she knew was wouldn't fire, the next."

"I see… you're attracted to my brains and my foolishness!" She knew Steve was trying to compliment her, as she resorted to good-natured torture. "If that's the case, you will fall head over heels for me when I show my organizational skills. I might even…"

She never got the chance to finish, as Steve leaned in and kissed her on the lips, pulling her arm toward him to bring them closer. Steve was looking into her eyes as their faces parted, expecting the look of mild astonishment he got.

"You might even what?"

She looked back into his eyes for a few seconds, luxuriating with the endorphins released from her brain, oblivious to the entire world as she savored the almost narcotic effect of the kiss.

"I might even ask you for another," She whispered, not waiting for his answer, she leaned in and kissed him back.

Fahd was watching from a café table down from where Steve and Beth sat. He was sipping a bottle of water as he watched them talk; it seemed endless to him as he sat. The area was too crowded for him to make a move; he followed them on foot and knew they would have to return on deserted streets. It would be a simple matter for him to walk up from behind and put a bullet in each of their heads from his silenced Glock.

"What the hell can they be talking for an hour and a half?" He asked himself, squirming to get comfortable in the aluminum chair. He shifted in his seat, glaring at the server when she asked him if he would order anything else. "No, nothing, this is it."

"I don't mean to bother you sir, but you have been here quite a while now. Are you ready to order? If not, we have people waiting." She pointed to a group loitering near the steps.

He held up the bottle of water and snarled, "I ordered this, now go away!"

"Please, Sir. The manager won't let me tie up this table for a bottle of water! If you don't plan to have dinner…"

Fahd interrupted with an evil stare. "If you don't get away from me, I will make you very sorry. Do you understand? Now leave me alone."

She stared in disbelief for a second before turning away, muttering under her breath, and walking back into her restaurant. Within a few seconds, two muscular men in aprons accompanied the server to the table Fahd occupied, their presence silencing the crowd at the surrounding tables, as the patrons watched to see what would happen.

Although Steve was not paying attention, a loud whisper from a teenager at a nearby table turned his head.

"Look, look! A fight!" The girl whispered to her companion.

166

Steve took Beth's hand as they both looked in the direction the teenager was pointing out to his friend. It was the same man Steve had seen going into the liquor store. He was standing now, an angry look on his face, waving off the two men in disgust as he left the café. As Steve watched him leave the area, he saw the man attempt a look back in their direction. When the man rounded a corner at the intersection and disappeared from view, Steve remembered why he thought it was so unusual for the man to be entering the liquor store. His dark features showing he was of Middle Eastern descent. Most Muslims don't use alcohol, and if they do, it's always in the privacy of a closed environment, never in public. He had never seen a Muslim at a liquor store. He stroked his waistband with his wrist, reassuring himself the gun Agent Graves had supplied for him was secure in its hideaway holster.

Steve stood at his chair, tapping Beth's hand. "Wait for me, right here. If I'm not back in fifteen minutes, I want you to call the Police."

"What's going on? Steve?" Beth looked around.

"I have to check something out, it might be nothing. There was a man watching us, so. I want you to stay here. Remember, wait fifteen minutes." He slalomed his way through the café tables to the sidewalk and disappeared around the corner.

Beth scanned the tourists eating and talking nearby, all seemed unaware. She had only glimpsed the man the teenagers were pointing to before he rounded the corner, and she thought he looked typical of the dozens of cab drivers she had seen on their walk in the old city.

After Steve left the table and rounded the corner at the next intersection, he ended up on a side street containing a few empty shops. He made a left and headed into a dark alley, figuring it would take him in the direction the Arab needed come if he was trying to watch Beth and him. Making his way down the narrow alley, he hurried between reeking restaurant dumpsters and the parked cars belonging to the employees working within. Withdrawing his gun from under his shirt he chambered a round, regretting now not taking the silencer agent Graves had offered. Hell, it was hard enough to conceal his gun; the silencer would be a major pain in the ass. He would have to carry it around in a back pocket, it was not as if he could take out and lay on a restaurant table. A quick glance at his watch told him he had twelve minutes to get back to Beth. Stepping around a large metal trash bin, his mind was racing with options should he encounter the man again.

"*Plenty of time to find out...*" He hesitated in mid-thought as he saw the Arab step out from behind a delivery van at the same instant he rounded the bin. They saw each other at the same moment, and both of them reacted by ducking back behind their respective covers.

"Damn!" Steve cursed through his clenched teeth, moving to the other side of the bin to see what the Arab would do. There was a small gap between the bin and the building beside it, and Steve used it to get a better perspective of the delivery van. He saw two shoes beneath the van, pointing towards the alley, waiting in ambush. They were in a stalemate; neither man could move without revealing himself. To one side he heard dishes clattering through the screen door of the restaurant beside him, and several voices within, conversing in Spanish.

The voices grew louder as a kick slammed the door open, and a teenage boy came out holding two large garbage bags. Steve wedged himself against the wall, hoping there wouldn't be enough light to see him crouching beside the bin. The boy was arguing with another man who remained in the doorway. His coworker yelled back as the boy slung the garbage bags into the open top of the bin. The heated conversation continued with the boy slamming the door behind him. As soon as he dared, Steve looked back under the van, to find the man vanished.

"He can't be far!" Steve took a chance, jumping to the other side of the alley, behind an old Honda. He stared down the alley looking for any movement at all. There was nothing, only the faint arguing emanating from the kitchen beside him. Keeping low, he crept around several cars, coming to the front of the delivery van. On one knee, he scanned the pavement under the van, although there was no sign of his adversary. He inched along the flat side of the van toward the rear, listening for any sound of movement, hearing nothing, except the muted beat of a Calypso band echoing from beyond the building. Everything was still.

"Where did he go?" Steve wondered as he scanned the end of the alley, knowing the man had not made it to the end undetected. He sensed an evil here, it smelled worse than the garbage fermenting in the overflowing bins, and he knew the Arab had to be nearby. Inching to the rear of the van, he saw the shiny tips of a man's shoes. His adversary was standing half on the truck bed, and halfway on the moveable delivery platform. Pressed against the closed door on the back of the delivery van, he waited for Steve to come past him. As he looked down, Steve spied the control lever for the platform. He shoved the handle forward, which caused the platform to fall to the street. Losing his foothold, the Arab grabbed at the doorframe and wedged his fingers in it to stop from falling to the ground. Although he had no way to see whoever had released the platform, he swung around and kicked from his elevated position.

Gun ready, Steve swung around the rear of the van, expecting the man to be at street level. A shadow flashed before his eyes, and a blow to the side of his face staggered him into the nearby wall. His elbow rammed into the wall to keep himself from falling, causing his gun to fall into the gutter at his feet. He looked up in time to see the Arab launching himself from a narrow metal ledge on the back of the delivery van. Steve ducked as the smaller man jumped onto his back, bringing a pistol down in a glancing blow off the crown of Steve's head. The Arab fell down hard in the street, giving Steve a split second to retrieve his gun. He spun around and pulled the trigger twice. There was no sound, no recoil, nothing... the gun had misfired. For a millisecond Steve remembered chambering a round a few minutes ago, there was no way this should be happening.

The Arab had ducked when he saw Steve's gun pointing at his chest, realizing what had happened, he brought his gun to bear. In a flash, Steve ducked to the dark shadow beside the delivery van. The Arab fired a wild shot, running around the corner of the truck. Steve had crouched down and now he sprang. Propelling himself into the smaller man, he grabbed the man's wrist as he squeezed off another shot. Steve shoved the barrel of the gun away, driving the Arab up and off his stride. Pushing his shoulder into him with all his might, he stood up and pinned the smaller man to the wall, slamming his head up into the man's chin. Stunned, the Arab clawed at Steve's eyes, trying to inflict enough pain to cause Steve to let go. They wrestled for a few seconds until Steve's side exploded in pain as Fahd brought his knee up and slammed it into his kidney, buckling his knees. Steve held on to the Arab's wrist and pulled his arm down hard, using his shoulder as a fulcrum. The pain of his elbow bending the wrong way was all it took for the Arab to let out a loud wail and drop the gun at Steve's feet. Steve then spun the man around and pushed him to the ground, landing him atop of the lowered power lift platform of the delivery van.

Steve pinned him with a knee to the chest and wrapped his big fist around the Arab's throat. "Who sent you? Who are you working for?"

The Arab kept struggling, trying to kick Steve in the groin. Steve blocked the kick with his hip as he grabbed the man's leg, jamming it under the scissors mechanism of the lift platform.

"You don't know how much, that pisses me off!" He groped around for his gun, only to discover they kicked both weapons down the curb in the melee. Turning back, he noticed the lever controlling the platform hanging near his head.

"I will only ask you one more time. Who sent you?"

The Arab sneered, "What are you talking about? You were chasing me!"

Steve pulled on the handle, engaging the hydraulic motor that raised and lowered the platform. He raised the platform until it squeezed the Arab's leg between the metal scissor mechanism, causing Fahd to let out a short scream. Steve held his hand over the man's mouth and tapped the lever to squeeze the Arab's leg. The pain was getting intense as the man's eyes squinted in pain, and a profuse sweat broke out on his face. Steve released the pressure on his hand.

"Was it Boulez? Tell me, or I'll tear your leg off!" Steve tapped the lever. The Arab grunted in pain, his eyes squeezed closed. With another tap on the lever and the Arab sucked in a sharp his breath, as the pain seared through his shinbone.

"All right, all right!" He gasped, "Ok, yes, Boulez sent me. I owe him, I am in his debt, and I had no choice!"

"No choice to do what, kill me? Why, what's he hiding?" Steve didn't want to let on he knew about the gold. He bumped the lever again, and the Arab let out a bellow.

169

"The hiding is over! Musa is in place! You cannot stop it..." Almost delirious in pain, he realized he had said too much.

"Musa? Who is Musa?" Steve spat. The Arab struggled with all his remaining strength to push the lever in the other direction, as Steve pushed him down and held him down with the force of his entire weight.

"It's too late for you, everything is in place, you'll never stop it, and soon it will be your turn to suffer!"

"Stop what?" Steve pushed. "What is he hiding on the ships? What's so important he needs to kill me? Tell me who Musa is and I'll let you live!"

Fahd was straining with all his might against Steve's arm, trying to push the lever in the opposite direction.

"Ha! Kill me now! It's a pleasure to die for Allah. My brothers will run blood in your streets, and none of you are safe. We will destroy you in ways you never imagined!" The Arab gasped, his face gone an ashy gray.

Steve saw he would get nothing else from the Arab, hatred had overcome any sense of self-preservation the man may have had.

"I'd love to oblige you, but I'm not filling out the paperwork for your worthless ass. I'll give you a souvenir to remember me by, though."

He held his hand over the man's mouth and gave a protracted pull on the lever. The raising platform crushed the Arab's lower leg bones, his stifled cries accompanied by the grotesque sound of bones snapping. With his leg bent at a sickening angle, Fahd lay writhing in agony, slumping into unconsciousness as the pain overwhelmed his senses.

"You will not be coming after anybody else soon, asswipe."

The kitchen workers who opened the screen door noticed the shots and muffled screams. They and came onto the concrete loading area at the rear of the restaurant, trying to locate the source of the screams in the dark jumble of vehicles and dumpsters. Steve collected both guns from the curb, and after removing the magazine from Fahd's weapon, he tossed it into the nearest storm drain opening. He tucked his own gun back into the waistband at the back of his pants. Fahd was laying still, his eyes glazed over, as Steve dusted off his clothes, and started back up the alley in the direction he had come. Checking his watch, he was glad to see the entire encounter had only taken twelve minutes.

"¿Todoestabien, Senor?" (Is everything all right?) An older man asked in Spanish, the dim light not revealing Steve to be a gringo.

"Sorry, no habla Espanol, Senor." Steve used his limited 'street' vocabulary to respond.

"Sorry, Senor. Is everything okay with you? We heard screaming, and gunshots!" The man switched to English.

"I'm fine thanks, but there is a man behind the truck in a real bind. He could use your help." Steve smiled at his little pun as he trotted back to the end of the alley, and into the glowing street light.

170

Beth was looking at her watch as she sat waiting for Steve, the tension building with each passing minute. She sat staring at the water bottle, trying not to draw attention to herself, still feeling a little self- conscious. Steve… she let her mind wander to Steve and their shared kisses a few moments ago. Her first impression of Steve had been of an aggressive military type, the haughty authoritarian attitude leaving no room for discussion. 'My way or the highway,' was the expression she associated with that behavior. Locked together in the container, her opinion of him had changed. He showed a genuine concern for her well-being, comforting her in her worries about their fate. It had meant a lot to her Steve didn't seem to feel the need to impress her with a lot of macho promises.

Steve had taken great pains, even risking his own life, to protect her when a lesser man may have let the cards fall where they may. She had fought off the feelings of attraction to him last night, while they sat talking in the Jaguar, chalking them up to wine and exhaustion, now she knew her heart had sensed what her mind had not considered. Then again, maybe he was just tired, not thinking with full clarity. He had been through just as much hell and a lot more. She didn't know what to think, she knew she didn't want to feel as if she were a schoolgirl with a crush on the star football player. The evening had become a roller coaster of exhausting emotions, fear, excitement, sexual tension, and apprehension, all ebbing and flowing with the disjointed thoughts tumbling in her head. The apprehension was taking control of her mind. She imagined the worst as she slid to the edge of her seat, panning up and down the street for any sign of Steve, or the mysterious man he chased after.

"Where is he? Maybe I should get help now… no, no, wait. He said fifteen minutes… not yet," she waited long enough she knew she had to act. She paid the check with the money from her envelope and left the table behind. Walking to the corner Steve had gone round, she saw an empty street, lined with the ubiquitous small Japanese or Korean cars everybody seemed to drive on the island. She hesitated for a second, aware two people seated near them in the café, were whispering assumptions about her plight… she saw just imagine what they thought. It did not matter to her, she was getting worried now, and it seemed an eternity since Steve left. She decided it was time to get the police involved, she wasn't waiting any longer, fifteen minutes or not. With a determined stride, she returned to the restaurant and ascended several steps to the vestibule. The small reception desk had an old rotary phone perched on one corner, serving as a paperweight for the single sheet menus printed with the night's fare.

Scratching names off a crowded reservation list, the rotund proprietor looked up to see Beth enter in a rush. He noticed her sitting outside a few minutes earlier and was ready for a complaint. Knowing the food service had been slow this evening, he prepared for a rebuke.

"Yes, miss. Can I help you, are you OK?"

"I need to use your telephone... I need to call the Police!"

"The Police? What's happened, a robbery?" He tried to look around her to the tables on the sidewalk, his eyes filling with consternation.

"My friend, the man I was with. He saw a man he thought he knew and followed him around the corner. I think he's in trouble."

"Lady, is this a joke? I am a very busy man." He stepped past her to scan the tables outside again, returning with a look of suspicion. "Is it possible you had a fight? Maybe the gentleman needed a few minutes alone. Why don't you go back to your hotel and wait for him there?" His answer infuriated Beth, and she started an angry response, "Why don't *you* go to...?"

All at once, a voice from the vestibule rang out, "Can you call an ambulance? There's a man in the back alley that ran into a little trouble."

The familiar voice startled Beth, and she spun on her heel to see Steve standing in the doorway. His shirt and pants streaked with grime, and his cheek had a fresh red contusion visible among the other recent battle scars.

"Steve!" Beth ran to him with an enthusiastic embrace. "I was so worried, what happened to you?"

Steve explained in her ear, "Our friend Boulez sent his man to welcome us to the island. Not the person you would want to have for a friend. I left him in the alley with a message for Boulez I'm sure will get his attention."

He knew what Beth was thinking when she looked up at him, eyes as big as saucers, "No, he's alive, but don't expect to see him running in any marathons soon." He took her by the hand as they headed for the door. "Let's get out of here."

"Well, it answers your question. Boulez must know we are alive." She said.

"Yeah, great," Steve replied.

They hurried up the street until they reached the main thoroughfare, hailing a ragged taxi to take them to their car. When they had settled in Beth examined the new bruise on Steve's face, with mock exasperation. "Such a handsome guy, can't you at least keep your face out of trouble?"

He smiled at the good-natured ribbing, directing the cabbie to stop as they approached the small parking lot where they had left the car. The old man had closed up his souvenir shop, he was still sitting in a lawn chair on the sidewalk, talking and joking with every person who happened by.

They alit from the cab to his boisterous greeting: "Dere dey are, now! How was yo' dinner, Mon, was I talkin' the truth?" His wide smile seemed to light up the area.

"Oh yeah, it was great. If you only knew." Steve patted him on the shoulder, as he peeled off a twenty and tucked it into the man's shirt pocket. He hurried around to unlock the door for Beth.

"Come on; tell me what happened in the alley. How did you get the bruise, and who was the man you were chasing?" She asked as Steve got in beside her.

He ignored her as he took the gun from his waistband and slid back the action. A bullet popped out, landing on the dash. He picked it up, holding it up to the light shining in the window from a streetlamp. Examining the firing cap embedded in the casing, he looked for the tiny imprint a firing pin leaves when it strikes. There was no imprint it was undamaged. Then he cocked the gun, running the tip of his finger over the trigger. With a perplexed look, he laid the gun on the floor.

"What's wrong?" Beth asked.

"Graves gave me the gun... there's no firing pin it."

"What does that mean, what's a firing pin?"

"It means I almost got my ass shot off because he didn't check it out."

"You mean the guy from the restaurant shot at you? Why, who was he?"

"I never found out who he is, although I found out Boulez sent him. He kicked me in the head when I wasn't looking." Steve touched his face, trying to access the damage in the rear-view mirror. "It got me pissed, so I uh, I persuaded him to explain himself."

"And...?"

"And not much. He said he was coming after us to pay off a debt to Boulez. Boulez called in a chit."

"Chit?"

"Yeah, it's called a chip, it's like an IOU. Boulez must have done a favor for him at some point, hid him from the authorities, you can use your imagination. To repay the debt, when Boulez called he had to jump, no questions asked, just do it."

"I see." Beth looked puzzled.

"He said something a little weird, though, I thought he said, '*It's already too late, you cannot stop Musa.*' I do not understand who or what Musa is." Steve explained.

"Musa, Musa, Musa... that doesn't ring any bells. I don't suppose he told you how to spell it? That's one of those words you can spell twenty ways... m-o-o-s-a,m-o-o-s-a-h, m-u-s-a-h... and on and on."

It perplexed Beth, trying to make sense of the latest information. "It's too late? Have they made enough gold?"

"No, they were still making plenty last night," Steve responded.

Steve watched the traffic behind them for the last couple of miles, taking several unnecessary turns through parking lots and hotel entrances. An ambulance rushing towards the old town passed them, causing Steve to make a mental note to send an agent to find the Arab. He might be a little more cooperative if he thought they might deport him. Assuring himself no one was following them, he made the turn into the wide entrance of the Sheraton. Parking under the canopy, he opened the door for Beth, whisking her into the lobby.

"We need to be careful, wherever we go, now we know Boulez isn't finished with us yet. If he sent one guy after us, he will have a dozen more right behind him."

As they stood to wait for the elevator to open, Steve noticed a man standing on the far side of the lobby, wearing a dark suit. When Steve looked at the man, he parted his jacket just enough for Steve to see the ICE badge clipped to his belt. An uneven lump beneath the man's left armpit announced a shoulder carry pistol. Steve smiled, touching his brow in a silent salute. Turning to Beth as the elevator opened, "Good, they have people in the lobby, and at every exit, too. We're safe here tonight."

"Safe, that word used to have meaning," Beth muttered.

Steve put his arm around her shoulder, remarking to himself how tiny she felt.

"I'll be in the next room, and our people are on both sides… you'll be okay."

She turned to him as the elevator glided to a stop, putting her hand on the back of his neck, and pulling his face closer to hers.

"Would you think I'm terrible if I told you I don't want to be alone tonight? Not tonight."

He looked deep into her eyes, almost black in the dim light of the elevator, savoring the look of desire he saw there.

"Then you won't be. Besides, don't forget, you're in my protective custody." Their lips brushed, closing together just as the door opened. It was only a dozen steps to Beth's door, a distance they walked arm in arm, anticipation filling each of them with a sense of urgency.

Steve closed the door behind them, hesitating in the small entrance while Beth turned on a bedside reading lamp. She cracked open the balcony door, allowing the gentle breeze to blow in from the ocean and fill the room with a little humid air. There was just enough light to chase the darkest shadows from the room.

"Are you sure about…" He never finished the question. Beth returned to him, reaching her arms under his, kissing him, as she pushed him against the door. He felt her engage the safety latch behind his back, realizing it was an unspoken answer to his unfinished question. They fell onto the bed, soon making it a tangle of half-removed clothes, scattered pillows, and twisted sheets. Through the open balcony door, the cool breeze was blowing the erotic smells of tropical shrubs and flowers around the room, and magnifying the dissolute experience to the point of overwhelming their senses. They were having sex, not making love, and they both understood it. They were not deep enough into the relationship to respond to each other with the emotions necessary to 'make love'. This was pure hedonistic pleasure, a release three days of mental terror, three days of intense emotional peaks and valleys demanded as a balm. It was unspoken, yet the acceptable

174

course of action. Love might come, or love might not, but tonight was for physical healing.

They both lost track of time, as they committed to total absorption with each other. Even had they wanted to look at the clock, it would have proved difficult to see after a flailing foot knocked to the floor. They had been enjoying each other for an hour, yet to them, it seemed as if it were only a few minutes. As their physical intensity waned and pleasant exhaustion took hold, forcing itself into every cell of their beings. They lay perpendicular to each other, Beth's legs across Steve's thighs, her outstretched fingers combing the hair on the side of his head.

"I needed that, you're amazing," Beth said in a soft voice, pulling the sheet over herself, a little self-consciousness creeping in.

"Amazing? The only thing around here amazing is how beautiful you are. I shouldn't tell you this but when you passed out in your Explorer, I noticed. I remember thinking, damn, this is one hot woman." He took her hand and kissed her fingers.

"Yeah, really hot," she cooed. "A big knot on my head must have been a real turn-on."

"I wasn't looking at your head!" He joked as he pulled her next to him, wrapping the sheet around them, enjoying the contrast in temperatures between their naked bodies and the sheets. They snuggled close together, her head on his shoulder. "I'm just kidding, you know. Besides, I'm more attracted to your mind."

"Fine, because I'm only attracted to your body!" They laughed and talked, as the night fell away into the early morning. Never raising their voices above a whisper, the rhythmic sound of waves outside their door induced them into a deep sleep.

175

Steve awoke to the sound of the telephone's insistent ring tone, sensing Beth was not beside him. Coming to full alertness, he realized Beth was in the shower. Her audible humming was filtering through the bathroom wall, the melody subdued by the sound of water rumbling against the shower walls. The phone rang again, and Steve considered for a second not answering it. He was sure it would be the Department, and he had no real desire to explain why he was in Beth's room at this time of the morning.

"Uh-oh," He muttered to himself, *"They've been calling my room."* t seemed to Steve to be bright outside for the time of the morning, as he looked around on the floor for the clock.

"You want me to get it?" Beth was standing at the foot of the bed, towels wrapped around her body and hair.

"No, I got it." Steve took his time, sitting up before picking up the handset, hoping it would stop ringing.

"Hello?"

"Oh… Steve? It's Barnes. I must have dialed the wrong room. I've been trying to get you in your room all morning. Aren't you in five fourteen?"

"Yes, but I came down to check in on Beth, I mean Ms. Williams. I will bring her down to breakfast as soon as she takes care of a few more things." He waved Beth off with a smile when she shook her head, feigning disgust.

"Gotcha… only you better make it lunch. And you better hurry, it's twelve-thirty!" Her tone of voice imparting a subtle levity, making it obvious she knew more than she was letting on. Steve hesitated, not believing he slept past noon without waking up. It was against his nature, he would work for two days straight and still wake up at his normal time of seven A.M. - without an alarm clock.

"Twelve thirty? Ouch… all right, we'll make it brunch. So, what's going on? Tyson put me on a forced vacation, at least for today."

"Vacations over, Beebe wants to meet with you, Mr. Tyson, and Beth Williams, this evening at about six."

"No problem, we have five-plus hours. Where do we meet?"

"Langley." Agent Barns said.

"Langley? You mean Virginia Langley, as in CIA Headquarters?"

"CIA Langley headquarters, six PM this evening. You two better hurry with your… ahem, brunch…" She gave him a good-natured tweak. I'll pick you up in the lobby in an hour."

"Yeh, yeh, yeh, give me a break. One hour, we'll be there. Oh, I almost forgot, you had better have an agent check all the local hospitals for an Arab dude with a broken leg. He jumped me in an alley last night. Boulez sent him to finish whatever they didn't get done on the ship. I think he knows about what is going on, he said something about everything being in place, they would get us…the

176

usual threats. Someone or something named Musa being ready. Maybe you can do a quick check, see if we have anyone in the files named Musa."

"I'll see what I can find, Steve. See ya."

Steve hung the phone up, and Beth saw he was deep in thought.

"What were you saying about us? Where will we be in an hour?"

"You better throw your things in a bag. We are going to visit CIA Headquarters today. Angie Barnes is picking us up in an hour."

Beth knew it would do no good to argue. She resigned herself to putting the few items she had purchased into a tote bag, "At least it won't be hard to pack."

After a quick lunch, they met Barnes in the lobby as scheduled. She carried a sheaf of papers and an envelope containing several photographs. She held them up for Steve to see.

"Is this the guy you ran into last night?"

Steve examined the two photos. Even though it had been dark, the shape of the man's head seemed familiar. "I think so, it was dark in the alley, but I'd say this is him. How is his leg?"

"Broken. Well, more like crushed. The nurse said he was in surgery all night. Even though they put half a dozen pins and screws in him, he will never walk normally again. What did you do to him?"

"He started it. He's lucky I didn't put him out of his misery. Does anybody know where I can find Graves? I have a bone to pick with him."

"I'm not sure; he wasn't at the hotel this morning. I guess he'll show up when he gets good and ready. He's been having a lot of trouble lately. I heard his wife is leaving him. He seems preoccupied."

"Yeah, well, whatever. Anyway, who is this guy? Do you have anything?"

"His name is Azziz, Hussein Azziz. He's been living here under an assumed name, Mohammad Fahd, for at least three years. He runs a gas station for a living."

"Big surprise," Steve said.

"It wasn't hard to find out who he is. His fingerprints are on file everywhere. Interpol wants him in Spain and Italy, and Germany has an interest in him too. He's been on our watch list for quite a while, although we lost track of him two years ago. Once he's lucid, we'll take him into custody, down to Guantanamo. They'll get whatever he knows."

"I wonder how many more sleepers Boulez has stashed around the globe. You can bet he has people in every port he uses and every big city. He's got a huge operation to pay for, a lot of expenses."

Beth had been sitting as they talked business. She interjected the obvious. "You can keep anybody happy with a few billion."

"Make it less the millions we found yesterday, and we are coming after a lot more," Steve said.

They slipped through a secure gate at San Juan International, where a U.S. Army Humvee escorted them to their plane. They followed it to a small private terminal near the end of the runway where a shiny blue Gulfstream G200 was waiting for them to arrive. Barnes escorted them to the side of the plane where she handed Steve a folder with a dozen loose pages of paper inside.

"Here, this will keep you occupied on the flight," She handed the folder to Steve. "I Googled the name Azziz gave you, Musa. I got a lot of hits, but I didn't have time to go through it, so have a ball."

Steve took the file, and they shook hands and said their goodbyes as the pilot helped them aboard, pulling the door shut behind them. Tyson and Beebe were already aboard, strapped into in their plush leather seats. Steve and Beth took their seats, and the jet taxied to the front of the queue of about ten aircraft waiting to depart.

Steve glanced at Tyson with a quizzical look. "Not bad! I didn't know you had this kind of pull."

"Now you know better, Beebe here has carte blanch," Tyson laughed. "We should fly with him more often."

Beebe tried his best to seem nonchalant as the powerful jet sped down the runway. Reaching critical speed, they launched into the air, the G forces pushing everybody to the back of their seats while the jet made a wide right bank, to head north. Steve as a little surprised at the steepness of the ascent as compared to a commercial airliner, it seemed to him as if the jet was climbing straight up.

The copilot appeared to announce a flight time of three and a half hours to DC. After instructing the passengers of the safety measures on board, and directing them to avail themselves of the stocked galley and mini-bar items, he returned to the front cabin. The passengers all unbuckled and stretched their legs as the jet reached an altitude of 38,000 feet. The air was so smooth, and the cabin so quiet, if you didn't know it, there would be no way to be sure you were flying.

"Sweet ride, don't you think?" Steve asked Tyson, as Beth and he walked over to sit on the sofa beside the two men.

"Nice. We're working for the wrong agency. We fly coach, and if ICE had its way, we'd fly in baggage." Everyone laughed as Steve laid out the folder on a small coffee table and scanned the papers inside.

He handed several pages to Beth. "We need your analytical skills again if you don't mind. Can you help to look through these? Does anything jump out at you?"

"All right, but somebody needs to put me on their payroll if you won't let me go back to work," Beth whispered.

"I said it before, you would make an excellent analyst, you say the word, and you're in," Beebe jumped in, "we're always looking for quality."

Beth nodded, but didn't answer; she held her head down, staring at the printouts of various web pages lying in front of her.

"I understand you had a problem last night, Steve, are you okay?" Tyson noticed the fresh contusion on Steve's cheek.

"Not as much of a problem as the other guy had. Boulez must have people on the ground in San Juan. He sent an Arab named Azziz, to watch us, and I'm sure a lot more. I followed him into an alley and he kicked me in the head when I wasn't looking." Steve rubbed his cheek, as he flipped through the papers, "He won't be any more trouble."

"So I gathered. They damn near had to amputate the man's leg."

"It only confirms Ms. Williams will need protection for the foreseeable future," Beebe added, catching a sharp glance from Beth.

"Speaking of Boulez, we tracked his private plane leaving U.S. Territory yesterday. He filed a flight plan for Dubai. We can't say if he was on it or not, I guess he knew things would get hot for him in Key West. What have you got there?" Tyson looked over at the printouts.

"I had Barnes do an internet search about what the Arab told me last night. You know how they all rant and rave about how they will kill us all soon."

"You mean blood running in the streets, and all that crap?" Tyson answered.

"Yeah, this guy had a new one I haven't heard before. He said Musa was ready, and you can't stop it. It was something to that effect. Angie did a search and came up with all this stuff." Steve pointed to the papers.

The information reminded Tyson of the conversation he had had a few days earlier with Dave Spellman, at the Customs computer labs.

"Musa? I know that name, hold on a second." He pulled his briefcase out from under his seat, placing it on his lap as he rummaged through several fat files; inside he found what he was looking for.

"Here it is!" He was holding a copy of the message Spellman had deciphered from the disc downloaded at Boulez's communications interface. "We think it's a log of gold shipments aboard Boulez's ships, eight hundred million dollars' worth. Look at the heading, the title of the whole thing is: 'MUSA'. We haven't been able to figure out what it stands for yet, as far as I know. We have people working on it."

"Wow!" Beth interrupted, holding a single sheet of paper out in front of her with both hands. "Here it is." She handed the paper to Steve.

"Mansa Musa," he read, 1312 to 1337. He was an African king who promoted education, commerce, and architecture in Mali. Legend has it he made Mali into an Islamic stronghold in the region. He was most noted for his hajj, or pilgrimage to Mecca."

Steve read on for a few seconds, until Tyson interjected, "So what? Everybody and their brother made a pilgrimage to Mecca back then. What makes him any different?"

Steve finished reading the paper, and then looked over at Beth, "Well I'll be damned." He handed the paper to Tyson, "That son - of - a - bitch!"

179

Alejandro Peña sat at his secluded lab table, holding his head in his hands. He had been checking on the microbes in the Petri dish every few hours for the last several days, now the fear was permeating through his bones. He peered into the microscope, his eyes seeing what he thought he had overcome, now knew was inevitable. The genetic trigger he had engineered a few weeks ago had accidentally contaminated the main microbe pool. Now it was pervasive in the latest generation. Samples from each of the twelve ships making port in Dubai over the last two weeks all displayed similar characteristics. Their reproductive cycles stymied after seventeen generations, always the seventeenth generation. Each new generation after the seventeenth was less efficient than the previous in producing the reaction necessary to remove the gold from seawater. It was serious enough it now affected production levels. He had been trying for the last two days to figure out how to reverse the generational decline, or to stabilize it, to no avail. There was a flaw in his genetic engineering model, a flaw should have made itself evident much sooner than this, but did not. What was it? He designed a mutation with the intent for its release as a fail-safe device, preventing future use of his process if something happened to him. It was his insurance against harm to him or his family, and only as a last resort, he would threaten Boulez. Somehow, the trigger he devised switched on, and the microbes were destroying themselves.

How can he go to Rahman now, and tell him production had plateaued, and soon would trend downward? Although he had a store of frozen 'seed' microbes, his "Adam and Eves" he called them, to start the process all over again from the beginning would be disastrous. The ships required constant modifications, as the process got refined with successive generations of microbes. The alterations took months to complete, and cost untold millions of dollars. His design would bring the entire fleet up to identical technological standards. From the onset, it was necessary to maintain a level of uniform technology in each ship, ensuring similar and predictable results. A certain distance traveled at a known speed would always bring in a volume of gold product within narrow parameters. As long as they regulated the 'process, and the microbial environment was identical. It would be impossible, and a logistic nightmare to maintain the complicated 'process' at differing levels of sophistication on each ship. Even if it were possible, it was difficult to find scientists qualified to maintain the delicate process. Even Boulez cannot force everyone he needed to work for him. The scientists he had now were adequate, and well paid, by design they were not privy to all areas of the research developed concerning the microbes. Boulez wanted to ensure only a few people had the knowledge to assemble the components necessary for producing the gold. While certain more trusted scientists had knowledge of sections of the 'process', Peña was the only person who had full knowledge. Now, if he can't stop the microbes from spiraling downward to mere natural levels of gold production after only seventeen generations, he would be in grave danger. Peña hoped Boulez might already have enough gold to do what he wanted, a plan of which he had no knowledge, other than to speculate it had to be financial shenanigans. By Peña's own rough calculations, Boulez should have harvested between five and a half and seven and a half million ounces of gold over the last two years, more. By anybody's calculation, it was a lot of money.

Peña's budget had been unlimited. His acquisition of research and technology equipment constrained only by the watchful eyes of the United States Commerce Commission, which had strict regulations for equipment useful in the manufacture of biological weapons. Although the Europeans and Chinese were developing good quality research equipment, the gold standard for equipment was American. The equipment he had was state-of-the-art and would be the envy of most of the best-equipped research facilities anywhere in the world. If he cannot overcome the unexpected problem with the 'process' within Boulez's time frame, Peña knew his life would not be worth very much. Patience was not a virtue possessed by Boulez, who had a strict timetable. Once the production had risen to satisfactory levels, he made it clear he expected to harvest at a rate no less than Peña's calculations had shown possible.

After coercing him with threats against his family, Peña knew Boulez was a man of few principles. At least not the progressive principles civilization had instilled in humankind over the last several centuries. Boulez ascribed to the medieval principles espousing religious convictions had more value than human life. To him and his ilk, life was a small thing to sacrifice to achieve his perception of God's desires. Far different from the Christian ethic he grew up with… considering all human life sacrosanct. He held no illusions about getting the research facility Boulez had promised to fund, a cynical ploy, he knew, designed to encourage him to expedite his research. Even though Peña had never met Boulez face to face, he knew Boulez was a Muslim, a devout Muslim. Many hard-liners considered scientific research as an affront to Allah unless it gave an edge to kill the infidels. He knew Boulez's would never keep his promises. He only wanted to placate him for as long as he was useful. Peña had long since given up on raising his family in a quiet academic atmosphere when Boulez finished with him. His only hope for the future was to get away from Boulez and safeguard his family. He would soon need excuses and subterfuge to explain away the reduced production. If only he had a way to get his family to safety, he felt sure he might make it to the American Embassy, and explain to them what he had been doing. He was fighting back tears of hopelessness, realizing even suicide would not assure him of his families' safety. Was he destined to never see his wife again, never hold his precious daughters? For a few weeks, he knew he had reason to stall, to blame the poor production on the lab personnel, or even claim to be near a repair of the genetic code. Deep in his heart, he knew it was over. He was tired, tired of trying to stay one step ahead of the second law of

181

thermodynamics, which implies trying to keep a complex controlled process from degenerating into a chaotic disaster, is futile. He made the sign of the cross on his chest, and then entwined his fingers and looked up to the ceiling, repeating a quiet prayer several times:

"Father, I ask nothing for myself, I ask only for my families' safety! If there is a way, please help. Please let an angel find this message. I give my humble life over to you."

Although his computer had all email sending capabilities removed, he had sent a coded message to several blog sites. He dare not make an appeal for help, he knew security checked and monitored all outgoing content. They allowed him to post anonymous messages in the guise of research questions, however since he had no way to leave an address for a direct response, he did not know if anyone had figured out he was sending coded messages. It was a simple code, and most chemists would be familiar with it. His only hope was a physics professor, or a chemist would stumble on his message, before whoever reviewed his computer transmissions stumbled on to it. He copied the message to fourteen sites with a push of his finger, knowing it was only a matter of time:

Requesting any known information on the effect on microbes of the following chemical element combinations:

1. (84, 37, 53, 21, 8, 11, 63, 37)
2. (8, 9)
3. (5, 8, 92, 3, 63, 39)
4. (53, 10)
5. (84, 8, 37, 81)
6. (32, 63, 5, 63, 3)
7. (31, 8, 3, 66)
8. (31, 3, 92, 52)
9. (66, 18, 7, 31, 63, 37)
10. (21, 63, 7, 66)
11. (1, 63, 71, 84)
12. (85)
13. (84, 63, 7, 85)

A sudden flurry of activity behind him interrupted his prayers, and he wiped his eyes as he looked in the commotion's direction. The security personnel assigned to "protect" him came to immediate attention, tossing the magazine he was reading on the small desk in front of him. As was Rahman's directive, the persons assigned to him for security were always changing, rotating days and evenings. A tactic Peña surmised was to ensure no possibility of establishing anything other than a strict business relationship with security. Although they kept a respectable distance while he worked, they escorted Peña everywhere

182

during the day. Peña's final curfew was at midnight, at which time he restricted to his small suite of rooms.

Through his blurred vision, and a tangle of lab equipment, he saw a group of men approaching. One he recognized, it was Rahman, and another, a shorter man he had never seen. The man was in the center of a small cadre of bodyguards nearing his work area. His dark suit was expensive, and his demeanor transmitted a natural authority. Where he walked, the group followed, moving in piscine coordination. He realized they were making their way to him, and he turned to cover attempts to wipe his eyes. As he pretended to examine a notebook lying open on his desk, he turned around to feign surprise as the group of men reached his lab table.

"Hello, Rahman. Is there a problem?" He felt a vague uneasiness.

Rahman and the other man walked closer. "Mr. Peña. What is troubling you? You look…"

Peña dabbed at his eyes again. "No, just ah, chemical fumes in my eye. I'm fine. What can I do for you gentlemen?"

"Mr. Peña, this is Jason Boulez." Peña looked bewildered. Neither man offered a hand. "He has come because we have concerns we want to discuss with you."

Peña did not know what to do. The man responsible for two years of anguish was standing not four feet from him. For a split second, he considered tossing the open beaker of sulfuric acid sitting on his desk in the man's face, if only for a second. As unhappy as he was, he did not wish to die this day.

"I have a small office, over there." He pointed to a nearby door.

"It will do fine. Security can wait out here." Boulez said as he followed Peña and Rahman into the small room. Once inside, Boulez took a seat behind Peña's desk, strewn with papers and research books. Peña and Rahman settled into two small chairs facing the desk. Peña was uncomfortable that Boulez was invading his space, and Boulez did not miss his sullen look.

"You seem displeased with me Mr. Peña; do I detect a touch of hostility?"

"Why would I show hostility to you? You took me from my family, threatened them, threatened me, keep me here against my will, what do I have to be hostile about?"

"I see your point, Mr. Peña. As a family man, I sympathize with you. My work separates me from my family often and, it is most unpleasant. I realize it is even more so for a man with small children. However, we are nearing the end of the project you have so developed for us. If all goes as planned, soon I will reunite you with your family."

"Well, you must forgive me Sir; it seems as if I'm out of the planning loop." He replied.

Boulez stared at him for a few seconds, unpracticed in swallowing insubordination. He paused to convey his irritation at Peña's response, knowing silence carried just as ominous a warning as any verbal threat. As distasteful as it was to him, he had to let it go. This man was more useful alive than dead, and for now, he had an advantage. He was the only person alive who knew the entire process.

"Loops can be dangerous. The less you know the better off you will be later. Take my word for it, if you do nothing else." His steely stare gave Peña the creeps.

"We have business," Rahman interjected, trying to diffuse the situation.

"Yes, we have business, let's not get sidetracked." Boulez had calmed down a little. "We are entering the final phase of our project. Until recently, gold production has shown a steady increase in efficiency. I can't say I'm displeased."

"So, what's the problem?" Was Peña's curt reply.

Rahman offered the explanation. "The problem is, for the last two weeks, the production has been going down. We have already produced a lot of gold. However, our project depends on maintaining a high level. A level you assured us obtainable with the modifications we made to the ships at your direction. All I need to know is whether this is an anomaly and if so, when we can expect the production to resume at the levels you attained, earlier. As Mr. Boulez said, we have to plan."

Peña tried not to show his astonishment. How can they know already? Production has dropped off so much they would notice so fast? Had they been examining his research notes? The scenarios ran through his mind as he struggled to come up with a plausible answer, not expecting to explain this problem so soon.

"I-I was not aware, I uh, I will have to look into it," He stammered, "it's just, um, you know, the procedure is not being followed as before." His body language belied the fact he knew it was doubtful. Peña was well aware, from talking with one of the onboard scientists a generous percentage of all they produced was theirs. It was all the incentive they needed to wring every molecule possible from their labs and to do it under the strict instructions Peña himself had issued.

Boulez suspected he was lying. Peña was a methodical scientist. There was no way an obvious production level drop had been overlooked by him.. Boulez was sure he knew more than he was letting on. Whatever was going on, this meeting would put Peña on notice to get it straightened out. Boulez stood up, supporting himself with both fists on Peña's desk, his dark eyes cutting into the scientist with surgical precision.

"Let me make myself clear, Mr. Peña. You will return the process to its former level of production, at a minimum. If you succeed, your time here will be short, and your reunification will happen soon. If you cannot, your time here will still also be short. However, any reunions will have to take place in the afterlife. The decision is yours. Do we understand each other?"

184

Beth took the piece of paper back from Steve and read. *"The Legend of Mansa Musa.* It says his pilgrimage, or hajj, included over a hundred camels loaded with fifteen tons of gold. Over five hundred slaves, each one of them carrying a golden staff weighing four pounds, accompanied him. His most senior wife, along with her hundreds of attendants, and many thousands of his subjects were part of the hajj. Mansa Musa spent his gold lavishly along the way, in Cairo and Mecca. He spent so much money he ran out and had to borrow money for the return trip at exorbitant rates."

"And let me guess," Beebe interjected, "he depressed the price of gold in the region?"

"More to the point," Beth continued, "he distributed so much gold, the price dropped to less than the price of copper. It took almost twenty years for the oversupply of gold to absorb back into the economy, toppling several kingdoms."

They all stared at each other for a few seconds as the gravity of the information sunk in.

Beebe was the first to comment. "So Boulez has a plan, 'Musa' as he calls it, is to depress the world gold market? I'll give him credit-it's an ambitious undertaking."

"It still makes little sense," Tyson said. "What can it really accomplish? Most people have no awareness of gold's effect on the economy. The most gold the average person ever sees is in a few pieces of jewelry, and no country is on the gold standard anymore. Can this make much difference? I mean if gold fell to ten cents an ounce, what effect would it have on my life? Not much, I'd say."

"Your life, and ours, you're right, not much." Beebe answered, "At least not for quite a while. Consider this scenario: Several African, South American, and even former Soviet Republics, countries with little in the way of natural resources besides gold, find the price of gold too low to mine it at a profit. A price we are close to, from the reports I received just a few days ago. Anyway, huge parts of their economies dry up, leading to economic chaos. They only have two options. One, open their borders to terrorist interests, people with money who now have unlimited access to gold, and will pay them for the relative safety of a government forced to look the other way. Or two, accept help from wealthier countries who have an interest in keeping the terrorists out requiring a quid pro quo in return. We might send help for allowing military bases, or missile launch areas, for example."

"Then we hope they choose option two, and why wouldn't they? They would keep their government's power base without having to deal with the instability the terrorists would bring. It would be an easy choice for me." Beth said.

"It would be logical, we can all agree. Few of the thugs in control of a few African countries would ever consider logic. Here's the rub, it wouldn't matter, both choices would devastate to the Western economies. With the first option, we end up with dozens of Afghanistans or Iraqs. We have spent countless billions policing and stabilizing just those two already, and no end is in sight. Take option two. We create perpetual welfare states in those countries, making them even more dependent on us as their workforce disappears, and whatever they have in the way of economic infrastructure disintegrates. Both ways, we pay, and we pay big. Think trillions, not billions. If Boulez can continue to make gold by the shipload, our economy will enter a death spiral attempting to offset either option. Then to make matters even worse, it would affect the economies of other countries, Russia, China, and South Africa. They could not help, even if they were so inclined."

Steve sensed the ominous tones in Beebe's voice. "What you're saying is this will throw us into a worldwide depression. It's a domino effect. First, the weakest countries collapse, and then on up the food chain until we have no way to sustain even ourselves. Game over."

"One of the first things to go out the door in those situations is democracy." Tyson seemed almost overwhelmed by the implications. "It's every man for himself, the law of the jungle, the survival of the fittest, whatever you want to call it. Nobody will vote to see who gets the last scrap of food. The strongest man takes it."

"I agree," Beebe said, "and any time you have the strongest man in control, it becomes totalitarianism, rule by brute force. The world has a long bloody history. Stalin, Hitler, Pol Pot. It's how the Taliban stays in power, and how most of the fundamentalist Islamic regimes stay in power."

"So, Boulez can cause most of the worlds' economies to tank, and then be ready to step into those places the West can't afford to subsidize. Since he will have already paid for loyalty with the tons of gold he has had to distribute to make this scheme work, it will be a cakewalk for him to take control." Tyson said.

Beth still tried to understand. "What's in it for him? He ends up with a boatload of worthless gold and control of a bunch of countries with no productive economy. What am I missing?"

"Good question and I think I have an answer," Beebe explained. "Unless I miss my guess, I'd say his goal is to control the Islamic population. No one has ever pulled all the various factions of Islam together into a cohesive unit. If they had, we would all be speaking Arabic right now. He has discovered the way to do it. If he can destroy the hated Western economies, and in doing so removing Islam's obsession with our dominance over them, he would have a massive population of the willing, all eager to recreate the world economy in their image. Since most of the world's Islamic population lives in poverty now, they would see any improvement as a sign from Allah. Once in power, he would bring back economic stability. By choosing which countries to stabilize first, he can control the balance of power. He controls the speed of the world economic recovery by controlling the amount of gold in circulation. What would he care if he took a few hundred tons of gold and threw it back in the deepest part of the ocean?" If he did, it would help bring back economic equilibrium to a world he controlled large parts of."

"So it's not the money he wants, it's the power!" Beth exclaimed, "The only thing money can't buy is love, until now. If he pulls this off, he'll have the adoration of millions of Muslims. He'll be a God!"

"As you said, it's one hell of an ambitious plan," Tyson added. "The question is what are we going to do about it?"

The pilot's voice crackled from the intercom to interrupt their conversation. "This is Captain James, we will land at Andrews in thirty minutes, please return to your seats now, and fasten your seat belts. Thank you."

"We'll figure it out when we get to Langley. I have the best people in the world working on this and we'll stop this." Beebe had a determined look on his face, as he buckled in.

Steve eased into his seat beside Beth, noticing she looked a little tired. "Are you going to make it?"

"Don't worry about me, I'll be fine. I didn't get a lot of sleep last night." She smiled up at him as he hooked his little finger around hers between the seats.

The jet was descending and their ears popped with the pressure difference. Steve found the runway of the Air Force base out of the window as they made the slow arc of their approach. The landing was flawless, a gentle bump and the sudden braking causing him to strain against his seat belt. As soon as the group exited the jet, another set of pilots met them and loaded them into two golf carts for a short ride to a waiting helicopter. A sense of urgency was in the air as they strapped into their new transportation, and in less than ten minutes, they were in the air, following the Potomac past the monuments, past the Georgetown waterfront, and into the Virginia countryside. From the air, the CIA complex looked to be a large college campus, with several buildings joined with various footpaths and manicured grounds lending a well-cared-for appearance. Several helipads were visible from their altitude, and the pilot headed for one atop the tallest building. Steve wondered how the people working in the offices below put up with the noise of helicopters taking off and landing throughout the day, until he realized the glass was bulletproof, which as a side benefit of not allowing bullets to pass through, also stifled sound waves with great efficiency. After another uneventful landing, a serious-looking security officer hustled them to a doorway at one side of the heliport which led to a stairway. They all remained quiet as they walked single file down the stairs to an elevator vestibule. Next, the security officer directed them to the proper elevator, and once everybody was in, he removed a security card from a lanyard around his neck and inserted it into the elevators' keypad. Descending several floors underground, the elevator glided to a cavernous hallway and opened to a man standing in a white lab coat, looking as if he had been waiting for a while.

Beebe stepped off the elevator first, reaching out to shake the man's hand. "How are you, Jack? It's been a while."

"Good, good as expected," Jack replied, "I see you are ganging up on me!"

"We'll do our best. This is Gene Tyson, Beth Williams, and Steve Ross." He waited for all to shake hands before explaining Steve and Tyson worked for Customs. He got a curious look from Beth as he explained her role as a consultant.

As Jack led them down the hallway to a conference room, Beth leaned in and joked to Steve, "Does this mean I'm on the payroll?"

Steve laughed, "The last thing you want, believe me!"

They entered the conference room, which held a large table surrounded by at least twenty chairs. There were five people sitting at the table, each had a large stack of files and notebooks spread out in front of him. Everyone exchanged nods of greeting as Beebe directed his group to sit. He began by introducing everyone, apologizing for only being able to identify the CIA people by their first names. Last names were only another possibility for a security slip, so they remained anonymous.

It took almost an hour for Beebe to outline the story to the five people sitting at the table who often interrupted with questions Steve thought unanswerable. It was as if they were creating a series of scenarios, asking those most involved to offer their opinion on the probability of them being viable. They threw everything they came up against the wall to see what might stick.

In passing, Beth mentioned the man she had heard was doing research for Boulez, the man she recalled as Peña. This caused an immediate reaction in one of the CIA people, who whispered in the person's ear who was sitting next to him. Together, they looked in their papers, until they found what they were looking for.

A middle-aged man, introduced as 'Bill' spoke. "I know the name. I have a report passed on to us by the FBI, mentioning a man named Peña. It seems a professor was doing a little blogging on a scientific site when he came upon a request for information concerning chemical reactions regarding microbes." He distributed a copy of the blog message around the table. He recognized what it was and thought it might be worth calling us on it.

"As you can see, the message contains a column of thirteen sets of numbers. We believe the numbers have no direct correlation to any chemical."

"OK, so do we know what they correspond to?" Beebe handed the page back to Bill.

"Yes. The professor, who is a chemist, recognized the numbers are a code. A code used by many college students studying chemistry, since it is very handy for them. It is easy to decipher. Each number corresponds to the Atomic Number of an element. If you look at a periodic table, the individual elements have an Atomic Number, and a one or two-letter abbreviation, Pb for lead, Fe for iron, and so on."

"So if you match the Atomic Number with the first letter of the abbreviation, you can spell out words. I remember the chemistry students' passing notes way back in high school! Unless you have a copy of the Periodic Table, you would never figure it out." Beth said.

"Well, it's not the Rosetta stone, but for a quick code, it works well. You've limited its decryption to people who might be familiar with the periodic table, which isn't many." Bill continued, "At any rate, we didn't have much to do on this; the professor did it for us. When he read the message, he gave the local FBI office a call, just for giggles. They had no file on a man named Peña. Since we have a request out for any intercepted communication including the keyword 'gold' among others, they sent it over to us. Beebe has been working on this gold problem for a while, and now with your information, it seems as if we have corroboration the message might be genuine."

"You said the FBI has no file on Peña. Isn't the FBI looking for him? Beth says he turned up missing almost two years ago, his family would have put in a missing person's report." Steve asked.

"It's the first thing we asked. We found out his wife notified the local police Mr. Peña had not returned home from a trip abroad as scheduled, and she feared foul play. After two weeks, his wife requested us to drop any investigation. She claimed her husband called her and said he left her for another woman. Since then, the locals closed their books on the matter." Bill explained.

Tyson had been waiting, "Can you tell us what's in the message?"

"Sure," Bill said, referring back to the sheet of paper."

PRISONER OF BOULEZ IN PORT GEBELGOLD GLUT DANGERSEND HELP-A PEÑA"

"Where is Port Gebel, located?" Tyson inquired.

"We're assuming it refers to the Jebel Free Port, in Dubai, United Arab Emirates. He spelled it with a 'G' since there is no 'J' in the periodic table." Bill held up the paper for them to see.

One analyst spoke up: "It would make perfect sense as far as handling a lot of gold. The Jebel port is a business enterprise zone…a euphemism for 'anything goes'. Almost everything shipped by sea from the east ends up going through it. They have no regulations on transferring currency, bullion, whatever. Because their oil supply is precarious, they are trying to develop other income streams. The port is their second-biggest moneymaker, after oil."

Bill continued, "After getting the information yesterday about the gold on the ship in San Juan, we began reviewing our tracking data of all the Global Shipping units we have been monitoring for the last several months. ICE has helped us out with their data. The review shows a definite constant denominator for as long as

189

our tracking records go back. Wherever a ship in the Global fleet sets sail, and no matter what the final destination, at least once every ninety days the ship will pass through the Jebel Free Port. Often, they stop several times during the same period. Those ships are carrying cargo destined for ports making Jebel an inconvenient destination. It makes no obvious economic sense to have a partially loaded ship go several thousand miles off the standard shipping course, to dock in Dubai."

Tyson rubbed his tired eyes, "obvious is the optimum word. Boulez needs to get the gold to a centralized location. There is no better place than Dubai. The cargo-hauling operation is just a cover for the gold production, anyway. It makes no difference to him if it makes a profit or not, he's not trying to make any economic sense. The information Steve intercepted from Boulez in Key West confirms it. Those ships were carrying thirty or forty million dollars' worth of bullion. In fact, one called the Sadim, we calculated to have fifty-three million in gold."

We don't know how long it took to produce it, although if ninety days is the cycle for Dubai, we have an idea."

Beebe had been sitting back on his chair, taking the information and theories in, weighing them, considering the options. There was only one option.

"What it tells me, is we have to find the gold. Boulez must stockpile it in Dubai, probably at the port. If we can find the main stockpile, we can do what's necessary to neutralize it."

"Neutralize it? I'm not sure I follow you." Tyson said.

"Let me answer that if you don't mind." Bill interrupted. "The only way we can bring the world's gold supply back into the equilibrium we enjoy now is to get rid of the sudden oversupply."

We have to find the gold and remove it from the marketplace. In addition, we have to ensure large quantities do not come back on the market. It's simple as that."

"Simple? You're talking about finding tons of gold in a foreign country and taking it from people who you can bet don't want to give it back. The only way to do it is with overwhelming force. We would need to do a virtual lockdown of Dubai, and a massive airlift to get it out of there. What happens if we can't find it? You'll be in deep shit." Steve was incredulous. "And don't forget Boulez has forty or more ships pumping gold out twenty-four, seven. How can you stop it?"

"First, let's understand one thing. There can be no overwhelming force." Beebe countered, "The United States is already in a precarious position in the Arab world. Can you imagine the repercussions if we blew into Dubai with an expeditionary force and took a few hundred million dollars worth of gold? How do we explain it? Besides making us out to be thieves, every country with deposits in our financial institutions would have a good reason to believe we were in danger of insolvency. There would be a massive run on our banks and massive dumping of securities and real estate. No, we have to do this in private."

"What about NATO? They would have to work with us on this." Tyson asked.

"A possibility, however the more people who know about this, the more chance for a leak. If Boulez gets wind we will close in on him, I'm afraid he'll disperse the gold even faster than he has been. The Hawala system can be efficient for moving large sums of cash or valuables."

"So let me get this straight. You want to go in in the middle of the night and take forty tons of gold, sneak it out of the country, and on the way out, throw a wrench in the machine making it. Don't you think it's asking a little much?" It amazed Steve Beebe would even consider it.

"It's a lot, and it will not be easy. That's why we're putting our best man on it." Beebe announced.

"Well, whoever it is, wish him luck. He will need it."

Beebe looked across the table with a wry smile, "good luck, Steve."

DUBAI

The Pactolus sailed into the Port Jebel Basin on a brisk wind, with Steve at the helm. A nondescript thirty-six-foot sailboat, it was grungy looking, care taken to make it look as if it was a beat-up live-aboard, traveling the seas on a wing and a prayer. Tattered, patched sails and faded teak trim completed the illusion of a carefree sailor, a threat to no one. Reaching the Harbor Master on the radio, Steve requested permission to moor as a tourist. The Harbor Police dispatched a two-man crew to meet him, boarding his little boat to do a thorough check of the vessel, as they explained, for "safety considerations". Steve gave the two polite harbor police his fake Australian passport, with visas stamped on the well-worn pages designed to show a long voyage through Indonesia, across to Sri Lanka, around India, and up the Arabian coast. His unkempt appearance, natural tan, and obvious disregard for housekeeping were enough to allay any suspicion of the supposed sailing vagabond, who would not be an unusual sight in an area clamoring for laborers to support the massive construction projects dotting the peninsula. The harbor police examined the boat's documentation and handed the tattered papers back to Steve.

"You can drop anchor over there and come with us." He ordered.

The boat's name caught the eye of one of the Police crew, a Turk. "Pactolus… funny name for a boat. That's the name of a river in Turkey."

"Tis true mate," Steve answered, trying his best to replicate a minor Australian accent. "It was the river that cured King Midas of his golden touch!"

The officer seemed to ignore him, and seeing nothing of concern in the disheveled sailboat, he directed Steve to follow them to a temporary berthing area. After securing the Pactolus, they led Steve to a small immigration office on the ground floor of a building on the pier. A spare looking office comprising one desk, a water dispenser, and two chairs testified this was not an area with a lot of tourist traffic.

"What's the purpose of your visit to Dubai, Mr. uh, Wilson is it?" A bored man in a trim official uniform asked him, straining to read the name through the creases on the tattered passport.

"Wilston," Steve replied, Jerry Wilston. Sorry, my passport is a little worn."

"Ah, yes, I see now, Mr. Wilston. You should have this replaced."

"When I get back, I'll take care of it. I've been away for a while," Steve lied as the man tried to flatten a page in the passport. "A few weeks of work are all I need to continue my travels. I'm hoping to catch on as a carpenter at one building up the coast."

The officer looked at Steve's photograph, and back at Steve with a steady, almost suspicious eye. You don't sound Australian. Where are you from?"

"I grew up in an Australian orphanage run by Americans. Been sailing since I was eighteen. Never took on much of an accent I guess."

It satisfied the officer, as he shrugged his shoulders as he slammed down a red visa stamp. "Enjoy your stay, Mr. Wilston."

Turning to leave, Steve touched the worn-out passport to his forehead in an informal salute. "G'die mite!" The officer let a slight smile crease his face as he pointed to the Harbor Police and directed him to moor his vessel in a buoyed area designated for the purpose. He waved a friendly goodbye as he climbed down a ladder to his deck level, smug in the knowledge beneath a few hidden floor panels lay the most sophisticated communications and surveillance equipment available in the world. Its protection assured by rigged explosive charges, set to destroy the boat if discovered.

Motoring at a leisurely pace towards the vacant moorage area, he had a few minutes to consider the events of the last few days. The meeting at CIA Headquarters had ended on an unexpected note, with Beebe announcing a joint operation with Customs to verify the location of Boulez's gold cache.

Given a few hours before the first mission planning session, Beth and he lingered over a late dinner in the CIA cafeteria. He tried his best to reassure her all this would soon be over. When a female agent came to tell Beth it was time to leave for a safe house in the city, he recalled with regret the look in her eyes told him she knew her life would be different from then on. Steve felt a pang of guilt as they stood, giving each other a tight embrace. They held it long enough to convey the emotion they would not verbalize. It was not time yet.

I surprised Steve when he got his assignment to be the undercover operative for the mission. It concerned him at first with the lack of preparation time for such a complicated operation. Soon he came around after an intensive forty-eight-hour strategy session. He felt not only ready, but he was also eager to start the assignment. Spending two days studying the satellite photos of the Jebel Port, technical data concerning the surrounding support facilities, his comfort level increased. His mission was twofold, gather whatever intel he could, and formulate a plan of action. One of his main goals was to determine if the gold was being stored at the port, and where. If he found it, the assumption was a second mission would go to secure it. Second, try to locate the scientist named Peña. The government figured he would be invaluable if he will cooperate. Because Steve worked alone, a necessity for keeping as low a profile as possible, he had to be cautious. No backup meant if caught by Boulez's people, they would give no quarter. A swift, sure death would be his fate.

After an all-night flight aboard a CIA plane landed in Kuwait, a helicopter dropped Steve on a small island in the Persian Gulf where a group of CIA operatives met him. The CIA set up as a sophisticated tracking station, and after an intense training session and instructions showing the capabilities of the sailboat, Steve, already a proficient sailor, made his way around the island, parallel to the main shipping lanes. Several hours earlier, one of Boulez's ships, the Global Ambassador, had docked in Jebel. It was a ship listed in the document retrieved from Boulez in Key West, and it listed over twenty-six hundred kilos of gold on board. He was hoping to get a visual on the gold shipment, and with luck, place a tracking tag on it.

Steve never felt comfortable being in the ocean at night, having seen a few too many shark attack movies as a teenager. The moonless night made the water black and eerie at the fifteen feet of depth he was trying to maintain. A small compass light was the only thing giving him a visual clue as the propeller whirred beneath his chest. It was four kilometers from the sailboat to the area of the commercial pier he wanted to go to, and he hoped the battery would last long enough to get him there and back on the return trip. By his calculation, it would take twenty minutes of hanging on to this water sled to reach the pier. He didn't relish the thought he might have to swim through this silent black universe of wet shadows, should the batteries die.

As he approached the area of the pier, he sensed a presence near him. Although it was impossible to see anything ahead of him, an almost magnetic attraction seemed to enter his consciousness, a sense of imminent danger. He slowed to a stop, glancing at his divers watch, to see fifteen minutes had elapsed since he left the sailboat. He felt vulnerable in the blackness, half expecting the rushing tentacles of a giant squid to drag him down into the silent depths of the ocean.

"Snap out of it fool! What the hell are you doing to yourself?" He slapped his head with his palm in gentle disgust and kicked for the surface. His head rose above the water with a muted splash and looking ahead, confused for a few seconds by the utter blackness surrounding his eyes. He had been expecting the lights of the pier to be close by now, but all he saw was emptiness so black he had to wave his watch in front of his face to make sure he hadn't gone blind. Treading water, he leaned his head back shocked at what he saw. The huge outline of a container ship was visible against the dim sky, only a few yards away from him. Its immense size magnified by Steve's proximity.

"Jeez!" He sputtered under his breath, realizing another few seconds and he might have collided with it. It was too dark enough for anybody to spot him from above, so he scooted along the surface to the rear of the ship, rounding the stern to see a pier supported by massive concrete piers. He heard the activity above, activity, which he knew continued twenty-four hours a day. The cranes were unloading the ship, men were yelling back and forth, and huge forklifts were transporting containers along the pier at breakneck speed. Steve dove beneath the water again to cross the last thirty meters between the stern and the pier, the lighting on the busy pier too much to risk. He surfaced again at one of the concrete supports, and looking up saw the name Global Ambassador emblazoned on the stern of the ship, the water's reflection creating a mesmerizing pattern on the giant white letters. There were metal catwalks connecting each concrete support, and at intervals along the catwalks were open metal stairways, reaching

195

up to the pier level. He saw several fuel barges moored in the spaces between the concrete supports, their decks only feet above the waterline. Several large hoses were hanging from swiveling arms suspended from beneath the pier deck, their loose ends ready to connect to a large manifold distributing the barges with the heavy fuel oil they transported to ships waiting in the harbor. The high tide stain on the columns showed the barges had plenty of overhead room to float under the thick concrete of the main pier deck. Skimming along the surface, he stopped at the far end of the catwalk, reaching down to remove the swim fins snapped onto the soles of his high-tech footgear. Threading the lanyard of the scooter through the fins, he tied them around a protruding pipe, and then pulled himself up onto the catwalk lit only by a series of weatherproof lanterns perched on metal pipes. He crouched, taking a moment to wait for the chemicals embedded on the surface of his wet suit to react with the dank air trapped under the pier.

After a few seconds, he sensed the gentle heat of a chemical reaction evaporating the water from the suit, making it dry to the touch. Designed to dry fast, it felt good not to have a wet, chafing, wet suit on while trying to complete a mission taking hours.

A muffled sound of voices and the staccato sound of work boots on the metal stairway alerted him workers were descending near him. He hurried to the rear of a barge where he saw an open engine hatch surrounded by parts strewn around the nearby deck. Buckets of used engine oil and a pile of dirty rags meant the barge was undergoing repairs. Steve slipped into the hatch, removing a small pair of field glasses as he did. A steady drip of water was draining from the end of an overhead pipe a few feet from, plinking on the metal of the catwalk. There were two men on the catwalk, each one seemed practiced in the chore they were doing. As one man removed a paper ticket and cranked it into a small metering device, the other selected a color-coded hose from the rack suspended above him and attached the snap-on coupling on the end to a fitting protruding from an adjacent barge. Removing a large padlock from a gate valve behind the meter, the other man opened the valve and threw a switch mounted on a pedestal engaging an unseen pump. With a slight whine of the meter, Steve heard the rush of heavy fuel oil flowing into the barge. He watched, as the men lingered near the meter, their small talk drowned out by the sound of the flowing fuel. After almost half an hour, the pump stopped. The water dripping from the pipe was getting annoying as Steve watched the men from his secluded vantage point. He glanced up to the pipe, wondering why they would go to so much trouble as to label what must be a drainpipe. He laughed to himself as he noticed the large letters stenciled on the end of the pipe:

"AC24/DC24"

Once the barge filled, the men reversed the process, replacing the hoses and locking the valve. After a quick check to make sure they secured the barge to its moorings, they made their way back up the steep stairway.

196

Steve remained motionless for a few moments after the men had left, the underworld of the pier his alone again. Traversing the catwalk, he wanted to find a way to the upper level where he could hide in the shadows. The pier was huge, the length of several ships, and further down he heard the activity of workers loading another barge. He made his way back to the barge he had hidden in, searching along the back bulkhead for a way up. Near the end of the pier, he found what he was looking for. A group of steel ladder rungs embedded in a concrete column leftover from the pier's construction.

He ascended the twenty rungs, which brought him to the lip of the pier. A quick glance gave him a view of the bustling action going on down the pier, dozens of men occupied moving cargo in a well-orchestrated mixture of finesse and brute force. Grabbing the railing overhead, he scrambled over the lip and squeezed in behind an old container the dockworkers used as a makeshift repair shop for the many forklifts zipping around the loading area. He needed to move around the dock without drawing undue attention to himself, and hanging on a hook inside the container, he spied just what he needed. A greasy pair of coveralls was hanging on a hook inside the door. With no one in the immediate vicinity, Steve jumped around to the front of the container, grabbed the coveralls and retreated to the shadows in the rear. He slipped the work suit on and found a pair of rubber boots tossed in the corner which fit over his rubberized footwear. Wedging a filthy baseball cap into the rear pocket of the overalls, and Steve donned them to complete the ensemble, grimacing at the smell of stale grease and body odor permeating the clothes. He walked to the front of the container, and picking up an empty propane cylinder from a large stack, he hefted it up onto his shoulder and walked out onto the pier.

Near the back of the loading area, he kept to the shadows carrying a gas cylinder on his shoulder to hide his face from the other workers. No one paid him any attention as he carried the cylinder across the dock. As he walked, he watched the large overhead cranes in constant motion, swinging back and forth, as they picked up and deposited containers in one fluid movement. The cranes staggered at even intervals down the pier, each one operated by a single man in a booth high above the concrete deck. Steve noticed one crane was not in use, it was near the stern of the Global Ambassador and another ship. Together, they rested beside a large area devoid of cargo. He began a quick walk to that area. Even though the cylinder was empty, it was getting heavy, so Steve switched it to his other shoulder. In the distance, a young Pakistani man sitting on a small forklift saw Steve carrying the cylinder. Waiting for a small pallet of cargo he needed to fill the last space on a flatbed truck, he did a good deed and helped his brother get the cylinder to the refilling station. After all, he loved zipping the forklift in and out, and around all the various obstacles on the dock, priding himself on his deft driving ability. He knew he could deliver the tank and get back losing no time for the driver asleep in the flatbed's cab. He spun the tires as he took off after Steve, reaching him with a squeal of brakes. It surprised Steve when the forklift slid to a halt in front of him thinking the man might run him down. The man gestured and spoke in rapid-fire Arabic, and although Steve discerned whatever the young man was saying was not threatening, he did not understand what he wanted. Steve looked dumbfounded as the Pakistani repeated whatever he had said, and tapped the lever on the forklift, raising the forks up a few inches. With that motion, Steve realized what was happening.

"Ay-wa, ay-wa," He said, swinging the cylinder down to the forks, while the Pakistani giving him a curious look.

"Shukran," he thanked him.

The Pakistani spun away, waving, and muttering gibberish Steve didn't understand. No matter now, he was only steps to the base of the empty crane, a huge metal structure with an enclosed spiral stairway leading to up the operator's booth. He wasted no time reaching the stairway door, and looking around to make sure no one was paying him any attention, he opened the door and slipped in. He hesitated inside the small landing, relieved to have slipped in unnoticed. The door had a small glass window in it, and outside Steve saw everyone going about the normal business of the pier. He had seen no military presence, nor any other security, although he was sure it was present on the docks. He kicked off the heavy rubber boots and began the climb up the dozens of steps to the operator's booth.

The crane operator made the trip to and from the operators' booth by a small elevator cage attached to the side of the crane support. He entered and exited through a small door on the booth's side. The stairway Steve was ascending was the emergency exit.

Breathing as he reached the top of the stairway, Steve opened the overhead hatch leading to the operator's booth. Once inside he saw a worn, well-padded seat, a bank of controls and dials, and a small mini-fridge. He slipped into the booth, thankful the large windows were all tinted. It would be impossible to see him from the outside.

He took a seat in the operator's chair, a perfect vantage point to watch the activity occurring near the Global Ambassador. Two large cranes were unloading containers from the deck of the ship, one stacking them in a double high pile to the backside of the pier, and the other loading a continuous line of large flatbed trucks queued around the perimeter. It worried Steve, the gold might be in any of the stockpiled containers, or loaded onto a truck for shipment elsewhere. For now, his only option was to lie low and watch. He would become familiar with the unloading procedure. Maybe then, he would infiltrate the onboard lab and tag the gold. The CIA operatives on the small island told him at least six more Global Shipping ships are scheduled to arrive in Dubai this week, so he would have several more opportunities.

198

It was one AM, and Steve had been sitting in the operator's seat for at least three hours. This was the part he hated about surveillance...the interminable hour upon hour of waiting for anything at all to happen. He stood to stretch his legs and checked the mini-fridge, where he found several bottles of water. He twisted one open and leaned against the back wall of the booth. As he gazed at the action on the pier, he noticed a small delivery truck pull up to the edge of the pier and stop. The driver put it in reverse, announced by a shrill back up alarm, and then backed up towards the edge of the pier. The truck seemed stout, heavy as an armored car; however, it had no names or lettering visible. Then, to the front of the truck, a black SUV pulled in to a slow stop. Steve was alert.

"What have we got going on here?" He said under his breath, glad to have something to concentrate on. From his waterproof wet bag, he removed a small digital camera with a slender telephoto lens attached to it, training it on each vehicle in succession. The driver of the truck remained in his seat, while another man got out of the truck and walked to the rear. There he slid up a door on the back of the truck, and then to the edge of the pier, taking a seat on one of the huge bollards where the ships moored. He lit up a cigarette, looking as if he expected to be there for a while. Two more black SUVs pulled up, spewing four armed men dressed in black military fatigues, joining four from the second SUV. Together, they created a wide perimeter around the group of vehicles. Used to seeing the operations, the dockworkers paid little attention other than keeping a wide berth from the vehicles.

Steve trained the camera on each man snapping images whenever their faces turned toward him. By then, the driver and passenger of the last SUV had exited and were opening the rear doors, of their vehicle. Steve observed two men exiting, the first a well-dressed man with a middle-eastern appearance. The other man was stocky, with jet-black hair, and he was wearing a white lab coat. Steve decided he wasn't Caucasian, but it was difficult to make out the man's ethnicity.

On the side of the ship, a small door Steve hadn't noticed before opened, and an aluminum gangplank extended to the pier. Escorted to the gangplank, along with the drivers, they disappeared into the ship. Once the men disappeared, Steve scrolled through the digital images on the camera's small viewer. He selected the best images of the two men from the SUV and downloaded them to his satellite phone. He then dialed a secure number to upload a copy of the images to a databank at CIA headquarters. If either of the two men were in the system, he would know it in a few minutes.

Several warning lights came to life on the operator's console, along with an angry-sounding buzzer. The diesel engine powering the crane rumbled to life, creating a brief white cloud to drift back over the pier. It startled Steve, as he jumped out of the seat to crouch beside the emergency exit. Through a small section of glass on the floor, he spotted the cable spool attached to the operator's cage begin to spin. "*Must be a new shift coming on.*" He said to himself as he

199

stuffed his equipment back in the waterproof pouch. It would be only a few seconds before the operator would open the side door to begin his shift. He slipped down through the floor hatch and began a rapid descent of the spiral stairs. After twenty steps, he reached up to his head, realizing he had left the cap lying on the console. Looking back up the stairs, and hearing the elevator basket latch into its docking port, he knew it was too late to retrieve it. His light-colored hair would stand out like a beacon in a sea of black now.

He chastised himself as he continued down the stairs, thankful his rubber-soled diving shoes were silent on the metal treads. Reaching the bottom, he caught his breath. Glancing out the small window, he watched several forklift operators near the crane base, scurrying with loads, and others side by side in conversation. Also in his field of vision were three of the armed guards from the SUVs. The only way for Steve to get to the relative safety at the back of the pier would be to cross in full view of about twenty dockworkers, and the armed guards.

He would need a diversion. He looked up at the dozens of stairs leading back up to the operator's booth above him, and with a resigned look on his face, started back up. Although he was in top shape, the lack of rest over the last several days was affecting his stamina. By the time he reached the top of the stairs, he had to rest for half a minute while the sharp pain in his abdomen subsided. The rumble of the diesel engine and the sounds of the mighty winch the operator controlled hid the sound of the hatch opening behind him. Steve cracked the hatch open, to see the back of the operator's work boots pressing the pedals and working the rotation of the crane. He watched the movements the operator used to control the winch. He was a quick learner, right pedal, rotate right, left pedal, rotate left. Right arm forward, load down, back, load up. Left arm forward sends the load out, pull in to bring the load closer.

He waited until the operator had hooked the harness dangling from the large steel cable to a container. He then reached around the man and jerked the headset plug from the control console. It frightened the man as he turned and saw Steve standing there with his pistol aimed at his forehead. Steve waved him out of the operator's seat with a flick of the gun, a motion needing no translation. He appeared to be Indian or Pakistani, a small man, whose look of confusion drew a powerful uppercut to the chin from Steve's fist.

"Sorry pal, I got no time for dicking around!" Steve said as he caught the unconscious man and dragged him from the chair. Looking through the floor as he took over the seat, Steve saw the dockworkers looking up, waving for the operator to pick up the container. Even though it had only been less than half a minute, the men who worked the docks were not used to delays.

"All right, all right, don't get your panties in a bunch!" Steve pulled back with his right hand, and the container zoomed higher. He had not realized how powerful the crane was. He jerked it to a stop, as the men below it watched it sway; unnerved by the jerky motion they saw as Steve rotated the container away from them.

"Come on baby!" Steve said as he tried to coax the box around in a fluid motion. He didn't have a long way to go. He bumped the control levers until he had the box where he wanted it... directly over the black SUVs. The men on the ground were not paying any attention to the container as Steve maneuvered the container to a halt. He took the cord from the headset and tied the lever all the way forward. Then, shifting the winch's transmission into its low range the box began a slow descent towards the pier.

Struggling to get past the tied off controls, Steve got out of the seat and ran down the emergency stairs as the container started to wind down towards the pier. He knew he could run down the stairs faster than the box would go in low gear. The handrail was already slippery with his sweat from before, and he slipped several times as he made the dizzying rotations down the stairway, again.

He reached the bottom just in time to hear a group of men shouting excitedly in Arabic. When he looked out of the small window, there were several forklifts rushing past toward the SUVs. The armed guards were missing as Steve slipped out of the door. Everyone running past him was watching the container drift lower and lower towards the black vehicles.

Steve tried to look inconspicuous as he jogged away from the scene. Looking back over his shoulder, he saw the security people had moved one of the SUVs, and now the box was perilously close to landing on the other, as they backed away. The shouting and blowing of horns on the forklifts were attracting everyone's as Steve slid to the shadows at the rear of the pier. From behind a container, he threw off the soiled coveralls as he watched the calamity across the pier. One quick-thinking forklift operator tried to get his forks under the container as it neared the roof of the SUV. He didn't realize that it tilted the box off-center, with its contents much heavier on one end. It tipped down onto the hood of the SUV, crushing a fender, its weight concentrated on the front tire until it blew out with a loud bang.

Men were rushing up the emergency stairs now, and all attention was on the damaged car as coils of steel winch cable unwound on the roof of the SUV.

Steve laughed to himself as he watched the scene unfold from the shadows. Until the operator he had knocked cold woke up, they would wonder what had happened. It didn't take long for the word to get to the people inside, and the two men from the SUV. They appeared at the ships' door soon after the winch stopped, and the container lifted from the front of the SUV. The well-dressed man seemed in control, questioning the security people, and examining the damage to the vehicle. He made several phone calls, while the other man with him waited on the fringe of the action, sitting in the open rear door of the smashed SUV.

From his new vantage point, Steve had a direct line of sight into the large doorway on the side of the ship. He watched as a small forklift came into view, with a pallet of small wooden boxes resting on its forks. The lift stopped on the extended platform, and the large heavy truck, the first to arrive backed up to it. When the lift extended its load into the back of the truck, the weight of the load caused the truck to settle several inches on its suspension.

Steve nodded his head in understanding, "I know what's going on here, you rotten candy ass!" He was thinking of Boulez, holed up in his nice digs now, the image sickening him. "I will rain down so much hell on you, and your gold, you sorry bastard, you'll never know what hit you!"

Steve looked down the pier, knowing he was at the wrong end to follow the truck. It had to go towards the other end, and he had to get there while there was still a chance. The well-dressed man had called for another car, which no doubt would be there soon.

He made his way down the pier, darting behind the containers stacked in piles of up to three high near the back of the pier. His black wet suit made him invisible, yet he had to be careful to stay out of sight of the crane operators. It was a cat-and-mouse game to time his movements to when the cranes were facing away from him. He tried to maintain visual contact with the men from the SUVs for as long as possible, however, he had traveled at least half a kilometer now, and the profusion of activity on the pier was blocking his view. He rested in the shadow of a stack of containers, alert at the sound of a siren in the distance. As he waited, he realized it was approaching in his direction, and the red reflections against the tops of several large white storage tanks in the distance confirmed its approach.

"Just what I need now, a bunch of cops after me!" He swore under his breath.

Up ahead, Steve noticed a small parking lot sandwiched between the last stacks of containers and the start of several low office buildings. Steve ran in a crouch to the edge of the lot, he ducked behind a small pickup truck as the vehicle emitting the siren turned the corner. It relieved Steve to see an ambulance instead of the police rushing towards the crane where he left the operator He stood and fished a pair of powerful field glasses from his small bag, training them on the unfolding scene. Through stacks of containers, he could spot the well-dressed man once, and see the ambulance was there to pick up the crane operator. The dockworkers had carried him down the spiral steps, and he lay on the concrete, unmoving as the EMT strapped a neck brace to him. Steve was unrepentant for having knocked the man cold because he knew it was for the greater good.

The sound of a car approaching from behind him caused him to duck again between the two trucks. He watched as a black limousine wasted no time in making it over to the area of commotion. Steve realized it was the replacement vehicle for the smashed SUV. He would have to act fast. Grabbing at the door handle of the truck next to him, he pulled, only to find it locked. He tried several vehicles in the row, finding them all locked. It was then he realized it must be the long-term lot for crewmember on ships at sea. Many of the vehicles looked as if

202

they had been there for weeks, and all had varying amounts of the silty sand covering them.

He picked an older pickup truck in the front row, suspecting it wouldn't have an alarm system, and he was right. "I guess I will use the old elbow key." He whispered as he smashed his elbow through the passenger side window and reached in, unlocking the door. After looking around to make sure nobody had heard anything, he crawled into the driver's seat and reached into his bag for the small universal tool he had brought with him. It had a small screwdriver, which he used to pry the column cover off, exposing the steering lock. With a deft punch of the screwdriver, he bent the bracket holding the locking pin, and the pin dropped out, freeing the wheel, and unlocking the transmission. From there it was a simple matter of punching the ignition lockout and twisting it with the screwdriver. The truck's motor jumped to life, almost inaudible in the thick ocean air.

After returning the tools to his bag, he noticed a small green light blinking on his little satellite telephone. He slid it out of the bag to see there was a message on the small screen reading: Text Messages Waiting (1). A small menu at the bottom of the screen prompted him to read, save, forward or erase the message. He chose 'Read', and at once, a small screen appeared with the following message:

Re Photos Sat Trans 0100 091618:
#1 Abdul Rahman STT VD NOIW
#2 Poss Alejandro PeñaRepmiss120401 NKTT NOIW

Steve understood the brief message all too well. Photo #1- name Abdul Rahman, suspected terrorist ties, very dangerous, no outstanding international warrants. Photo #2- Name Alejandro Peña, reported missing since December 4 2001, no known terrorist ties, no outstanding international warrants.

"Peña! He's the guy Beth said was doing research for Boulez. I will talk to him." Steve told himself as he put the phone back.

He was ready now, and just in time as the headlights of several vehicles lit up the entrance road to the pier. Lying over in the seat, he watched as the armored car, followed by the SUV and the limousine passed by him in a single file. The convoy did not take the exit road as he had expected, instead, turning up a short hill towards the line of office buildings.

Steve eased the manual transmission into first gear, holding on the clutch, waiting for the three vehicles to get far enough away for him to follow without drawing undue suspicion.

203

Alejandro Peña was nervous. The microbes on the Global Ambassador had not lost efficiency as he had expected. Perhaps the fact the ship had spent over two months of its voyage in the frigid waters of the South Atlantic had helped. He did not know, nor did he care. It would all fall to pieces soon enough, he was sure. When it did, he knew the blame would fall on him.

What choice would Rahman have? Let him go? Say it was fun while it lasted? Yeah, right! They would never believe his excuses that the death of the 'process' was inevitable when the other biologists discovered he had designed a genetic trigger as a fail-safe. Had it worked, he would have been able to hold it over Boulez as a trump card. Boulez was greedy, always pushing for more gold. Peña had assumed it would be a safe bet...after all they say you can never be too rich.

Soon, the cost of running the ships would surpass the value of gold produced. Although expected and tolerated in the development stages of the program, returning to a lower level of production now, after all the modifications to the ships he himself had claimed as necessary would be intolerable to Boulez. He had made a mistake in the trigger, and now if he could not reverse it, it would mean his death. There had to be a way to get out of this! He resolved himself to escape; convincing himself it was better to go down in a hail of glory than to help this bastard achieve his goals. It placated Rahmin for now, because they had unloaded about one hundred forty million dollars' worth of gold from the Ambassador. The armored truck in front of them labored up the slight hill, the six thousand pounds of gold causing its automatic transmission to shift down into a lower gear with a pronounced 'clunk"!

Peña reached down, pretending to pull up his socks. He felt for the keys he had been carrying there every day now for almost two weeks. He had been sitting on a bench, dressing after a workout in the gym set up for residents of the secure dormitory residence where he lived. The ever-present security person assigned to Peña always took a seat in the gyms' lounge area as Peña showered and dressed. One biologist from the lab, an Indian named Gupta, had gone to the sauna, forgetting to snap the lock shut on his locker. Peña, having just returned from the weight room, noticed the locker door was ajar as he was changing back into his white lab suit. When he reached up to close it, he noticed there was a set of keys lying in plain sight. Without thinking, he grabbed the keys, taking care to wipe his fingerprints off the metal door of the locker after he clicked it shut. Entering the restroom, he examined the keys as he sat in a closed stall. There were six keys on the ring, along with a cheap plastic key ring. One key was a door key to a house or an apartment; one had a stylistic 'H' Peña recognized as the symbol for Honda. One of the other keys drew his scrutiny. He had seen a similar key used often by the security people escorting him between the residential building and the lab building. It was larger than the rest, an odd gray-green color he recognized as titanium, and it had the logo of Global Chemicals etched into the side. While key cards controlled access to the exterior doors of the residence dormitory, the titanium keys operated all the interior doors. This key accessed all the individual residence rooms, including the kitchen, janitor's closets, and offices. Gupta having the key in his possession meant Rahman's security detail, must trust him. He did not know what the other keys were for, so with a trace of desperation, he removed both the Honda key and the titanium key from the ring and buried them in his sock. The other keys he put in his lab coat, and made his way back to the lounge, telling his guard he needed to get back to the lab.

He had been doing experiments with acid to determine the purity of the gold the 'process' was producing and had several large bottles of acid on his lab desk. Taking a bottle of sulphuric acid, he filled the bottom few inches of a large open beaker. With a quick glance around to make sure he was alone, he reached into his lab coat and removed the remaining keys, dropping them into the beaker of acid. A sudden sizzling sound rushed from the beaker, and bitter fumes poured into the air around his table. With a flick of a switch, the fume hood kicked on, sucking the fumes out, as Peña watched the keys dissolve into small particles. In less than a minute, they dissolved, leaving only the plastic keyring which he placed into a heavy metal pan and held over the Etna until it melted into an unrecognizable glob. He disposed of the residue in a hazardous waste container, confident his actions had gone unnoticed. Deep in the recesses of his brain, the keys dissolving impressed a memory into his subconscious. Little did he know it was an impression that would be very important in the hours ahead.

For now, as he rode in the limousine with Rahman, he was trying to figure out what to do. He had the framework of a plan mapped out in his head. He planned to use the titanium key to find a room in the dormitory building with access to a telephone, or the internet. Then, he would either call or email his wife and tell her to go to the FBI. They would at least keep her and his daughters safe. As for himself, he would need to get out of the residence building unseen. It was his biggest problem, finding a way out of the building without drawing attention from the security people. At the least, he would need a key card to open one of the exterior doors, and a disguise. He knew how to get one, and it would mean an all-out commitment to escape, there would be no turning back. Rahman would take an escape attempt as a personal affront and be furious. If it did not work, Peña felt sure it would cause his immediate execution. If he made it into the parking garage, it would be easy to get away from the port area. He felt confident if the biologist had taken the keys from the lab, or the residence area, the car would have to be in the parking garage. He had been watching the man, noticing he must be off on Saturday and Sunday because he did not stay in the dormitory those days. Every other day, he slept in a suite near Peña. If he took the man's car, in less than two hours' drive down the coast to Abu Dhabi, he would turn himself in

205

at the US Embassy. He was sure the story he had to tell would set off an investigation into his kidnapping.

The plan had problems, and he knew it. He knew there was no guard station on the floor; however, there were video surveillance cameras mounted at each end of the hallway monitoring his door. Once each hour the dull footsteps of a security guard passed as he did a door check on the hall, testing each door to make sure it was secure. Since there was a mechanical lock on the door and not an electronic key card, he believed no one had connected the door to an alarm. Although not intended to house prisoners, the security measures added for the residence dormitory were for his benefit. As far as he knew, he was the only person there against his or her will. His suite was on the fourth floor, and the windows sash would not open far enough for a person to get out. He had a small kitchenette equipped with a few basic implements. A microwave and a one-burner hot plate were the only appliances except for a small refrigerator. There was an alcove with a television displaying a few Arab channels, and radio off to one side, and an austere bedroom was on the other. He found nothing much useful in an escape attempt.

What he knew was the titanium key operated the lock on his door. After waiting three days from when he took it, he tested it out on the lock in the middle of the night. Although he didn't open his door, he saw the bolt slide back from the jamb.

Rahman talking in Arabic on his cell phone interrupted Peña's thoughts. His tone was becoming more and more animated during the short ride back to the residence building. The container dropped onto Rahman's SUV was causing quite a stir, as several Port Police cars were heading into the port with their lights flashing, as the armored car and its escorts left.

"Did you find out what happened?" Peña asked Rahman, expecting a rebuke for daring to ask. It surprised him when Rahman gave him an answer.

"Right now it looks as if the operator passed out for and hit the release lever. He is conscious, and he cannot remember anything after he got in the crane elevator. My people on the pier have vouched for him, so, for now, we will consider it an unfortunate mishap. Nothing for you to worry about, you are safe in the residence building."

"I guess safety is in the beholder's eye," Peña replied as the limousine pulled up to the residence building. His stomach churned as he realized with all the attention back at the pier, tonight might be his best chance to slip away.

Rahman watched as Peña's security guard opened the door to escort him to his suite. When the door shut, Rahman slid over and pushed the button to lower the tinted window.

"Mr. Peña!" Peña and his guard heard the window motor, and they stopped and turned to see Rahman's icy stare. "Remember one thing. I hold your safety and your family's in my hands. I trust you keep that in mind for the next few weeks as you address the problem we discussed earlier."

Peña just stared back as the window rolled back up, for a second he thought he might spit on the ground in front of Rahman. He clenched his jaw, watching the limousine roar away until his security guard motioned for him to enter the building.

Upon entering the building, Peña noticed a security desk in one corner of a small lobby. Sitting there, behind a bank of only four monitors, was the night's security crew, one to watch the desk and lobby, and the other two to make rounds. They would rotate, with each taking a turn at the desk, then doing the inside check, and the outside checks on an hourly schedule. It ensured there was always a fresh guard on each detail.

Peña noticed the man at the desk was about his height and build. He looked to be in his late fifties, hair still dark, the lines on his face from exposure to the sun formed deep creases in his skin. Peña picked up his pace to the elevator. This would be the night.

CHAPTER 49

The approaching flashing blue lights on Harbor Police cars caused Steve to freeze just as he was ready to pull out of the parking lot.

"Dammit!" He seethed, fearing he would lose the armored car in the maze of warehouse buildings and storage tanks further up the road. He waited for the cars to stop in the distance and then pulled out into the street. There was a little traffic ahead on the road leading to the warehouses, so he would not draw the attention a single vehicle might. He zipped up to the crest of the hill, slowing as he tried to decide which would be the best way to go. To his left, he saw a chemical tank farm with a concrete retaining wall built around three sides and a low office building with what looked like an underground parking area. Just beyond was what Steve guessed to be an apartment building. He saw people walking about inside, and several rooms had television sets on, the changing bluish hues visible through gauzy curtains in several units.

Then, a faint sound echoed through the buildings and tanks. He heard the unmistakable sound of the same backup alarm he had heard earlier, on the armored truck. From where he stopped, he observed a small windowless building built into a low area between the large chemical tanks and the parking office building. He saw the tank farm's retaining walls continue along one side, designed to shield the loading and unloading of the chemical trucks from the view of the adjacent offices. He coasted the pickup into the loading area, pulling the parking brake to stop, to keep the brake lights from coming on. The concrete wall would hide the truck, as there was no lighting on around the small building. He would go on foot, sticking to the shadows, quickly making his way around. The building seemed to have minimal exterior lighting, and no outside security personnel was present at all.

Steve heard the backup alarm start and stop twice more as the truck maneuvered to the loading dock, allowing Steve to zero into its location. It wasn't far off, in fact, it sounded as if it was under the office building beside him. He grabbed the small bag of equipment he had been carrying around from the seat beside him; he set off on foot beside the shadows of the concrete wall. He made his way around to the far side of the building, staying out of the line of sight of the security cameras he saw located high on each corner. Once he got around to the side of the building containing the ramp leading to the underground parking, he darted through an opening in the shrubbery to the side of the building. He inched his way along the edge of the building, trying to find a spot allowing him to enter unseen. It would be difficult, as the ramp descending into the levels beneath the structure opened to the level above. If he dared follow down the narrow sidewalk beside the ramp, any vehicle entering or leaving would come upon him. There had to be a better way. Another few feet ahead, and Steve came upon a concrete slab surrounding a large thick metal grate. He recognized it as an

208

electrical transformer vault, typical of anyone might see beside buildings on a city street. A transformer mounted at the bottom of a deep pit, sucked air through an open grate allowing ventilation and cooling air to circulate down in the pit. This one was no different. Steve shone his small flashlight down into the abyss beneath him, its beam strong enough to reflect off a large green transformer bolted to the floor below. He estimated it to be at least thirty feet to the bottom, and he knew there would be an access door from whatever level it was on. The grate had a large movable hatch section, secured by a solid billet steel padlock. To saw off the heavy lock would be difficult, and to break it would take time and tools, neither of which Steve had. What he had was a small lock picking set, which he unrolled from a cloth storage bag, and worked at the lock. He had not seen this lock before, and it was proving difficult to pick. He spent almost a half an hour working on it, trying not to become frustrated as he looked for the proper combination of small picks and levers. The voices echoing up the ramp told him whoever had come down into the garage was still there, and the muffled repetition of bangs and clicks gave him the impression work was going on below.

With a crisp mechanical snap, the heavy padlock came open. The sweat was dripping from his brow in tiny rivulets as he rolled up his little packet of tools. He strained to lift the large grate, heaving it up and leaning it against the wall of the building. Hidden from outside, the shrubs did an excellent job of camouflaging the area. Gripping a small flashlight in his teeth, he swung down on the metal rungs embedded in the wall and made his way to the bottom. It was further than he thought as he stepped into the last rung, shining the light onto the water-covered floor. Small pieces of trash plugged the drain creating a slimy reservoir on the floor.

It was close in the pit and the transformer was humming with an ominous sound, the fear of electrocution gave Steve an uneasy feeling as he brushed against the vibrating equipment. He crept to the far side of the pit where a single metal door appeared to be the entrance to the garage level. Again, Steve had to get his lock picks out and wedge them in the door's keyhole lock. There was a large PVC pipe attached to the wall near the door. It came up through the floor and ended with an elbow. Steve paid no attention to it, until a slight vibration in the floor and a sudden blast of air from the pipe, blew a blast of chilly air through his hair.

"What the...?" He looked up, annoyed at the distraction. The top of the pipe was open, and he realized it must be some kind of vent. It was white plastic and painted in block letters near the top were the letters BC2/DC2. Something seemed familiar about the lettering on the pipe, but absorbed in his lock picking he paid it no mind. He made a mental note, filing away a tidbit of information that may come in handy.

The door lock picked more than the padlock, and soon he was opening the door. Instead of opening to the garage area, it opened out into an electrical equipment room. He crossed the small room to another door, which he knew must open onto the parking deck. He twisted the doorknob to unlock the door and opened the door just a crack. When he looked out, the bright headlights of a vehicle were shining at him, causing him to jump back in a subconscious reaction.

One hand shielding his eyes, he looked through the crack in the door to realize he was face to face with the armored car. Not ten meters in front of him, the truck idled, with a ring of armed guards facing away from it in a semicircle. It looked as if the truck backed up to a small loading dock. Just beyond the loading dock, Steve saw the man identified as Abdul Rahman exit an elevator, although he did not see Peña. He saw the edge of a forklift waiting near the rear of the truck. The repetitive thud of objects dropped onto a wooden pallet and a muted conversation was the only sound audible to Steve.

After a short while, two men in blue jumpsuits closed the rear doors on the armored car. Steve closed the door he was spying from as he heard them get in the truck and drive away. The armed guards were all collapsing their perimeter around the loading dock, and Steve glimpsed the forklift, loaded with few stacks of small wooden boxes. Rahman waited for the forklift to enter the elevator, got in beside it, and closed the door, while the security guards remained on the loading dock. Beside them on the floor, were two of the small wooden crates. As soon as the armored car left, Steve heard a vehicle approaching. A few seconds later, a small sedan stopped at the loading dock, its driver an older-looking man, Indian or Pakistani. He opened his trunk, as the security guards loaded both of the small crates into it. Not a word broke the silence between them, other than a grunt of appreciation from the older man as he got back in the car and left.

Steve closed the door he was at, pushing the lock button as he sat back on his haunches to consider what he had seen.

His mind raced with an explanation. *"The elevator must go down to a vault. Under this garage would be a perfect place. Close to the pier, easy to defend, a solid concrete structure with at least five levels of parking and offices over top. This had to be the central distribution point. They bring cars in here all day long, loading a few bars of gold at a time, taking them to wherever they want. They would have to follow every car leaving here to see where the gold was going."*

He wondered where Peña was, he had not seen him on the loading dock. Was it was possible he was down in the vault? How was he involved in all this? He had posted the message on the internet. He wanted to be found.

The same slight vibration he had felt earlier interrupted his thoughts. Now he knew what it was, the elevator motors coming on. The air blowing on his head from the pipe in the transformer pit must have been from a vent to equalize the pressure of the elevator.

Steve was trying to decide what to do next. His assignment had been to find the main stockpile of gold, get any information on how it was being distributed and most difficult, and provide scenarios to help the CIA destroy or take

210

possession of the gold. He believed he had found the main stockpile and surmised runners must distribute it in small amounts. The old man had to be one of many. If everybody had been right in the hypothesis Boulez wanted to distribute gold to reduce its value, then he didn't care where it ended up, or who got it. As long as a government didn't take possession, it would serve its purpose anywhere in the world.

The question was how much gold was in the vault? Determined to find out, he waited for the vibration to tell him the elevator was returning. When he felt it, he again cracked the door open to see a black SUV and a black limousine parked at the dock. The elevator doors opened, and Rahman came out with two men dressed in blue jumpsuits. Rahman got into the back seat of the limo alone, while the security guards and the two other men got in the SUV. Two security guards remained behind as the vehicles roared out of sight. They walked to the backside of the loading dock, to a small glass-enclosed cubicle Steve had not noticed earlier. Through the tinted glass, Steve made out the flashes of a lighter as they lit cigarettes. A steel mesh curtain unrolled from a slot in the ceiling, closing off the entire loading dock.

Steve had seen enough for now. He needed to get back to the Pactolus and contact Tyson and Beebe. He would need help if he would find a way past all this security.

Making his way back to the transformer pit, he locked the door behind him. As he fumbled with the lock picking tools, he felt the smooth PVC vent pipe against his shoulder, surprised at cool it felt in the humid night air. It must be cold in the vault he thought to himself. Then he realized, the pipe connected to the vault! It was as if a comic page light bulb flashed in his head. His next step became clearer. With a little luck, he would soon know what was in the vault.

Satisfied with his nights' work so far, a sense of accomplishment entering his thoughts as he ascended the rung ladder to the surface. He had a confident feeling he would take Boulez down. It was just a glimmer of hope, and it felt good. He put the lock back on the grate, adjusting its position so it would look locked if anyone happened by.

Shadows and bushes concealed his progress as he made his way back towards the little pickup.

CHAPTER 50

Unable to eat anything, Peña took a swig of liquid courage from the bottle of vodka he kept in his suite. He was running his plan over in his head, trying to ignore the parts out of his control or subject to chance. When the guard making his rounds got there, Peña would have to be quick or it would all be over before it began. He inhaled and exhaled as possible, trying to suck in confidence and exhale the fear making his knees weak. Soon, he heard the dull sound of footsteps plodding on the hollow metal treads of the stairway at the end of the hall. It wouldn't be long now. He wiped the sweat from his palms and got a fresh grip on the table leg he had removed from the little coffee table in his room.

Before switching the light off, he looked around to make sure everything was ready. Earlier, he had packed a small bag containing several computer discs of notes, and a change of clothes. He parked the bag on the floor near the door where he could grab it as he ran out.

Peña twisted the titanium key he had been hiding, unlocked the door and then braced himself against the wall. He held his breath as he heard the guard stopped to try the knob on the door to the room across the hall from him, verifying it was locked. Peña's door was next, and it pushed in when the guard reached for the knob. A little surprised, the guard pushed the door open, bending in to peer into the darkened suite. He felt no sense of danger; in the three years he had been working here, he had never had a problem with Peña, much less any occasion to draw his weapon. He reached for the key on his belt, cursing the sloppiness of whoever locked the biologist up for the night. His head hung just past the door, as he called, "Peña! Peña?"

The split second it took for him to decide whether to enter, or just lock the door, was all Peña needed. He slammed the table leg down into the top of the guard's lowered head, making a hollow-sounding pop. The guard staggered back against the doorjamb with a loud grunt, and Peña grabbed his lapel and jerked him inside the room, closing the door behind him. The guard had fallen to his hands and knees, trying to find the walkie-talkie he had dropped, when Peña crashed another blow to the back of his head. With a sharp, "crack!" the table leg broke into two jagged pieces, one of which skittered all the way across the floor of the living room. The guard fell in a heap to the floor unconscious, with a rush of thick blood showing through the dark hair on the back of his head, making its way to the tile beneath him.

Peña worked with determination, turning the man over, and unbuttoning his uniform shirt. He peeled it off and slipped it over his own tee shirt. As planned, he was already wearing black pants similar to the guard's uniform, so he didn't bother with those. Then, he tied the man's feet and wrists with the cords he had removed from the window blinds, and dragged the unconscious man into the bathroom. Next, he took the keys attached to the guard's belt and hooked them to his own belt. The plastic key card for the exterior doors was on a lanyard around the guard's neck, and Peña reached down and snapped it off, stuffing it into his pants pocket. The guard was regaining consciousness, his moans becoming louder, a problem Peña had not foreseen. He assumed a severe clubbing to the head would have either have knocked the guard out cold for quite a while or maybe even have killed him. Peña didn't have time to remove another table leg to hit the man with, and he didn't think he was venal enough to kill him in cold blood.

He muttered to himself as he ran to his drawer and removed a pair of socks, winding them up into a ball. He returned to force the man's mouth open, and then he stuffed the socks between his nicotine-stained teeth. Then, taking a short piece of leftover cord, he wrapped a length around the man's head and tied the socks so the guard could not spit them out. The man strained to suck air through his nostrils, accompanied by a panicked wheezing sound. Even in his frantic haste, Peña realized the socks were close to asphyxiating him. The man was regaining his senses now, struggling against his bindings, and struggling for air. Peña removed the guard's pistol and holster, and pressing the gun to his bloody head, he leaned down close to his ear.

"If you don't lay still and be quiet, I will put one right behind your ear, do you understand?" Peña took a second to pull half of the roll of socks out of the guard's mouth. The man, who did not speak a word of English, nodded his head, indicating he received the message loud and clear. Then, he curled up in the shower pan, lying still as he watched the blood dripping from his head and running in a thin stream to the drain.

This had all taken just two minutes, and Peña was still worried. If the other guards in the lobby had been watching the monitors and had seen this guard open Peña's door and not come out, they would most surely be on the way. Since they had not tried to contact the guard on his walkie-talkie, Peña hoped they had not been paying attention. He figured his room was about the halfway point on the route of the guard's rounds, and each round took forty-five minutes to an hour, so at a minimum, he should have over twenty minutes before anyone would start wondering what happened to this guard who lay bleeding in his shower stall.

The rush of adrenalin from implementing his plan was diminishing now, forcing Peña to breathe deep to regain his composure. He wasted no time, methodically buttoning up the uniform shirt, and tucking everything in place. His confidence building, he strapped on the holster and grabbed his little bag, and the walkie-talkie from the floor. He opened the door a little, pausing to listen for any unusual noises.

Summoning courage from within, he stepped into the hallway with a determined step and pulled the door shut behind him. With a quick flick of his wrist, he held the small bag to his chest, trying his best to look nonchalant as he made his way towards the stairway at the end of the hall. Just as the security

213

guard would, he stopped to check each door as he made his way down the hall, knowing it was possible the guards in the lobby were watching on the monitor. Forcing himself to walk at a normal pace, he turned the corner at the end of the hall without looking back. The door to the stairwell was in front of him as he leaned against the wall, taking a second to catch his breath. He looked down at his feet, just now realizing the sticky substance on the sole of one shoe. He must have stepped in the blood back in his suite, and now he had tracked it all the way down the hall.

"Oh my God," He reacted in dismay. Taking a quick glance back up the hallway, only to see an obvious trail from his suite to where he stood.

"Keep going now!" He told himself as he ducked through the door and made his way down the stairs. His plan was to have time to find a room with a telephone in it and call his wife to warn her about his escape. It ruined his idea. If a guard came along and saw blood, it would only take a few minutes to get in his room and figure out what had happened. He planned to get out of the building and drive to Abu Dhabi as fast as possible. If he was quick, he could get out of the port area long before they figured out had a car. While they wasted their time searching for him close by, he would make it to the embassy, and safety. He was sure the embassy would help him get his family to safety. His confidence was growing by the minute.

Determination set in as, he made his way down to ground level, staying silent in the hollow stairwell. The stairway ended at a ground-level landing with an exterior exit which was a fire door. An alarm would sound throughout the building if a door opened. The local fire code would not allow a lock preventing egress in the case of a fire. Peña wouldn't need the key card to get out. The landing also had a door opening to the interior Peña hoped would afford him a quiet exit. He cracked the door to see what was on the other side, and when he did, the sound of excited voices speaking in a rapid Arabic staccato was audible from the far end of the hallway.

Peña froze, realizing the worst must have happened, causing panic to rise through him with an icy chill. All the commotion only meant one thing...a guard found the blood in the hallway, and the bound guard. Why hadn't they tried to contact the guard on the walkie-talkie? He yanked it from his back pocket to find the battery case was missing its cover. There were no batteries in it!" The security guards must have a prearranged call interval when they make rounds. When the guard whom Peña knocked out didn't check in, they sent another to look for him, and in the process discovered the blood.

Voices yelling from above snapped him back to attention. Above him, footsteps began pounding down towards him, and simultaneously the low-pitched whoop, whoop, whoop of the security alarm began sounding through the hallways.

214

"Good God, what have I done?" He cried to himself in despair. The sound of the approaching footsteps caused him to panic, so with no other choice, he bolted straight through the fire door. He shoved the door open to find himself outside, at the rear of the building. The door opening set off a piercing wail of an alarm, the cacophony fueling his desperate rush towards the parking garage. He ran crouched over as fast as the low shrubbery allowed, holding the security guard's gun in his hand. If he was going to go down, then he would take as many of these bastards along with him as possible!

CHAPTER 51

Steve stopped dead in his tracks when he saw a rear door on the apartment building ahead of him swing open. The light from inside the building chased a figure in dark clothes as he ran out of the door accompanied by a harsh pulsating alarm siren. A group of low bushes to one side offered Steve a little cover, and he dove in, crouching as low as possible. When he stuck his head through a thin spot in the foliage, it surprised him to see the man was running right for him, along the same pathway he had just used for cover.

"No way he saw me!" Steve said to himself in amazement, as the man got closer and closer. It was a short man, and he was looking back over his shoulder as he ran.

"He's not running after me, he's running away from someone!"

The rear door on the building slammed opened again, revealing three men silhouetted in the light, each holding a flashlight. They appeared to be searching the bushes near the door and shining the lights in wild arcs around the perimeter. The man running on the path was only steps from Steve and closing fast. Steve pulled his razor-sharp diving knife from its sheath near his ankle and flipped it open with a deft twist of his wrist. It locked with a metallic click as Steve steadied himself. If the men with flashlights saw the other man running from them, it would draw them to where Steve was hiding. He was determined not to let it happen. With a powerful lunge, Steve tackled the man as he ran by. It surprised him at how heavy he was. A soft grunt was the only sound emitted by the man as he hit the ground, the wind knocked out of him.

Steve caught the glint of black metal in the man's left hand, and he pounced on his back, pinning the arm to the ground. Even as he was tackling the man, he was considering whether he should cut his throat to ensure immediate silence. To do so, he would have to pull back on his head to expose the man's neck, but he didn't have enough arms. One held the knife, and the other was pinning the gun to the ground.

Steve waved the knife in front of the man's eyes, "Ekhrass, ekhrass!" Steve hoped he had said 'shut up!' with enough clarity for the man to understand.

Peña knew enough Arabic to realize the man whose forearm was pinning his neck to the ground was no Arab. He took a chance. "American," he whispered, "I'm an American!"

Steve grabbed the pistol from Peña's hand, keeping pressure on his neck.

"What the hell are you doing here?"

Peña was trying to look back over his shoulder enough to see who was holding him down and speaking with perfect English. "Are you American?"

"I'll ask the questions. Who are you?" Steve looked back around towards the building. The three men were waving their lights, one of them talking on the walkie-talkie. Soon they would fan out to look for this guy.

"My name is Peña, Alejandro Peña. They've been holding me here for over two years against my will. I have to get away!"

"Peña? You're the Peña Jason Boulez has his hooks into, the biologist?"

"How do you know that? Who *are* you?"

The noise of both alarms died out after a few minutes, and an eerie silence encompassing the darkness behind the building.

"I'm the guy who came to get your ass out of here. Come on, stay low, we have to move!"

Steve led the way back towards the chemical tanks on the far side of the residence building. The shadows afforded good cover, and the sounds of shouting from behind them meant more people had joined the search. They needed to get away from this area, now!

Steve pointed out to Peña the roof of the small pump building near where he had parked the truck.

"I didn't have time to introduce myself," he held out his hand. "Steve Ross, Customs and Immigration."

"You don't know how glad I am to meet you," Peña whispered, giving him a firm shake, "my friends call me Ali."

"Okay, Ali, I have a little truck parked down there. We have to get to it so we can get down to the backside of the pier before they can organize enough to catch us. Can you swim?"

"Swim?" Peña looked confused, "yeah, I've spent a lot of time in the pool."

Nearby, the roar of a large semi-truck coming around the corner intruded into their conversation. Two angry pulls of his air horn signaled the driver's displeasure at finding a vehicle in the loading rack of the pump house. Steve held his hand up for Peña to be quiet.

"No way we can get to the truck now, we will go to Plan B."

"Plan B? What is Plan B?" Peña wondered

"The plan after Plan A and I hope to come up with it any second now." Steve quipped.

They watched as a small Honda sedan with a rotating blue light on the roof drove up to the pump house, a powerful spotlight trained on the little truck. Two men got out with weapons and flashlights drawn and waved for the men searching behind the building to come over. Peña recognized the car as the same model he drove back in the States, a Honda Accord. Then he realized all at once, the key! Peña fished deep in his pocket for the precious Honda key, showing it to Steve.

"Look, Plan B!" He whispered.

"A car key? Are you telling me you have a car here?"

"No, it's a key to a Honda; I took it from a biologist that spends nights here during the week. He's inside, so his car has to be here in the garage. It's how I was planning to get away."

217

Steve took the key, and after holding it up to the ambient light to verify it was, in fact, an ignition key, he tucked it into a small pocket on his hip. "You know, I like you already, Ali! Let's get out of here."

Steve led Peña back around the dark perimeter to the edge of the parking garage. He was sure there would be security at the entrance, so they slipped back around to the grate over the electrical transformer. Steve removed the open padlock, and Peña reached down and lifted the heavy grate to the side, impressing a silent Steve with his upper body strength.

"Put the grate back when you come down," Steve directed as he lowered himself into the black pit. "It will take me two minutes to unlock the door."

He was glad he had done it before, so he knew just what technique to use on the lock this time. When Peña joined him, he gave the small flashlight over to him to hold as he worked the lock. In less than a minute, they were in the electrical room. Steve led the way to the exit, knowing there would be two security guards on the other side of the door at the loading dock entrance to the vault on high alert.

Steve motioned for silence as he opened the door just enough to verify there were two security guards. One was standing outside the small booth, and the other was visible behind the darkened glass of the security booth.

"We will take them out, are you up to it?"

Peña nodded. "Just tell me what you want me to do."

Steve looked around the small electrical room, noticing a coil of thick wire in the corner, and a small fire extinguisher mounted on the wall.

"Help me unroll the wire across the floor!"

They laid the wire out across on the floor, and Steve handed Peña his knife.

"Skin off a little of insulation from both ends of the wire."

While Peña worked on the wire, Steve found an electrical panel on the wall and removed the cover with the small universal tool he carried in his little bag.

"This will work just fine. I want you to wedge one end of the wire into the keyhole on the doorknob. Make sure it's good and tight."

"Okay, what's the plan, we juice them?"

"We will try. Come over here, and. I'll show you what to do." Steve waved for Peña.

"When I tell you to, I want you to hold the wire against this copper lug. Make sure you keep your hand off the bare metal, or you'll light up like a Christmas tree."

"Got it. How long should I hold it?"

"I'll wave you off. Once we get the first dude, the other one should come out of the booth. I'll jump him, and I might need your help if the first guy doesn't stay down."

"Right behind you!"

"Okay, wait for my signal."

218

Steve returned to the door and opened it just enough to see one of the security guards was still outside the booth.

"Okay, go ahead." He told Peña.

Peña wiped his sweaty hands off on his shirt and touched the wire to the copper lug. A small spark startled him for a second, but he held the wire tight. Steve took the little fire extinguisher from its hanger and heaved it with all his might against the rear door of the electrical room. The resounding thud and the clatter of the extinguisher falling against the floor were enough to get the immediate attention of the security guard. He looked at the door curiously, wondering who was in the room. Then, he walked over to the door, leaned in close, listening for any other sounds.

He heard nothing as he pushed the door with the edge of his boot. It seemed shut and locked, so he withdrew a bundle of keys from the lanyard attached to his belt. Searching for the proper one, he inserted it into the lock. With a sudden jolt, he stood straight up, his back arched, and his face contorted into a horrifying grimace. The electric charge forced his fingers to clench the key as if by an unseen, pulsating force. His eyes rolled back in his head, and his teeth ground shut, as he stood trembling. After what seemed an eternity to him, he lost consciousness, falling straight back onto the concrete floor. The other guard, watching from the booth, rushed out with his weapon drawn to kneel at the man's side. He did not understand what had just happened. Since he did not hear the noise of the fire extinguisher from the booth, it looked to him as if his partner was making a routine check of the door to the electrical room.

"Hussein, Hussein!" He called to the unconscious man, shaking his shoulder to wake him. His first thought was to summon an ambulance, and he stood to take the walkie-talkie from his belt. Just as he did the door to the electrical room burst open, and a large man stepped out, pointing a shiny black gun right at his chest.

Steve had been waiting behind the door, and when the man called out his associate's name, Steve knew it was time to go. He shoved the door open, surprising the security guard, who jumped back. The guard instinctively turned the muzzle of his weapon in Steve's direction. Even before the barrel finished its arc, Steve unloaded two rounds into the security guard's chest, knocking him flat on his back, spread eagle to the concrete. He was dead when he hit the ground, even before the echo of the last bullet stopped resonating in the garage.

Peña stood in the doorway of the electrical room, a look of shock on his face. The deadly violence he had just witnessed causing his face to turn white.

Steve knew they didn't have much time. He reached over and grabbed Peña by the shirtsleeve. "Come on, we have to find the car. Somebody must have heard those shots!"

They ran up the ramp to the next level, seeing only a few cars none of them Hondas.

"It should be on the ground level." Peña offered, "There's a covered walkway to the residence suites from that level."

"Okay, let's make it quick!" Steve said, grateful Peña had regained his composure and had no trouble keeping up with him. They passed the next two levels, each empty at this time of night because they housed the office workers and field staff of the chemical tank farm right beside the garage.

The exit ramp to the fourth level led them around a corner to several dozen cars parked neat rows. Behind one the ducked and waited for two cars with 'Port Security' in large letters on their doors to go down the entrance ramp.

"We better get our asses out of here, because they will find our two buddies down there any minute." Steve pulled the Honda key from his pocket. "I don't suppose you know which one it is?"

Peña took the key from him, pressing a small button on the plastic case. About halfway down the row across from them, they heard a chirping sound, and a silver-colored Honda's lights flashed. Peña handed the key back. "I believe it's that one."

Steve grinned as he gave Peña a good-natured shove.

"Let's go, smart ass!" Steve enjoyed Peña's sense of humor. Anyone who can laugh under these conditions was all right with him. They ran up to the Honda, and jumped in, the doors having been unlocked. Steve put the key in the ignition, and the little V-6 came to life. He looked over at Peña, who was fastening his seatbelt.

"I hope you don't get car sick, this might be a rough ride."

"The car ride doesn't bother me, it's lead poisoning I'm worried about!"

Steve laughed as he backed out of the space. There was only one exit for the garage, putting them on a perimeter road, which wound around the back of a group of large chemical tanks. When he stopped at a dark intersection, it relieved him to see the activity near the small pump house had moved off. The tanker truck had backed into the unloading area, and a long hose connected it to a pipe protruding from the side of the building.

"What's in all those tanks?" He asked Peña.

"As far as I can tell this is a major chemical transfer station. The ones I've seen from the lab windows have been acids. I gather a lot of it gets shipped out on boats to places like India and China. They use it in manufacturing processes."

The glare of headlights in their rear window interrupted the conversation. Two dark sedans cars had pulled up behind them with their headlights off. Now they both flashed their high beams on and turned on their rotating lights. A voice on an external speaker shouted an order in Arabic.

"They want us to get out!" Peña translated.

"I'm going to get out all right, hang on!" Steve mashed the gas pedal to the floor, causing the front tires to spin on the sandy asphalt. They took off with a lurch, the Honda's motor responding with a high-pitched whine as Steve wound out the gears. He knew it would be very difficult to lose the Police on the pier. Although it was huge, it was a closed-off control area. If they did not get to the far side, they would have no way out. No, they would have to get out of the port. If they got to the nearby town, Steve felt it would be easy to lose any pursuers in the narrow back streets. The lights of the Port Police cars followed in their direction, although not putting a lot of effort into a pursuit. After rounding a few corners, there was no sign of the flashing lights behind them anymore. Steve watched in the rear-view mirror for another mile, realizing the Port Police had given up. Perhaps they had not gotten the word about the escape. Unless Boulez had paid off all the port officials, the police were still a government entity. Boulez's people didn't expect the Police to put out a lot of effort into a private matter.

"The Port Police didn't come after us. It must mean Boulez doesn't control everything at the port. Once we left the port, they radioed a watch notice to the local police in this area. They told them we were burglars. We still have to be careful."

"Don't count on it," Peña said. "Rahman has his fingers in everything. He runs this place with an iron fist."

Steve slowed the car as they passed a small industrial area containing several construction storage lots. Neither he nor Peña saw the two black Mercedes pull from the shadows of a warehouse building, and into the road behind them. They were running with their lights off, the light of the stars was enough for the drivers to follow them down the black pavement that contrasted with the beige sand of the desert.

Soon, both of the more powerful Mercedes had both caught up with the Honda. They were following in a single file, and from the one behind the Honda, the passenger leaned out of his window, taking careful aim at the driver of the little car with a large handgun. When his sights lined up with the back of the driver's headrest, he pulled the trigger. In the same instant, a small dip in the road threw his aim off as he squeezed the trigger, causing the high-speed bullet to veer to the left, and the rear window of the Honda shattered into a million pieces, and a bullet whizzed by Steve's right ear and splatted into the windshield beside the rearview mirror. He and Peña flinched instinctively, ducking as low in the seats as Steve tried to see where the shot came from. Tapping his brakes, the red light lit up a familiar grille following not far off his bumper. He steered with his knees as he reached into the center console for the gun Peña had laid there and pulled back the slide.

"What was that?" Peña cried out.

"That was the lead poisoning you worried about!" He yelled as he handed the gun to Peña.

"Can you shoot?"

"I can try…" Peña took the gun and cocked the trigger.

221

"Hold it tight! Steve yelled. Put a few rounds in their direction, it should make them stay back a little!"

It was the first time Peña had ever fired a gun, and the power of the recoil surprised him when he pulled the trigger. The discharge, much louder than he had expected, stung his ears as he struggled to aim the gun at the car just yards behind him. Steve was veering from side to side, trying to block the dark sedan from coming up alongside. With the element of surprise gone, the Mercedes turned on its bright halogen headlights, blinding Peña. His first shot pierced the metal at the edge of the rear window, loosening a large chunk of glass. Trying to anticipate Steve's turns, he braced himself against the foot well and squeezed off three more rapid shots. One shot passed through the radiator of the Mercedes, careening into the plastic fuse box beneath the hood. It smashed a block of fuses, which caused the car to stall. The driver coasted to the side of the road, steam blowing from the small hole in the grill. The other car pulled to take its place, the driver shooting from his window. He kept the sedan behind their rear right corner, a position making it difficult for Peña to get off a shot.

Steve knew the driver of the sedan was trying to shoot his tires out, he heard several shots hit the back of the Honda. Peña was having a hard time holding on and getting off a shot from the passenger seat. They were traveling at over ninety miles an hour, the sedan behind them was half in the lane, and half on the shoulder. A sturdy guardrail lined both sides of the road, built on an elevated bed of rocks to keep it out of the marshy coastal sand.

Up ahead, Steve's eye caught the red glow of a vehicle's rear reflector. As he approached a curve, he saw it was a truck parked on the narrow shoulder, a white handkerchief tied to its door handle. He inched the car over towards the right side, blocking the truck from the view of the sedan behind him.

"Sit down and hang on!" He shouted to Peña as he gripped the steering wheel with both hands, jamming the gas pedal to the floor with all his might. They headed for the rear of the parked truck, causing Peña to cover his face with his arms in what would have been a futile attempt to protect himself. Steve let off the gas a few seconds before impact, causing the sedan to close the gap between them to only a few feet. Peña yelled in fear as the Honda came to the brink of collision. Steve's timing was almost perfect, he waited just a hundredth of a second too long before he jerked the wheel to the left. The rear wheels of the Honda skidded, and with a loud 'Bang!' it clipped the back corner of the truck. The Honda spun around in two 360-degree circles, with Steve losing all control. On the first rotation, the sickening sound of metal slamming against metal seemed to come from every direction. A second rotation brought the sight of a massive crash, and the orange light of an explosion flashed in the windshield. The Honda stopped spinning, with the sound of small pieces of metal raining down in the road, and on the roof of the Honda. The truck had lurched forward, now rolling to a gentle stop near the Honda.

Peña slowly uncovered his face, the destruction laid out before him unbelievable. What he assumed to be the dark sedan was a crumpled twist of unrecognizable metal, flames shooting from every crevice of the mangled body. The torso of a human being was lying face down in the road, its dangling entrails exposed in a grotesque display across the road.

"Are you okay?" Steve asked as he tried to restart the stalled car.

Peña gave him a blank look, and in a barely perceptible voice, and answered: "I have t-to call m-my wife."

223

LeGionne was an elegant restaurant, in one of the most exclusive five-star hotels in Abu Dhabi. Obtaining a reservation for most people takes at least a month in advance. Only then may they sample the exquisite French cuisine of Chef Daniel LeGionne. When Rahman called earlier in the day to talk with the owner, there was no problem getting a special table set up for Boulez and his party. He loved the perks of being wealthy, even though it was in direct conflict with his Muslim beliefs. He justified his actions and shortcomings as a necessary means to an end.

Jason Boulez was eating a filet mignon steak smothered with blue cheese, as fine as he had ever tasted. He barely had to chew the succulent meat, but he wasn't enjoying it. Rahman, impeccably dressed as he sat across from him, making small talk about his oldest son's accomplishments at the university in Germany he attended. Distracted, Boulez tried his best to concentrate on what Rahman was saying, the excitement and anticipation of what he had planned for the next few weeks were gnawing at his stomach. Although he would never drink alcohol in a public place, he longed for the soothing feeling a shot of aged Scotch would give him.

It was a small restaurant, and he was glad to see Benny Chavez sitting at a table in a corner near the entrance. Chavez was in a position where he could see Boulez, watch the front door, and watch the kitchen door. The slightest hint of trouble would bring out the considerable firepower concealed beneath his suit jacket. Even though Chavez was in his doghouse, Boulez felt secure with him present. He was aware of, although not concerned with Rahman's security detail, which he observed through the large windows facing the street. By necessity a perceptive man, he noticed a flurry of activity among the men as he caught glimpses of them between the window supports. They were standing around the two stretch limousines parked in front of the hotel, talking on cell phones, and glancing back inside. Something was up, and they were debating whether to risk interrupting his meal.

"Rahman, look outside." Boulez interrupted.

Rahman turned to see the head of his security on a cell phone, his face showing obvious impatience as he gestured with his free hand.

"It's woman trouble," Rahman guessed without concern. His lack of concern wouldn't last long.

Rahman's head of security, Hussain entered the restaurant, bringing Chavez to his feet. Anybody carrying a loaded firearm, even a trusted person in the organization, drew a cautious look when near Boulez. Chavez stepped in front of him, hand inside his jacket, and whispered in his ear. He looked over to Rahman, who gave him an almost imperceptible nod. Nodding back, Chavez took Hussain by the arm, bending close to his ear.

Chavez was almost happy with the information the man told him. This would draw the attention away from him, and the situation his flunkies had screwed up back in Key West and beyond. He walked over to Rahman to tell him the news from the security.

Rahman stood as Chavez and Hussain approached, and Chavez said in his gravelly voice," Mister. Boulez, sir, I am sorry to interrupt, we must speak."

Boulez spread his hands open, waiting for the response.

"Sit down Abdul. So, what is going on, Benny, what is so important? We are almost finished here." Boulez had an impatient look on his face Chavez had seen before. Whatever it was, it had better be important.

"Sorry, sir, Hussain apologized. I have to tell you we had a problem out at the port. The biologist, Peña, has escaped."

"What?" Rahman, who had not finished sitting, jerked straight up, incredulous. "He would never do that, he knows what would happen!"

Chavez was gloating inside; happy he was not the one in the hot seat for a change.

Hussain continued, "The Port Police say he had help, and they had a car. They followed him to the port limits and notified our security. We still have people out looking for them. As of a few minutes ago, there is no sign of them."

Rahman stood from his seat again, livid. "That scum bag!" he seethed. "He must have been planning this for a long time. He screwed with the microbes, and now he's running like hell. We have to find him!"

Boulez, with a calmer head, jumped in, addressing Hussain. "Did you said you they followed them from the port?"

The man looked uncomfortable addressing Boulez face to face. "N-Not exactly. We had two cars in the area. Our people saw them on the coastal road, heading in this direction, and tried to chase them down. I don't know whom the biologist was with, but they put a bullet in the radiator of one of our cars, and then they blew the second one all to hell. The local police are still trying to figure out how many people were in the car. There are arms and legs and guts on the road everywhere."

Boulez's mind was spinning. "He must have found a way to communicate with the FBI or Interpol. He told them he is captive here, held against his will. You can bet his wife and children will not be walking around in Central Park, now. They'll be under the tightest security. Getting him away from us is one thing, not everybody is capable to transport him out of the Emirates. We have many people in our pocket, so this happened with the diplomatic auspice of a foreign country. The question is whose embassy?"

Rahman eased into a chair, the initial shock of Peña's escape wearing off. He addressed his security: "The American Embassy. If he headed in this direction, he was trying to get to an embassy. He is an American citizen; the American

225

Embassy would be the best place for him. We have people everywhere, if he's on the road you will find him. Go and don't disappoint me!"

The security guard had a sinister look on his face. "And when we find him...?"

"Alive. Alive if possible," Rahman saw the question in the man's eyes, "We still have a use for him. He is not a man who can do this alone. Bring them back alive."

Rahman watched his security leave, and then he turned to Boulez, who looked tired. He knew he should at least try to mitigate the damages. "It's a problem, but maybe not as great as we think. As for Peña, he has no way to know what we are trying to do with the gold. The only thing he knew is we have a lot. Anyone he tells will look at this as a profit-making enterprise. We have established the 'process' onboard each ship, and they are all producing good quantities of gold. The people running the programs are doing a great job. Even if production continues to drop, we can meet our timetable. I'm sure we can find Peña or another biologist just as good if you want to continue after Ramadan. For now, we have to concentrate on moving the gold, if it is what you wish."

"I hope to not have these problems. If we are careful, we will not expose our plan. Already I am seeing news stories telling of gold originating on the Arabian Peninsula helping to drive down world prices. The Westerners, the Jews, they are no fools. If they can pinpoint the source of the gold, they will take steps. Legal, illegal, sanctioned, unsanctioned, even militarily, it makes no difference. They will do whatever they need to do to safeguard their economies. We have begun our assault, and we have seen it bear fruit. We have caused billions upon billions of value to disappear in a puff of smoke. Now we must strike with a killer blow. We must not give them time, or opportunity to counter what we do. Once we get the gold to our distribution points, it will be impossible to stop us!"

"Is the gold we have now enough to do it?" Rahman asked.

Boulez contemplated the question for a few seconds before answering. "I'm not sure, maybe. If we can flood the market now, and nobody will know we can't keep the production levels up, it will have the same effect. Gold will lose its true value, the value of its security. If no one is sure where the bottom is, no one will be willing to invest in it."

"Financial anarchy," Rahman smiled, "even better than political anarchy!"

226

CHAPTER 53

The Honda was flying down the four-lane road, this time Steve kept a wary eye in the rear-view mirror, and checked every crossroad for suspicious vehicles. Even though they were over five miles from the scene of the crash, a pale orange glow was still visible on the horizon.

"I need to warn my wife," Peña repeated. When Rahman finds out I've tried to escape, he will send someone to kill her and my daughters. We have to stop at a phone!"

"They kept you here, by threatening little girls? They are the worst pricks. Anyway, we can't stop now, not here. Can you hand me the bag on the back seat?"

Peña snatched the small backpack Steve had been wearing when they ran into each other. He hauled it to the front seat where Steve reached in a zippered compartment and brought out the small satellite transceiver stashed there.

"Keep an eye out for any approaching vehicles." He instructed Peña as he thumbed in the code to Robert Beebe's encrypted cell phone. Although it was only a few seconds, it seemed as if it took an hour for the connection to make its way through the series of buzz tones, clicks, and rings. As he waited Steve noticed the smell of salt air…they were close to the ocean.

After a quick double beep, Beebe's sleepy sounding voice answered with a cough: "Khak, khak! Steve! Sorry…"

"You don't sound so good."

"Terrible cold, what can I do for you? We sent the IDs on the pictures you transmitted, did you get them okay?"

"I got them, and even better, I got Alejandro Peña, he's sitting right here beside me!"

"Excellent work Steve, I'll find out how later."

"Look, Beebe, we have a problem here," Steve interrupted, "You need to get out to Peña's family. He has a wife and two daughters Boulez has been threatening to kill if Peña doesn't cooperate. He's afraid they will make good on it now he got away. Can you do it like yesterday?"

"I'll put it in motion as soon as we hang up. They'll be under guard and on their way to a safe house as soon as they can be located. Do you want to save a few minutes and tell us where they are?"

Steve handed the phone to Peña. "It's Robert Beebe, CIA. Tell him where he can find your family."

As Peña spoke to Beebe, the Honda started to lose speed. Fighting against the steering wheel, Steve struggled to keep the little car going in a straight line. Then, a rhythmic 'clap, clap, clap,' sound accompanied the smell of burning rubber, forced Steve to pull to the shoulder. Peña had given Beebe as much information as he remembered; afraid his wife may have had to move to a more economical

227

place in his absence. Beebe promised to do everything in the departments' power to get them to safety, a promise that gave Peña a glimmer of optimism. He handed the phone back to Steve.

"Beebe, Ross here. We have to go. I'll be back in touch soon." He didn't wait for an answer as he flipped the cover down on the transceiver. Peña was already out of the car, staring at the shredded rear tire on the Honda when Steve came around the back.

"Bullet must have grazed it. It took a while to blow."

Steve looked around in the darkness, struggling to read a sign advertising a marina, just ahead on the side of the road. With a glance up and down the flat road, it relieved him to see there were no headlights within sight. At least not yet, he was sure there would be all hell breaking loose as soon as they discovered the wreck. He ran to the back of the car to open the trunk.

"Let's hope the spare survived-keep a watch on the road and I'll try to change the tire." The trunk opened to a black hole, the courtesy light shattered into a dozen pieces. Steve felt around in the darkness, coming across one small wooden box, and then another. They were the size and shape of ammunition crates, and when he tried to slide one out of the way, its weight convinced him what it was.

"I don't know what the guy you got these keys from was into, but he has a trunk full of ammo, we were riding on a bomb back there!" Steve took the first box out, setting it on the ground behind the car. He pulled the second box closer to him, feeling a piece of damaged wood along the side.

"Must have taken a bullet," He thought as he gathered it up, sensing it may not hold together enough to get it free of the trunk. *"That's all I need now, live ammo bouncing around."* He squeezed the box tight as he picked it up, intending to set it on top of the first box. As it cleared the lip of the trunk, it started to come apart, and Steve fumbled with it until it fell to the ground with a solid 'thump!'

The sound brought Peña back to see what had happened, and he found Steve on his knees staring down at the broken box. Almost luminescent in the ambient light, were six reddish bricks splayed across the asphalt.

"I'll be damned," I thought he was carrying ammunition. "He's got gold bricks here!" Steve exclaimed.

"And six more in the other box, I'd say!" Peña squatted down, picking up the box. "Ugh, this must weigh at least eighty pounds!" He slammed the box to the pavement, the gold bars inside sliding out of the box with an almost musical clatter.

"Do you think he was stealing them, would he be that crazy?"

"He didn't need to steal. I saw your friend Rahman give them to him. Before I met up with you, I was watching them load boxes into a vault. At least I think it was a vault. They saved these two boxes back and loaded them into a silver-colored car. I didn't see what kind of car it was, so now it turns out to be this car. I'm betting Rahman gave these to him to spread around. He was one of many…"

A spark of light on the horizon caught Steve's eye, making him pause mid-sentence.

"Car coming, come on, help me throw this stuff in the sand and cover it up!" They buried the bars by digging a small trench in the loose sand with their bare hands, and after placing all except one side-by-side, they threw a deep layer of sand on top. When they finished, it was impossible to see where they disturbed the sand.

"Good enough. Grab your gun, let's head for the marina." Steve pointed to the sign ahead. Steve was holding the last brick upright in his palm, as a waiter might hold a tray of food.

"Evidence." He said as he caught the curious look on Peña's face, not waiting to give him any further explanation. Although there were no boats in sight, he had been hearing the familiar clanking of mast rigging hitting against the hollow aluminum masts in the distance as the gentle breeze rocked the sailboats. He took his backpack and gun from the Honda and led the way across the sand toward the marina. The car's lights were still over three miles away Steve calculated as he glanced back over his shoulder. There wasn't much time.

Peña was breathing hard as they made it to the marina gate. The gate was a rolling gate, the type opened by a card, and the perimeter of the parking area enclosed by a tall chain-link fence with three strands of barbed wire jutting out from the top.

"Can you make it over?" Steve asked as Peña wheezed beside him. Peña could only nod, as Steve entwined his fingers and bent low, offering a foothold for Peña.

"Try to swing over in one movement so the barbed wire doesn't get you."

Peña placed his foot in Steve's hands, bounced twice, and then nodded he was ready. With a mighty heave, Steve propelled the smaller man up towards the top of the fence. Peña could grab the top strand of barbed wire, and with luck, continued the push from Steve to land crouching atop the wire fence, the wobbling wire determined to throw him off balance. He regained his equilibrium and jumped to the ground, rolling over in the sand to help absorb the shock. Standing to his feet, a slight sprain of his ankle sent a dull, unpleasant pain up his leg.

"You okay?" Steve asked as he tossed his backpack over for Peña to catch.

"I'll make it, as long as you don't throw the brick over!"

"No way, my man, the brick is coming under." He slid the gold brick under a gap in the fence, and then climbed the fence overhand, reaching up to grab the barbed wire with both hands. Two bounces gave him enough inertia to swing himself up to the top of the wire, and springing against the taut wire, he jumped to the ground beside Peña.

From down the road, squealing brakes, the headlights of two vehicles, and the rapid jabbering of the occupants were more than enough to announce the search party had arrived.

"You head to the docks," Steve pointed as he picked up the brick, "we need a boat." The marina was not large, with berths for at the most a hundred and fifty boats, none of them over thirty-five to forty feet long. Small low voltage mushroom lights, mounted at short intervals around the edges lit several workboats tied up along the bulkhead. A line of pleasure boats up in the berths of finger piers extending out perpendicular from the main bulkhead. Steve chose the pier furthest from the small building, which appeared to be the dock master's quarters. There was a light shining in the window, but no sign of any human activity.

They ran out onto the dock, with Steve quickly assessing each boat as they passed by. He was hoping to find a 'go fast', the term ICE used for the high-powered speedboats drug smugglers had a penchant for using. They were not much more than slick hulls and a couple of high horsepower engines and capable of speeds over one hundred miles an hour over smooth water. No such luck here, most of the boats berthed here appeared to be older cabin cruisers.

Steve held his arm out to stop Peña near the end of the dock. He was looking at a small open console sport fisher. A Grady White, it was only about twenty-five feet long, and it had two 225 horsepower outboards hanging from the stern, enough power to outrun anything in the marina.

"This is the best we will get."

He unzipped the access panel in the canvas cover and crawled in. Peña came in beside him. Exploring on his hands and knees in the dark, Steve felt a carpeted storage area in the gunwale beside him and lay the gold brick in it. He then groped in his backpack looking for the small flashlight. It was pitch black inside the boat's canvas cover, not even a hint of light visible around the tarp.

"I don't suppose they left us the keys," Peña whispered, already knowing the answer.

Steve found his light and adjusted the focus to a narrow beam. He shined it on the ignition switch. "Not a chance, we're not that lucky."

"Can you hot-wire it?"

"I'll tell you what. If you can get a bunch of little bugs to shit gold, then I can damn sure spark these bad boys up!"

Peña chuckled, "I should have expected it. What can I do?"

"Drop those outboards down, as quiet as you can, then untie the lines."

Back outside, it took Peña a few minutes to figure out how to lower the heavy motors into the water. His task completed, he made his way around the narrow ledge on the boat serving as a walkway and unhooked the lines from the small stainless steel cleats holding them. The current was pulling the last line tight, making it difficult to unhook. As he fumbled with it, the harsh beams of

230

headlights cut through the black night over his head. Two sets of headlights had pulled up the automatic gate at the entrance to the marina.

Two angry blasts on the horns brought the dock master, in boxers and a tee-shirt, to his door. After a brief exchange, comprised of a threatening sounding yell from the cars, the gate came to life, sliding open at what seemed to be a maddening slow pace. Peña crouched beside the cabin cruiser next to him, watching as several men fanned out, running towards the main bulkhead of the finger piers. His experience told him they were all holding one hand out in front of themselves they were armed and ready.

"Uh oh!" He muttered under his breath as he scooted back under the canvas to Steve. "We have company…five or six guys with guns. They'll be coming this way soon." He was close to hyperventilation.

Steve was holding the flashlight in his mouth as he twisted two wires together. He took it out and turned it off, knowing it would be a dead giveaway if anyone saw it from outside the boat. The thin canvas would glow as if it was a lampshade.

"Don't panic, we'll be all right. Are we ready to go?"

"Yeah, yeah, come on, let's go!" In his excitement, Peña had forgotten he had not released the last line. From further down the pier, Steve heard the echo of hard-soled shoes on the wooden dock approaching, hesitating, and approaching with a staccato rhythm. He chambered a round from the magazine of his gun, tucking it into a back pocket for easy access. A move would soon save both their lives. Reaching to his ankle, he removed the diving knife and cut a long slit in the canvass over his head. Poking up from a crouch, his view blocked by the cabin cruiser next to them, he glimpsed at least two men maybe ten or twelve slips down the pier. He said a silent prayer, as he got ready to push the starter button. The boat was clean and new. If the boat's owner was a stickler for cleanliness, it meant he was a stickler for keeping his mechanicals in good working order. Steve needed the boat's motors to start on the first or second try in order for them to have time to get out of range.

"Hang on." He said in a low voice and pushed the red starter button. The whine of the electric starter motors broke the night's silence when Steve mashed the button with all his might as if the extra force would help start the outboards. With a roar and a puff of white smoke, the twin engines came to life, startling the men down the pier. Steve rammed both throttles forward, and the boat stern dropped as the propellers grabbed hold of the brackish marina water. The small boat lurched forward, and then slammed to a halt, the slack in the nylon dock line snapping taut. Steve held on to the windshield as the boat jerked sideways, then grabbed the edge of the canvas to steady himself. He glanced in dismay to see Peña had missed a line. It stretched tight as a piano wire, still tethering them to the dock. The half-inch thick nylon rope had a tensile strength of seven thousand pounds, much more than the motor's ability to overcome in such a short space.

231

Although the motors were revving at top speed, they did not mask the loud "POP, POP, POP!" sound of semiautomatic gunfire. Steve sensed bullets rushing through the air near him and ducked. He came up with his gun in hand, seeing the muzzle flashes of guns coming from near the back of the cabin cruiser. His eyes followed the bright yellow spring line holding them back, to the stainless steel cleat near the stern. It was too dark to see anyone on the pier, so his hand aimed toward the flashes and peeled off four shots in rapid succession. Whoever was shooting at them ducked in behind the cabin cruiser for cover as Steve continued to pull the trigger. He knew he had thirteen shots, and he meant to make use of them. As fast as he pulled the trigger on the .40 Smith & Wesson, he drove lead into the fiberglass beside the cleat. The throttles were still at full speed ahead, and with his left hand, Steve steered the bow of the boat towards open water. His gunshots kept the pursuers pinned behind the cruiser until with a loud 'CRACK!' the cleat gave way.

Again, the stern dipped as the propellers grabbed water, this time the boat zoomed away from the pier. Steve answered several more muzzle flashes from the dock with a hail of bullets. He pulled the trigger until he emptied the magazine, only then turning to see where he was steering the boat.

"Ugh!" He cried, jerking the wheel as he barely missed hitting a buoy marking the entrance to the inlet surrounding the little marina. He cleared the jetty, heading straight out into the Arabian Sea. It had become cloudy, so now there was no separation at all between the black water, and the black sky. It felt to Steve as if he was heading into the ebony abyss of hell. The deep water was rougher than Steve had expected, and the waves bouncing the little boat caused his feet to slip on the fiberglass floor. When he felt safe, he throttled back, looking down through the slit for Peña. Instead of the clean white surface he had been crawling around on earlier, he detected the black streaks of a viscous fluid running across the floor in several spots. Whatever it was, it was causing him to slip around on the deck.

"Ali, are you okay?" Steve worried about the dark mass lying prone, his body contrasted against the white insides of the boat. There was no response from Peña. Steve took out his knife and cut several slits in the canvas cover, an ominous feeling in the pit of his stomach. From his front pocket, he took out the little flashlight, cupping his hand around the lens before he turned it on. He had to be careful not to shine a light in the dark where it would be visible for miles. He reached down to find Peña lying still on his back.

"Peña... Ali?" There was no response. Steve kept the light as low as possible and shined it on Peña's face. Then he realized what was so slippery. Blood covered Peña's forehead and the left side of his face. His eyes were half shut, and there was a small stream of blood dripping off his ear. He had taken a round to the head.

232

CHAPTER 54

A powerful beam of light stabbed through the pitch-blackness. Steve looked back towards the shore, which was at least two miles away. The running lights of at least two small boats were in the water, one of them shining a spotlight in wide arcs into the hazy blackness beyond. Steve realized the light did not have enough power to reach him at such a distance, and he didn't want to find out. He reached down to Peña's wrist, encouraged when he felt a strong pulse. Unzipping the top section of his wet suit, he slipped out of his black tee-shirt and wrapped it around Peña's head. Steve folded the piece of canvas he had cut from the boat cover to make a small pad, and Peña moaned as Steve laid the injured man's head down on it. It would be difficult to keep him from rolling around on the deck as the little boat jumped from wave to wave. There was no choice for now. If Peña's injuries were serious, he would die. Steve had come too far to jeopardize the mission now. He had to get back to the Pactolus... now.

Steve found a small bucket in the stern compartment, and he used it to dip into the seawater surrounding them. He sloshed it on the small deck, washing Peña's blood through a scupper and into the black water.

"I'm sure it will wake up any sharks sleeping around here." He quipped tossing the bucket down. He risked a quick look with the flashlight, noticing Peña's head seemed to have stopped bleeding, or at least the shirt was soaking up the blood. Peña's eyes remained closed, while his mouth moved as if he was trying to speak. Whatever it was, it was not loud enough to overcome the noise of the motors idling on the stern.

"Hang on bro, hang on. I will do my best to get us out of this." Steve eased the twin throttles forward, trying to minimize the boat's movement as much as possible. Checking for the boats he assumed were searching for him, he watched them as they hugged the shoreline, the spotlight alternating between sweeping the open water and checking hiding places on the uncrowded shoreline. He was not concerned about them now, confident the twin 225s on the center console would outrun them. Pointing the little boat towards the Jebel Port, he saw the glow of its lights visible against the blackness several miles ahead. He would stay close to shore to avoid the slim possibility he would show up on radar.

Although it only took forty minutes to get to the main channel of the Jebel Port, Steve was getting tired. He fought for balance as he powered the boat up and back to maintain a smooth ride and kept watch behind him in both the air and water for any pursuers. There were several large ships and barges in the channel which forced Steve to turn on his running lights. Someone would report a boat running without lights and draw a visit from the port police, not what he needed right now.

Steve powered down to check on Peña, who had moved a little now. He had braced a foot against a bench at the back of the boat, and his arm was clinging to the storage area of the gunwale. The light from the port area was enough for Steve to see Peña's eyes were open, although he didn't seem to focus.

"Ali... Ali...Can you hear me?" Steve whispered.

"Wa..." Peña's voice was only barely audible.

"I said, can you hear me, are you all right?"

Peña shook his head in slow motion. "Wa-water, please water."

Steve realized the loss of blood made Peña dehydrated and woozy. "Hold on man, I'll see what I can find."

Steve pulled the snaps loose holding the remaining canvas cover on. Working his way around to the bow, he found what he knew every fishing boat had: a drink cooler. He tossed the canvas overboard and opened the cooler. It was still too dark to see inside, so he stuck his hand in to find several aluminum cans floating in lukewarm water. He held a can up to the dim light to see it was a brand of cheap European beer. He picked two others out, both beers as well.

"Crap, he can't drink beer." Steve thought as he tossed the can back with a splash. Then it hit him. The cans were floating in the water, no doubt water from bagged ice... freshwater ice. He popped the top on a can and drained it overboard. Filling it with the water from the cooler, he took it back to Peña.

"It might not be too clean, but it's all we have for now. Just take a sip or two."

Peña looked as if he was drunk as he tried to hold the can to his lips. Steve helped him, tilting the can until water flowed from Peña's mouth, dripping to his shirt. All Peña could muster was a faint nod of thanks, as he lay his head back on the canvas.

The sound of a far off helicopter brought Steve back into focus. He had to get back to the Pactalus before daybreak. If not, he would be an easy target to spot from the air. There were not a lot of pleasure boats active at this time of the day. He spotted a large ship headed to the port and set a course to fall in behind her. A few minutes of choppy water and careful seamanship over the huge wake she left, brought the small fishing boat to calm water behind the great ship. Steve followed at a safe distance until he saw the group of pleasure boats moored off to the port side. There, right where he left her, the Pactolus bobbed in the calmer shallow waters.

Steve approached the sailboat, looking for any sign of compromise. It looked as he left it, including the boat hook he had left propped up against the main hatch an intruder would have to move to enter. Everything was in order as he sidled up to the hull and jumped aboard. He tied the center console alongside, and it surprised him to see Peña struggling to get to his feet.

"Take it easy, take it easy, Ali. Let me help you. Not many people can take one to the head and get up and walk around."

"Any skis in this thing?" Peña managed a grimacing smile.

"Come on fool; get your ass in here. You can do your comedy act later." Steve grinned with relief, sensing Peña's injuries might not be as bad as he had

234

thought. He hauled the weakened scientist onto the deck and found the hatch key he had secreted under a cushion. Opening the hatch, he helped Peña down the steep steps to a narrow berth.

"Are you going to make it?"

Peña nodded, "I think so, what happened?"

"All the joking around about lead poisoning and you got one in the kisser. A half an inch to the left and you would be on the breakfast menu for a bunch of crabs by now."

Peña looked confused, and Steve didn't have time for an explanation. "Lay down here until I get back, I have to get rid of the Grady White before daylight. Try not to bleed all over everything."

As he ran back up to the deck, his mind started racing. He had no way to deal with an injured man, and no way to get him to safety. He needed to return to the parking garage to verify the main cache of gold was there, and to determine how it where it was going. Part of his mission was to come up with an "end game" scenario, a way to get control of the gold, to prevent its distribution. Playing nursemaid to an injured scientist would make it even more difficult, if not impossible. The only advantage he had coming in here was insignificance. Just another drifter looking for short-term work, an itinerate wanderer. These waters were full of people down on their luck, dropped out of successful lives, or just wanted the unencumbered lifestyle of an ocean nomad. Now, any outsider would be suspect. Even though it had been accidental, they had to believe Peña had help to escape. The Pactolus showing up with a westerner, the same day Peña escaped would draw immediate scrutiny. Eventually, Boulez would come looking, and if he looked hard enough, he would find. Steve gritted his teeth as he jumped back into the Grady White.

"We'll meet up soon enough. This time it will be on my terms," he promised himself as he got the gold ingot he had stored in the gunwale and reached it over to the deck of the Pactolus. He untied, and shoving it away from the bigger boat, he eased the Grady White about fifty yards off her bow, facing to the open waters of the Arabian Sea. A small coil of line found beneath the seat was all he needed to tie her steering wheel solid. The fuel gauges read just over a quarter, it should give her an hour running time, Steve calculated as he reached down at the back of the stern, removing the small rubber drain plug from below the waterline. He pushed the throttles to half and dove off the side as she headed out to sea.

"Nice little boat, shame to waste her." He thought as he swam back to the Pactolus. The Grady White would travel out to sea until she ran out of gas, or hit another boat. As long as she was moving, no water would come in the drain hole until she ran out of gas. Then, in a matter of minutes, the water entering her bilge would overpower the small pump, and the weight of the motors would drag her to the bottom.

235

It only took Steve two minutes to get back to his boat, and as he climbed the ladder from the swim platform, he realized how tired he was. It seemed as if he had been going at full speed for over two weeks. He had had time to collect his thoughts, Jim Ragan, Beth Williams, Robert Beebe, all people who had a great influence on him in a short time. He needed time to process, time to unwind. Thank God, it would be daylight soon. His nocturnal duties required him to sleep during the day, and he was ready for it. First, he needed to hide the gold ingot, it might be hard to explain if anybody came snooping around. He carried it to the bow where he pulled the remaining two hundred feet of anchor line from the small storage space beneath the bow platform. Stuffing the gold to the back, he piled the jumble of rope on top. It would take a concerted effort to find it.

A light shining up through the deck hatch told him Peña must still be kicking. He opened the hatch and made his way down, eager to be out of the wet suit he had been wearing all night. The door to the head was open, water was running, and Peña was bending over the sink inside.

Steve's face appearing in the mirror startled Peña, who gave a little cry of surprise.

"Jesus, you scared the piss out of me!" Peña gasped.

"Sorry, I thought you heard me come in."

"The way my head is aching, I can't hear a thing."

"Let me look." Peña winced when Steve pulled his thick hair back, revealing a deep gash running from the near the corner of his eye to over his left ear. "Wow. That will leave a serious mark. The good news is it's not bleeding much now."

"Tell me something I don't know."

"Okay, try this. There's no way I can get you to a doctor. We will take care of this right here."

Peña hesitated, "I what I am afraid of. At least tell me what happened. The last thing I remember is climbing over the fence."

"Boulez's men found us at the marina. You must have missed a line, and when I started the boat, all hell broke loose. One of them got lucky and clipped you on the side of the head. Knocked you out cold... I thought you were dead, you lost a lot of blood."

"Head wound. You always bleed like a stuck pig."

"Right. You should lie down. Let me find the medical kit."

"I don't feel too bad. I must have a concussion. You wouldn't believe the headache I have."

Steve returned with a briefcase-sized medical kit, and a large bottle of clear liquid. "I know how you feel. One of Boulez's thugs gave me a going over a few days ago. Pistol whipped me."

That reminded Peña he didn't know who Steve was, and what he was doing in Port Jebel.

"So what is going on here? Who are you? How did you know about me?"

Steve was laying out bandages, a suture kit, and antiseptic. "You want to chit chat, or you want me to sew up the hole in the side of your head?" He set the bottle and a plastic glass in front of Peña. It was a bottle of Stolichnaya vodka. "It's all I have for a pain killer. Take it or leave it, it's up to you."

Peña looked at the large curved needle Steve was threading, and picked up the bottle, pouring himself a healthy shot. "I'll take it."

Steve took his time readying the sutures, not looking forward to sewing up Peña's head. He had received limited medical training in his Ranger days, the only real instruction he had in suturing was watching the many ones he had received himself.

Peña had several shots of the vodka, while Steve a makeshift operating table using the little table in the dinette. He directed Peña to sit and lay his head on a towel as he maneuvered a wall light to shine on the wound. Peña didn't move as Steve separated his hair, exposing a wide purplish gash.

"You ready for this?" Steve asked.

"Do I have a choice?"

"I can drop you off back at the pier. Take your chances."

"Thanks, but no thanks. Go ahead." Peña squeezed his eyes shut.

Steve pinched the two sides of the gash closed, and poked the needle through the swollen scalp tissue, as Peña stiffened and clenched his fists. Steve tried to work as fast as possible, trying to distract his patient with small talk.

"Tell me how you got here, what happened?"

Peña answered through his clenched teeth. "I was doing research at the University of Illinois on microbes reproducing using gold for an energy source… Aggh!" He complained as the needle snagged his skin.

"Sorry, my good man. Sit still, you only need a couple more. So how did you meet up with Boulez?" Steve hoped the conversation would distract him from the pain he was inflicting.

"I didn't. I never met the man until the other day. He's here in the Emirates. Early on, they approached me and offered to fund my research. I worked for them in the States, and when I informed them about my breakthrough concerning the microbes, they came in one night and grabbed me. They packed up my entire lab and shipped me over here. My wife knows I'm here, but not where. She gets a check from Boulez every month. I can't leave or have any contact with her, or anybody else. They don't want to take a chance I'll reveal the process I've developed. I know they threaten my wife and tell her they will kill her if this gets out."

"Don't worry about it now. If Beebe said he'll get them to safety, you can bank on it."

"Ok, now it's your turn. How did you find out about me?"

237

Steve had finished the sutures, he was dabbing at the wound with a ball of gauze as he applied an antiseptic cream. "Finished, unless you want your appendix out."

Peña sat up, probing the bandage Steve had applied.

"Thanks, Doc, I'll pass on the appendix. So tell me, how did you find me?"

"Have you ever heard of a lady named Beth Williams?" Steve replied.

"No, I don't think so, not that I can remember."

"Well, it's a long story. She's a microbiologist I ran into. She and I witnessed the gold-producing process on one of Boulez's ships. We weren't sure what was happening until she remembered an article she read about you and your disappearance. She even remembered your name. When we were being briefed by the CIA, your name came up regarding a message you posted on a blog."

"It got through? I'll be damned. I had no way of knowing, I thought it was a million to one shot."

"It got through. A professor noticed it and decoded it. He forwarded it to the FBI when he read it, and then it set off a keyword alert, and Ta-da, we knew about where you were. They sent me here to find you."

Peña looked tired, the vodka had made him sleepy, and he was leaning back on the dinette bench holding a towel to his wound. Steve felt worn out also, the aches and pains were catching up with him.

"Let's catch a little shut-eye. You can take the side berth." Steve pointed to a narrow sleeping area inset into the side of the boat. His own sleeping quarters were on a vee-shaped mattress at the bow. He did a quick rigging check and made sure his marker light was on the outside before he came down and crawled into the vee berth. Peña was already sound asleep as he passed by, his bloody shirt tossed in a heap beside his berth.

Steve wanted to sleep, but he thought he should check in with Beebe, after their earlier conversation. He removed the small trigger wire concealed at the base of one of the galley cabinets and rolled back a short piece of carpet revealing a small storage compartment. Moving aside the items stored there, two rolls of duct tape, and a few hand tools, Steve pulled a hidden lever. When he did, the section of the deck popped open, revealing a deep compartment. Inside were several electronic components, all operating with a dozen or more blinking status lights and LED readouts. There was a small jump seat mounted to the floor, into which Steve squeezed his oversized frame. To the front of the boat, the compartment had a bulkhead with several firearms clipped into brackets. There were three handguns, two rifles, and a miniature RPG type weapon. Steve brought the satellite phone with him, and now he plugged it into its charging base.

It took a few minutes for it to recharge. When it was ready, he dialed Beebe. Beebe picked it up on the first ring, his voice still hoarse.

"Steve... I was getting worried. How's it going?"

Steve briefed Beebe and then verified the FBI had found Mrs. Peña. Beebe told him her and her two daughters, and her mother was on the way to a safe house in Chicago. After making a tentative schedule to report back, Steve hung up the phone. He remained sitting on the jump seat in tired contemplation. It would relieve Peña to know his family was safe. That was the easy part. Now he had to deal with the gold. First, he had to verify the main cache was in the parking garage vault. Then he needed to come up with a recommendation for gaining or controlling it. His thinking was as long as the U.S. Government controlled it, the gold would not enter the financial markets. Problem solved. The excess of gold in the market now would take several years to assimilate, and the gold market would stabilize.

How can he get it? He asked himself. Identifiable U.S. forces overrunning the port would be unthinkable. It might throw the world economy into an uproar. Government sanctioned thieves running roughshod over foreign nationals on their native soil. There was no way it would happen. No, it would be a force of unidentifiable commandos, special ops people who can get in, get the gold, and get out.

Steve had heard rumors of a CIA group called the 'Black Legion', an extra-legal commando force operating outside of any congressional oversight, trained in remote areas of South American and Eastern European countries. Before planning anything else, Steve had to get closer. He had to find out how much gold was in play, and he had to do it quick. Time was of the essence now, and he would do everything in his power to conclude this situation. He wanted to get this over and get back to the States.

It had been a long time since he had a reason to look forward to going home. With an empty apartment facing him, he was happy when immersed in his work. Now, the imperceptible movement of the boat lulled his mind into a trance, and he drifted back to his last evening with Beth. He didn't realize how much missed he missed her until now. In their short time together, they had connected in a way he had forgotten. The physical part was nice, yes, but he felt a rare depth to her personality that he found extremely attractive to him. He wanted to talk to her, tell her what is happening, tell her found Peña, and he is safe.

He looked around at all the high tech gadgetry surrounding him, the best communications equipment available anywhere in the world.

"Why not?" He asked himself, dialing her cell phone number into the satellite phone.

Beth was having her second cup of coffee when the cell phone the people at WITSEC gave her rang. The dining table in the little apartment they put her in covered with several newspapers, the Washington Post, USA Today, Wall Street Journal, all the major dailies. In addition, FOX News was on in the background, feeding her insatiable desire for any information giving her a hint of what was going on in the Arabian Peninsula.

239

"Hello?" She answered. There were several beeps and clicks as Steve's phone received authorization through the WITSEC database controlling all calls on Beth's phone.

"Beth, it's Steve."

Concerned, she asked, "Steve! Are you okay... what's going on?"

"I'm good. Just getting ready to hit the sack over here, and I was thinking about you. It seems like a year since I saw you last."

"I know, I feel the same way. I'm worried about you. Gene Tyson took me to lunch yesterday, he told me about Agent Graves. He wouldn't even tell anything about you, other than you were okay. I feel like I'm in solitary confinement."

"Agent Graves, Bob Graves? What happened to him?"

"He came up missing, nobody has heard from him since we left San Juan. Tyson is worried about him."

"Don't know him well... quite standoffish. What do they think happened to him?"

"Tyson wouldn't say. I got the impression he might have been having financial problems." Steve thought it was odd, after seeing Graves wearing a twenty thousand dollar watch.

"Right, you never know. Anyway, I didn't call to talk about him. I want to find out how you are doing."

"Oh, I'm fine and in a safe place, and I find I'm missing your company."

"I know, I know. This will all be over soon." Steve wasn't sure who might listen in, so he had to speak. "You know I can't get specific. I believe I've found the main cache. I have to figure out what to do about it."

"What *can* you do about it?" She asked.

"Not sure, but I'm working on it."

"I'm sure you are."

"I'm also working on a serious case of the Beth withdrawal."

"Hmmm, I think I can help you with that as soon as you get back."

"You don't know how good that sounds, right now. I'm not alone. I'm with Alejandro Peña, the biologist you told us about. Remember the one who left the coded message?"

Beth knew Steve was being vague with details. "You're with him? How did you... is he okay?"

"Well, he's been better, but I think he'll make it."

"Excellent news. I knew it wouldn't take you long to stir things up over there."

"It's stirred all right, and now the 'you know what will hit the fan."

"Be careful Steve, remember, it's the little things get you."

Steve knew he had already spent too much time on the air. Beth's voice was such a pleasant contrast to the harsh sounds of explosions and gunfire he experienced recently, he was having a hard time ending the conversation.

240

"I'll do my best..." Steve's eye caught the lettering on a small black plastic case stored in the tiny compartment he was sitting in. White letters labeled the contents as 'Motorized RC-LCD Unit'. Steve was wide awake, "Beth, sorry, something just came to me. I'll call you again as soon as I can."

"Understood, secret agent man. I'll be waiting."

Steve smiled at her good-natured ribbing as he removed the plastic case from its compartment. He opened it to find a tiny battery-operated camera, mounted on a small four-wheeled motorized device. The case contained several types of interchangeable wheels. There were wheels intended for use over smooth ground and ribbed ones for use over rougher ground. It also had a flotation set for crossing water, and, the set Steve needed. He held up a wheel, shaped like a small umbrella from the side. Gauging them with his hand, he guessed they were about six inches in diameter. Perfect.

His mind was churning as he closed the hidden door to the compartment and headed for his berth. Fatigue flooded over him as he lay down, and even the plan of action forming in his head was not enough to stave off the onslaught of weariness forcing him into a deep sleep.

CHAPTER 55

Steve was lying face down on the shoulder of the highway. Huge tractor-trailers were whizzing by, only inches from him, each one giving a blast of its air horn as it passed. Each truck came closer and closer, their vibrations rocking him, yet he was incapable to force himself to move away. Paralysis stiffened his arms and legs, and he tried to inch himself out of the way with the tips of his fingers. Another loud blast of an air horn, and the gravel gouging his lower lip melted into the soft cotton. He raised his head with the realization he had been having a dream. The light streaming through an overhead hatch was bright, too bright for the morning. It must be near noon. The familiar blast of the air horn from his dream sent him bolt upright. It was no dream.

He grabbed a shirt, noticing the noise had Peña stirring. "Stay put." His tone of voice imparted seriousness that brought Peña to full alert.

Steve climbed out of the hatch, closing it behind him when he saw the blue and white Harbor Police boat ten yards off his starboard beam. Besides the driver, wearing the standard blue uniform of the Port Police, there were four armed men aboard. Men who did not appear to be harbor police, they were a paramilitary unit. They wore desert camouflage, red berets, and each carried an automatic rifle.

Steve gave a wave and pretended to tend to a windlass as the men in the boat waited for the current to bring it alongside the Pactolus.

"What can I do for you, mate?" Steve tried his best to look unconcerned.

The police officer spoke in accented English. "We are coming aboard; we have orders to do a customs inspection."

"Not good." Steve hissed under his breath. He had left his gun was lying on the counter below. If they saw it, this would get out of hand in a hurry. He did his best to stall them. "I passed through customs yesterday, in the port. I'll get my certificate."

In an instant, four rifle muzzles pointed at him. One man jumped over onto the deck of the Pactolus, the name 'Kibar' stenciled on the tag sewn over his left breast pocket. "It won't be necessary. Where is your passport?"

Steve's throat tightened as he realized he didn't have a lot of options. "It's down below."

"Are you alone, anybody else on board?"

'Just a friend, a guy I, um, we're trying to find work at the port." Steve knew Peña didn't have any identification. It would be impossible to bluff his way out of this. For a split second, he considered diving overboard, trying to swim beneath the boat out of danger, but it wouldn't be right to leave Peña hanging alone. He waited for an opportunity below. He might have a little advantage in the closer quarters.

Steve slide the hatchway open with, leading the way down the several steep steps. Peña was not in his berth, and when Steve glanced at the small counter, he was confused to see his gun was not where he had left it. In its place were the items from the concealed storage area beneath the rug. Peña had slipped into the secret compartment. Below decks, it was crowded, even though one man in camouflage and the police officer stayed topside.

"Where's your friend?" Kibar asked, his suspicious eyes roaming the small cabin.

"I dunno... I was sleeping. He musta gone for a swim."

The man nudged the pile of bloody towels Steve had left from sewing up Peña's head. "You have an accident?"

"I was cleaning a fish, mate. Got the blood all over meself." Steve hoped his attempt at an Australian accent was passable.

Speaking in Arabic, Kibar gave a brisk order to the other two. They searched under cushions and looking for compartments large enough to hold a person. A glint of metal in the corner caught Steve's eye. Someone exposed the tripwire for his hidden compartment, and the piece of carpet covering it was askew. If one man spotted it the wire, it wouldn't take long to find out where it led.

"Who are you guys, what do you want?" Steve asked, trying to keep their attention on him.

"Don't worry about it. Give me your passport."

Steve kicked a cushion over the tripwire as he reached into a small cabinet for his passport. Kibar watched him, never breaking eye contact with Steve until he opened the document.

"Jerry Wilston, Australian," Kibar mumbled as he matched Steve's face to the passport photo, satisfied it was the same man. "You are a long way from home, in a dangerous part of the world. What are you doing here, besides killing our fish?"

"Looking for work. I'm just trying to make enough cash to get to South Africa."

Kibar studied Steve, looking for any sign of guile. "And your friend... does he have a name?"

"Moboud, Mobuta, something," Steve lied, "I called him Mo. Just a drinking buddy I met in town. He didn't have a place to stay, so I told him I have an extra bunk."

Kibar picked up the half-empty bottle of vodka from the sink, holding it up to the light.

"Lucky we came along Mr. Wilston. Picking up guys in bars can be a deadly habit." Kibar motioned for the soldiers to leave as he tossed Steve's passport to the counter.

"Now wait just a damned minute, mate. It wasn't nothin' like that!" Steve followed them out with mock indignation.

Kibar turned as he balanced on the gunwale of the sailboat, a menacing look in his eyes. "Consider looking for work elsewhere. This is a dangerous place."

Steve sat in the cockpit of his boat as he watched the Harbor Police boat head for a large catamaran moored about a half a mile away. The men didn't respond as he gave them a wave and a smile, the relief palpable on his face as they sped off.

Steve wanted to run below, he knew the place Peña must have hidden, although he didn't know how he found out about it. He watched, waiting until the boat was engaged with the catamaran before he went below. They must check all the boats moored in the vicinity. It meant they had no reason to suspect him any more than any other boat. Peña and he would be careful now. They were probably watching from shore watch with high power telescopes.

Once below, he locked the hatch behind him and dropped to his hands and knees.

How had Peña known about the compartment? He was thankful he had not replaced the tripwire when he had finished talking to Beth last night, or this would have a different ending. He reached in to open the hidden latch and then hesitated. The stereo was in a cabinet over his head, and he reached up and clicked on a CD. A Beatles album spun up, and in a few seconds, the song was flowing from the six speakers situated around the cabin. Steve lifted the hidden panel a few inches, seeing Peña in the jump seat, a relieved look on his face.

Steve held his finger to his mouth, whispering, "Quiet now, no noise."

Peña nodded, fear showing in his eyes.

Steve pointed to a small electronic device, tucked in a slot at Peña's feet. It was about the size and shape of a child's paddleball paddle. He motioned for Peña to hand it to him.

"Stay here, I'll be right back." He said, closing the hidden panel.

Waving the paddle in front of him as he walked around the little cabin, Steve held it close to the cushions and storage shelves the uniformed men had searched while inside the boat. It made no noise, but two small yellow lights were blinking near the edge of the paddle, alternating from side to side. Coming to a light attached to the wall with a short swivel, the blinking lights on the paddle blinked much faster. Steve held the paddle against the light shade, and the blinking lights converged to the middle of the paddle, turning to a steady red. Steve rotated the shade away from the wall, and there it was. He found a small plastic disc about the size of a dime attached to the shade with an adhesive pad. The edge of the disc held a silvery metal wire, its two ends sticking out on opposite sides. Whoever the men in the desert camo were, they were no amateurs. Steve peeled the bug from the shade and attached it to a nearby stereo speaker.

He returned to where Peña was hiding, whispering. "They planted a bug, keep your voice low." He gave Peña a hand up from the compartment, pointing to the disk stuck on the speaker. "How the hell did you know about the compartment?"

"I woke up last night when you were opening it. I saw how you took the tripwire off and released the latch. When I heard the voices outside, I grabbed your gun and jumped down here. I thought they might look for me."

"Man, you don't know how glad I am you did. There was no way I would take five out."

"So they were looking for me?"

"I can't say they were looking for you, but it's a good probability. Anyone without ID would have been fair game after last night. They dressed in camo, not U.A.R. forces uniforms. It was private muscle, and around here, that means Boulez. It would be easy enough for him to pay off the Port Police to help him monitor everybody and everything in the port."

"Why would they leave a bug?"

"Why not? For twenty-five bucks, they can check up on me any time they want."

"Then I have to leave now. I'm a sitting duck out here."

"We're both going to leave here soon, but I need your help first. We need to verify the gold is in the vault, and how much of it. I think I have a way to do it."

"I don't know what help I can be, I feel like they beat me with a shovel." Peña reached up and touched his bandaged wound. "Thanks for the repairs."

"You might not be so thankful when you see my stitching job."

"It's okay, my hair will cover it. It beats bleeding to death."

"You were lucky. Take my advice, and don't block any more bullets with your head, capiche?"

"Capiche. Now, you say you have an idea?"

Steve snatched the hatch door open again, reaching down and removing the plastic 'Motorized RC-LCD' case he had seen earlier. He opened the case, showing Peña the little motorized device inside. His contacts on the small island had demonstrated its capabilities. Its small size and silent operation allowed it to travel unseen into places inaccessible to humans. A small digital television camera transmitted pictures to an operator controlling it from a remote location. It had the ability to cross water, climb short steps, and most important to Steve, travel inside of pipes with its special tires.

"We have to go back to the parking garage, and we have to go tonight. I don't want them to find you, I can't afford the time it would take me to get you to safety. If I leave the port area, I will go through customs again, and we saw is in control here."

"What will we do until then?" Peña asked.

"You will cool it down below. I know it's cramped so you'll have to make do. Maybe you should try to get some shut-eye; we may be out for a while tonight. Touch nothing, and whatever you do, don't come out of there. I have to run an errand. I should be back in an hour."

245

"See you later." Peña looked down into the open compartment, a shudder coming over him as he thought of its similarity to a coffin.

Steve replaced the bug back on the lampshade before he returned to the deck, just in case the Police boat returned. The afternoon sun beat down with a vengeance as he scanned the horizon, the soft rippling of the water lapping against the hull was the only sound, as even the gulls were trying to cool off in the distance. The public moorage area held about a dozen yachts, with no evidence of the police boat in the vicinity.

Unhooking the inflatable dinghy from its davits on the stern, Steve climbed in and started the little five horsepower outboard motor. He knew it was dangerous, but he needed to retrieve the water scooter he had left tied up at the pier yesterday evening. He knew Peña would be in no condition to swim such a distance, so they would need it tonight. As an afterthought, he tossed an old cooler into the dinghy and shoved off. He took his time, heading for the small customs dock near the end of the pier. When he arrived, the few people toiling on the pier paid him no mind as he tied off the dinghy and took the cooler up the steps. There was a small convenience store attached to the customs office, a store catering to the dockworkers. Steve looked around to see most of the workers were on a midday break, the heat nearing 115 degrees making it impossible to touch any exposed metal, making their work difficult. He purchased two bags of ice and a six-pack of bottled water and returned to the dinghy. A new, larger container ship had docked since he was on the pier last night. The 'Sadim' was several hundred yards away, yet the name on the stern read, the letters at least thirty feet tall. Steve stole glances down the pier, looking for any activity showing an increase in security. It looked much the same as it had last night, with no great show of force. It wouldn't last long. With Peña gone, Boulez had to expect he would tell the authorities about the massive quantities of gold stockpiled here. Eventually, someone would come looking for it… thieves, enemies, traitors, soldiers of fortune… everyone will want the gold. Every hour delayed would make his job more difficult. He meant to get it done in a hurry. From the customs dock, he cursed the entire length of the pier. There were several large container ships and a few barges tied up alongside, and the walkways beneath the pier were deserted. Untying the dinghy, he slipped into the gap between the pier and the great ships. It only took him a few seconds to reach the pipe where he had tied up the scooter and swim fins. The tide had gone out since the night before, and it exposed the pipe he had tied his equipment to last night. The scooter and fins were gone.

He gave a silent curse as he double-checked his location. The plate on the pipe over his head read AC/24-DC/24. He was in the right place. He spun the dinghy around and motored past the rudder of a huge chemical tanker, popping back out into the open water, trying to convince himself whoever found the scooter didn't even know what it was. A dockworker found it tied up there, took it, and threw it in his trunk. It'll be for sale at a middle-eastern flea market this weekend. The more Steve thought about it, the more he decided it didn't matter. Even if security had found it, there would have no reason to suspect it was his..., he's just an Aussie looking for work. All looked calm as he tied back up to the Pactolus, and climbed aboard. When he opened the hatch, he found Peña reading a small instruction manual by flashlight. He helped him from the compartment, not saying a word, as Peña stretched. Wary of the bug, Steve found a small notepad, and jotted down a short note, sliding it to Peña: <u>We go tonight.</u>

CHAPTER 56

It was almost dark outside now, and Steve was on deck, trying to jam all the equipment he needed into a waterproof duffle bag. Peña was below, struggling to get into a wetsuit Steve had found in the diving locker. It was an old suit, and it would have to do. With the RC-TV unit, night vision goggles, the satellite phone, various hardware, and rope, and a couple of bottles of water in the wet bag, there wasn't enough room for the two guns, they would have to carry them inside their wetsuits.

Steve made Peña stay below, just on the off chance they were being watched from shore with night vision scopes. Boulez wasn't shy about buying or using the latest technology and Steve wasn't taking any chances. He had gone over the plan of action with Peña, writing notes and whispering until they felt safe enough to put the bug back on the stereo speaker. All they needed now was the cover of darkness. It would be a black night, the new moon and low hazy clouds ensuring the only light would be manmade. If things go wrong, they might never get the chance to come back to the Pactolus, so Steve attached the wire to the compartment cover. The device would fry the electronic components of any classified equipment while blowing a hole in the hull big enough to sink the Pactolus within a few minutes. It was enough to ensure no usable components fell into the wrong hands.

One last run-through of his checklist and Steve was ready. He held a portable two hundred thousand-candle power spotlight ready and motioned for Peña to come up from the cabin. With the spotlight trained on the shore, it would blind anyone watching them with night vision equipment.

Peña crawled across the deck and slid off the stern, laying on the floor the dinghy. Steve clicked the light off and tossed it back on deck as he shoved the dinghy away from the Pactolus. With no running lights, the black inflatable would be invisible crossing the water to their destination.

The silky smoothness of the evening water contrasted with the tension both men felt as the dinghy motored across the mouth of the port. Steve kept his distance, knowing the bustle of dock activities would drown out the little outboard's sound.

When the stern of the Sadim came into view, it surprised Peña.

"Look, it's the Sadim. One of the largest ships in Boulez's fleet. I'm a little surprised to see her back so soon."

"Why?" Steve asked.

"It can't have been over seven or eight weeks ago she dropped off a huge load of gold. I knew theoretically, what my process would produce given perfect conditions. Until I saw it, I never conceptualized it in my head. It was over five tons."

"Five tons!" Steve whistled. "Are you sure?"

"Oh, I'm sure all right. She used to be the 'Global Pursuer, but they renamed her Sadim. Sadim is a Muslim name, and I thought they renamed it after an ancient leader, an Imam, a cleric. It wasn't until the last time they took me to check on her lab I realized what it means."

"What happened?"

"Nothing happened in the lab. When we were leaving, I looked in the rearview mirror and saw the name of the ship. Backward it reads 'Midas'. Although it might be the coincidence, I believe Boulez is just flipping the proverbial bird, daring anyone to figure it out. He thinks he is King Midas."

"It fits in with what Beth Williams said. She called what you are doing the 'Midas Effect'."

"Close enough, everything King Midas touched turned to gold. My microbes can only extract the gold already in the seawater, but I'm working on it."

"A week ago, I would have said all this was a fairy tale. Now, I think given enough time, you will find a way," Steve replied.

"I was only trying to reduce pollution from land-based gold mining. After seeing what devastation this will cause, I wish I had never started." Peña sighed."As they say, no good deed ever goes unpunished," Steve smirked. Peña sat at the front, enjoying the cool breeze against his head, while he tried to convince himself everything would turn out all right. Steve offered to let him sit this out, hidden in the secret compartment of the Pactolus. He felt he owed it to Steve to be of help. To have a stranger come from halfway around the world to help you, putting his own life in jeopardy, demanded nothing less. Coming so close to death, made him realized every day of his life from here on would be a bonus. Because he could not reverse the deteriorating microbial output, Boulez would have killed him or his family. He felt a great debt to Steve, and to the United States government. If he had to die tonight helping Steve, then so be it. It would be far better than disappearing from the face of the earth at the hand of one of Boulez's misguided goons.

A change in the outboard motor's pitch broke his concentration. Steve had reduced speed, pointing the dinghy into the shore, towards a dark bulk headed area past the end of the pier.

"Get ready and remember what we talked about. We're in no hurry tonight. Let's take our time, get what we want and get out safe. Everything else will take care of itself. Got it?"

"I'm with you; just lead the way, Steve." Peña held out his hand. Steve gave it a firm shake, as he looked up at the bulkhead for any sign of human activity.

The bulkhead rose five feet out of the water, topped by a tall chain-link fence. A drainage pipe from an unseen curb drain was producing a little waterfall of dripping water, and several short lengths of jagged steel rebar were protruding from the face of the bulkhead. Steve tossed a rope with a small grappling hook up over the top of the fence, pulling it tight as it snagged the wire mesh.

"Tie the bowline to that piece of metal." He instructed Peña, as he yanked the rope. When he was satisfied it was secure, he pulled himself up to a narrow ledge on the bulkhead and tossed the rope back down to Peña.

Peña struggled a little on the slimy concrete and made it to the ledge beside Steve. Several piles of what looked to be surplus building materials were stored haphazardly on the other side of the fence, along the edge of the bulkhead. A few concrete pipes, stacks of masonry blocks, electrical conduit, and nearly empty spools of wire. Beyond the building materials were a few rows of cars, the entire lot lit by tall security lights. Separated from the lot by an access road and a large grassy area, was the building Peña had escaped from the day before.

"Look, the residence building!" Peña whispered, a slight edge to his voice revealing his excitement.

"I planned it that way," Steve winked, "follow me."

To their left was a tangle of thick honeysuckle brush growing, and intertwining with the fence. Steve crab-walked to the end of the ledge and swung himself onto a little clearing in the brush. It was barely big enough for two or three people to stand. The cigarette butts and empty beer cans were strewn in the brush beside an old lawn chair signaled this place is where the workers came to sneak a few drinks or do a little quick fishing during a lunch break. It also meant there must be a path to the road.

Peña jumped to the ground beside Steve, thorns grabbing at his wet suit. "It looks spooky as hell. Is there a way through?"

"Got to be a way, look at all this trash. People from those offices are using this as a personal getaway spot."

Steve kneeled on one knee, reaching into his waterproof bag. He pulled out a pair of night-vision goggles and snapped them over his head. It only took a few seconds for them to gather enough ambient light to show the well-trodden path winding through the brush.

"Sorry, I only have one pair of goggles. Remember, take it easy, try to step where I step, keep your head low. A little thorn in the wrong place will be big trouble."

"I understand. Don't worry, I can do this."

Steve clapped him on the shoulder. "This will be a great story for your grandkids."

"To get grandkids, I have to get back. Let's get this over with."

Steve started up the path, with Peña close behind. What Steve had assumed to be honeysuckle were wild rose bushes. The thorns grabbed at their wet suits as they walked in a crouch toward the road, making them stop several times to unhook the stubborn barbs.

"You can kiss this wetsuit goodbye," Peña said as they arrived at the grassy strip beside the road.

"Don't worry about it. You're only wearing it because it's black. I don't plan on swimming tonight."

They were in a low spot between the pier and the parking garage. From their vantage point, they scanned the pump house where Steve had parked the night before. Several unoccupied tanker trucks were parked to the rear, and they had backed one truck into the loading area, its driver standing by as a pump labored to the accompaniment of a steady whine. Close by and to its left was the parking garage and the transformer pit where Steve wanted to go. To the rear of the parked tanker trucks sat the chemical tank farm, and a short way up the road stood the residence building. Several armed guards were milling about at the entrance to the parking garage, evidence Boulez suspected Peña's escape was bound to bring unwanted attention to his cache of gold.

"When the tanker leaves, I'll go across first. You wait until I signal." Steve was in full stealth mode now, his communication short and to the point. When the tanker finally ran dry, it seemed as if the driver was moving in slow motion. He took his time disconnecting the large hoses attached to the chemical pumps and was unhurried as he stowed them in their respective troughs along the side of a concrete wall shielding the area from view. Each second dragged on until finally, the tanker pulled out onto the access road towards the exit.

"Damn, can he go any slower?" Steve said impatiently, waiting for him to put distance between them. "We better do this before another one comes along."

He waited until there were no cars within sight on the access road and sprinted across. Once he was safely across, he waved Peña over, surprised at how he ran.

"Not bad for a desk jockey." Steve joked.

"It's the only thing I can thank Boulez for. The only way to kill time was to go to the gym. I'm twenty pounds lighter than when I got here."

"Good, it sounds like you're ready to kick ass. Let's go."

Keeping low, Steve led Peña around the perimeter of the parking garage to the steel grate covering the transformer. Everything was as they had left it the previous night. Steve worried the security patrol found the open padlock on the grate, and it relieved him to find it still there unlocked. They must have stopped searching once they realized Peña got out of the area.

Steve gave Peña a small flashlight. "You go down first, keep the light shining down. I will lower the equipment bag down to you."

Peña took the light, holding it in his mouth as he climbed down the ladder. The lights from the parking garage gave off enough light for him to see Steve's form at the top of the transformer pit.

"Send it down!"

Peña caught the bag, and unloaded the equipment, just as Steve and he had discussed. The clandestine operation's excitement left his mouth dry as sand. He was glad Steve had thought ahead to bring two bottles of water. As he unscrewed the cap on a bottle, he noticed the lettering ink, an innovation for a Syrian businessman. Fluorescent glow in the dark letters…"Never lose your water at night!" He had seen the advertisement on the TV in his room. Peña smiled as he read the label, 'AQUA REGIS'. "Hmm, Royal Water, what a joke," he thought to himself. Steve replaced the heavy grate before descending, and soon he was kneeling next to Peña. He assembled the special wheels on the motorized RC-TV unit, while Peña calibrated the picture on the little video screen in the cover of its plastic case.

"Which pipe?" Peña asked, noticing several similar pipes running up the wall.

"This one, 'BC2/DC2," Steve pointed, placing the motorized unit on the floor. "Turn on the light."

Peña keyed a tiny button with a metal stylus, and a bright headlight-camera combination, no bigger than the butt of a cigarette, shone across the floor. They checked the unit to make sure it was responding to the radio control's signal. Everything was working as planned.

"Here we go," Steve said as he shoved the unit up into the PVC pipe.

Peña sent a signal for it to expand its axels, which made the umbrella-shaped wheels hug the inside of the pipe with its soft rubber tires. With a miniature joystick, Peña guided the unit down the PVC pipe. It was disorienting watching the picture on the video screen, as the unit made several slow revolutions inside the pipe. After a few minutes of practice, Peña made the unit respond as if he had been doing it all his life. Steve had expected the pipe to intersect the other pipes, and so far, this pipe had no branches. A digital counter on the screen told them how many feet the unit had traveled. After about fifty feet, Steve worried they might be in the wrong pipe, or it might not end up in the vault.

"Any time now..." Steve was anxious.

"Amazing what you guys come up with, TV cameras in the sewer. I can't imagine what the CIA spent to develop this technology." Peña said.

"Not a dime, big guy. They developed this for sewer inspections. It's much easier to dig up a stopped sewer if you can pinpoint its blockage location to the inch. In shallow ground, a locator will find this thing, and all you have to do is dig a small hole to fix your pipe."

"I see... that's why plumbers make the big money."

"You can say that again... whoa, stop it right there."

Peña stopped the unit at what looked to be small slats blocked his progress.

"Damn! It's a grate or grille. We must be at the end. We will not be able to get a picture through it." Steve sounded dejected.

"Wait... look at this." Peña reversed the unit and focused on the end of the pipe. "The grille has no screws through the pipe. It must be friction fit. Maybe I can push it out."

"Okay, give it a shot." Steve wasn't optimistic.

Peña pushed the control forward, nuzzling the remote unit against the grille. He tried to dislodge the grille, but it seemed solid.

"No way, it's not budging."

"Ram it."

"Wha...?"

"Ram the damn thing, what have we got to lose?"

Peña looked over at Steve, "What if we lose the camera?"

"Then we'll go back to Plan B. Just do it, we've already been here too long."

"I know all about Plan B!" Peña mocked, backing the unit up in the pipe. With eight feet of clear pipe ahead, Peña shoved the control forward. The RC unit sped down the pipe, slamming into the grille. The image on the video screen tumbled with incomprehensible images until just as they stopped. The transmission of a nondescript flat surface was the only thing visible. Aside from a black circle surrounded by the letters DC2/BC2, there were no clues to what they were looking at.

Peña worked the controls in vain. "It won't move. I think it landed upside down. It must have broken."

Steve stared at the image on the video screen. "It's the ceiling."

"Excuse me?"

"The black circle is the end of the pipe. The RC unit fell out, and now the camera is pointing straight back up at it."

"DC2/BC2." Peña read the letters surrounding the hole, glancing at the top of the pipe near Steve. "Look, the pipe you inserted the remote unit into has the same letters. Only here it's BC2/DC2, and inside it's just the opposite. It must be a pipe labeling scheme. If you know one end, you can determine where the other end comes out. Very important when you have dozens of pipes running everywhere."

"Let's run the last few seconds of video back. Maybe we can get lucky."

Peña worked his way through the various menus of the remote device until he found a replay function.

"Here it is. We can go frame by frame."

They both watched in silence as Peña advanced the image through the many frames. Although they were in a grainy black and white format, the images gave enough detail for them to follow its progress through the pipe. The grille impact resulted in a sudden disorienting view of a large open space. Advancing each frame they followed the camera's eye view as the RC unit tilted straight down at the floor.

"Stop it right there!" Steve said, "what does it say?"

Peña squinted at the screen where he saw another black circle surrounded by block letters.

"OC24/AC24… no, let me try to focus it a little better." He fumbled with the image control, tweaking the picture until the letters came into focus.

"D-C24/AC24. It's a floor drain. The other end is AC24/DC24. I saw where it comes out underneath the pier." Steve said.

"How can you remember anything that arcane?" Peña asked in amazement.

"No big deal, it's stupid. AC/DC is the name of the old rock group. You know, Highway to Hell, You Shook Me All Night Long…"

His eyes conditioned to the dark now, Steve realized Peña was drawing a blank. "I know AC/DC can't be before your time."

"No, I listen to Salsa... look, look!"

Peña stopped advancing the frames. The picture on the screen was astounding. On the way down, the camera had rotated to one side, catching a view of several pallets. They were stacked with what had to be hundreds of ingots of metallic bars, and others were stacked similar in fashion to the wooden boxes Steve had found in the Honda's trunk.

"Ali, what have you done?" Steve intoned.

Speechless, Peña did not understand Boulez had so much gold stockpiled in such a small area. Working the image controls, he advanced a few frames to get the best picture.

"It has to be most of the gold we harvested, 75-80 percent. I would have thought he had distributed it by now."

"We discussed a scenario concerning this back at CIA Headquarters. The head-slappers there think to disrupt the Western economies; he will need to flood the market over a short period of time, as little as a month. It will cause panic in the markets and give Western governments no time to plan a coordinated response." Steve explained. "It's our worst nightmare."

Peña was being quiet. He was holding the bottle of water in one hand, alternating looking at it, and looking up with a faraway look in his eyes.

"I can see the gears turning in your head, Ali," Steve said, "what is it?"

Peña hesitated, the idea he was mulling over in his head was so farfetched he was almost afraid to say it aloud.

"When you said Boulez has to flood the market, it gave me an idea. It's crazy, so crazy you might just think I'm nuts."

"I already think you're nuts, besides, it's time for a good laugh."

Peña knew Steve was joking, but after what he was about to propose, he might change his opinion. It bordered on the ridiculous but it did not bother him. What worried him was he knew it was possible.

"Suppose we don't wait for Boulez to flood the market with all the gold. Suppose we flood his gold first... with acid!"

"What are you talking about?"

"This," Peña held the flashlight on the water bottle, showing Steve the label.

"A bottle of water... so what?"

"It's not the water, it's the name. 'Aqua Regis', is Latin for Royal Water."

"I'm not following you here, Ali." Steve was showing his impatience.

"I'm talking about Royal Water... a mixture of two acids. Royal water is one part nitric acid to three parts hydrochloric acid. Those two acids in combination do what no other acid can do. They dissolve gold."

Steve looked incredulous. "You are crazy. I've always heard gold is inert. It won't rust or corrode...nothing affects it. Now you are telling me you want to mix a little acid and hocus-pocus, we dissolve this huge pile? Come on."

"No, no, it's true, someone can do it. During World War Two a famous chemist hid a gold medal from the Nazis by dissolving it in Royal Water. After the war, he returned to find his jar of acid right where he left it. It's a simple procedure to precipitate the gold back out of solution."

"Are you serious? Even if it were possible, how much acid would it take? How would we..."

"If I estimate the size of the pile," Peña interrupted, pointing at the video screen, "I believe about nine thousand gallons would do it... give or take a thousand."

"Nine thousand gallons, only nine thousand? I'll have the GSA ship it right over." Steve still hadn't picked up on Peña's idea.

"No need. You are standing maybe a hundred feet from a chemical tank farm, and at least twenty fifty thousand gallon chemical tanks. Hydrochloric and nitric acid are two of the most common acids used in manufacturing. I've seen both tanks when I was traveling back and forth from the pier. Everything we need to ruin Boulez is right outside."

256

"How many trucks can you get?" Boulez asked Rahman, leaning back in the plush leather chair complimenting the mahogany desk in his office. Peña's escape brought a sense of urgency to the late-night meeting in the office of Boulez's opulent penthouse apartment.

"I only have thirty couriers standing by, and I told the others to be available after Ramadan."

"I'm afraid we will have to start now. We have to disperse before any pro-western government takes it upon themselves to intervene. Remember, this will affect the entire world economy. Until we weaken the West as much as possible, we will be very unpopular. Even Arabs don't want to see the value of their holdings disappear. I'm worried Peña will put two and two together when he is in Western hands. They have been monitoring the price of gold for the last few months."

"We may have made an error, trying to keep the gold in a central location. It will be harder to get long distances now." Rahman offered.

"It may be so, but we have to deal with it now. The Hawala system will allow us to move quickly, we will need to deliver the physical product soon. No dealer will risk his reputation and his life by not having the gold he promised." Boulez said.

"Our brethren will be in difficulty if they are holding too much gold. Remember, the price will drop for them too. If we go too fast, they will stop taking new supply orders." Rahman stated the obvious.

"We are so close, we must not fail," Boulez was circumspect. "We must make a bold move, a move to bear witness to our vision."

"What move are you speaking of?"

"Let's start with the Hawala brokers. They will not have to worry about the value of the gold they are sending. I will give it to them. I will give them as much as they want!" "What are you saying? Do you mean…?"

"Yes, Rahman, I am committed to my purpose. On the grave of my father, I vowed to bring the people responsible to account. Now I have the means. I will drown them with the gold they hold so dear. We will not keep records or ask for repayment. Give the gold freely, with only one stipulation."

"What stipulation?"

"Whatever gold you receive, then you must divide into ten parts. Then you must give away seven parts through a Hawala broker to one who has no gold. The person who receives the gold must do the same until the amounts are not worth breaking up. With seven Hawala receipts, you may receive another share, and so on until we have dispersed all the gold in the vault."

"I see, I see," Rahman nodded, amazed that Boulez came up with such a simple, yet efficient plan, on the spot, "it will .happen. With a few telephone calls, we can have millions and millions of dollars' worth of gold transferred to anywhere in the world. Our trucks will then have a few days to deliver the physical product in bulk, we will break it into ever-smaller amounts... none of which is illegal to transport."

"I predict within five days of beginning, the price of gold will drop by at least a thousand dollars an ounce." Boulez looked smug.

A sharp rap on the door startled both men. "Yes?" Boulez asked.

Chavez stuck his head through the door. "I have important news."

"Come in, come in. We are finishing."

As with the rest of the apartment which occupied the entire floor of the exclusive building, the office exuded wealth to Chavez. Accustomed as he was to seeing Boulez with the best of everything, this... this was a step above.

"Yes, Benny?"

"We received a message from our friend back in the States. He says the Customs agent, his name is Ross, and he's here in the port. He came in undercover two days ago on a sailboat with Australian papers. We checked out the boat earlier today before we had this information. The ICE agent was there... alone. We have our people watching the boat and there has been nobody around it all evening."

"Good work, we'll get him this time. I want you to make sure it's the last we hear of him. And make sure to compensate our special friend in the States."

"Yes sir, and that's not all. I have even better news. Peña is with him. As far as we can tell, both of them are still here in Port Jebel."

Boulez had a faraway look in his eyes deep in thought. "Why would they stay here? If he came to get Peña, he accomplished his mission. Why stay?"

"The gold," Rahman hissed. "Peña knows about it, he knows where it is. I don't think he has a way to know how much is there. The only reason to stay is to find out."

"Possible," Boulez agreed. "If the United States or its Western allies suspect we have a large stockpile here, they must verify it before they can take any political or military action. Can you imagine the diplomatic nightmare they would bring on themselves if they tried to confiscate the gold and found nothing?"

"The Middle East is already a thorn in their side. They have hidden their agenda with quests for 'WMDs, and the supposed 'liberation' of Arab dictatorships, all with enough of a smell of truth to encourage their allies to take part in their imperialism. Now, the last thing they need is getting labeled as international thieves, trying to loot the ill-gotten wealth of foreigners on their own soil."

"If they find the gold, they will have the evidence of our plan, and international approval for stopping it. We must not give them the chance," Rahman said.

Boulez stood from his chair, "we have work to do. They must not find the gold."

CHAPTER 58

The tank felt cool to Steve as he leaned against it, catching his breath. Peña was waiting for him back in the shadows of the parking garage. Steve was still skeptical about the plan to dissolve the gold, so he decided there was nothing to lose. His mission did not include any orders to take action on his part if he found the gold, just his recommendations. It also didn't prevent any action on his part either.

"This might be my first and last job for Beebe," He thought, "in more ways than one." He calculated the worst that would happen, aside from capture by Boulez's people, was that they would flood the gold with acid and Boulez would have to deal with it. If he planned to move it soon, it would at least slow him down.

"What the hell, I'm in this to take Boulez down, it's personal now."

Steve was looking for a tank with the UN Number 2031, the United Nations universal chemical code for nitric acid. They had found the hydrochloric acid in two large tanks right beside the pump house. He was near the far end of the tank farm now. Having darted between the huge tanks, and hopping over the overflow dikes and the myriad pipes and valves running all directions, he was running out of steam.

He ducked as the second security patrol car to pass by in the last ten minutes drove up the access road at low speed, watching it until it rounded the corner towards the pier. Something was going on. The schedule had been a drive-by about once every twenty minutes, and Steve sensed the increased activity wasn't coincidental. It was not a secure facility. There were civilian workers, itinerant port workers, and government workers, all allowed in certain areas, all under the control of Boulez's operation. Boulez had not chosen the port only for its unhindered financial freedom. By placing large quantities of his financial resources in the hands of the right people, he trusted them to maintain a high level of security without drawing undue attention to himself. It was security by intimidation. Nobody knew who might be on the inside, so it paid to watch your back.

A military fortification here would have drawn the curiosity of the CIA long ago. Only now the importance of the port came into the picture of declining gold value was a testament to Boulez's grasp of human nature.

Steve had a different vision, and tonight was the night to put it in play. Crawling to the far side of the cool tank, he hopped over the last overflow dike on the edge of the tank farm and looked up to see a large black stencil on the side of the tank

TANK # 27 - Prod. UN2031.

"Hot damn, tank number twenty-seven," Steve muttered, looking back in dismay at the industrial jungle he had to cross to return to Peña. "Figures it would be the last tank."

Adrenalin was pumping now, with the thought of what lay ahead. If Peña were right, this would all be over soon. He took a more direct route around the perimeter of the tank farm, crouching low behind a short concrete wall serving as the last defense if one of the chemical tanks failed. Designed to contain any chemical spill inside the tank farm, they would be inadequate considering the amount of chemicals stored there.

Without incident, Steve made his way back to where he left Peña, surprised to find him wrestling a long chemical transfer hose down the access grate of the transformer pit.

"I knew there had to be nitric in there, so I got a head start on these hoses." Peña was breathing hard.

"You're right. The nitric is in tank number 27. I noticed the drive-by patrols have increased, and I'll bet it won't be long before we see foot patrols... maybe even dogs. We have to hurry."

"We're set in here. I got the vent cap off the pipe. This hose fits down over it a little loose, but when the juice flows it won't matter."

"Good deal. Come on, let's pump acid."

Their plan was to use the tanker as a giant manifold. They would run the three to one ratio of acid into the tanker, and then drop it into the vault, letting it flow as they made their escape.

Steve led Peña to the pump house, where it surprised them to find the door unlocked. They slipped into a small dark room, the acrid smell of chemicals lingering in the air from the last delivery. Steve shone his small flashlight around the room, revealing a bank of valves connected to a complicated looking manifold system. Six large explosion-proof pumps sat lined up on pedestals, each had a flexible hose attached, the loose end secured to an overhead rack with a hook.

"We need to bypass the pumps." Peña said, "The acid will flow out by gravity almost as fast. Can we do it?"

"If I can find the right valves, we should be able to." Steve agreed, realizing it might be better to sacrifice speed for the advantage of silence. He handed the light to Peña. "You work on the valves, I'll go hook up the hoses."

261

Steve hurried back outside, listening for any sign of activity. Looking at the luminous dial of his watch, he figured it was about time for another drive-by patrol, he would have to be quick. The retaining wall blocked the view to the pump house from the road on one side and the parking garage on the other. The patrol would have to attempt to see what was happening in the recess between them. He was counting on them to be too lazy.

There was a large tanker truck parked in the cleanout rack beside the loading platform. It was in the area where they flushed the inside of the tank after each delivery, preventing contact between dissimilar or reactive chemicals. A long discharge hose connected to an underground waste tank stored the rinse chemical and any residue from the tanker. Peña said he noticed the truck in the same place almost every time he had passed by the tank farm on his way to and from the pier. It appeared to be a plant vehicle, a tanker used for moving chemicals between locations on the pier. Divided into four compartments, the numbers painted on the side reading 2,500 - 2,500 - 2,500 - 4,000, displaying the gallon capacity of each compartment. Steve climbed a small ladder on the back of the truck, and crawled down the top of the tanker, opening a small hatch on each compartment making sure they were empty. Peña had warned him of the danger should the tanker contain any chemicals. Lethal gas, explosion, any number of dangerous reactions were possible. The white plastic coating on the inside of the tanker revealed it was empty. Steve slid back to the ground, dragging the heavy discharge hose towards the transformer pit beside the parking garage. It wasn't long enough. He needed another section of hose to connect with the hose Peña had placed over the vent pipe. When he returned to the loading area, Peña was looking through the pump room door.

"I'm all set in here, are the hoses hooked up?"

The sound of an approaching car caught their attention at the same instant. Steve ducked into the pump room just as the brilliant shaft of light from a spotlight played over the cab of the tanker, and then on the door of the pump house. Steve reached for his gun, watching the light linger for a few seconds, shining through cracks in the door.

"They're hunting you, there's no time," Steve said, cracking the door open when the light dimmed, relieved to hear the patrol heading away. "I need another section of hose to get to the vent, give me a hand."

He pointed to the hose hanging beside them on the wall. It was a heavy, stiff hose, but the two of them made quick work of the connections. Running back to the pump house, they connected two more hoses from the bank of outlets to a manifold on the side of the trunk. Everything was in place.

Peña looked over at Steve, "Are you ready?"

"Let'er rip."

Peña pulled on the large circular valve handles, and the hiss of flowing liquid was audible through the hoses.

"How long do you think it will take?" Steve asked as they took cover back inside the pump room.

"I'm not sure about filling up the tanker. The volume in the storage tank will determine it. The more in the tank, the faster it will push out. I guess it might take fifteen or twenty minutes."

"And draining it into the vault?"

"It will be easier. These hoses have about five inches of inside diameter. A hundred fifty gallons per inch, per minute," Peña took just a second to murmur the calculations under his breath, "nine thousand gallons divided by seven hundred fifty gallons a minute… twelve minutes."

"So it should be about half an hour for both." Steve rubbed his temple, concerned.

"Don't hold me to it." Peña wavered, seeing the concern on Steve's face. "What are you thinking?"

"Damn it." Steve cursed, the realization coming to him they had made a major blunder. "How long will it take to dissolve the gold?"

"I don't know. It will start slow, and then the reaction will build a head of steam. It will take an hour, maybe more. What are you…?"

"We forgot about the floor drain! The acid will drain off almost as fast as it goes in. I have to get to the other end and plug the drain!"

Peña threw up his hands in disgust. "You're right! How did both of us miss something so obvious?"

"Don't worry about it. I have to go, or we will lose this whole operation. Stay here. As soon as the tanker fills up, cut the acid loose just like we planned. Once you do, head for the dinghy. Get yourself back to the Pactolus." Steve seemed out of breath as he looked down at his watch. "If I'm not there by 4:30, you haul ass. She has a diesel motor that can get you away quickly."

"But, but…"

"We don't have time for buts, Ali, just do it. I will get underneath the pier. Remember I told you about the floor drain pipe, AC24/DC24 - DC24/AC24? I know where it is. I have to get to it and plug it up before the acid drains out."

Peña nodded, "I'll wait as long as I can. How will I know if you're ready?"

Steve tried to sound calm. "You won't. You release the acid in ten minutes." He handed the waterproof bag to Peña, taking out the satellite phone. "I will stay at the drain to make sure it stays plugged up long enough for the acid to work. We have to know whether all this worked, we're not coming back for this gold. Remember, four-thirty. If I'm not there by then, head to open water, don't wait! Hit any of the preset numbers on this, it will connect you to our people. They're not far; they'll come to get you."

Peña stood speechless, satellite phone in hand, as Steve slipped out of the door?

CHAPTER 59

The glistening paint of the tanker's tractor cab gave Steve an idea. Taking a minute to crank the legs down on the tanker, and to disconnect the air and electrical connections between it and the cab, Steve climbed up into the driver's seat. Amazed at his good fortune, Steve found there was no key required to start the truck as it had a pushbutton starter. On the passenger side floor was a small, insulated cooler, not much larger than a lunch box. Making a quick assessment of the controls, he then glanced down to the access road, his finger pausing on the starter button. From the air cushion drivers' seat, he was high enough to get a good view of the road. His good fortune continued as it looked deserted. With a deep breath, he pushed the fuel lever all the way in, tapped the starter button, and the diesel motor roared to life, spitting a cloud of white smoke into the humid air. Steve pushed the air brake release, cringing when it released a sudden loud blast of compressed air and eased the truck into gear. Inching forward, the well-greased fifth wheel disengaged as the cab slid out from the tanker trailer.

He took a quick look back at the pump house door, seeing the dark form of Peña's head sticking out of the door. With a quick wave and thumbs up, he jerked down the loading ramp towards the road, sweat beading on his forehead.

Turning the corner at the end of the ramp, he squinted at the bright lights of the pier, with several large ships tied up alongside. Keeping the headlights off, he roared towards the pier, building up speed as he worked his way through the many gears. He passed by the corner of the parking garage, surprised to see what looked to be fifteen or twenty trucks lined up single file at the entrance. Several men dressed in the same uniforms as the men wore who visited the boat earlier, were milling about, their weapons at the ready.

Ahead he followed two Port Police officers stationed at the gate to the pier. They were leaning against their car talking, and as he approached, they waved for him to stop, pointing to a small paved area where they wanted him to stop.

"Sorry, no can do, pecker-head!" Steve's adrenalin was flowing now, it was pure aggression fueled by fear and determination. His thought processes converging to a narrow focus: find a way to complete the mission

The Policemen had to dive out of the way as Steve careened past them, bursting through the chain-link gate as if it was so much paper. Heading straight for the opposite end of the pier, Steve knew it would take more than luck to make this work. He said a silent prayer as he reached back for the shoulder belt, clicking it into the receptacle, as he fought the steering wheel with his other hand. The center travel way running the length of the pier was open, and Steve streaked down it past the stacked containers and pallets of freight. Yanking the air horn cable, he drew as much attention to himself as he thought possible. He wanted to draw any security patrols in his direction, away from the pump house.

The end of the pier was getting closer, and more congested. Steve veered to miss a forklift carrying a pallet of cement bags zipping around a container into his path.

With containers on both sides of the travel way, there was not enough room to avoid the inattentive forklift driver. Fighting for control, the truck skidded sideways and clipped the pallet, sending bags of cement spraying their dust in a wide arc. The forklift spun violently, the centrifugal force wrenching its bottle of compressed gas from the thin bands holding it, and flung it down the pavement. It slammed into the corner of a container with such force the steel bottle ruptured, the gas catching a spark and exploding with a huge orange ball of fire. Steve heard the explosion but had no time to look back. The end of the pier and the jet-black water of the sea beyond loomed ahead. He held the accelerator to the floor, picking a clear spot between two sea containers. The truck plowed through the short cinder block wall on the end of the pier and became airborne. Steve shut his eyes and took a deep breath as the world became almost silent. For what seemed an eternity, all he heard was the air rushing by his open window.

A chaotic rush of nearby dockworkers to the edge of the pier slowed the Port Police car near the gate, as it tried to catch up with the truck. It took only a few minutes for a rumor to start flying the shipping containers contained bombs, and they were set to detonate at several places on the pier. Sirens, flashing lights, and the Police shouting instructions through portable bullhorns added to the scene of mass confusion.

266

Steve tried to keep his body loose as the truck flew through the air. He knew rigidly braced limbs would snap with the force of impact. He had seen it a hundred times. A loosey-goosey drunk would walk away from an auto accident unhurt, while the sober driver who had braced for the collision had serious injuries. He wrapped his arms up over his face, and squeezed his legs together, trying to protect two critical areas of his body. The truck was airborne for about three seconds, with the front dropping as soon as it left the pier. Steve waited for the impact he knew was coming, the three seconds seemed like three minutes. Suddenly, with a violent jerk, the truck hit the water nose-first.

The bumper dug into the water, flipping the cab over on its top, where it rolled to the side and began to sink. The impact slammed Steve against his safety belt, punching the air from his lungs, and wrenching him to one side. A sharp pain stabbed his shoulder as the cool water enveloped him, driving the cobwebs from his head. The truck had rolled over on its side, disorienting him as he struggled to release the safety belt. Pressure building in his ears told him the truck was still sinking. He had no way to know how deep. Finally, after 30feet, the truck came to a gentle stop, landing on the driver's door in the soft sand of the seafloor. He struggled to release the seatbelt for a few seconds, freeing himself from the jumble of straps, the burning in his lungs consuming every thought. He had managed a quick gasp of air before the truck submerged, but his lungs were his enemy now, demanding air, fighting his resistance to suck in the surrounding water.

As he reached up to unwind the passenger side window, the drink cooler floated up from the foot well and bobbed in front of his face. He was about to push it aside when he felt the small drain plug on its side.

He pulled it open and a torrent of bubbles started flowing from it. Wrapping his lips around the small spout, he sucked in the precious air, stuffing his lungs to capacity, as he let the cooler float him up out of the window.

Once free of the truck cab, the cooler towed him toward the surface of the water above.

Nearing the surface, he opened his eyes to see the lights of the pier reflecting in the small choppy waves above him. With a final inhale of the stale cooler air, he pushed it away, began paddling towards the source of the light. He knew the dark water and his black wet suit would render him invisible from above. Even so, he took no chances, doing his best to maintain a depth of about eight feet.

267

The truck had ended up about twenty yards off the pier, a difficult swim for him underwater. The stabbing pain in his left shoulder was robbing him of his usual superb swimming efficiency, and again, his lungs were protesting. He surfaced under a metal walkway, sucking in a silent lungful of blessed air as he surveyed his surroundings. Across the surface of the water, the white cooler was bobbing in the current, eliciting the shouts of the dockworkers above, as it reflected the strobe lights of the official vehicles parked along the edge. Steve checked his watch... seven minutes had elapsed... eight to go.

The lower pier area appeared to be deserted. Everyone was up on top or had left, worried about possible bombs. Steve swung himself up on the metal walkway with difficulty, the searing pain in his shoulder weakening his knees for a second. He reached up beside his neck to feel a large, tender knot pushing against the muscles of his shoulder. He winced from the pain of touching it, realizing the shoulder harness had broken his collarbone.

"Let's get this over with!" He said through clenched teeth, crouching low and running back towards the area of drainpipes. He reached into a zippered pocket and withdrew his gun, sliding a bullet into the chamber as he ran. He would stop the acid, and no one had better get in his way.

The pipe labeled AC24/DC24 was easy to find, it was right beside the broken down barge he had hidden it in the day before. Directly below the drainpipe was a barge not there the previous day. The oily residue of diesel fuel had not yet smeared the fresh paint of the new fuel barge. Checking his watch again, Steve calculated he had only four minutes to find a way to stop the drain up. The only activity in the lower pier area was a fuel barge leaving the fueling berth at the far end. Steve heard its diesel motor blowing bubbles in the water through its underwater exhaust pipes. He ducked to watch as a single deckhand threw off the dock the lines and guided the pilot who steered the barge between the concrete pilings towards the open water. The barge headed to a ship moored in the basin beyond the piers.

Steve studied the overhead drainpipe. It had a metal fitting on the end, with a shallow rounded groove inset about an inch back from the lip. It was the male counterpart to the fittings on the fuel loading hoses, which had a female fitting of the same size on both ends. If he clamped a hose to the drainpipe, he could hook the other end to the fill valve on the new barge. With the fill valve off, the acid would stop, backing it up into the vault.

268

Steve ignored the pain in his shoulder as he fought the heavy hose up over his head. As he tried to guide the hose fitting together, the timer on his watch announced time had run out. Peña should be running the acid into the vault now. The sweat was flowing off his head in buckets as he strained with every ounce of his strength to connect the hose. A blast of dank smelling air erupted from the drainpipe, spraying Steve with stagnant smelling water. The surprise dousing energized whatever strength he had left, and he managed to lock the hose onto the end of the drainpipe. The loose end was spewing the foul water onto the deck of the barge, and Steve was aware at any second the hose would start spraying its deadly mixture of acid.

He jumped to the end of the hose, struggling to align it with one of several fittings protruding from a rack of large valves mounted to the deck of the barge. Steve was able to snap the cams shut on the hose as the acid-filled it, the full hose becoming heavy with the weight of the liquid.

The stench of chlorine gas accompanied by a rumble from beneath his feet subsided as he spun the round handle furiously, closing off the valve. Only about a hundred gallons of the acid had dropped into the empty hold of the barge before Steve was able to shut the valve. He backed away from the strong-smelling fumes, retreating to the shadows at the rear of the barge to catch his breath. The stabbing pain in his shoulder was demanding attention. He eased his arm into a less painful position and glanced at his watch, noting the time. If Peña was right, in about an hour the gold in Boulez's vault would be reduced to nine thousand gallons of steaming liquid hell.

CHAPTER 60

An entourage of security guards accompanied Boulez and Rahman as they made their way to the vault. Rahman was the only person other than Boulez himself whose weight and retinal scan were stored in the vaults' computer. The reason they rarely met at the same place. Should anything happen to them both, it would take a massive operation to cut into the stainless steel door securing the vault.

Boulez sensed the imminent danger of the situation. If the CIA was closing in on his operation, his only advantage was speed. It took time, even for the CIA to move the assets they would need to stop him. It was especially so in the Middle East, where certain Arab governments derived great pleasure 'tweaking' the tail of the Great Satan. Even though they usually agree to the requests of the United States Government in time, they seldom did so without receiving a quid pro quo. Those things took time, and time was in Boulez's favor now. If he dispersed the gold over the next few days, the Western governments would be powerless to stop him.

He said a silent prayer to Allah, asking for help in staying humble in the weeks ahead. The destruction of the Western economies would bring a realignment of world powers more catastrophic than the fall of the Roman Empire. Nations who were not industrialized would suddenly be on a par with those whose economies based on the value of this yellow metal responsible for so much death and destruction over history.

With no money to fuel their military might, they would leave the Holy Land. This would unite the Arabs in one voice, destroying the fear and restraints placed upon them by the wicked culture of the West.

With Israel on its knees, the Dome of the Rock would be in Arab hands again.

Of course, a newly united Muslim world would need help to lead it and who better than he? He was the architect of his new world order. He, of humble origins, was about to slay the dragon. His place in history assured, and his reward from Allah a certainty, his brethren would look to him as a modern-day prophet.

Boulez was almost euphoric as the thoughts danced in his head. The limousine stopped near the vault elevator door, with security vehicles both in front and back of it. His years of hard work about to bear fruit, and he was eager to get started. He didn't wait for his door to open, as soon as the limo stopped, he pulled the door handle. Swinging from the limo, he noticed an unpleasant smell in the air, as did everyone else.

"What is that smell?" He asked to no one in particular.

"It's chlorine, it smells like bleach." Rahman had come around the limousine. "I've smelled it before when they deliver it to the tank farm."

"I thought I made it clear. I want all outside deliveries stopped until we see how our operation goes." Boulez said.

"We have stopped them. No freight enters the pier by truck tonight, period. It might be the plant. They transfer chemicals all the time. I'll check it out." Rahman dialed security at the garage entrance and told them to find out what was causing the smell.

Boulez was mollified for the moment. "Then, let's get started."

Rahman nodded for the security guards to open the elevator door. The forklift operators and four helpers had gone down to the vault to wait for Rahman a few minutes earlier. Boulez, Rahman, and 4 security guards entered the elevator, each trying to ignore the acrid smell of chlorine wafting in the humid air.

When the door opened at the bottom, the smell of chlorine was stifling. The forklift operators and the workers were waiting as usual, and after being exposed to the noxious gas for several minutes they d began coughing, and their eyes were red and tearing.

"What the hell is going on, Rahman?" Boulez was becoming annoyed, waving his hand in front of his face.

"I don't know, I will find out. I'll get maintenance to check on the exhaust fans." He dialed his cell phone once again, and after an animated conversation, reported back to Boulez.

"I have people on the way. They can hook up fans to blow the fumes out of here. It will probably take a few minutes."

"Good, open the vault. I want to see what I have been working so hard on."

Rahman held his handkerchief to his nose as he stepped on the metal plate inset in the floor. The retinal scan screen came on and verified his iris, as the computer verified his weight.

Rahman stepped onto the scale, causing the green light to flash with the weight acceptance message on the LED screen. He wiped his burning eyes and placed his face into the scanner's rest to allow it to match his iris. The machine hesitated, and then the recorded voice announced "Incomplete image. Please retake the iris scan. You have fourteen seconds until system reset." The fumes were causing his eyes to tear. He wiped his eye and blinked several times before placing his face in the scan rest. Red light filled the LED screen, as the recorded voice announced: "Unauthorized entry attempt. System reset has occurred. Please wait two hours to re-initiate vault entry."

"What?" Rahman exclaimed.

By then, everyone was coughing and gasping for air, and one of the forklift drivers had vomited in the corner. The smell of chlorine had grown stronger in the few minutes they had been at the vault.

"Let's get back up and find out what's going on before we all end up dead." Boulez wheezed as he got back in the elevator.

Rahman had stepped away from the scanner and glanced at the front of the large stainless steel vault. Noticing a trace of white-colored smoke rising from a crack near the bottom of the massive door, he bent to take a closer look.

"Wait a second!" He yelled to the group, nearly gagging on his words.

He knelt next to the door, seeing a tiny rivulet of a yellowish colored liquid seeping from between the elevated threshold and the door. The concrete dripped onto was foaming and emitting the whitish colored smoke.

When manufactured, the door was machined to very exacting standards. Although it weighed several tons, it pivoted on its huge hinges with the ease of a refrigerator door. Designed to be air and watertight, the tolerances for the fit of the door were comparable to a watchcase, a single sheet of paper would not slide through the space between the door and the jamb.

The door felt warm to the touch, in contrast to its usual subterranean coolness. He reached down, touching the seeping liquid with the tip of his finger. Rubbing it between his thumb and index finger, he first noticed it had an unusual viscosity, then an overly warm sensation. Within a few seconds, it grew from uncomfortably warm, to very hot. Shaking his hand violently, he tried to wipe the liquid off on the concrete floor, only to spread the painful substance further. Finally, spitting onto his outstretched fingers, the pain subsided, leaving the tips a bright, crimson red.

"Acid..." He said under his breath, dumbfounded. He wiped his finger on his jacket sleeve as he headed for the elevator.

"We have to get in the vault!"

CHAPTER 61

Peña had no idea how to work the night vision goggles Steve had left behind in his waterproof bag. He kneeled at the entrance to the pathway leading back to the dingy, fumbling with them as he watched across the activity across the access road. Several security vehicles were circling the tank farm after finding the tanker hooked up to the vent line.

"Too late, suckers!" He laughed to himself as he watched from the security of the dark bushes. He had released the acid exactly as planned, and now it had been over half an hour, plenty of time for the acid to drain from the tanker into the vault. All the security forces found was a tank filled with the chlorine gas backed up from the vault, the sickening smell permeated the entire area.

An idea was brewing in the back of Peña's mind, and he was trying desperately to push it away.

"It's enough, don't worry, it's enough." He told himself, finally getting the goggles to come on. He wound his way down the dark path, his thoughts making both sides of the argument within himself.

"No, it's not enough, they'll figure it out. They won't get it all back, but they'll get a lot of it. There's nothing you can do, get away alive, it may be your only chance."

"Steve risked his life, other people have died. You have to get to him, help him figure this out; you owe it to him…"

He reached the end of the path, relieved to see the dingy tied up, as they had left it. Swinging back onto the bulkhead, he retraced his steps to the rope and climbed back into the dinghy. He untied it, pushing off into the darkness, not starting the little motor. Peering out across the water, he identified the lights of the boats in the yacht basin on the horizon, the Pactolus was among them. It looked so tempting.

With a sharp yank on the starter rope, the motor snapped to life.

"As you said, we're not coming back for this gold!" He spun the dinghy away from the open water and headed up the pier. He had no way of knowing if Steve had been able to plug off the drainpipe, he was sure he would see evidence of an acid spill if he had not.

What he did know was Steve had said to find the drain labeled AC24/DC24, and from his vantage point in the dinghy, he could see the ends of dozens of pipes, all with a different number and letter codes. The one constant was the letters were trending downward, the further he made it towards the far end of the pier. TR16/RT16 gave way to GH10/HG10 and so on.

273

He was surprised there only a few workers on the lower pier and wondered if the explosion he had heard after Steve left had anything to do with it. Did Steve have had time to improvise a bomb to draw their attention away? He didn't see how, but if anyone could do it, it was Steve Ross. He was careful to weave his way behind the concrete piers, staying out of view as much as possible. As dangerous as it was, he felt he had to press on. He had to be getting close, as the pier ended only a couple of hundred yards ahead.

Steve's shoulder was growing stiff as he waited in the shadow of the wheelhouse on the broken down barge. There had been no activity for at least twenty minutes at this end of the pier, the excitement on the upper level coming at the beginning of the lunch hour, and drawing any remaining workers up to gawk at the mayhem.

From farther up the pier, he heard the soft putter of an outboard motor, approaching slowly, hesitating from time to time as if it was searching the darkened barge berths. His thumb automatically clicked off the safety of his gun as the motor stopped directly in front of the disabled barge. He blended into the darkness, although from where he was it was impossible to see how many men were in the boat, or what they were doing. Glancing at his watch, he realized it had been almost an hour since the acid had flowed from the vault. Peña said it would take at least an hour. He needed a few more minutes.

A loud whistle blew on the top level, giving notice for the workers to return to their stations. Steve strained to catch a glimpse of whoever it was on the boat. He stood, weapon pointed straight ahead as the shadow of a man played on the wheelhouse of the new barge.

Above him, the sound of laughter and the rapid Arabic patter of workers returning to the lower pier resonated against the water. Steve spied a man crouching behind a row of barrels at the front of the barge, and he appeared to be alone. The man darted to the side of the new barges' wheelhouse, a stanchion pipe blocking him from Steve's view until he leaned forward. There in the polished glass of the wheelhouse, Steve saw Peña's reflection.

"What the...?" He exhaled under his breath, standing in the wheelhouse door.

"Ali?" He whispered as loud as he dared, "Ali!"

Peña jumped in surprise, heart in his mouth, at the sudden apparition of Steve.

"You scared me half to death!"

"What are you doing here? You're supposed to head back to the boat."

They hunkered down in the shadows of the broken down barge.

"I had to find you before you left here. I'm worried we may not have thought this through... entirely." He had a sheepish look on his face. He caught a grimace of pain on Steve's face and asked, "Are you hurt? What can I do?"

Steve didn't respond for several seconds, he stared at Peña in disbelief. Then in his most serious tone, he said:

"I'll be okay. I think I sprained my shoulder. Don't tell me this isn't going to work. It's too late now, we've tipped our hand. They know we know where the gold is."

"No, no, no," Peña interrupted, "it's going to work. I released the acid. If you plugged the drain, I guarantee there's a lot of very valuable acid floating around in the vault, right about now."

"I plugged it, I plugged it. So what's the problem?"

"The problem is, if we leave the acid they are going to figure out what we did. The other chemists will conclude a lot of acid, plus no gold equals Aqua Regia. They'll know exactly what we have done. They'll pump the acid out and reclaim the gold. It's a matter of time."

Steve looked at the hose attached to the barge, then grabbed Peña's arm. An idea flashed in his head. "Come on."

They jumped over to the new barge where Steve reached up to the hose rack. "Help me hook this hose up."

"What are you doing?"

"You said they'll pump the acid out and reclaim the gold. They can't pump what they don't have. I'm going to run the friggin acid right out into the water, right here, right now!"

Peña reeled, grabbing his temples with both hands, making an effort to concentrate. He felt they were still missing something. He stepped back, raising his hand to indicate he wanted Steve to wait for a second.

"Come on, what now?" Steve asked.

"It's no good, they'll dredge."

"Dredge?"

"Dredge the sand, under the pier. If they know we dumped the acid into the water right here, they'll figure the gold will settle to the bottom. The acid is a lot heavier than water, and there's not a lot of current, so the gold will settle out in the sand. They'll suck up the top few inches of sand and be able to reclaim it, eventually. It'll take time. For hundreds of millions of dollars' worth of gold, believe me, they'll find a way to get it. We've slowed them down, but we haven't stopped anything."

275

Steve was weary, as he leaned back on a fifty-five-gallon drum of motor oil. For a second he almost allowed himself to believe it was over. Boulez would do what he had done all his life: come out on top, find a way to win. He tried to shake off a feeling of dejection as he looked past Peña, into the wheelhouse of the barge. Although new, it was fitted with the old style spoked ship's wheel, designed to pay homage to an earlier time.

For an unknown reason, it jogged his memory to an image of Jim Ragan. Jim was at the controls of a fishing boat, a boat with the same type of wheel. Steve remembered the day clearly. Jim and he had spent the day deep sea fishing off the coast of Miami in a boat confiscated from smugglers.

They had caught and released several fish over the course of the day, and upon pulling one particularly active fish aboard, Jim had lost his favorite diver's watch overboard. He had impulsively jumped in after it, knowing he didn't have a chance in hell of getting it back. Steve still remembered what Jim had said when he climbed back on the swim platform, in response to Steve's question about his sanity.

"Sometimes it doesn't matter, you do something! At least I tried."

Then an idea clicked in Steve's head. He looked over at Peña, with a renewed intensity in his voice.

"Ali, open the valve," he pointed to where he had attached the hose from the vault drain. "I'm going to have to jump-start this scow."

CHAPTER 62

They loaded a few ounces of acid from the vault door into the labs' spectrometer. Chief Chemist Amir Faruk was studying the readout for the analysis displayed on the computer monitor. Boulez and Rahman entered the lab, walking in lockstep. The dour look on their faces left no room for misinterpretation: this was serious.

"Well?" Rahman demanded. He, and Mr. Boulez, wanted answers, and they wanted them now. The entire pier seemed to be descending into chaos. There was acid dripping from the vault, the smell of chlorine was everywhere, and a truck had run off the pier... explosions. This cannot be the work of one or two men. What did they hope to gain by flooding the vault with acid? It had to be a delaying tactic. It means they know, and they are coming for the gold. Boulez was not prone to apoplexy; however, this delay had changed his demeanor from the steely calm he usually exhibited to one of silent rage.

"I'm almost finished," Faruk said as he scanned the results of his tests displayed on the computer screen, "I want to make sure. If this is what I suspect, we can't be too careful." He was comparing the information on the screen to a large scientific manual spread on the desk, his chin in his hand.

Less than an hour ago, a hazardous material response team investigating the chlorine smell permeating the building discovered the tanker beside the parking garage and the bodies of two security guards in the pump house. The guards had been overcome by the chlorine fumes trapped in the pump house, after notifying Rahman's security they had found a tanker hooked up to a pipe going into the garage. Now they knew they pumped acid into the vault through the vent pipe. Who did it, what kind of acid is it, and most troubling, why?

"This is unbelievable, unbelievable!" Faruk seemed mesmerized by the data on the computer screen. "It's as I thought, one part nitric acid, to three parts hydrochloric acid. It generated chlorine gas. When the gold dissolves, it gives off chlorine gas."

"Dissolves... DISSOLVES? What the hell are you talking about?" Rahman's eyes bulged from his brow.

"Yes, dissolved. One part nitric acid combined with three parts hydrochloric acid make a solution called Aqua Regia, or Royal Water. It's called royal water because it dissolves the royal elements. It's a process usually done to reclaim small amounts of gold from computer components, alloyed jewelry scrap, waste gold. I doubt if they could get enough acid in there to do much damage."

"How much acid would it take?" Boulez felt a glimmer of relief.

"Depends on how much gold was in the vault, and how much time they had."

Rahman looked at Boulez, who nodded his approval to divulge the information.

"The vault is five meters square. It had about 150 thousand kilograms of gold in it, maybe a little more. We don't know how long the acid has been in there, we started smelling it about ninety minutes ago. Figure two hours."

Faruk seemed unsure he had heard Rahman correctly.

"Don't you mean 150 thousand grams?"

Boulez stepped forward, his voice an icy whisper. "He said exactly what he meant, kilograms. One hundred fifty thousand kilograms. Now, can you see why this is so important to me?"

"Of course, Mr. Boulez, let me do the calculations." Faruk's hands were shaking, as he punched the numbers on his scientific calculator. He looked unsure of himself as he read the results. "I must be calculating wrong, I'm coming up with... uh, almost seven. Seven cubic meters of gold, can that be right? I don't believe my math; let me check my calculations again."

Rahman was trying to visualize the gold he saw on his last visit to the vault.

"There was one pile of ingots, and another pile of ingots we put in wooden transport cases. I'd say in total it was about three paces square, and past my waist, about here." He held his hand up to indicate the height of the stacks.

"Then this is right, a little less than seven cubic meters of gold. Aqua Regia works best at a ratio of six parts acid to one part gold. It would take forty-two cubic meters of acid, which is forty-two thousand liters."

"How many liters does the tanker hold?" Boulez asked Rahman.

"Let me find out." Rahman dialed the chemical plant office on his cell phone. After a few minutes, the plant manager was located, and Rahman posed the question to him. He listened to his response, slowly closing it when he got the answer.

"About thirty-eight thousand liters, an equivalent to ten thousand gallons." He announced.

Faruk had been searching frantically through his reference books while they waited. "It's a good thing you didn't get the door open. You would be dead now, and a most unpleasant death it would have been."

"Allah was watching over us, now we are being tested," Rahman said.

"So how long would it take to dissolve the gold, is it gone?" Boulez asked, his face suddenly looked years older.

"It's impossible to tell," Faruk explained, " this reference tells me the reaction feeds on itself, gaining speed as more and more chlorine atoms are released. It's like throwing wood on a burning fire. The new pieces heat and burn much faster than the original pieces. My best guess is the gold is already dissolved."

"No!" Boulez was ashen, his knees week as he propped himself against a lab stool.

"It's okay, Mr. Boulez, Sir. It's okay; we have not lost the gold." Faruk tried to console his employer.

"What do you mean, you said it's dissolved... gone! Is it or isn't it?"

"Yes, it is probably dissolved, but it is not gone. It's still right there in the acid, and it's relatively simple to get it back. All we have to do is pump it out of the vault and set up a reclamation operation. Within a few days, I can get most of your gold back."

"A reclamation operation, what is a reclamation operation?" Rahman asked

"Without going into technical detail, I can tell you the gold is still in the acid, however, it is in another form. If we can set up large tanks, I can add the right chemicals to the acid, and the gold will precipitate back out of solution. It's not hard, but it takes time."

"Then you must get started. I will have the chemical plant supervisor pump the acid right back out of the vent and put it back in the tanker." Rahman was glad to have things in his control again.

"Yes," Faruk answered, you will need quite a few tankers. Remember, the gold is still in the acid, so the acid will be much heavier than normal. I can certainly find the chemicals I need either here or on the pier.

"You take whatever you need, you spend whatever you want, Faruk. If you have the slightest problem, I want you to let Rahman know. We must not lose any more time." Boulez said, his color returning to his face. He clapped Faruk on the shoulder as he turned to leave, indicating with a nod of his head for Rahman to follow.

Rahman spoke quietly as they walked towards the exit. "I am troubled, Mr. Boulez. Nothing seems right."

"Yes, I agree. Not all is what it seems. Whoever did this, planned carefully. Why did they go to so much trouble to dissolve the gold, why? Surely, they know this is one of the most modern labs in the world, with the brightest chemists found anywhere. Of course, they know we would figure out what they have done. If they are smart enough to use this Royal Water, then they are smart enough to know we would figure it out and reclaim the gold, as Faruk indicates."

"As we said earlier, we think they did this to delay us. They must have other plans they need time to implement. They will not let us keep this gold without a fight."

Boulez stopped in his tracks, spinning towards Rahman, a sudden realization striking fear in his eyes. "How do we know the acid is still in the vault? It was only leaking out at the very bottom of the door. Why wasn't it leaking out all around? Maybe the tanker truck was a decoy. They pumped the acid out already and left it to confuse the situation!"

"Remember the truck that ran off the end of the pier? I'll bet they used it to draw attention away from what they were doing here. It would only take half an hour to pump out the acid. For all we know, the acid had been inside the vault for hours. Faruk said the reaction increases over time, so by the time it generated enough chlorine to become noticeable, they must have been set up to pump it out."

Boulez noticed two HAZMAT suits hanging in a glass front locker beside them. He reached in, taking them both out and handed one to Rahman.

"There's only one way to find out. We must open the vault. Go up and reset the vault computer. Don't forget to weigh the suit. I'll meet you back at the vault elevator in ten minutes... hurry!"

Escorted by his security detail, Rahman was able to get back to his office, reset the computer, and return to the vault elevator in twelve minutes. Normally a chore he would leave to underlings, Boulez had donned the HAZMAT suit in preparation to enter the vault. He had to see with his own eyes the ruination of decades of hard work and planning.

They had set up large fans to blow the chlorine fumes from the parking garage, and the self-contained re-breathers in their HAZMAT suits would keep them safe for approximately twenty minutes. Looking strangely extraterrestrial in their white Tyvek suits, the two men descended in the elevator to the vault level. Apprehension gripped them as the door opened up. A faint white mist hung in the air as Rahman approached the security station. He craned his neck to look at Boulez, fear showing in his eyes.

"Maybe you should wait in the elevator."

"Why?"

"What if we're wrong, what if it is full of acid? There's no point in both of us dying."

Boulez smiled, the specter of death bringing an uncharacteristic charm to his voice. "My dear Rahman, we have been together thirty, thirty-five years? If Allah is calling us, let him call us together. It will be better for us both. Open the door."

Rahman drew strength from the older man as he walked through the security routine necessary to open the door. Surprisingly, the clear plastic face shield did not affect the iris reader. When the recorded voice announced the authorization to open the vault, Boulez walked confidently to the door and pulled with all his might. Both men stepped back in horror as a surge of dark brown liquid, as thick as molasses rushed from the door. Boulez clung to the vault door handle trying not to slip in the viscous goo, as Rahman edged back towards the elevator.

The surge of liquid stopped after a few seconds, leveling in the elevator area to a depth of only about four inches. The rubberized HAZMAT boots were more than enough to protect them from the minor deluge.

As Boulez peered around the vault door, it surprised him to see the lights still on in the vault. Not even a third of the way up the wall was a brownish mark, indicating the highest level the acid had reached. Below the mark, the concrete walls were rough and pitted; the acid ate away the porous concrete. Rahman came up beside Boulez, both men staring at several yellowish lumps of grainy material on the floor.

The material was bubbling with an effervescent hiss, and small pools of brownish liquid trapped in pockets were emitting a yellow-brown smoke.

Boulez was speechless, as Rahman kicked at one of the lumps. It disintegrated into dust right before their eyes, sending up a cloud of smoke when it contacted the liquid on the floor.

Boulez turned, carefully making his way back to the door. Emotion overcame him as he realized he was ruined. "No, no no! Allah, why? Have I not been an obedient son? Have I not sacrificed family, self, and everything for you? Why have you let everything be ruined, why destroy everything when we were so close? Why?"

Rahman hung his head, watching the dust he had made flow in the sluggish liquid towards the floor drain. A whirlpool spinning over the drain mesmerized him for a few seconds, until he kicked at another yellow lump, crushing it into dust. He watched the dust move slowly towards the drain, and then it hit him.

"Look, the acid!" He pointed at the floor drain. "Look!"

281

Boulez nearly fell as he returned to the spot where Rahman was watching the acid flow down the drain. The cast iron grate was gone, eaten away, by the acid. The six-inch hole in the floor was gurgling with the remnants of the thick slop.

"Are you telling me it all went down the drain? We lost billions of dollars' worth of gold down a floor drain?" The irony of his question would have been funny if it had not been true.

"They didn't pump it out… they ran it out of the drain. I know this drain, I designed the vault. It comes out under the pier where the fuel barges are berthed."

CHAPTER 63

The rumble of thick acid dropping into the fuel barge resonated from the open deck hatch. Peña finished spinning the valve handle as the white chlorine smoke began streaming from the hole in the deck. He ran over, holding his breath and slammed the hatch shut, sealing the fumes in the large cavern below. This was a small barge, used for refueling the ships berthed at the cargo piers. The capacity was around 100,000 gallons; it was powered by a pair of diesel motors located in a small engine room behind the rear bulkhead of the product tank. Not designed for speed, or looks, it was wide and squat, with only about three feet of freeboard.

Steve worked on a clump of wires behind the small console in the barge's pilothouse. Pilothouse is too generous of a term, as it consisted only of the most basic of controls. He found a throttle for each engine and a steering wheel. There was not much else other than the standard gauges, compass, and depth finder. It was cramped, and Steve's shoulder was aching, the fingers on his left-hand tingling.

Not making a lot of progress finding a way to get the motors started, frustration was setting in. The wires ended at a relay panel, which had several safeties and overrides for the motors. Low oil, high temperature, RPM limiter, all modern safety devices would make it difficult to hotwire the motors.

"The acid is rolling!" Peña stuck his head in the door. "How are you doing?"

"Not so good, this might take a while. How long will it take for the acid?"

"It'll be a little slower than it was running it into the vault. It's as thick as motor oil now. Count on at least a half an hour."

"Do you still have your gun?" Steve asked.

Peña patted his pocket. "Got it."

"Move the dinghy to the back of the barge, tie her up secure. Then keep an eye out. If anyone gets near, give me a yell."

"Will do."

Steve returned to the relay panel, hesitating, "Maybe I'm going about this the wrong way. I wonder who keeps the keys to this bad boy."

He looked around the tiny booth housing the controls. There was a ledge of curled up metal where the roof was bolted to the walls, and he ran his hand around it, only finding several packs of matches and a half-eaten bag of peanuts. Near his feet was a round plastic cylinder, about the size of a large coffee can, attached to the wall with a metal band tightened with a thumbscrew. He bent down and snapped it open, and there were several highway type flares, a flare pistol, several 12 Gauge flare loads, and a set of keys, which were hanging from a miniature plastic buoy.

"Hot damn!" He grinned, realizing his luck.

Peña crouched behind the barrels at the front of the barge when he heard the diesel motors turn over. So far, the only activity on the lower pier was happening at the far end where a similar barge was preparing to leave its berth. He walked back to the pilothouse, to find Steve on his way to the stern of the barge.

"You're crazy. You should have been a locksmith."

"It would have been a lot safer," Steve answered. "Anyway, I can't take credit for it; I found a set of keys."

"What are we going to do now?"

"We're not going to do anything. I want you to help me throw these lines off, and then I want you to take the dinghy and head back to the boat."

"But…"

"No buts just do it. Take the boat out into the shipping channel and punch up the number nine speed dial. They'll come and get you."

"You can't do this Steve. The acid is going to eat a hole in the bottom of this thing. It might not last an hour!"

"Don't worry about me. My job was to deal with the gold and to get you out if I can. I have the gold, and now all I need is to get you away from it. We have to split up if the worst happens to both of us, how are we going to let them know back home we did it? I don't want anybody else coming over here and getting killed for nothing, do you?"

Peña knew Steve was right, he also knew there had to be a better way. "If you take this barge out into open water, it'll be a death sentence. If she breaks up, you won't be able to swim away fast enough to…"

"Let me worry about it. The acid is slowing down, it must be almost finished. You gotta go, now."

Peña considered refusing, realizing it was no use. He held out his hand to Steve. "If anything happens, I want you to know that…"

"Something is going to happen. You will be on your way back to your family, so don't screw this up. Now get out of here." Steve squeezed Peña's hand, pushing him towards the dinghy.

"Nice and easy for a while, don't make it look as if you're running."

Peña reluctantly glided away from the barge with a sullen wave, and Steve watched him round the bow of a freighter, disappearing in the early morning light.

The fumes were growing stronger around Steve as he waited for the acid to stop running. He was feeling a little nauseated and lightheaded. He realized it would be extremely dangerous to disconnect the hose too early... the acid would still be flowing too strong to control. He had to wait, wait until the last second, and even then, the flow may be too strong. There was no way to know how long this would take. If anyone came by, he would be a sitting duck. He decided he needed a backup plan.

Steve jumped over to the broken down barge beside him and started looking around the piles of equipment and spare parts strewn around the deck. Towards the stern, he spied a pile of heavy chain, and something even more familiar. A short stout tube with what looked to be a steering wheel attached to one end. It was his water scooter!

"I'll be damned;" he said quietly, "one of the mechanics working on the barge must have found it." He grabbed it and took a heavy chain with a hook on one end, and a large shackle on the other the mechanics used to hoist the barge's motor out.

He felt his shoulder getting numb, as the sharp pains became a steady ache. With the chain and scooter, he jumped across to the new barge and secured the hook end of the chain around the hose attached to the vault drain.

The other end was long enough to loop around a short steel stanchion, one of two that rose from opposite corners of the stern. He inserted the threaded shackle pin through two links, and with a short length of rebar, he found nearby and tightened the pin snuggly. As an afterthought, he slipped a length of rope he found coiled near the stern through the handle of the scooter and set it to one side.

Peña was motoring out into the harbor, between the eerie metal behemoths, aiming for the masts of the pleasure boats in the distance he barely made out in the dim light. He had never felt so lonely, heading for the Pactolus and knowing Steve would not share his voyage to freedom. He knew Steve well enough by now to know he must have a plan to save himself, so what was it? If he took the barge into the open water, how would he get back to shore? He might be ten or twelve miles out by the time the acid ate a hole in the barge's hull. Peña began to regret leaving Steve back at the pier.

"I should have stayed to help him. I should have refused to go." He thought as he looked back over his shoulder, to the area where he imagined the barge was moored.

It seemed so far away, and from this distance, all the piers looked the same. For a second he considered going back, the little outboard coughing for a second made him realize he might be running out of gas. Turning back towards open water, he started to be able to pick out the individual boats moored in the yacht basin ahead. It was slow going, a light breeze, and the current was flowing against the dinghy, and he felt as if he was making little headway. Anxious now, he pushed the dingy on, ready to get far away from Port Jebel. He was still a hundred yards off when with a quick sputter, the little motor died. Reaching down, he picked up the small metal gas tank lying in the back of the boat. It was empty.

"Damn it," he cursed at it under his breath, "can't give me two more minutes?" Little did he know, it had probably saved his life.

Peña fumbled with the small wooden oar tied under the dinghy's seat. Paddling for a minute, he paused, sensing danger. The sound of garbled voices carried across the water ahead of him.

He peered through a slight mist starting to rise from the water; he could swear he was looking at the Pactolus up ahead. The mast and rigging looked familiar, and the outline of the hull seemed misshapen and unbalanced.

Drifting a few yards closer he swore he recognized the shapes of two or three people moving on deck. He froze, ducking low in the rubber boat, as he looked around in a near panic. There was no question in his mind who it was, and no doubt what they would do if they caught him. The sun would be up in a few minutes, and he could never paddle fast enough to get out of sight. The nearest boat was a large sailboat moored a half a mile further out in the yacht basin.

Peña no longer heard voices as he started paddling furiously back toward the pier. Daybreak was only minutes away. If he put distance between himself and the Pactolus, there was a chance if they saw him; they would mistake him for an early morning fisherman. He dug deep with the oar, using all his strength to pull himself along until a cramp in his side required him to rest. Craning his head back, he noticed the men he had seen standing on the Pactolus's deck had gone below. Reaching behind him, he felt the gun tucked into his waistband. It might be his only hope.

Suddenly, a flash of light accompanied by a muted explosion sent pieces of the cabin roof and the entry hatch soaring high into the air. A man stumbled from the hatch holding his hands to his face, screaming in pain. His shirt was on fire as he twisted blindly around the cockpit. His fate sealed when he tripped on a coil of rope, slamming his head on the gunwale as he fell overboard.

Peña looked on in horror as the man surfaced once, arms flailing, and then again, face down and still. Heavy smoke was billowing from the cabin door, and the Pactolus began to list to one side. Orange flames soon began roaring from the open portholes, and the sickly smell of burning flesh and fiberglass wafted in the breeze.

The Port Police boat had three heavily armed men aboard, approaching the barge area cautiously.

After leaving the vault, Rahman had radioed the crew investigating the truck that had run off the end of the pier, ordering them to head for the fuel barges.

Returning to his office with Boulez, he had found a set of construction plans for the vault showing the exact location of the floor drain, and where it ran to on the pier. Rahman ordered the patrol to be on the lookout for any unusual activity at or near the drain location. He, Boulez and a large security detail were on the way.

Steve sensed the danger before he saw it. The sounds of footsteps running above him on metal catwalks were not the sound of employees returning from a break. They sounded too quick and too determined. The echo of an outboard motor coming down the pier meant only one thing: the para-military patrol was closing in on him.

The acid was still flowing, although the sound was decreasing with each passing minute. Steve was squatting down in the barge's pilothouse, trying to stay below the level of the glass. The patrol boat was visible, passing between several concrete pilings a short way up the pier. They seemed to be looking for something, pointing to the underside of the metal catwalk suspended over the barges.

"They know! They're looking for the drain pipe." Steve tensed closing the door behind him, as a sudden feeling of claustrophobia enveloped him in the little pilothouse. He would have to move fast, there would be no time to disconnect the hose from the drain. He rammed the throttle to the barges diesel motor forward, creating bubbling maelstrom around the underwater exhaust ports. Ahead of him was an open space between the bow of one container ship, and the stern of another. The barge wallowed in the water for a few seconds, before gliding out of the covered berth. The chain wrapped around the beam behind him quickly snapped taut, pulling the drain hose out of the manifold connection. Heavy brown liquid gushed out, spraying the door of the pilothouse, spilling over the rear deck, and running into the scuppers.

The patrol boat immediately gave chase, quickly coming alongside the slow-moving barge. The pilothouse was mostly glass on the upper half, so allowing the pilot to see three hundred sixty degrees around the boat. The hull was made from heavy steel.

Steve hunkered down below the glass level, the barge making near top speed of almost seven knots. The breeze had picked up after the early morning calm, and the sea had a small chop.

While the barge was unaffected, the small patrol boat was fighting the chop and the wake of the barge as it tried to come alongside. Steve ignored the shouts he heard coming from the boat, no doubt orders to stop, which was not in his plan. He spun the wheel to the side, hoping his large wake might capsize the patrol boat, but with a flick of his wrist, the driver avoided the wave.

Suddenly the window over his head exploded into pieces, and a shower of thick shards rained down on him. It was reinforced plastic, designed to protect the pilot in the event of a large wave hitting the pilothouse. A high-powered bullet was about the only thing able to go through it. Soon, loud rapidly-paced thumps on the metal wall beside him left no question about the pursuers' seriousness. The steel was protecting him from the bullets for now, but a well-placed shot or a ricochet would be all it took. Steve swung the barge into the patrol boat's path again, causing the driver to swerve. When the shooters grabbed the nearby railings to steady themselves, Steve popped up and fired several shots through the broken window. He hit one man full in the chest, knocking him over flat on his back. Steve guessed he was dead before he hit the fiberglass.

The patrol boat broke off, falling in behind the barge, out of pistol range. Steve watched them there, waiting to make his move. As long as he stayed low, even the high-powered rifles were not a worry. He took time to glance down at his watch. He had been underway for about fifteen minutes, and Peña said the hull might not last the hour. He hoped Peña was right, and it would hang together long enough for him to reach the deep shelf located about six miles offshore. If he dumped the acid there, it would be impossible to reclaim it. First, he had to make it there.

For the next several minutes, the patrol boat followed at a distance. From their hand gestures, the men inside seemed to be making a plan. Steve kept an eye on them over his shoulder, as he made a beeline for open seas.

After a few minutes of following at a distance, they seemed to have come up with a plan. The two riders trained their rifles on the pilothouse as the driver gunned the twin outboards. Steve watched them approach warily.

If he opened the pilothouse door to fire at them, he would be without cover. He tried reaching around the broken window to shoot, but the patrol boat was agile enough to stay out of his line of fire, and he wasted several rounds. Keeping as low as possible, Steve checked the rounds in his magazine. He had only two left. He would have to make each one count.

The patrol boat was at the stern of the barge now, and Steve knew exactly what they would do, yet he was powerless to stop it. The barge seemed to be getting less and less responsive. He had no way to know the acid had already eaten a football-sized hole in the hull, and it was taking on thousands of gallons of water.

Two men were standing in the open bow as the patrol boat bumped the stern of the barge. They jumped onto the back of the barge, assault rifles trained on the pilot's booth. They both ripped off several shots, blowing the last piece of glass from the pilothouse door.

"Come out. Come out, and it will not harm you!"

Steve needed time, and more ammunition. They had too much firepower. He reached up and shut down the engine, removing the key and shoving it into a flap on his wet suit.

"No! You throw your guns overboard now, and I'll let you live!"

He knew how melodramatic it sounded, as he stalled for a few more seconds. As the boat neared, he removed the flare canister from the wall and scrambled to attach the 12 Gauge projectile flares to the highway flare with the metal band that had held the canister to the wall. A striker would light the highway flare, and if it burned enough, it would burn through the plastic cases of the projectile flares, setting them off with a ball of fire. At least that was the plan. Steve did not know if it would work, and he had no choice it was now or never.

Fortunately, the flare was almost new, and when he struck the lighter, it lit immediately. Steve held the blinding package for a couple of seconds and then tossed it through the window to the deck. The two men jumped back, stunned as the bright pink light burned for another few seconds, and then when with several loud explosions, the projectile flares ignited in rapid succession.

Steve kept his eyes diverted while the flares spun around spewing white-hot light, and sparks on the deck. Dodging the sparks, one of the men slipped on the acid spilled on the deck, falling hard on his hip, and dropping his assault rifle. It slid over the edge of the barge and fell into the water before he made a desperate lunge for it. Steve stood and fired one round at the other man, who had not averted his eyes from the bright light. It grazed his shoulder, spinning him off balance as he fired several wild rounds, his eyes blinded by the flares. Steve had no choice, so he fired his last round, hitting the man in the throat above his ribcage. He staggered, taking several steps towards the patrol boat before tripping on the hatch cover and collapsing in a gurgling heap.

His fallen comrade stood to his feet, grabbing at the strap securing his sidearm while backing towards the stern. He saw the patrol boat had drifted about fifty yards away and was caught in a cross-current moving back towards the shore. A powerfully built man, he seemed familiar to Steve, who reacted by kicking the now dying flare in his direction, following it with a bull rush to his midsection. Steve had hoped to knock the larger man into the water, where he was certain he would have an advantage. Surprisingly, he barely budged him. The man got Steve in a headlock as he managed to clear his gun from its holster. Steve locked his own powerful hand around the man's wrist, pulling his arm toward the ground. With his head in proximity to the man's chest, Steve read the nametag on his military-style uniform shirt: Kibar.

"I know you!" Steve spat, realizing it was the same person who had boarded the Pactolus yesterday.

"You should have taken my advice and left when I gave you the chance." Kibar groaned in pain as Steve twisted his wrist to an unnatural position.

"Take my advice now, and let go of this gun, and we'll both live." He spun out his hold, wedged his foot behind his heel and shoved with all his might. They both fell over in an awkward pile, Steve maintaining his grip on Kibar's wrist as they writhed on the slippery deck. The acid was starting to soak through Kibar's shirt and pants, and he noticed an uncomfortable stinging sensation increasing as the acid mixed with his sweat. Steve's rubber suit was protecting him from the acid, and Kibar became more and more distracted with the burning as it starting to become intensely uncomfortable.

Within seconds, Kibar lost all interest in the gun. He had no idea why his skin was on fire, although he knew he had to do act quickly.

"Arrrggghhh!" He yelled, tossing the gun into the water with a flick of his wrist while staggering to his feet, Steve's grip on his wrist released.

Steve was on his hands and knees, the acid starting to generate heat where it touched his skin during their struggle.

Kibar was fully distracted now, trying to rip the wet uniform shirt from his body, realizing the brownish fluid on the deck was a caustic material. Steve stood, taking a second to debate whether to shove Kibar into the sea or try to incapacitate him with brute force. He took a step forward, but never got a chance to make the decision. The unmistakable sound of a high-speed boat and the splatter of lead against the pilothouse drowned out Kibar's high-pitched screams.

Steve whipped around to see a large open cruiser, maybe forty-five feet long, approaching from the starboard stern and closing fast. He recognized half a dozen men dressed in uniforms similar to Kibar's, with automatic rifles aimed at the barge, and two or three other men in civilian clothes holding onto the rails in the cockpit. Once the cruiser swung around, all the men with rifles began to level them at Steve. As the bullets started raining onto the deck, Steve turned, and with a great leap, dove into the water beside the barge.

CHAPTER 64

Rahman was at the wheel of his forty-two foot Sea Ray, a boat he enjoyed cruising up the coast of the Emirates whenever he felt a need to get away from the pressures of his job. An experienced yachtsman, he prided himself on his ability to do difficult docking maneuvers, navigate in open water, and find the best fishing spots for his guests. The boat also served as an ultra-secure meeting spot for those times when his associates did not want to risk a meeting on foreign soil.

Earlier, when the security patrol came upon the barge leaving the pier and the remaining acid draining from the hose, they immediately notified Rahman, who instructed them to give chase, and under no circumstance damage the barge. Notifying the Dock Master to prepare his private yacht, Rahman passed out new polo shirts he kept in his office dressing room to Boulez and Benny Chavez. It would be hot today, and suit jackets and dress shirts would extremely uncomfortable on the open water. As far as the security detail, they would have to make do.

Rahman and Boulez were not concerned about the barge getting away. With a top speed of seven knots, the Sea Ray would overtake it within minutes. However, they wasted no time getting to the boat, keeping a quick pace as they discussed the events of the last few hours. "I don't believe they want to destroy the gold," Rahman said. "If so, they would have placed explosives… or if it's the CIA they would have dropped a bunker bomb on it." "I think you are right." Boulez agreed. "They are determined to steal the gold. The western countries would use the gold to stabilize the markets at whatever level they wish. They could control the fluctuations in the value of their currencies." "Yes, and don't forget their latest tactic, offering millions for information on people they consider terrorists. There was a bounty of fifty million for bin Laden, and twenty-five for al-Zarqawi. With our gold, they could afford to splurge. Why not two hundred fifty million for the next guy? Eventually a price would be reached to induce an informant to come forward."

"We won't let it happen, let's go get our gold back." Boulez was feeling a renewed vigor and a newfound sense of purpose.

They followed the flashing blue lights of the harbor patrol boat on the horizon as Rahman eased the big SeaRay out into the channel and slammed the throttles to the powerful twin diesels all the way forward. There were nine men in the cockpit. The six heavily armed men from Boulez's personal security detail, Chavez, Rahman and Boulez.

The sport cruiser cut through the small choppy waves with ease, its engines reaching a sonorous harmony, a pleasant accompaniment to the sound of rushing water beneath its hull. They closed in on the drifting patrol boat after several minutes, confused to find it appeared abandoned.

While the SeaRay slowed beside the patrol boat, a sickening tenseness was welling up in the pit of Boulez's stomach. He was watching Rahman scan the area with a pair of high power binoculars, trying to fight a feeling of impending doom. How can they be so close, yet so far away?

The sound of several rounds of gunfire brought their attention to an area ahead hidden in the glare of the early morning sun.

"There she is! Over there!" Rahman pointed. Several hundred yards away was the barge, its gunwales barely above the water level of the sea. Its gray color rendering it nearly invisible against the water, they watched two men in an obvious struggle on deck.

Rahman nudged the boat into gear and set a course for the barge. As they closed, Chavez saw the Caucasian dressed in a dark wet suit and knew instinctively who it was. "I don't believe it, I know him, it's the American!" He yelled, grabbing an assault rifle from the man standing beside him. "Let me have him!" Chavez slipped the rifle to full automatic and squeezed off two short bursts. An unexpected roll skewed his aim, and as he steadied himself, the customs agent took two quick steps and dove into the water on the far side of the barge.

Rahman eased the boat alongside the barge, to the peculiar sight of one of his special unit personnel doing what looked to him to be a wild dance. He had stripped off his shirt and was rubbing his hands over his arms and trying to reach his back. Finally, in desperation, he jumped into the water at the back of the boat.

"Spread out, he's not going to swim back," Chavez ordered as he jumped to the barge, his men close behind.

"Forget about him, he'll never make it back. Let's start this thing up and get it back to the pier."

One of Boulez's security men checked the pilothouse, searching for the keys.

"No good, he must have taken the keys with him." "Then tie it up to the boat, we'll tow it back!" Boulez shouted from the cruiser's cockpit.

"Rahman, let's move!" In his struggle to crawl out of the water, Kibar pulled on a chain he found a chain dangling in the water off the barge' stern. The loose chain slid from the deck hitting him on the head. Dazed, he stumbled onto the Sea Ray's swim platform. Desperately he tried to pull himself up, the saltwater burning into the lesions from the acid.

On deck, Boulez watched in disgust as the big man's blistered arms slipped on the fiberglass, his back, half out of the water, a grotesque skinless mess. Foam was dripping from his mouth as he whimpered in pain. Opening the short door leading to the platform, Boulez stepped through, and putting an expensive shoe on Kibar's shoulder, gave a surprisingly powerful shove.

"We have no time for you now. The next life will be your reward."

Steve took a quick gulp of air before he hit the water, diving straight down as far as he dared. He was expecting the slivers of white water that follow bullets fired into the water to search for him. Above him, the dark hull of the Sea Ray contrasted against the lighter sky as it sidled up to the barge, the twin propellers under it coming to a gentle stop. He had no problem holding his breath for over three minutes; however, the quickly forced gasp he took as he dove into the water would not last long. If he swam away from the barge, he was reasonably sure they wouldn't spot him for the two seconds it took to steal a breath; he would need help to get back to shore.

By his quick calculations, they were about six and a half miles out, a swim he had made many times in his life. Normally, he would have little doubt about taking on such a swim, but the nagging pain in his shoulder was sapping his strength as he fought to stay underwater. He was going to need help this time, and dangling from a rope off the back of the barge, he saw his salvation.

It was the water scooter, knocked overboard in the scuffle on deck. He tried to untie it, cursing the over-tightened knot. His lungs started demanding air, pushing back against his diaphragm with an imperative: Get air!

Abandoning the knot, he gave a powerful kick and propelled himself to the far side of Rahman's cruiser. He surfaced in the curve of the bow, an area out of sight from both the barge and the cruiser. After several deep breaths, Steve dove again, staying under the cruiser and heading for the scooter. From beneath the barge, a trail of brownish fluid was draining from a large hole and mixing with the seawater. The current seemed to be dragging it out to sea, and the water was burning his eyes. He swam to the back of the barge, surprised to see the chain hanging down into the water. He started to work on the knot again, recoiling in shock when from above the lifeless body of Kibar sank down and bumped into him. He shoved him away, the chain snagging the disfigured body for a second as it drifted to the depths. Steve watched him disappear and then snapped his head back up to the chain. In a split second, Steve saw a way to make sure the golden acid sank to Davey Jones' Locker, and to send a boatload of seriously bad people along with it.

The shadows of men jumping from the barge to the cruiser spurred him into action. If he was lucky, he might have twenty seconds. Even underwater, the chain was heavy, and Steve called on a deep reserve of strength to swim it over to the two large propellers protruding from the bottom of the cruiser's hull. He wrapped it behind the shaft supports, and threaded it through the blades, fumbling with his sore arm to slip the hook over a link to lock it in place. If the starter button was activated now, he would end up as human sushi. Timing a wave that gave the chain a little slack as it lifted the barge slightly; he managed to secure the chain. Again, his lungs were complaining, there would be no second rest period. Heading back for the scooter, he heard a loud clank, and saw the blade of a propeller whiz past him, following Kibar's body to the bottom. He flipped over on his back, to see the chain straining against the weight of the cruiser. It tangled around the props and the shafts, and as long as the shackle held on the other end there was no way to separate the two… short of an underwater torch.

Steve was barely able to keep his eyes open. The water was becoming cloudy as the acid, which is heavier than water, drained from the hole in the bottom of the barge. He finished untying the knot by feel and hit the thumb switch on the scooter. To his relief, it felt strong as it pulled him through the depths away from the barge. He concentrated on his chest, willing it to stay calm, as he rode behind the scooter until there was no choice, it was either breathe water or breathe air. He chose air.

CHAPTER 65

Aboard Rahman's cruiser, confusion was setting in. Boulez had gone below cursing. He was cursing Rahman, cursing the American, even cursing Allah. He had never known such depths of despair. Every time he thought they were in the clear, another disaster would come up as if an unseen force was waiting to sabotage their every move. When Rahman hit the starter button, the SeaRay jerked violently into the side of the barge, the chain hanging from the rear stanchion becoming piano wire tight. Rahman knew the chain was tangled in the props, and he did what any good sailor would do, he tried to bump them in reverse to back the tension off. It was to no avail, the chain had bent the soft bronze props, trapping the chain. As Rahman sat back in the pilots' seat rubbing his brow in disgust, he noticed the waves were breaking ever so slightly over the deck of the barge. Although it struck him as odd, he dismissed it as the consequence of having several tons of cruiser attached to its side. Half of the security detail was making a desperate bid to unscrew the shackle pin from the chain; the weight of the barge had bent it enough to ensure the futility of the attempt. They were locked tight to the barge, and there was no way to get away. The other half was attempting to do what even Steve could not do - hotwire the barge's motor.

Chavez was pacing the length of the barge, rifle in hand. He knew the customs agent was still there, still alive. The only he wanted was the sight of the man's body floating on the sea face down. Had they realized the acid had been eating away at the hull for over two hours now, they all might have spent the time planning to abandon the unwilling flotilla. Rahman stepped below to find Boulez."I have radioed the Port Police. They will dispatch a couple of towboats. They should be here in twenty minutes. Not all is lost, Mr. Boulez. We will have the gold."

Boulez looked up from the sofa. "No, my friend, unfortunately," he paused, the weight of his vision of his destroyed plan pushing his shoulders into a slump, "unfortunately, the gold has us."

Those prophetic words would be fulfilled in the next few minutes. Under the barge, a seam, corroded through from the acid, split amidships. The acid was now flowing out in a torrent, its place displaced by the lighter seawater.

Chavez was standing in the cruiser's cockpit when he heard what sounded to him to be metal rubbing together. The cruiser was leaning at an angle, leaning into the barge listing heavily and the entire port side sinking a few inches beneath the water.

"Rahman! Rahman!" He shouted. "This damn thing is sinking!" Boulez and Rahman were well aware of the situation. A large crack had opened up on the bulkhead beside the kitchenette, and water was spraying into the cabin. They ran up the few steps from the cabin to the cockpit, shocked at the sight of the barge, now half underwater. "Life jackets are in the storage area under the seats!" Rahman pointed. Chavez threw the seats open and began tossing the bright orange jackets to the frightened security detail, men not known for their swimming prowess. Rahman ran back for the radio, falling to the deck as the stern of the cruiser suddenly shot up at a steep angle. With an ear-splitting crack, the barge folded in the middle, forming a steep vee shape, the bow and stern jutting out of the water. Brown acid was staining the water all around the barge as the last of the acid gushed from the broken hull. The men standing on the cruiser ended up against the cabin wall, and Chavez and Rahman were tossed back down into the cabin. The brownish acid, diluted by the seawater, still extremely caustic, exploded through the cracked hull into the cabin and washed over them. It took only seconds for the burning liquid to begin eating away at their flesh, exposing billions of enraged nerve endings. The excruciating pain induced a hysterical gasping and wailing, which in turn allowed the acid to splash down their throats. Chavez held on a few seconds longer than Rahman, unconsciousness relieved their misery as the acid roasted them from inside and out at the same time.

Boulez was afraid of the sea, the unknown depth always spooked him the few times he swam off the end of his own yacht. There was no flat place for him to stand in his slippery Italian street shoes, so he sat on the stern of the Sea Ray, struggling to untangle the straps to a bright orange life jacket. He saw three of his security people drifting in the water not far from the barge, what happened to the others he did not know.

They were yelling for him to get away from the boat and the acid, as great bubbles of air were rushing from the depths below the barge. It was filling with water.

Boulez reached behind him, passing the crotch straps of the life preserver through his legs, and up into a double safety snap. It's designed made it impossible for the jacket to slip back over a person's head, even if they jumped from the side of a tall ship. He rested for a few seconds as the barge and cruiser stabilized, searching the horizon for the towboats. He wanted to delay his plunge into the dark water as long as possible. Even now, he hoped he would be able to tow the barge back to the pier and salvage the golden acid. He had no way to know of the severity of the split in the barge's hull. The top deck which was not in contact with the acid was still intact, although bent at a severe angle. Quickly, the pockets of air in the barge were finding their way out with each roll of the waves.

Finally, the rage building inside him caused him to try to stand. He realized he was snagged, and rather than take the time to free himself, he began to scream at his unseen enemy.

"I will be back! I know you are out there, I know you can hear me! Don't worry, I will be back! I have the technology, I have the money! Do you hear me?"

Suddenly a huge belch and metallic groan emanating from the barge frightened him to silence. The barge was completely awash now and listing so heavily to one side, the Sea Ray was nearly out of the water. Boulez clung to a handrail, trying to swing himself off the stern into the water. He reached down between his legs and pulled on the safety strap, only then realizing he had inadvertently looped it under the stainless steel handrail. The Sea Ray rotated slowly out of the water and Boulez hung in the air, his full weight suspended by the life jacket. He clawed at the release to no avail. The barge spun in a death roll, exposing the cracked hull to the sky for a second before slamming the Sea Ray upside down into the water. The barge, engulfed in water, sank rapidly, dragging the SeaRay along with it.

Boulez screamed through clenched lips, holding his breath until it was no longer possible. The last sensation to register in his brain was the bitter taste of the golden acid as it flowed over his tongue.

CHAPTER 66

It was a hot day in Key West. Steve hated wearing a suit, and even worse, a tuxedo. A yellow jacket attracted to the scent of perfume made its rounds among the guests, each taking a turn swatting at it. As he waited patiently, he found himself daydreaming. He had been back from Dubai for over seven months now and seeing Beth walking towards him on the arm of her father was the best outcome he might have imagined. Gene Tyson stood at his side, as best man, and Alejandro Peña was among the ushers. Still, it was a bittersweet day for Steve. There was one less usher than bridesmaids, a silent tribute to Jim Ragan. He had always expected Jim Ragan to be his best man, and vice versa, and when Beth suggested they do a tribute similar to the missing plane in a flyover formation, Steve readily agreed.

Beth had asked Angie Barnes to be one of her bridesmaids, an assignment she gladly accepted, returning to active duty after spending two months testifying in the espionage trial of Bob Graves. Convicted on several counts of tax evasion and dereliction of duty, Graves received a life sentence in the penitentiary. It was Graves who gave up Tom Miller, the agent Boulez killed for discovering his shipboard laboratory. In addition, Graves provided intel keeping Boulez one-step ahead of ICE.

"Steve, are you okay?" Beth leaned in with a puzzled look on her face.

He snapped into focus, surveying the small group of people gathered at the little chapel on the Gulf of Mexico. He took Beth by the hand and turned to face the Pastor.

"I'm fine, I'm just fine."

EPILOGUE

"I see you did the wise thing, and held on to your gold, sir." The vice president of the Abu Dhabi National Commerce Bank, Mohammed al-Aslan said. "This time last year, we were seeing prices in the two hundreds... a disaster."

Alejandro Peña smiled as he waited for the cashier's check. A metal detector and a couple of hours spent along the road holding such terror for him last year were now paying off big. He had five ingots of pure gold totaling over a hundred pounds. When he had told Steve he was returning to Abu Dhabi to find the gold they had buried in the sand, it surprised him that Steve didn't try to dissuade him from the endeavor. With Boulez dead, his lab was one of the first things to go bankrupt. Then, the cost to remove the labs from his ships was putting the shipping line in a crisis, and now the headless organization was in turmoil. The danger was minimal now, and the rewards great. Besides, Boulez owed him for two years of his life. This wouldn't bring those back, however, it sure would help make the rest easier.

Steve had said as much last year when Peña had found him swimming three miles off Port Jebel towards the beach. By a stroke of good fortune, the patrol boat had drifted away from the barge, floated within eyesight of Peña, who was trying to row the dinghy to open water. Peña caught up with it, watching the barge and cruiser sink from a safe distance. Knowing if Steve was alive he had to be trying for the sandy beach past the pier, the closest land, he circled the area for over an hour. Vowing not to give up, he stopped to call out Steve's name across the water every few minutes until he felt hoarse. Steve had seen the patrol boat circling near him several times, not knowing Peña was at the controls, he dove from sight each time it came close.

Had it not been for the fact the scooter died, he might never have found Steve. Unable to make it to shore with his injured shoulder, Steve caught the attention of the patrol boat. His plan was to overpower the operator and then head out to open sea to find Peña. On the next pass, the boat stopped fifty yards from him, and the driver began shouting over the water. To his amazement, it was his name being shouted and shouted in a familiar voice. They soon connected as he shouted back, waving furiously.

Now he was dressed casually, sitting in a plush chair, in a private office. Al-Aslan entered the office and shut the door behind him.

"Here we are Mr. Peña, a cashier's check for five and a half million Dirham. You should be able to convert this to about one and a half million American dollars and change. If you can sign these few papers, sir."

300

Peña stared at the check for a few moments, its value almost beyond his comprehension. "I don't want to insult you, sir, are you sure this check is good... I mean in the United States?"

"I take no offense, Sir. This check is drawn on one of the most stable banks in the world, Abu Dhabi National Commerce Bank. The wealthiest people in the world use our services. Do not worry, the check, sir, is as good as gold."

The End

If you enjoyed this book, please take a moment to leave a brief review. Thank you!

https://www.amazon.com/dp/B07PLMZQ85

Made in the USA
Monee, IL
23 June 2021